LINGARD
was originally published by Crown Publishers, Inc.

LINGARD

A Novel By

COLIN WILSON

PUBLISHED BY POCKET BOOKS NEW YORK

LINGARD

Crown edition published June, 1970

POCKET BOOK edition published December, 1972

This POCKET BOOK edition includes every word
contained in the original, higher-priced edition. It is printed
from brand-new plates made from completely reset, clear, easy-to-read
type. POCKET BOOK editions are published by POCKET BOOKS, a division
of Simon & Schuster, Inc., 630 Fifth Avenue, New York, N.Y. 10020.
Trademarks registered in the United States and other countries.

L

Standard Book Number: 671-77598-7.
Library of Congress Catalog Card Number: 77-108077.
This POCKET BOOK edition is published by arrangement with
Crown Publishers, Inc.

Printed in the U.S.A.   Cover art by George Ziel.

LINGARD

ONE

The most dangerous criminal I ever met was not confined
in the top security wing of Durham Jail; he was in the Rose
Hill experimental prison near Sedgefield—an open prison run
along Swedish lines, where the seventy-five internees are
given the minimum of supervision. He was Arthur James
Lingard, serving the last years of an eight-year sentence for
second-degree murder; he had accidentally killed an old man
in the course of a burglary. Lingard had served three previous terms in prison, twice for breaking and entering, once
for fraud. He was regarded as moderately intelligent, but
temperamental, and he had been a sufferer from childhood
from epileptic seizures. No one, as far as I know, suspected
that he was the minicar murderer of the A.26, the Leeds silk-
stocking killer, and the man responsible for the Doncaster
orchard murder of 1957.

Lingard placed me in the strangest dilemma of my whole
career. As a prison psychiatrist, my first duty is obviously
to the public and the prison authorities. As a doctor, my duty
is to my patient. Moreover, I have always believed that the
psychiatrist stands the greatest chance of success if he can
empathize with his patient, enter into his world; the ideal
relationship would be one of love. I soon became aware that
a dangerous psychopath was being treated as more or less
harmless and trustworthy. I knew it was my duty to warn
the prisoner governor. I also knew that if I did so, I would
betray the tenuous links of trust that had sprung up between
Lingard and myself. I decided that I would take the risk; as
a result, I gained a unique and terrifying insight into the mind
of one of the most complex psychopaths of the twentieth
century.

1

On June 19, 1967, I had been working at Rose Hill for only a month, and had not yet seen Arthur Lingard. When I arrived that afternoon, the governor, Mr. Frank Slessor, told me that Lingard had had some sort of attack, and seemed to be in a state of intense depression. Slessor accompanied me to Lingard's room—it could hardly be called a cell—and I saw him for the first time. He was sitting in a corner of the neat, pleasant room, his fists clenched, looking as though he wanted to push himself backward through the wall. The position was fetal, with the knees drawn up to the chest. Both fists were pressed tight on his knees. He showed no sign of interest in our arrival, staring into space with a tension that was so great that I would have thought it impossible to maintain. This, the governor told me, was the second phase of the attack. It had started at eight the previous evening, when he had allowed his supper to fall into his lap. After that, he had seemed confused, uncertain where he was. I moved closer and saw that he was trembling slightly, and the look on his face was dull and fixed. He was like a miserable animal, shivering with cold.

Lingard had rather a fine face, although the inactivity of prison life had made it fat. The forehead was high and rounded; the nose beaky, almost aquiline, the chin round. The mouth was sensual and drooped weakly at the corners. The bulging eyes gave him the appearance of a startled squirrel. The hair was dark and curly. For some reason, he immediately aroused my pity.

I bent over him and snapped my fingers in front of his eyes. They remained glassy, unblinking. I pulled the skin underneath them down; they were bloodshot and swollen, as I would have expected from the intense concentration of his stare.

I said: "Arthur. My name is Kahn, Samuel Kahn, and I'm the prison doctor. I'm here to help you. What's worrying you so much?"

It was hopeless; he might have been alone on a mountain-top.

I pinched the back of his hand, clapped my hands in front of his face. He was obviously unaware of me.

It was baffling. I asked the governor if the attack had been preceded by the scream of the epileptic, and whether he had shown signs of confusion or disorientation during the earlier part of the day. He said no. I wasn't surprised. This was less like epilepsy than catatonia. But except for the occasional epileptic attacks—four in five years—his case history was negative.

There was nothing much to do. I decided to leave him for the rest of the afternoon, and told the guard to watch him carefully, observing if he relaxed when we had gone. On the way out of the door, I noticed the photograph on the small table—a shiny brown one. I picked it up and stared at it. It was a family group, and the woman was remarkably beautiful, dressed in the pretty off-shoulder dress of the time. The husband was a tense, square-faced man with an angry, traplike mouth. Although the resemblance was only slight, I could detect signs of Arthur Lingard there.

The girl of six or seven who was obviously the daughter was as strikingly lovely as her mother, with tiny, regular milk teeth like the young Shirley Temple, and the large, dark eyes and crinkly hair of her mother. Finally, there was Arthur, who was hardly more than a baby. He looked as expressionless as most babies, in his sailor suit, staring into the camera with mild interest. His face also resembled his mother's; chubby, earnest, not as attractive as his sister. The mother brought back a flash of memory; of a nurse I had known before I graduated, and wanted to marry. But since the governor was beside me, I did not stare as long as I wanted to. We left the cell, and as I glanced back, Arthur Lingard still looked tense and miserable.

I spent the next three hours talking to other inmates about their problems. With the exception of a gentle manic-depressive, none of them was seriously ill; they wanted to talk about their families, about what to do when they got out of jail. They enjoyed talking with me because it flattered them to talk with a psychiatrist who had written a popular paperback about his profession, and who treated them as serious, decent human beings, not as patients. On the whole, things were working out well at Rose Hill; I liked the place and the people, and had a feeling that I was doing good work. But the Arthur Lingard problem bothered me; it looked as if things were not going to be smooth after all. At five o'clock, I went back to his room. He was in the same position.

His tension worried me. So far it was not unduly pathological, but I had had experience of this condition leading to hypertension and then to acute catatonic excitement with

3

its threat of exhaust status and death. I decided to administer a sedative before I left. Two guards held him, but it was unnecessary. He remained perfectly still as the needle jabbed into his upper arm. After that, I told the guards they could go, and sat on the bed. I sat there, staring at the photograph, a few yards away from me on the table. Why did it fascinate me? Because it seemed to be the photograph of a happy, healthy family group. The husband must have felt a great deal of satisfaction when he looked at his softly beautiful wife, and then saw her reflection, with some subtle addition of sheer vitality, in the daughter. The small boy was leaning back on his mother's knee, his hand resting on his sister's shoulder. If asked to base a prediction on that photograph, I would have said that he would grow up happy and secure, with all the affection he needed from attentive womenfolk and the knowledge that his father was always there to protect them. What had happened to change the secure child into the trembling animal crouched in the corner? Suddenly all my scientific and human curiosity was aroused; I wanted to know.

I sent one of the guards to the governor's office for Lingard's file. It came with a note saying: "Call in and have a drink before you go."

The report told me little that I did not already know. Arthur Lingard's crimes had been petty: juvenile burglaries, a halfhearted attempt at fraud. The crime for which he was now serving an eight-year sentence took place in February 1963. He had broken into a remote farmhouse on the Yorkshire moors, stunned a dog that attacked him, and proceeded to slash the furniture—apparently in search of money. The farmer, a man of seventy-three, heard the noise and came down with a loaded shotgun. He managed to surprise Lingard, and made him put up his hands. While the farmer was telephoning the police, Lingard attacked him and tried to wrest the gun away. In his statement afterward, he claimed it had exploded in the struggle. The barrel was under the farmer's chin at the time, and blew away most of his face. The police were actually able to hear the struggle over the telephone, but it took them half an hour to get out to the farmhouse. The burglar had fled, leaving no clue behind; but the farmer's wife who rushed into the room after she heard the shotgun blast saw him clearly as he rushed to the door. She described him as a big man, about twenty-five,

4

with a round face and bulging eyes. The bulging eyes were the clue. A detective remembered seeing the face of such a man in the wanted file. The farmer's wife identified Lingard as the burglar. He was picked up in Manchester the same day, having hitched a ride there in a lorry. At first he denied the crime, and persisted in his denial until his lawyer told him that the police had decided that they had enough evidence to convict him even without a guilty plea. At this, he pleaded guilty, and the charge was reduced to manslaughter. The chief controversy at the trial hinged on whether he had really snarled: "I should have killed her too," when told that the farmer's wife had identified him. A psychiatrist at the trial had argued: "This man is an inadequate personality; such people do not murder to steal."

The psychiatric report that had led to Lingard's transfer from Strangeways Jail, Manchester, to Rose Hill stated that his behavior had been consistently good, in the sense that he never quarreled with other prisoners or gave trouble to prison officers. The majority of prisoners detest the guards, whom they refer to as "screws." Lingard was always polite to the "screws," and had never been known to respond to provocation. The report stated: "Emotionally inadequate and intellectually subnormal. Refuses to carry on any kind of discussion, apparently because of an inability to concentrate, and never reads." But this, I noticed, seemed to conflict with another medical report from Strangeways that mentioned that Lingard had worked in the library for a while, and proved to be a moderately efficient librarian. No doubt there are many librarians who are mentally inadequate and never read; but it had the ring of a contradiction. There was also evidence that Lingard had begun to show signs of mental disorder in Strangeways; he had been withdrawn from library work when he had been caught smearing a book with excrement. The title of the book was not given.

The sedative was working; he had ceased to tremble; the stare had become duller. It was half past five. I made my way to the governor's office. I accepted a whisky on the rocks, and we went out to the terrace that overlooks the main prison area. The heat of the afternoon was bringing a fresh breeze from the moors beyond, and many of the inmates were taking the opportunity to do a little gardening, or sit outside in the late sunlight. Rose Hill has an ideal situation, with the bare hilltop beyond it in one direction, and the river winding below past newly planted woods. The electrified fence around it is not obtrusive. The well-designed chalets and the fountain in the center of the lawn make it look more like a holiday camp than a jail.

I was glad of the opportunity to talk. I told him I'd given the patient a sedative, and that I had no idea of what had caused the crisis.

"Could it be organic—some brain disorder connected with epilepsy?"

"I doubt it." I described briefly two other cases of catatonia that I had encountered during medical training. In both of these, the symptoms had borne a striking resemblance to Lingard's, but in both, there had been enough premonitory symptoms to warn us what to expect. It was the unexpectedness of Lingard's attack that puzzled me.

I asked: "Didn't Dr. ——— [my predecessor] take any interest in him?" The doctor in question had moved to London, where he was now sharing a practice.

"Ah, that's possible. I've still got most of his files in the pending cabinet." He went into his office and came out a few minutes later with a single sheet of paper. It was handwritten, which is why it had not yet been incorporated in Lingard's file. It was only a few lines long:

"Arthur James Lingard, born Barnet, North London, 1937. Orphaned in early years of war; went to live in Warrington with relatives. Placed under care of probation officer, 1951; stealing, general disobedience. Attempted sexual attack, age sixteen, followed by suicide bid. Two burglaries in following year; spoils included ladies' panties. Probation. 1955, six months' sentence for burglary. 1956, washing machine fraud, six months. 1959, six months for burglary. 1963, eight years for burglary and manslaughter, Knaresborough. History of epilepsy. Docile and below normal intelligence."

Here there were three items that immediately attracted my attention. He had been orphaned at the age of five or so. That went a long way toward explaining what had happened to the secure family group. There had been an attempted sexual attack when he was sixteen, and the spoils of his burglaries included panties. There could be many reasons for taking a pair of panties; he might have taken them with other clothes, meaning to sell them, or have intended them as a present for a girl friend. (I knew of a petty thief who kept his wife for years in underwear by stealing from clothes-

6

12 OCT 74

$10.95   1
$10.95   1
$10.18   2
$30.08 total

lines.) But with the knowledge of the earlier sexual attack, the likeliest explanation seemed to be the sexual aberration called fetichism.

I asked Frank Slessor what he made of it. He produced two observations that had escaped me.

"I don't know whether you know High Barnet. I had an aunt who lived there. It's a pleasant, residential sort of district. In 1933 it would have been pretty well out in the country. If his family lived there, they were probably moderately well off—semidetached suburban villa. On the other hand, I think of Warrington as a pretty grubby sort of place —industrial suburb of Manchester. If he moved there from Barnet, I can imagine he wasn't too happy."

I studied the whole case file again.

"I need to know more about him. Unless I can get him to talk, it's hopeless."

I finished my drink, and went back to Lingard's room. He had fallen asleep on the floor, and the guard had covered him over with a blanket. Even under sedation, his breathing was still tight and abnormal.

As I sat in my car, waiting for the gate to be opened, the gatekeeper came over to me.

"Mr. Slessor would like a word with you, sir. He's in the admin building."

I assumed it was some other business he had forgotten. But when I got back to his office, there was a warder sitting in a chair.

"I think I've got something for you, Sam. That mention of Knaresborough rang a bell. This is Mr. Jenkins, who lives in Knaresborough."

I shook the hand of the heavily built, middle-aged man who looked like a farmer. I asked him: "Do you know anything about Arthur Lingard?"

"I've heard a story, sir. I can't say if there's anything in it. I used to be very friendly with the sergeant in the Knaresborough police station. When this bloke got arrested for killing old Benson, he told me he'd been a suspect in another murder case—a girl down near Stocksbridge—I can't recall her name."

Slessor reached into his desk drawer. "Easy enough to find out. Stocksbridge, you say?" He took out a duplicated telephone directory. "We may as well be accurate." He asked the prison switchboard to get him the Stocksbridge police station. A moment later he was saying: "Could I speak to the sergeant in charge, please? Governor Slesssor of Rose Hill prison." The conversation went on for ten minutes, while he made notes on a writing pad. When he hung up, he said to the warder: "You were right. Lingard was a suspect." He read from his notes: "The girl's name was Evelyn Marquis. In February 1960, she was found near Ewden, on the Midhope Moors. Apparently she was the daughter of a man who ran a garage, and she occasionally helped out with taxi work. Late on a Friday evening she answered a telephone call to drive a man to Leeds—about twenty miles away. She picked him up at a hotel at ten thirty. At two the next morning, a passing motorist saw a burning car fifty yards from the road. The girl was found lying next to the car, with her clothes on fire. She'd been killed by a violent blow on the back of the head."

"Was she raped?"

"Yes. The medical report established that she'd been a virgin before the attack."

"And why was Lingard suspected?"

"The girl's father thought he was a man he'd seen hanging around the garage—he drove a television repair van. They questioned him twice but there wasn't any evidence. They must have decided he was innocent, because they later arrested a man called Evans."

Jenkins said, "That's something I didn't know."

"He was never brought to trial—lack of evidence again."

I was surprised at my own reaction to the words "They must have decided he was innocent." After all, it made no real difference to me whether Lingard was guilty or innocent; he was only a "case." But the possibility of his being a sex murderer might have offered me a clue to his present breakdown.

I took the governor's notes home with me; I had decided it was time to start a new file on Arthur Lingard. That evening I wrote to the psychologist who had made the report from Strangeways, asking if he could give me the title of the book that Lingard had been caught smearing with excrement.

Frank Slessor rang me before nine the next morning. "You told me to let you know if any change occurred. He's almost back to normal this morning. He won't speak to anybody, but he's eaten his breakfast."

8

"Good. Try giving him a pencil and paper." I knew from past experience that this method often works with patients who are still too withdrawn to want to communicate verbally.

West Hartlepool—where I had bought a house—is about an hour's drive from the prison. There was not enough work at Rose Hill to justify the full-time services of a psychiatrist, and I usually spent two or three afternoons a week there, dividing the rest of my time between the local mental hospital and my private practice. Although I was not due to return to Rose Hill until the following day, the problem of Arthur Lingard nagged me all morning, and I drove out immediately after lunch.

He glanced at me without recognition as I came into the room, and ignored me when I spoke to him. He was drawing with a red ball-point pen. Several sheets of paper lay on the floor beside the bed. I picked them up. They all seemed to be roughly the same: bulging masses like clouds or low hills reflected in water. As I stared at them, it struck me that they also resembled intestines. I held one in front of him and asked: "What is it supposed to be?" He stopped drawing, politely, while I waited there, but remained silent. When I took the paper away, he returned to his drawing. I asked the guard: "Who gave him a red pen?"

"He chose it hisself, sir." He pointed to a cheap pack of pens on the chest of drawers; Lingard had selected the red one from seven different colors.

I sat and watched him for ten minutes. The tension was still there and showed itself in the pressure on the pen. A lead pencil would not have lasted more than a few seconds. His face was still rigid and strained.

Lingard ignored me while I sat there, but when I stood up to go, I received a long, searching glance from the bulging eyes. I felt encouraged. This at least was some form of communication.

I looked in again before I left. He had covered another twenty or so sheets. It seemed to me that the drawing was becoming more careful; he appeared to be deriving a sensual pleasure from the undulating movements of the lines. I sat on the bed for another ten minutes. As he was about to throw a drawing on the floor, I reached out and took it. He looked up at me, and the unblinking eyes stared into mine. They seemed expressionless, yet at the same time I felt that he was trying to beat down my stare, or even to hypnotize me. He stared for several minutes, apparently unaware of the passage of time, then returned to his drawing.

I said: "Tell me something, Arthur. Would you like your sister Pauline to come and visit you?" He glanced up at me without interest, then went on drawing. I tried a shot in the dark. "How about Evelyn Marquis?" Again he looked at me blankly; then his eyes suddenly flickered to a point over my shoulder, and a look of alarm crossed his face. I looked around. There was nothing there; just a blank wall. I leaned forward and asked: "Did you know Evelyn Marquis?" As I stared into the dull eyes, it seemed to me there was a response: a look of caution and cunning. But it was gone immediately. After that, he ignored my presence completely. I left a message asking the governor to ring me if there was any further development, and drove home.

At eight thirty that evening, the guard who brought Arthur Lingard's supper found him staring fixedly at the wall opposite his bed and trembling. The guard asked what was the matter, and Lingard muttered something about someone looking at him. The guard went to the window. "There's no one there." "No," Lingard said irritably, "*there*," pointing to the wall. "I can't see anybody." "It's a mask, an electric mask." The guard gave him his food, and reported to the governor. Slessor decided not to contact me, since Lingard was not actually violent. The next morning, Lingard was still talking about electric masks, and also drawing them. They were twisted, gargoyle-like faces.

On the following day, I stood and watched him draw them. The pen would hover over the middle of the page for a while, then make a sudden stab, and begin to draw an eyebrow or the nose. Then the eyes or the mouth. Sometimes the pencil poised uncertainly, as if he wasn't sure where to begin; then the quick stab, and another line would appear. The odd thing was that the last part of the face to be filled in was the outline of the head. It was almost eerie, the way that this last line could change the whole character of the face, making it menacing, or lewdly suggestive, or merely sleepy.

At one point, he glanced toward the window with a look of alarm. I asked: "Is it an electric mask?" He shook his head. "What then?" He glanced up at me sullenly and muttered something that sounded like "dog."

When I left the room, I asked the guard if Lingard had

ever mentioned dogs. "Oh, yes, he talks about them now and then. Seems to think they're after him." I knew that Lingard talked to the guards; for some reason, he was more cautious with me.

As I walked toward the administration building, a picture flashed into my mind. It was a photograph of the dead farmer that had been included in Lingard's file. His face had been obliterated by the shotgun blast. Two walls of the room were visible behind the body, and there were pictures of dogs on both walls. Could this be a clue to his psychosis— that he had repressed the image of that gruesome, faceless head, and that this was the root of the disturbance? It sounded plausible—images of masks, to cover up the sickening pulp, and guard dogs that were tracking him down to revenge the farmer's death.

It was one of those ideas that appeals by its tempting simplicity. But when I tried it on Frank Slessor, he seemed dubious. I pressed him to explain. He said finally: "What bothers me about him is that he's more intelligent than he lets on."

"What makes you think so?"

"I talked to the librarian about the books he's read since he's been here." He handed me a paper from his list. I looked at it unbelievingly.

"Are you sure there's not a mistake?"

"Quite sure."

It was incredible. Lingard had been in Rose Hill for just over six months. The books he had borrowed during that time included Freud's *Civilization and Its Discontents*, Ardrey's *African Genesis*, Doughty's *Arabia Deserta*, Lorenz's *King Solomon's Ring*, E. H. Carr's *The Romantic Exiles*, a history of the Spanish civil war, and John Cowper Powys's *Owen Glendower*, as well as a number of science fiction books.

Slessor said: "That's the man that two psychiatrists described as intellectually subnormal."

I said: "There are two possible explanations. Either the psychologists didn't know what they were talking about. Or Lingard *was* subnormal at Strangeways and has improved since he's been here. That might help to explain the breakdown—increased mental activity, weakening of old repressions."

11

"There is, of course, one other explanation. That he meant the psychiatrists to believe he was subnormal."

"But why should he do that?"

He shrugged.

I went down to see the prison librarian—an energetic little man who was serving the last year of a sentence for rape. He confirmed that Lingard had always made full use of his allowance of two books a week from his admission to Rose Hill until a few days before his breakdown. I asked his impression of Lingard. "Fairly intelligent sort of bloke. Doesn't say much." "Did he ever talk to you about books?" "No. The only thing he ever said was 'that's one of the best books you've got in this library.'" "Which book was that?" He went over to the shelves and handed me a bound Penguin. It was E. H. Carr's *The Romantic Exiles.* "He really liked that one—had it out once or twice." The book was subtitled: "A portrait gallery of some nineteenth-century refugees from Tsarist oppression." It fell open naturally at Chapter 14: "The Affaire Netchaev: or the First Terrorist." I looked through it. Someone had made a number of marks in pencil on the margin. On the first page, the sentence, "In a meteoric career, which ended at the age of twenty-five, he achieved literally nothing," was marked with two exclamation marks and a question mark. Occasionally passages in other chapters were marked, but the Netchaev contained more markings than any other. I borrowed the book and took it home with me. I also took a pile of Lingard's sketches. My wife's intuition often works when my own clumsier intellect marks time.

That evening, I read most of the book. And as I read, a pattern began to emerge. When the author describes idealistic revolutionaries, the exclamation marks indicate disagreement or sarcasm. "The kiss in human love," says Herder, "is a proof of the nobility of man." There was an exclamation mark and a question mark. A small arrow pointed to the bottom of the page, where someone had sketched two dogs, one sniffing the other's rear.

The chapter on Netchaev showed evidence of careful reading—Netchaev, the most ruthless and amoral of all revolutionaries, the man who thought of revolution as a purpose in itself, and who believed that any crime is justifiable in its name. It was Netchaev who arranged the murder of one of his followers to bind together his revolutionary group. On the last page of the book was penciled the comment: "Mostly fools."

I made a mental note to check on Lingard's file the next day, to see if his signature matched the handwriting. But there was no need for this. My wife was sitting opposite me looking through the drawings. She said: "That's odd." "What is it?" She handed me one of the drawings. In the upper right-hand corner, Lingard had written: "It stinks." I compared the writing with that in the book. It was larger and more spiky; but they were the same hand.

The drawing itself, I noticed, differed in a basic respect from the earlier billowing masses. This was more angular, as spiky as the handwriting. For some reason, he wanted to escape from the soft curves, wanted something more disciplined and abstract. Instead of the masses of intestines, this pattern looked more like mountains reflected in a lake.

"Here's another." She handed me an "electric mask" drawing. Written across it were the words: "God created the world, but it has been taken out of his hands."

I was more interested in the American-sounding phrase "It stinks." Did he mean the drawing was so bad that he couldn't bear to look at it? Then I remembered that psychotics are often oddly literal. Why should it stink? What stinks? The answer was obvious: Shit. I reached over and took one of the other drawings from my wife's knee. Now I had the key, it was obvious. These bulging, twisted sausages were strange-looking masses of excrement. But excrement from a healthy person is not bulgy or curved. Only the excreta of a constipated person comes out in these round-looking masses. Lingard had been drawing the shit of a constipated person—a symbol of his own inner rigidity and stagnation. And then there was a revolt. "It stinks," and the lines became angry and spiky. And then, almost immediately, following his revolt, came the electric masks. Perhaps they had always been there—I remembered the look of fear he had cast over my shoulder when I asked him about Evelyn Marquis. But now they were there all the time.

All this may sound arbitrary; but I was trying to make use of some of the intuitions built up over twenty-three years of practice. For some reason I myself did not understand, Lingard fascinated me. I felt like a child consumed by curiosity. I wanted to know his secret. And now I seemed to be getting indirect glimpses of some drama that was being played out inside his mind. This man was no fool. The problem of Arthur Lingard could not be summarized in terms of weakness and inadequacy. This man was beset by demons. He had tried to escape them by retreating into the world of catatonic passivity; but a part of him refused to surrender. And now he was again fighting alone in his strange private world, like a man trapped with monsters in a glass bowl. My task was to break the glass, to try and get in there and help him.

But what kind of a man was this, who had convinced two psychiatrists that he was mentally subnormal and emotionally inadequate, and who actually had dreams of violent revolution—who identified himself with the fanatical loner Netchaev? This was a man who thought of human beings as dogs, of human affection as two dogs sniffing each other's arses. And now something had convinced him that he was in danger from the "dogs," and he was afraid.

It came to me, late that night, just before I fell asleep, that the killing of the farmer might well have been deliberate. He was caught in this absurd situation by an old man in a nightshirt, who intended to hand him over to the police like a boy caught stealing apples. He waited his chance, then attacked. He silenced the old man as quickly and ruthlessly as he had silenced his dog, then went out into the night, ignoring the screams of the old woman who stood at the bottom of the stairs.

And if he had killed the farmer deliberately, then it was also possible that he had killed Evelyn Marquis. It dawned on me then that Arthur Lingard might be a very dangerous man.

That night, Lingard began screaming. He was convinced that something was trying to get in at him through the window. It took three guards to subdue him and get him into a straitjacket. The prison doctor gave him a knockout dose of sedative, but he was awake again a few hours later, screaming about a man with a knife. The next morning, they removed him to the remotest room in the prison, where his screams were less likely to disturb the others, and sent for me. The doctor had suggested moving him to a mental hospital. I flatly rejected the idea, pointing out that it could only do him harm to place him in an overcrowded ward with other mentally disturbed patients. I recalled a trick that had worked

14

on a number of previous occasions with highly disturbed patients, and suggested that they offer him warm milk in a baby's feeding bottle. An amazing number of psychotics seize on this suggestion that they are babies with great relief. When I arrived at Rose Hill two hours later, I discovered it had worked. Lingard had drunk three bottles of sweetened milk, and was now lying on the floor, staring at the ceiling.

I was shocked at the way his cheeks had sunk. The face had become yellow and exhausted. On the forehead there was an enormous bruise—the guard told me he had rolled off the bed in the straitjacket. There were traces of blood on his cheek. The guard said he had been babbling about an electric man with a carving knife.

Since he now seemed calm, I untied the strings of the straitjacket. He kept licking his lips and swallowing, and muttering things that I could not catch. I helped him to his feet and onto the bed. On the table there was a pile of drawing paper and the red pen. I placed these by the side of the bed and left him.

An hour later, I heard his screams from the other end of the prison. I hurried back to his room. He was crouching under the bed, and two guards were trying to persuade him to come out. When he saw me, he seemed to become calmer. I sat on the floor, and asked him what he was afraid of. He ignored me, then suddenly pointed at the window. "Look! The man with the knife." "What does he want?" Lingard screamed, "You're not going to stick that up me."

I picked up some of the pages that were lying scattered on the floor. The first one showed a hand grasping a penis, which is being cut in half by a huge, triangular-bladed knife of the type butchers sometimes use. The knife figured in a number of the other drawings. In some of them, it was cutting off the noses of the gargoyle-like masks. In one, it was driving into an eye.

Half an hour of soothing talk induced him to climb into bed again. I offered him the baby's feeding bottle, but he brushed it away impatiently. When I restored the drawing pad and the pen to his knees, he seized it and began to draw knives.

I slipped the drawing of the knife cutting the penis into my pocket. It seemed too obvious a Freudian symbol—fear of deprivation of genitals, the result of some guilty fear. But what was its relation to the drawings of excrement and electric masks? "You're not going to stick that up me." Who had threatened him with a knife? The question remained at the back of my mind all the time I talked to other prisoners. The outline of a solution came to me as I was crossing a sunlit lawn, and made me stop and stare at the grass. The triangular blade of the knife reminded me of the jagged points that had replaced the soft curves of excrement in his drawings. Those jagged points represented aggression, revolt against his own passivity. Suppose the knife also represented aggression— *aggression against someone else's penis?* Suppose that "You're not going to stick that up me" referred to a penis, not a knife?

I had one more visit to make that afternoon—to a hard-faced little cockney who had been having nightmares that made him wake up screaming and sweating. Bert had responded well to ordinary suggestive treatment; the mere assurance of a doctor that everything was going to be all right was enough to start the process of improvement. He was crooked and immoral in an open, cheerful way, and I had got to like the incorrigible little rogue, while recognizing that it would save the country money to have him quietly "put down" like a dog that kills chickens. He was the kind of criminal the public hears little about; he was a crook as other men are plumbers or carpenters, and there was nothing mixed up or inadequate about him. When I asked him if he intended to go straight when he got out, he laughed. "Why should I? What's the point of being in here if you're going to go straight? I'm in here because I'm hoping to do the big job one of these days—something I can retire on. I've got a right to a bit of comfort as I get older." He felt it was no more antisocial to plan a robbery than to plan a coup on the stock market or the Grand National. His philosophy was based on ignorance and downright stupidity, but, such as it was, it was consistent. If his attitude had been known to the governor, it might have led to loss of parole, so I took care not to mention it.

As I was leaving Bert, I asked him, "Do you know anything about Arthur Lingard?"

He shrugged. "Not much."

"What do the others think of him?"

"Quiet sort of bloke—not very bright."

"Would you think he *might* be cleverer than he looks—for example, that he might be some kind of a big-time crook?"

Bert guffawed. "Not on your life. 'Scuse the comment, gov, but you don't know big-time crooks. They're not modest wallflowers. If they're in the big time, they let the others know it."

"What about his sex life—do you know anything about that?"

This was, strictly speaking, an unfair question. There was a certain amount of homosexuality in the jail, as in all jails, but I had no right, as a representative of officialdom, to expect him to betray what went on. Luckily, he trusted me.

"I've never heard a thing about him. He's got no special mates."

"How about the guards? Do you know if any of them are queer?"

"I don't want to get nobody into trouble."

"He won't get into trouble."

"Well, there's 'Arry Tebbut. He's as queer as a nine-bob note. Doesn't seem to be a bad sort, though."

I winked at him. "Thanks, Bert."

Lingard was sitting in bed, his sketch pad on his knees. He was not drawing, but staring at the wall with narrowed eyes, and swaying back and forth with the movement I have often seen in affection-starved children. I sat down on the bed and glanced at the drawings. There were several more of knives cutting penises or testicles. Suddenly, his head jerked, and he stared at the window like a startled animal; a dribble of saliva ran down the side of his mouth.

"What is it, Arthur? Another electric mask?" Without taking his eyes off the window, he nodded imperceptibly. "What's his name?" He shook his head violently, as if I was an irritating fly. "Is it Harry Tebbut?" The reaction was unmistakable. It was as if I had thrown cold water over him. There was a sharp intake of breath, a convulsing of the muscles, and a terrified glance at me. I said soothingly: "Don't worry. Harry Tebbut won't be allowed near you. He won't be allowed to stick it up you again." This seemed to have no effect; but I went on repeating variations on it, slowly and quietly, and watched him gradually relax. He closed his eyes and breathed deeply. I wondered if he was falling asleep. Then his hand groped out and found the pen. He began to make lines on the pad on his knees. The pen moved very slowly, and its point traced the soft, bulging curves that I already knew. For the first time since I had been called to see him, I felt a surge of delight and triumph, mingled, to my own surprise, with an almost fatherly feeling of protectiveness. I got up and left the room.

I found Harry Tebbut off duty, drinking tea in the guards' canteen. He was a big, good-looking man in his thirties, with powerful shoulders and a deep chest. The face was not prepossessing—bony, almost fanatical, with a hatchet-like nose. The huge, soft brown eyes were a little disconcerting in a man; they claimed one's attention. At once, I understood how Arthur Lingard would feel if he believed this man had designs on him. Anyone who has seen an old woman with some arresting sexual feature—good legs, a sensual mouth, even attractive eyes—knows the sensation; the good legs automatically draw the thoughts toward bed; the sensual mouth makes one think of kissing; but the idea of sexual intercourse with a matriarch is repellent, frightening. Harry Tebbut aroused this same mixture of attraction and revulsion —at least, in me.

I came to the point immediately.

"There's a certain amount of talk about you in the prison."

He paled, in spite of his attempt to seem unworried.

"Oh? What about?"

"I think you know what about." As he started to protest, I interrupted him. "Look, it's no business of mine what you do with other consenting males. It's legal now." He looked relieved. "So long as you don't use your position as a guard to force yourself on prisoners." He stared to protest again. "And I've no doubt you're too sensible to do that." He smiled with relief.

"Then what was it you wanted to see me about?"

"I want you to tell me something truthfully. If you answer me honestly, I promise it won't have repercussions on your job. I want to know about you and Arthur Lingard." I stood up. "Think about it while I get myself a cup of tea."

I came back and sat opposite him. "Well?" Some other guards came in, so we were no longer alone. He said, "Come on outside and I'll tell you about it." We walked outside, toward the wire. He said: "Look, there's something you've got to believe. I didn't try to force myself on Arthur."

"I believe you. Tell me how you got to know him."

"I got interested in the books in his room. He's a bright bloke, you know. At first he didn't want to talk, but after a while he opened up, and we'd have a jaw about politics and books. And . . . well . . . one day in his room, I . . . well, I sort of got the impression he was asking me to come on."

"Had you discussed homosexuality?"

"Well, a bit. We talked about sexual perversion. I got the impression he'd . . . well, he'd had plenty of experience, put it that way."

"So what did you do?"

He looked at me anxiously and said nervously, "Look, I don't . . ." but my face stopped him. I wasn't playing the judge and inquisitor, but I was determined to know. I said: "Remember I'm a doctor, and tell me all the details."

"Well, I kissed him." He was looking at his big, raw knuckles. "And then?" He went on with a rush. "Then we played with one another, and got on the bed. Then we both came."

"He came?" I was interested in this point.

"Oh, yes, he came all right. Like a bomb."

"What happened then?"

"Nothing . . . on that occasion."

"But there were others?"

"One other. The next day. I went back and we did it again."

"But this time you went further?"

He had decided to be open about it. "I got the feeling he wanted to. So I asked him to bend over the bed. I knew from the way he did it that this wasn't the first time."

"There was no question of him wanting to bugger you?"

"No."

"What happened when it was over?"

"He said: 'Go away and let me alone now.' I said 'How about tomorrow?' and he said, 'No, never again.' So I left it at that."

"You say you got the impression it had happened before. Was he physically easy to enter?"

"Well . . . er . . . no."

"And how did you manage it?"

He put his hand into his overall pocket, and drew out a small tin of vaseline. I said: "All right, thank you, Tebbut,"

19

and went back into the canteen to have my tea. He did not follow me.

I kept my promise to him and said nothing to the governor. There would have been no point. I believed Tebbut when he said Lingard had consented. Tebbut was, of course, a guard; if he had been a fellow prisoner, I believe that Arthur Lingard's reaction would have been positive rejection. But guard or not, there was nothing to prevent him rejecting Tebbut. It was a nasty episode. Lingard made a habit of keeping himself to himself. Then he made the mistake of allowing himself one friendship. It turned promptly into a betrayal, with the indignity of being sodomized over a bed.

(I was relieved when, two months later, Tebbut was caught behind a local cinema, engaged in sex play with a twelve-year-old boy. The governor took action, and he left for parts unknown.)

I walked back slowly to Lingard's room. This certainly looked like the clue to his breakdown—or at least, one of them. The psychotic is in a perpetual state of fear: he swims in fear like a fish in water. The fear tinges everything he sees or thinks about. Every shadow on the wall can produce that sinking of the stomach, and the psychiatrist is as much an object of fear as anything else. The problem is how to break into his enclosed world, to reverse this negative flow in at least one particular. I now had the means to enter Lingard's inner world. And now I was possessed by an excited desire to use my key. And because Arthur Lingard was *my* patient, and I had discovered the key, I felt a protective warmth toward him. It made no difference that he might be a deliberate and calculating killer. That was merely another aspect of his sickness.

I sat on the end of his bed and watched his hand trace out a knife blade. When I spoke to him, he ignored me. He drew the glans of a penis. I pointed at it, "Whose penis is this?" He ignored me. "It's Harry Tebbut's cock, isn't it? You want to cut off Harry Tebbut's cock?" The line he was drawing wavered; then he dropped the pen. A film of sweat suddenly appeared on his gray skin. "Nobody minds if you cut off Harry Tebbut's cock. He deserves it, doesn't he? He makes you do things you don't want to do?" His head leaned back against the pillow, the eyes closed. He looked sick and old. My whisper made me feel like the devil tempting some

20

medieval ascetic. "Go on, cut it off. Don't be afraid." Suddenly, his face turned sharply aside, and he vomited onto the drawings on the bedside chair. It smelled foul and sour; I felt sick too; but it was no point for squeamishness. I watched the convulsing of his shoulders, watched for five minutes or more until he leaned back, vomit running down his chin. "That's better. You're getting him out of your system now." I felt that a part of him was still resisting me; but he was weakening. I talked on softly. Every time I mentioned Tebbut's name, there was a reaction. His fist clenched. "Go on, take the knife in your hand. That's right. Grip it. Hold it tight." I saw his other hand close, and interpreted the movement. "That's right. Cut it. Don't be afraid." His left hand— the hand with the knife—wavered. I said sharply, "Go on. *Now.*" The movement that followed was so savage that it startled me. His hand rose violently, the sweating face expressed loathing. With all his force, the hand crashed down, striking his knee violently. For a hallucinatory moment, it seemed that he was actually holding a knife in one hand and a severed penis in the other. I said, "There. You've done it." His face convulsed with released tension, and the sweat ran down it. He looked like an exhausted runner after a race. I went on talking, slowly, drowsily. "There, it's gone now. You can throw it away. . . ." I was not assuming that his single act of violence had somehow released all his hatred of Tebbut. Why should it? He had been expressing the hatred ever since he began making the drawings of knives. What mattered was that he had let me into his fantasy, allowed me into his private world. One of two things could happen. I might become a part of some other hate fantasy, or he might accept me as someone who wished him well, as a force of benevolence. As soon as that happened, the battle was half won. The negative circuit was broken. I talked on for over half an hour, praying that no one would interrupt us. I watched his face relax slowly. He was becoming drowsy. After a while he began to mutter. I caught the words, "Yes, he's a swine, a filthy swine." They were said sleepily, without hatred, and I felt a flash of triumph. The glass bubble was broken. For the moment, he was back in the world of people.

When I left him, half an hour later, he was sleeping peacefully. After the stench of vomit, I was glad of the scent of flowers.

TWO

It is sometimes difficult for a doctor working with the mentally sick to preserve a sense of humor. But I had to smile the next day when I went to Arthur Lingard's room. The subject of his drawings had changed. Instead of knives slicing into penises, he was now drawing razors slashing into female genitals. Lingard's drawings showed a basic artistic talent; the open thighs and the pubic hairs looked real. I said: "How are you?" He looked up at me and nodded. "Have you seen the electric man today?" He said, without looking up, "He's gone." He said it with finality. I sat down on the bed and picked up one of the drawings. "And who is this?" He pointed to the fold of the vulva. "This is the world, and this is God's razor." "But why is God cutting open the world?" "To let out the . . ." He groped for a word. "To let out the muddy water." "Muddy water?" "Yes, water with green stuff floating on it, and frogspawn and mud like jelly."

It produced intense satisfaction to hear him answering like this, communicating again, even though it was obvious that I was still a long way from curing his sickness. With a psychotic, it is essential to let him talk, and to listen carefully, waiting for him to provide a clue. Often he tries to avoid the subject that is at the forefront of his mind, to disguise it, to wrap it round with layers of evasion. Now I was past the first stage—getting him to talk freely. But I had only to look at his drawings to see how far there was still to go.

That afternoon, before I went to join Frank Slessor for our usual sundowner, I sat beside Arthur Lingard's bed, trying to get some meaningful response. I said: "You're a clever man, aren't you? Do you know who you remind me of? Netchaev." There was no response. "You know Sergei

22

Netchaev, don't you, the Russian anarchist?" He looked up, his eyes showing surprise.

"Oh, Neechev!" That was why he had not reacted immediately: he had worked out his own pronunciation of Netchaev (which I pronounce with three syllables—Nechay-ev.) He went back to his drawing—an electric mask—but I noticed that his hand was hesitant.

"Yes, you're very like Neechev in some ways. You believe in revolution at all costs, don't you?"

He grunted; I sensed that he was pleased. But all he said was, "Perhaps I do."

"Is that why you want people to think you're stupid?"

"Who said I did?"

"Dr. Massey" (this was my predecessor). "He said you tried to convince people you were stupid, but that you were actually well above average intelligence."

He looked at me oddly. "Did he say that?"

"Yes." It was untrue, but I was feeling my way.

"Are you sure?"

"Quite sure. Would you like to see the report?"

This seemed to convince him. I said again, "Why do you want people to think you're stupid?"

I had no particular aim in asking this question. I simply wanted to establish a two-way relationship between us. He glanced at me cunningly.

"You know why?"

"No, I don't. Tell me."

He looked up at me, then tore off a strip of paper from his drawing pad, and scribbled something on it. He passed it to me. I read: "They'd get me." "Who'd get you?"

"Sshh!" He snatched the paper from me, and pushed it into his mouth. He chewed it and swallowed it. I looked around me in a conspiratorial manner.

"Who'd get you?"

I bent my face close to him. He muttered out of the corner of his mouth, "The black guards."

"What, the prison guards?"

"No!" He smiled pityingly at my stupidity. "Why do you think I'm in here?"

"I don't know. Why are you?"

"To hide away from them. These guards are here to protect me."

"But who are the black guards?"

"Don't you know?" He looked incredulous.

"No, I don't."

He whispered, so quietly I could hardly catch it, "They're from the Black Bailiff."

"And who's he?"

"You don't know?" This time he was amazed, almost scandalized. I shook my head and tried to look stupid. He said: "No. I suppose a lot of people are as ignorant as you." He stared at me penetratingly, and stopped trying to keep his voice down. "Well, there's a war. The universe is at war."

"But who's fighting?"

"God. He's lost control of his universe. There are black powers from outside the universe trying to get in at us. I know about them, so they want to destroy me. That's why I came in here, to hide from them." I began to understand why his betrayal by Tebbut had been so traumatic; one of his protectors had turned against him. I wondered how long Lingard had suffered from these delusions.

It took me half an hour to get him to tell me all about the "great war of the universe." What he said eventually was that forces of immense evil had entered the world, and that he could see and feel them. The "old reality" was at an end, or superseded; now there was a new, horrible reality that threatened the whole human race. It would do no good to tell people about it, because it would only terrify them, and there would be fighting in the streets.

However, *he,* Arthur Lingard, had the secret answer to the problem. He was one of a new species of man who would develop extraordinary powers, the power to look into the profoundest gulfs, to understand the most terrible secrets, and, eventually, to destroy the Black Bailiff himself. He told me confidentially that he could destroy a man by pointing his finger at him. I risked provoking his hostility by asking why, in that case, he had not destroyed Harry Tebbut. He smiled at me pityingly.

"Because I don't want people to know who I am. *They* might find out where I'm hidden."

His fantasy was extraordinarily elaborate and terrifying. These creatures could change their shape at will, but mostly they became a cloud of electricity, vaguely in the shape of a human being, full of glowing red points of energy like a swarm of fireflies. Sometimes they came into his room, but it was only a routine check; he did not think they suspected his identity. The Black Bailiff himself was a monster something like an octopus or a black jellyfish, but he could also assume different forms; his favorite one was of a bird-man. Their world was completely unlike ours, and earthly minds could not even begin to understand it.

The details he had thought out were amazing, and I found myself reflecting, as I have about a number of psychotic patients, that if he had had the power to organize his fantasies, he could have made a living writing science fiction.

I asked finally, "And when do you think this great battle will take place?" (The battle when God, with the help of Arthur Lingard, would defeat the Black Bailiff.)

"Soon. Very soon." He looked out the window and stiffened. I followed his stare, and saw a motorcycle policeman walking past. He wore black goggles pushed up on to his forehead, and a crash helmet. I said: "What is it?"

He pointed. "I've just seen one of them, one of the black guards."

Here, I thought, was my opportunity, the opportunity to insert the first thin wedge of doubt into his insane structure. I said: "Are you sure?" "Quite sure." "But I recognize the man. It's Police Constable Hammett, who patrols between Sedgefield and Darlington."

He smiled contemptuously.

"You think it is. He's in disguise."

I walked to the door, and looked out. I called, "Hammett! Constable Hammett!"

He looked around, saw me, and came back. I said, "Would you come in here a minute, please?"

"Why, certainly, sir." He followed me into the room. I said to Lingard: "There. You know Constable Hammett, don't you?" I asked Hammett if he would mind removing his goggles and helmet, giving him a faint wink. He obliged. Then, to avoid watching Lingard, I carried on a brief, friendly conversation with Hammett, asked him how his wife was, whether his child had recovered from chicken pox, and so on. He played up admirably; a west countryman who had come to live in the North, he had a pleasant, burring voice and a down-to-earth manner of speaking. Anyone who thought he was a black guard would need considerable powers of self-persuasion.

When he had gone, I turned to Lingard, and was glad to see that the superior smile had vanished.

"Well?"

He nodded. "I could have been mistaken. He looks very like Liafail, the head of the Deathwatch division of the guards."

I felt that this opportunity was too good to miss.

"But are you sure Liafail exists? Have you ever seen him?"

"Several times."

"But how can you be certain it wasn't Police Constable Hammett, or another motorcycle policeman? You just mistook him for Liafail."

He shook his head. "That isn't certain. Perhaps it *was* Liafail. Their disguise is often perfect."

"But I thought you could always penetrate it?"

This worried him. He considered for a few moments. He had been very insistent about his ability to penetrate the deceptions of the emissaries of the Black Bailiff. I pressed my advantage.

"You're a highly intelligent, reasonable man. Surely you must admit that you're capable of being mistaken about the black guards?"

He rubbed his eyes, and said in a bored voice, "What you're suggesting is that it's all my imagination—repressed unconscious urges distorting my natural perceptions? You think I'm sick?"

It was my turn to be taken aback. I could not have been more surprised if my Alsatian had suddenly addressed me. Lingard did not make an impression of brightness, but he now talked of "urges distorting my natural perceptions" as if he was thoroughly accustomed to using such terms. I began to wonder if he was not making a fool of me. I tried not to show my surprise.

"Quite. Why don't we suppose, just as a hypothesis, that you may be suffering from auditory and visual hallucinations?" (I had decided to work on the assumption that he would not be worried by big words—in fact, would be flattered that I should treat him as an intellectual equal.) "This doesn't imply that you're insane. I'm perfectly willing to admit that my unconscious mind can interfere in my everyday life without my being aware of it. In fact, I suffered from auditory hallucinations myself during the war, after the house I was in was hit by a bomb. I'd hear my mother's voice calling to me quite distinctly, although she'd been dead for ten years." (I was trying out Paul-Charles Dubois's

26

persuasion method—establish a close, human relation with the patient.) "In the same way, I once suffered severe delayed shock after a motor accident, and it took me some time to work out why I suddenly began to tremble and feel weak. The subconscious is, after all, hidden from us by definition."

Lingard listened to this judicially, his head on one side, his finger resting against his cheek. Then he nodded slowly: "I see your point of view, of course. And I understand why you think so. But why don't you consider the opposite hypothesis—that I may be right? You admit you don't understand when your subconscious may be interfering in your everyday life. But you'll agree that you prefer not to think about unpleasant things? For example, that in thirty years from now, your body may be turning to liquid under the ground?"

"That is true."

"You admit it's true, but do you really think about it? Can you really look at your hands, and imagine what they'll look like without skin on the bones?" I did so, and winced. "You don't think about it normally, because you'd blow your mental fuses. It's necessary to human happiness to ignore anything that would endanger mental fuses. Do you agree?" I said yes. "In that case, isn't it more likely that I'm right than that you are? I'm trying to face facts that you prefer to ignore. You have to admit that you'd *prefer* the Black Bailiff to be a figment of my imagination, wouldn't you? How do you know your preference isn't blinding you to his real existence?"

I began to get a very uncomfortable feeling. The relation between a doctor and his patient is supposed to be based on the doctor's feeling of superiority. But Lingard was making me feel defensive, almost angry.

He went on reasonably: "The trouble with most people is that they can't concentrate. Isn't that how you felt when you kept hearing your mother's voice? Did you feel confused and unsure of yourself? And how did you manage to get over it? Wasn't it by concentrating on trivial, everyday problems and forgetting about your fears?" (This was a particularly good shot; I had, in fact, regained my balance by learning to paint.) "Do you think that's really honest—to try to forget what's worrying you instead of facing it? I've never run away from a problem. I decided I had to learn to concentrate more than other people. And as soon as I learned to concentrate, I began to suspect the existence of the black guards."

He argued lucidly and reasonably. Basically, it was an unanswerable argument. Anyone can prove anything by pointing out that the universe is full of unanswered questions, and that we know almost nothing. I said as much to Lingard, and he said, "Exactly. So how can you be sure you're right and I'm wrong?"

"But I can't see your black guards. If they existed, surely I could see them?"

"They don't want to be seen. If you could learn to concentrate properly, you'd be able to see them. And if you had a little more imagination, you'd see that everything I say is possible."

It was the first time in my life that I had been in this position: completely checkmated by a patient. It struck me then that there is something very dubious about the usual methods of psychiatrists. If you tell a patient that he can't think straight because his judgment is distorted by subconscious factors of which he is unaware, he has a perfect right to retort that the same applies to you, and that your whole treatment may be founded on your own obsessions.

But although it seemed clear that I could not win this argument, I was winning in another sense. I was closer to Lingard, and he was talking freely to me. It was the first big step. Thinking about it that evening—and describing the afternoon to my wife Evelyn—it struck me that part of Lingard's trouble may have been his loneliness. In telling him that Dr. Massey considered him brilliant, I had made an inspired shot in the dark; it had been the key that opened his mind to me. He *was* brilliant, or at least, highly intelligent, and he had been in prison for nearly five years, keeping himself to himself, hiding his thoughts from others. This, I saw, explained the Tebbut episode. Tebbut was fairly bright, as I discovered in a talk with the governor. That was why Lingard had encouraged him. He had decided to risk a closer relation. And the result had been betrayal. He was thrown back into his wilderness.

And this presented the most interesting question of all. Why the hell *should* he be so determined to keep himself to himself? It wasn't natural. An intelligent person needs sympathetic human intercourse more than a stupid one.

It was at this point that I had my second break in this

case. I have mentioned that I had written to Strangeways jail to see if I could find out the name of the book Lingard had been smearing with excrement. Their first response was negative. It had been burned, since it was now unreadable. But two days later, I received a paperback in the mail. It was called *The Kid from Louisville* by Idris T. Moroney, and seemed to be a boxing novel of the kind issued by the thousand every year. The letter from Dr. Alan Buckle that accompanied it said that the assistant librarian was quite certain that this was the title of the book, and that they happened to have a second copy of it, which I was asked to return. He had, of course, no idea of the page that Lingard had smeared. I settled down one evening and read it. It was the usual story of the boxer's rise to success, and the writing was below average. Halfway through, the hero meets the manager of the ex-world champion, and his beautiful mistress Pauline. "Her warm skin glowed with health. Under the smooth black sheath of the dress, her nipples stood out like small spikes. As she walked away from him toward the bar, he could see the outline of diminutive briefs under the glossy silk. . . ." Later, when they are alone, Tex leans forward and bites her nipple through the dress, then pulls up the bottom over her waist. "The ripe red mouth opened in a groan of ecstasy, and her eyes closed tightly. He leaned forward, took her lip between his teeth, and bit it so the blood came. One jerk of his big hand tore away the flimsy panties and tossed them into the fire. His other hand reached up under the dress, and tore loose the black bra. She leaned against him weakly, as if her legs were turned to water. He pushed her away for a moment to bare his own throbbing flesh, then picked her up and carried her to the divan. 'The door . . .' she whispered, but he ignored her. 'Please . . .' Then her protest broke off in a groan of pleasure as his mighty loins thrust forward, splitting open the waiting bud of flesh. . . ."

This scene was the high spot of the book. I skipped through the rest, and assured myself that there was nothing, as far as I could tell, that would excite Lingard. In any case, I had felt a flicker of recognition at the name. Arthur Lingard's sister was called Pauline. I copied out the passage, and returned the book. Two days later came another surprise. Dr. Buckle had looked into the files of *his* predecessor, and had found the carbon of a report dating from the 1955 sentence for burglary; he sent me a photostat of this. It consisted of three typed sheets, and I saw immediately that it represented a conscientious attempt to trace the course of Lingard's development into a habitual petty crook.

Arthur Lingard was born in November 1937—an ominous date, with the clouds already gathering over Europe. His mother was killed in an air raid on North London in 1941; Lingard and his sister Pauline, five years his senior, saw the body when it was dragged from the burning building. Lingard told the psychiatrist that he could recall every detail of the scene, although he was only four at the time. They had been on their way to the air-raid shelter when the bomb hit.

They were evacuated to Warrington, in Lancashire, to the home of his father's brother. Six months later, his father was also killed. His uncle and aunt kept that secret, but one of their cousins told him toward the end of the war.

Their mother had owned a little property in East London; it was bought by the London County Council for a few hundred pounds, and a block of flats rose on the site. Pauline and Arthur inherited the money. Uncle Dick Lingard became their official guardian when he learned about the money. All that was left when Pauline came of age was twenty-two pounds.

Arthur was in trouble from the age of four, when he went to nursery school; he seemed to have an obsessional need to smash things—toys, windows, bottles, flowerpots. He was beaten a great deal, and in 1951, when he was thirteen, his uncle asked a probation officer to have him committed to an approved school because he was completely beyond control. Arthur ran away after six months, and a kindly magistrate ordered his uncle to take him back home and try again. A few months later, his uncle was arrested; Pauline was pregnant, and alleged that Dick Lingard was the father of the child, and that he had been having sexual intercourse with her since she was twelve. He was sentenced to three years in prison. At sixteen, Arthur had a long period of intense depression that may have been associated with fear of his uncle's return from prison. He stopped eating, and told a social worker that his food was poisoned. He attacked a ten-year-old schoolgirl with a flatiron, and attempted rape. A juvenile court ordered psychiatric treatment. Twice during the next year, he was caught burgling houses; on each occasion, he

30

escaped with a warning, since he was under treatment. On the second occasion, his spoils were a gold watch, a knife, and five pairs of ladies' panties. When he was eighteen, a judge sentenced him to six months in prison for burglary. On his nineteenth birthday, he tried a new way of making money; he obtained from somewhere a pile of brochures of washing machines, and went from door to door in South London offering the machines on exceptionally good terms, and accepting a deposit from housewives. This business prospered; it was three months before he was caught and sentenced to another short period in jail. Almost immediately, on his release, he was caught in the act of breaking into a shop; he pleaded guilty to breaking and entering, and received another six months. After that, he managed to keep out of trouble with the police for nearly four years, until the farmhouse burglary. During that time he was questioned several times about burglaries, and once about the murder case I have mentioned, but never detained. He was also accused by the husband of his sister Pauline of coming to the house one afternoon and severely beating her. His sister refused to charge him, and the matter was dropped.

It seemed a fairly straightforward case history; early deprivation and shock; a brutal foster-father with a large family of his own. (Dick Lingard was often in trouble with the police for violence when drunk.) The school record was better than might be expected, but otherwise, all the signs indicated a youth with a deep resentment about society. I wondered how far he had been responsible for getting his sister to implicate Dick Lingard in the matter of her pregnancy? Was he, perhaps, sexually jealous of his uncle? After the death of his mother, his sister Pauline was all he had in the world, a substitute mother. If his uncle committed a sexual act on Pauline when she was twelve, then Arthur would have been seven at the time. Might this not account for the various acts of destruction and defiance that culminated in Dick Lingard's request to have him sent to an approved school?

The trouble was that the case records were not full enough. I needed to know a great deal more about Arthur Lingard's development. And at present I knew of only one person who could tell me: Lingard himself.

He and I had now established an interesting relationship. We had agreed to differ. He understood that I considered his visions of electric men to be hallucinations; I understood that he considered me well-meaning but rather obtuse. Sometimes, he would unbend to the extent of entertaining the hypothesis that they were unreal. On other occasions, he was tense and worried, and then I listened to him seriously, as though I was convinced he had something to worry about. A week after our first conversation about the Black Bailiff, I found him looking haggard and exhausted. He told me that he had information that the invasion was due to start almost immediately. Thousands of black guards were pouring into England through remote areas in the north of Scotland, and exterminating every living thing they encountered. What is more, he was afraid that he was their objective; they knew he could destroy them. The following day, I found an article about the Loch Ness monster, datelined from Inverness the previous day. I took this to show him, to prove that no one had noticed the black guards yet. He shrugged.

"Naturally. They've got tremendous organization. Every time they destroy a village, they leave people behind to answer the telephones and answer letters. No one knows what they've done."

"But what about people going into the district?"

"If there's any danger of discovery, they're killed or held prisoner."

He read the newspaper story carefully, then pointed out several misprints. "You see, they give themselves away in small things. They can't spell yet."

"You think that article was written by the black guards?"

"I know it was. Inverness was overrun by them last Sunday."

"How do you know?"

"Someone came and told me in the night. An electric woman."

"What does she look like?"

"She's just a head. She knows that if she appeared with a body, I'd have bad thoughts about her. So she leaves her body behind when she comes to see me."

The next day he was worse. He was convinced that black guards had infiltrated the prison, with instructions to poison his food, and if possible, to stop his heart by sending out "electrostatic waves." They would appear behind the guard who brought his food, leering at him, and one of them had an enormous erect penis, over a foot long. He would make obscene twitching motions with his hips, implying that he intended to rape Lingard as soon as he got the chance. Once, when I was waiting outside the lavatory for Lingard, he gave a loud scream and rushed out with his trousers around his ankles. He said that he was reaching behind to wipe himself when he discovered there was already a hand covering his anal orifice. He turned and found the leering black guard, holding his penis in one hand. He was completely convinced of the reality of the guard, and I had to look into the lavatory and assure him there was no one there, then stand beside him as he wiped himself and flushed the toilet. He was trembling when he got back into bed, and on the point of tears.

The time for argument had gone past. I tried another approach: "Listen, why don't you stop fighting so hard? Why don't you simply relax, and stop fighting? They can't mean to harm you, or they wouldn't be watching you like this. They're only keeping you under observation. Why don't you simply let yourself become wide open. Accept everything. Behave as if you're simply an observer, watching them."

Surprisingly enough, this worked. He promised to try it. While we were still talking, I saw his eyes wandering over my shoulder. I asked him if he could see anything.

"Yes, he's there, right behind you. He keeps grinning at me and waving his penis."

"That's all right. Let him. It doesn't matter if he listens in to what we say, does it? Treat him as something completely natural, like the furniture. Make notes of everything they say to you."

He relaxed quite visibly; he actually sank back into the pillows, and allowed his bent knees to straighten out. Again, my instinct had led me to make the right suggestion. And in fact, this was the turning point in the case. He stopped reacting to his delusions. He simply observed them, bore them as inevitable, and carefully wrote them all down. A huge black dog sat outside his window and growled periodically. The woman who brought him news of the advance of the black guard allowed her body to accompany her. She was dressed like a nurse and carried a cane. He accepted her so completely that she began standing by his bed, smiling at him in a suggestive manner.

33

I said, "Why don't you see what happens if you make an advance to her?"

"She might take offense and go away."

"That wouldn't matter. Accept whatever happens."

The next time I saw him, he said triumphantly, "I did it."

"What happened?"

"She outsmarted me. I got my hand on her thigh, and she didn't try to stop me. So I lifted her skirt and pulled down her pants. But there was nothing underneath them. They were empty."

"Fascinating," I said. "You see how much you've learned by becoming an observer?"

He nodded, seriously and thoughtfully. I knew that our relationship had changed. Once again, I was the doctor, he the patient. He had decided to trust me. At my request, he made drawings of everyone who appeared to him, and of the black dog outside his window. Rather to my surprise, this latter proved to be an excellent sketch of my pet Alsatian, Skinner, black but quite unmistakable. Lingard had never seen my dog. I cannot explain the coincidence, and do not attempt to, except to say that a doctor and his patient can sometimes establish a strangely close relationship.

The result of all this was an immense improvement in Arthur Lingard's general health. He began to walk around again and to take an interest in his own patch of garden; he could even keep up a normal-sounding conversation with other prisoners, although he soon tired and would break off abruptly. His relationship with me became the usual one between a doctor and a neurotic patient. I noted down his dreams, discussed his hallucinations, listened to his fears—of being attacked by a giant dog, of turning into a tortoise (another symbol of claustrophobia), of having a snake climb up his behind when he was seated on the lavatory (another obvious symbol). The governor congratulated me on my success. But I knew this was premature. He trusted me, but there was still much that he held back. Fundamentally, he was still a mystery to me.

One day when I left him—about five weeks after treatment commenced—this sense of frustration, of having glimpsed a fragment of a mystery, was so strong that I brooded all the way home about it and, that evening, actually discussed it with a medical colleague from Lancashire who called on me. What intrigued him most was Lingard's

34

sudden switch from a semimoronic state to a highly articulate level. He described a similar case he had known—of a banker who had experienced delusions after a serious accident, and who actually seemed to become two different persons, one lethargic and half-witted, the other cultured and intelligent. I tried hard to put my finger on some elusive insight.

"But Lingard isn't quite the same kind of thing. His stupidity—his assumed stupidity—seems to me a kind of permanent disguise, which he's decided to drop with me."

"You mean he's normally afraid to show he's intelligent?"

"Well, something like that."

"Then he's really a weird case. I've known people who spent their lives trying to conceal their stupidity, but never the other way round."

That night, as I lay in bed, this comment came back to me, and I half sat up in bed. Because I felt like shouting the question: *Why* should Lingard want to conceal his intelligence? It just doesn't conform with the criminal mentality. Criminals are boasters; again and again they spoil a perfect crime by wanting to be admired by other criminals. Was he so disgusted and bored with his prison surroundings that he relapsed into apathy? Or had he always been like this? There was a possible way to find out: to investigate his background.

THREE

I am not fond of the industrial towns of Yorkshire; so I drove across the Pennines to Burnley, then south to Manchester. It had rained in the night, and the July morning was fresh and full of the smells of summer. As I drove down through the golden and green countryside, I listened to a concert of Elgar and Delius on the car radio, and the beauty of the day made me understand the nostalgia in their music. Then the hills gave way to the grime and cobbles of northern Lancashire; the factory chimneys of Burnley belched smoke, and the air smelled of soot. On the outskirts of Manchester, a signpost pointing to Saddleworth reminded me of the Moors murder case, and I suddenly felt I understood it. All this dirty brick was without glamour, without charm. The leggy girl in the red miniskirt who walked over the level crossing had the look of someone who had lost her virginity behind a dance hall at the age of thirteen; in a few years' time she would be pushing a pram along this same road, with another child trotting alongside and complaining.

I spent half an hour in a traffic jam in the center of Manchester, now sick of the July heat. I reached Warrington slightly before midday. I parked my car and drank a pint of beer in a pub before getting out to look for Penketh Street—the street where Arthur Lingard grew up. I had never been in Warrington before, but it was somehow what I had expected; another Lancashire industrial town, with railways and canals and the River Mersey looking brown and oily. On the wall of the pub's gents' toilet, there had been a drawing of a girl seated on a toilet, pressing open her sexual organs with both hands, and an obscene caption underneath. This conjunction—of female genitals and a lavatory—seemed to fuse in my mind the many impressions of the past hour or so.

Children were playing hopscotch in Penketh Street. It stretches between a main road and the Manchester Ship Canal; a yellow-fronted, ugly Methodist chapel stands at the end of the street. The modern self-service grocer on the opposite corner looks completely out of place. This is a street that has not changed since the 1880s, and it could have been a street in Arnold Bennett's potteries or D. H. Lawrence's Eastwood; the cobbles, the smell of the gasworks and the canal, the distant crash of trains being shunted into sidings, the chalked wickets on a garden wall. The front door of number seventeen was covered with the scales of a varnish that had probably been there in Arthur Lingard's childhood.

I raised the knocker; it made a thudding crash. There was no reply. I knocked again, and waited, then went down a narrow entry that smelt of cat pee, and into the backyard. Flies buzzed around the dustbin; what had once been a small plot of garden seemed to be used as a rubbish dump. The back door stood slightly ajar, but repeated knocking brought no reply. Then the gate opened, and a woman came in, carrying a shopping bag. She was small, and her face was flabby and unhealthy. She looked startled and rather alarmed to see me; I quickly introduced myself as "Dr. Kahn," and asked her if she was Mrs. Lingard. She acknowledged that she was. I said: "I'm from the prison. I want to speak to you about Arthur, your foster son." "You'd better cum in." I followed her into a kitchen that was full of steam; a copper bubbled away in the corner, with the smell of boiling clothes. "I've got to get me 'usband's dinner, so I can't sit down. Is Arthur in trouble again?"

I told her briefly about Arthur's breakdown, and I was interested to observe the way she seemed to cheer up when I talked about it. I have come to regard this as a useful method of assessing personality; the more someone has succumbed to fatigue and defeat, the more news of disasters cheers them up. Elsie Lingard struck me as a person who had sunk into defeat up to her neck, and has finally achieved a kind of miserable stability. I watched her lighting the gas stove, dropping the used match into a huge tin of used matches that stood on the corner of the kitchen table. The walls were painted a dirty brown. It would have taken her a single morning and a tin of cheap paint to brighten the whole place beyond recognition; but she couldn't be bothered. The dirty oilcloth that covered the table was almost colorless, and was full of cuts where she had sliced onions or potatoes without bothering with a plate. The smell of grease hung over everything. She took down a frying pan in which grease and fragments of bacon had been allowed to harden, and set it on the gas; the kitchen filled with a slightly rancid smell. She took an egg from the shopping bag and cracked it on the edge of the pan; the yolk broke as she pulled it apart, and ran across the pan.

"Is your husband at home?"

"Yes. He's in bed."

"Is he ill?"

"I suppose you could call it that. Will they put Arthur in a lunertickersylum?" (She pronounced it as one word.)

"There may be no need for that: I'm hoping to cure him."

"Oh." She obviously lost interest.

It was hard to penetrate her indifference. I said, "How do you feel about Arthur now?"

"You can't expect me to feel much, can you?"

"No? Why?"

"You know what he did to Richard?" (Her husband.)

I pretended ignorance. "No, I don't. What did he do?"

"Split on him to the police" (gave him away).

"You mean about his sister."

"That's right. It was 'im that made Polly go to the police."

This is what I had suspected. "Didn't they like each other—your husband and Arthur?"

"I s'pose not. 'E was too clever to show it. You could never tell what he was thinkin'. 'E was a sly un."

We were interrupted by the arrival of a girl of about twenty, who introduced herself as Jane. She seemed one of those girls who are born for a lifetime "on the shelf"; a sallow face that could have been pretty if it had possessed a gleam of vitality, straight, mousy hair, arms and legs like sticks, no breasts; she also showed the characteristic gleam of pleasure when I talked of Arthur's breakdown. "Yes, I always thought 'e'd go bats." Mrs. Lingard remonstrated: "Hush, gel, you mustn't say that to a doctor."

I wondered whether it would now be tactful to pursue the subject of Dick Lingard's period in jail for carnal knowledge of his foster daughter; I said cautiously, "You were telling me about Arthur's attitude toward your husband."

Jane said, "Dad hated Arthur's guts."

"But why?

"Wouldn't you? Dad brought him up, treated him like a son, and all he does is gets him took away."

"I thought it was his sister Pauline who was responsible?"

"No. 'E was be'ind it all right."

I decided to risk the question I had meant to ask Mrs. Lingard before Jane arrived.

"And was he guilty?"

I looked from one to the other. Jane shrugged slightly.

"Depends what you mean by guilty, don't it?"

"In what sense?"

Mrs. Lingard, who was peeling potatoes by the simple expedient of removing huge slices and converting them into cubes, said, "He wasn't the first."

"Course he wasn't," said Jane.

"No? Then who was?"

Jane said: "Could have been anybody. She was that sort. She'd 'ave it off with anybody. Dad 'ad to belt her a dozen times. She used to get lads in the entry."

"Was Arthur very attached to her?"

38

Jane laughed shrilly.

"Oh, yes. He was attached all right. So attached you couldn't prise 'em apart."

"You think Arthur was one of the boys who . . . who got her in the entry?"

"He didn't have to, did he? They slept in the same bed."

"The same bed?"

Perhaps I looked scandalized, because Mrs. Lingard said quickly: "Not alone, of course. There was three of our lot as well, Albert, Ted, and Maggie."

"All in one bed?"

"It was quite a big bed. It's still up there."

I saw that I would learn as much from Jane as from Mrs. Lingard, so I suggested that we allow her mother to cook in peace. She accepted the idea with alacrity.

"Yes, cum and sit down." The living room looked as if burglars had been through it. "This is a bit untidy. Cum on in the front room." I followed her past a piece of dyed sacking that hung in a doorway, into what was obviously the "best room." This was tidy enough, but the layers of dust, and the smell of damp and disuse, made it a depressing room. The July heat had not penetrated; it was distinctly chilly.

When we were seated in lumpy armchairs, I said, "Could you begin by giving me a list of your brothers and sisters?"

She ticked them off on her fingers.

"Well, there's Jim, the eldest. Then Albert, Ted, Aggie, and me. There was Maggie, but she's dead."

I wrote them down, then asked, "Would you say that Arthur was very clever?"

She shrugged irritably. "He tried to be."

"But *was* he?"

"No. He was morbid. He liked to frighten the kids in the street with tales about ghosts and monsters." She pulled open a cupboard at the side of her chair. "This is the sort of thing he read." She handed me a magazine, *Terror Tales*. The cover showed a drooling man with a whip, and several girls in torn underwear chained against a wall. "He tortured women to satisfy horrible lusts" read the caption. I opened it. There was an illustration of a girl tied to a bed, with her legs spread wide open; the same drooling maniac is approaching her with a red-hot poker.

I looked in the cupboard. There were piles of these magazines, as well as of copies of *Weird Tales, Ringside,*

39

True Detective, and *True Confessions*. There were also a number of paperback books. One of them immediately caught my attention. It was called *Marvo the Magician*, and the cover showed a man in a red cloak with signs of the zodiac on it, bending forward, his hands outstretched toward a beautiful girl, who is obviously hypnotized. On the ground at his feet, a man is crouched in the posture of a frightened animal. "He turned human beings into dogs," said the legend on the cover. Jane saw it.

"Oh, yes, that was one of his favorites. You can see how much he read it." It was true; the book had been carefully repaired with cellotape and gummed paper, and the covers strengthened with the cardboard from a cornflakes packet. I said, "I must ask your mother if I can borrow some of these."

"Oh, she won't care. She never reads."

I asked, "Where is Pauline now?"

"She married a lorry driver. She lives in Stockport."

"Do you ever see her?"

"No. But I hear about her sometimes."

She said this in a meaningful way. I raised my eyebrows.

"She's a right tart. She always was. 'Er 'usband goes away nights. It's a good thing he doesn't know what goes on."

"What does go on?"

"She'll sleep with anybody. I'll tell you a story I know to be true. She loves bingo. A bloke I know runs the one near where she lives. She comes in one evening, goes to his office. She says: 'I haven't got any money, but will you take it out of this?' and she pulls up her skirt. He said she'd got all frilly underwear on, and she just stood there so he could get a good look."

"And did he?"

"No!" She spat it out with contempt. "He wouldn't take the risk. You could catch anything off a type like that."

I began to find Jane Lingard depressing. She talked readily enough, but everything she said seemed to be saturated in meanness and envy; moreover, she seemed to take it for granted that everyone felt as she did. Perhaps I was looking too sympathetic and encouraging. I felt that I had made my most important find of the day—the magazines. I was relieved when Mrs. Lingard called, "Jane, come and get yer dinner." We went back into the other room. She had cleared some of the breakfast dishes off the table, and laid out her daughter's midday meal—egg and chips, all of it discolored by the brown fat. There was a heavy thump on the ceiling, and Mrs. Lingard yelled "All right!" in a voice that made me jump. "That's Dad," said Jane, "I 'spect 'e's 'ungry."

As Mrs. Lingard came through the living room with another plate of egg and chips, I said, "Could I see your husband?"

She looked startled.

"If you like. Better let me tell him first."

Jane said confidentially, "She wants to tidy the room up."

A few minutes later, Mrs. Lingard called, "All right, you can come up now." I went up stairs that were so dark that I felt my way up with my hands. Dick Lingard's room overlooked the backyard. The window was tightly closed and the room stank of sweat and urine.

Dick Lingard was sitting up in bed, and my first sight of him was a surprise. I knew he had been a powerful man; but nothing of this remained. He looked seventy. The face was as white and soft as uncooked dough, the mouth sunken in (his false teeth were in a glass of water on the table). He was wearing a string vest. He gave an impression of being humpbacked, but after a while I realized this was because he had allowed shoulders that were once powerful to droop forward.

Mrs. Lingard said, "This is the doctor." He looked at me and nodded, then began picking up chips with his fingers and putting them into his mouth. I said, "Don't let me disturb you," but he ignored me. He sucked rather than chewed his food. Mrs. Lingard cut his egg in half and offered him some of it on a spoon. He opened his mouth, showing shrunken gums and unswallowed potato, and allowed her to push it in. I tried to move toward the window, past the bed that occupied most of the room; my foot caught a chamberpot and it slopped over my shoe. I said awkwardly, "I don't want to disturb you now. I'll go downstairs." Mrs. Lingard nodded without speaking. I found my way back to the room below. Jane was mopping the fat off the plate with bread. She said, "Now you can see what Arthur did to him."

"What's the matter with him?"

"I dunno." Her voice seemed to imply, "You're the doctor."

"Doesn't he ever speak?"

"Only when he's had a few."

41

"Is he allowed to drink?"

"He does whether he's allowed to or not."

I was beginning to get a feeling of claustrophobia. Twenty minutes later, when Mrs. Lingard had still not appeared, I said I had better go. "Yes, I've got to get back to work meself."

"Do you have Pauline's address by any chance?"

"Oh, you're going to see 'er, are you?"

"I'd like to."

She opened a cupboard and took out a tattered handbag. From this, she pulled old letters, slips of paper, photographs. I looked at these latter with interest.

"Do you have one of Arthur?"

"I 'spect so." She made no attempt to find one, so I began to look through them myself. There were old, brown photographs of wedding groups dating from the end of the century, and creased snapshots of groups of smiling people raising pint glasses. I came upon a photograph of a plump, strikingly pretty girl of about fifteen. "Who's this?"

"That's Polly."

I stared at it with interest. The curve of the cheek was soft, the chin tilted upward; it was a picture of a girl full of vitality, untouched by defeat. I could see why Jane hated her. I soon found other photographs of Pauline; apparently people had enjoyed snapping her. And in one of them there was a child who was unmistakably Arthur Lingard: the face looked thin and pinched, but the bulging eyes were recognizable anywhere. He looked very seriously into the camera, while Pauline, standing beside him, laughed merrily. I could almost read his thoughts: I am being photographed; perhaps one day people will look at it and say: That was Arthur Lingard before he became famous. . . . Jane looked over my shoulder.

"Yes, he was always sullen."

But he was not sullen; only very serious.

I found another snapshot of a family group that seemed to have been taken at a picnic. I pointed to a girl of Pauline's age who had rested one hand on Arthur's shoulder.

"Who is that?"

"Oh, that's our Maggie, my sister."

"Did she like Arthur?"

"Oh, yes. She's dead now."

"What did she die of?"

"Pneumonia."

Yes, I could see it in her pale face, the face of a victim. But the photograph told me something else. Arthur stood between Maggie and Polly: two girls who were fond of him. So his childhood was not affection-starved. What had caused him to develop into a rebel?

I asked Jane, who was putting her coat on, "Why do you think Arthur got into so much trouble? Did he hate anyone in the family?"

"Not that I ever noticed. He just wanted to . . . to be boss, cock of the walk." She put her finger on the reinforced cover of *Marvo the Magician*. "Like that bloke. He always fancied 'imself as an itnertist."

For a moment I failed to grasp what she meant.

"As a hypnotist?"

"Yes. He was always trying to itnertize people. I reckon that's what killed Maggie. He made her weak."

"Did he ever try to hypnotize you?"

"No, I was only a kid. But he used to do it to Aggie. She was his slave."

"In what way was she his slave?"

A factory hooter sounded. She jumped to her feet.

"Sorry, I've got to get back. They dock off sixpence for every minute you're late. There's Polly's address."

She hurried out. I was left alone with the photographs. I was tempted to borrow some of them, but decided I had better ask permission. I called softly up the stairs, "Mrs. Lingard?" There was no reply. I called again, and when everything was still silent, I decided to go. I took some of the magazines and paperbacks with me. On the back doorstep of the house next door, a man stood with his hands in his pockets, watching me curiously; a woman looked out of the kitchen window. I could imagine them saying, "Now who the hell could that be?" In Penketh Street, the neighbors are curious.

It was pleasant to step into the sunlight, and breathe air that smelled of the gasworks and the canal. At least they were open-air smells.

As I drove into Stockport, I threw off some of the depression; I analyzed what I had seen, and it made me understand how fortunate my own life has been. What is so hard to grasp about an environment like the one Arthur Lingard had grown up in is that it is so *self-enclosed*. While I had sat in the Lingards' front room, I had seen a newspaper with the headline: "De Gaulle says Non!" and it had seemed unreal. Outside the church at the end of the street, there was a board that said, "Defy the Devil in the name of the Lord." De Gaulle, God, the Devil, Shakespeare . . . they all belonged to some distant realm of legend, of unreality. *This* was reality: "Our tea still fourpence a cup," "Send the Pakistanis back home." Once you were in it, this world was like a bog; your feet sank in, and every effort to escape made you sink deeper. So Arthur Lingard dreamed of secret powers, of being Marvo the Magician, of making men grovel like dogs with a keen glance from his hypnotic eyes and a few passes with his magic fingers. But in practice, the only effective method of expressing rejection of this environment was to break into the confectioner's on the corner, or sketch a girl in an obscene position on the wall of a public lavatory. As a doctor, I had escaped all this; I lived in a world in which Freud and Darwin and De Gaulle were not mythical characters but a part of everyday reality. Arthur Lingard's psychotic world of the Black Bailiff was only an extension of the unreal world of Penketh Street.

The street in Stockport where Pauline Lingard—now Sparrow—lived was less depressing than Penketh Street; socially speaking, it was one step higher. Although the houses all looked identical, and there were broken milk bottles in the road, each house had a tiny front garden behind its wooden palings. An errand boy had left his carrier-bike, loaded with greengroceries, leaning against a fence; this was something he would not have risked in Penketh Street. And the houses, although small, were semidetached.

The front garden of Pauline's house had a scanty privet hedge, and a dry, half-bald patch of lawn. I raised the knocker on the green front door (all the front doors in the street were green) and tapped gently. The windows of the house next door were wide open, and a radio blared loudly:

> "I've thrilled to many a kiss before
> But darling, never like this before. . . ."

I rapped again, more loudly, in case my knock had not been heard. A woman appeared on the doorstep opposite, drying her hands on a tea towel.

44

"She's not in. She's out at work."

This was a setback. "What time will she be home?"

"About six. Shall I tell her you called?" She obviously hoped to start a conversation. I said I would return later, and left.

With more than two hours to kill, I had a Chinese meal, wandered around a secondhand bookshop, and looked at boats in a showroom. At half past five, I drank two gin and tonics in a pub, then drove back to Pauline's address. There was still no one in. The lady emerged from next door to tell me that she sometimes went out for the evening. "Her husband's a long-distance lorry driver, so she doesn't have to get his supper." I sat in the car for half an hour. If I intended returning home tonight, now was the time to set out. But I had a curiosity to see Pauline Lingard. I drove back into the center of Stockport, and booked myself into a hotel. I spent half an hour in the bar, then another hour watching television in the lounge. After this, I was hungry and ate dinner. It was now nearly ten. I drove back to Pauline Lingard's house through the dusk. The lights were still out. The next-door neighbor must have been watching out of the window; she came out to tell me that Mrs. Sparrow often stayed out until after midnight. This was a depressing thought, but I was determined not to give up. I went and sat in the car, and listened to the radio. At eleven o'clock, the news came on. Then I saw the front room of the house light up; she had gone in without my noticing her.

I went and knocked on the door, aware of eyes watching me from the house next door. There was no reply. After more knocking, I heard a lavatory flush, and a voice called, "Who is it?" Since I could hardly shout my name through the letter box, I knocked again. Then the door opened with a jerk, and Pauline Sparrow said, "Who are you?"

"My name is Dr. Kahn. I'm from the Rose Hill prison, and I'd like to talk to you about your brother."

"What, now?"

"I came here this afternoon. I've been trying to see you all evening."

"Well, I suppose you'd better come in then." She looked at me keenly as I stepped inside, and was evidently reassured. I followed her into the living room. It was pleasant enough; not tidy, but not shabby either.

Polly Sparrow was a woman in her mid-thirties, with large

45

hips and large breasts. Her hair was thick and dark. The face had lost its soft outline and become coarser, the mouth was full and sensual, the eyes very striking. She impressed me as a vital, healthy animal, the kind of woman who looks completely natural when she stands with her hands on her hips, her legs braced apart with the skirt tight across her thighs, the shoulders well back.

I asked, "Have you ever visited Arthur in prison?"

"Not much. My old man hates him. He wouldn't like me to have anything to do with him. How is he?"

I told her in detail about Arthur's breakdown, the delusions about black guards, and so on. She listened intently, but her only comment was "Poor sod." But at least, I felt that I was communicating. I told her about my visit to the Lingards in Warrington.

"Did they tell you anything useful?"

"No. I don't think they understood the problem."

She laughed; it was a strident laugh, but not unpleasant. "I could have told you that. Aunt Elsie's as thick as two planks. And Jane's not much better."

"What about your Uncle Dick?"

"His brain's gone completely. He's an alcoholic. He used to be violent, but he's burned himself out. The doctor gives them drugs to keep him quiet."

I tried to explain what I wanted to know. Why did her brother try to conceal his intelligence? What had turned him into a petty criminal? Why, for example, had he not been able to get a scholarship to a university?

"Well, to begin with, he used to have fits. Did you know that?"

"I knew he was an epileptic. How often did he have them?"

"About twice a year."

"But that wouldn't have prevented him from taking a scholarship."

"That wasn't his idea. He had big ideas."

"What kind of big ideas?"

She opened her handbag and took out a packet of cigarettes.

"If we're going to start on that, we'd better go in the other room. It's more comfortable."

I followed her into the front room, and she lit a gas fire. "How about a drink?" I said that I could perhaps manage a small one. She went into the kitchen, and came back with a bottle of gin, a bottle of lime juice, and two glasses. "Say when." I stood looking at some of the framed photographs on the sideboard. One of them showed Pauline and Arthur, standing on a pier, with the sea in the background. Arthur looked about fifteen; thin, pale, with the brooding, serious face and bulging eyes. Pauline, as usual, looked intensely vital; two men in the edge of the picture were looking at her. Arthur's face caused a memory to stir. What did it remind me of? Then it came: of an early photograph of Hitler I had once seen: the same intense, slightly wistful stare.

A wedding photograph showed Pauline, looking dazzling in white. It was dated: January 19, 1960. As usual, the eyes of all the men in the group were fixed on her. Her husband was a big, handsome man; he looked easygoing and not particularly bright, and it was plain that he felt uncomfortable in his wedding suit. Pauline came and stood by me as I looked at it. She reached out and pointed. "That's Ernie. That's George, our best man." She indicated a tall man with a moustache, who looked quite comfortable in morning dress. She giggled. "He wanted to marry me too." Her cheek rested against my sleeve for a moment as she pointed.

"He's very attractive," I said, feeling that she wanted prompting.

"Yes. I'd have married him. But he'd have been more trouble that he was worth. He was a devil for the girls. . . ." So Pauline had preferred George, but married Ernie, because she knew he was reliable. She was a hardheaded woman who knew what she wanted.

"Have a seat." She waved me to an armchair near the fire. I saw that she had poured me a very large gin and lime. Her own was even larger. She sat on the settee, and arranged a cushion behind her head. "Well, go on, ask me any questions you like." She lit another cigarette.

"Are you fond of your brother?"

"Well, let's see." She had a decisive, forthright way of speaking. Her accent was an interesting mixture of London and Manchester; but far less broad than her aunt's. "I s'pose I used to be very fond of him when he was a little lad. He changed a lot when he got older."

"In what way?"

"He got queer ideas. He got very broody."

"What kind of queer ideas?"

47

"Oh, I dunno. He never really talked to me. He used to talk to Aggie a lot more—that was his cousin. She used to think he was marvelous."

"Your cousin Jane described her as his slave."

She laughed. "Oh, yes. She'd do anything for him. And did."

Her manner invited my next question.

"You mean he had sexual intercourse with her?"

She shrugged. "Oh, well, yes, of course . . ."

"Why do you say 'Of course'?"

"They all did in that family. The boys thought about nothing but sex. The oldest one, Jim, was the worst." She took a long drink, then, seeing me attentive, went on: "I got the shock of my life the first time I realized what was going on. 'Course I knew they used to play games and all that. We all did. The lads used to feel us and get us to feel them. But one night, I woke up and heard Aggie crying, so I said, 'What's up?' She said, 'I'm frightened—Jim's hurt me.' Jim was the oldest. So anyway, I ended by creeping downstairs with her and putting the kitchen light on. She was wearing an old nighty, and she'd got blood all over the back of it. We were talking in whispers, so as not to wake Uncle Dick. I said, 'What did he do?' and she said, 'I think he's torn something inside me. See if you can see anything.' So she sat in the chair with her knees up, and I looked inside her, but all I could see was blood. I got a bit of cotton wool, and we put some zinc and castor oil ointment on it, and she put it inside her, then we went back to bed. The next morning, she'd stopped bleeding."

"How old was she at the time?"

"Oh, about twelve, I suppose."

"Did her brother force himself on her?"

"Oh, no. Jim wasn't that type. But he was a couple of years older than Aggie. And whenever their parents were out they'd play doctors and nurses, if you know what I mean. They'd sit on the bed, and he'd take off his trousers and she'd take off her knickers, and they'd just play with one another. So it was bound to happen sooner or later, wasn't it?"

"What would their parents have done if they'd found out?"

"Oh, he found out all right. He walloped them both."

"So he disapproved of it all? Yet he ended by doing the same thing to you."

48

She smiled and shrugged; I could see she was enjoying the conversation.

"That's not the same thing, is it? He liked walloping us. He especially liked walloping me. It wasn't so much fun with his own kids, but he always had a bit of a thing about me."

"You think he was a sadist?"

"Not exactly. It was just an excuse to get my knickers off and get me across his knee. I could feel him getting excited as he did it."

I said, "I hope you'll believe me when I say that all this is not mere prurient curiosity. I'm trying to understand the atmosphere your brother grew up in."

"Oh, that's all right. I don't mind talking about it. Ask me anything you like."

"Your uncle ended by raping you when you were twelve?"

"I suppose you could call it that." She stood up to replenish her glass, and glanced disapprovingly at mine, which was still half full.

"Did he or didn't he?"

She said: "Look, I'll be frank with you. You gather that none of us were angels. We all knew plenty about sex from an early age. I guessed why the old man liked smacking my bottom, even if his old lady didn't. I wanted him to know that I knew what he was up to. Well, one day, it was a Saturday afternoon, he came home from the football match, and I still hadn't washed the pots. I was alone in the place, all the others were out on the recky.* So he says: 'I think you need a good talking to. You're going from bad to worse. I've decided you need a good lesson.' I said: 'All right, I know what's coming,' so I pulled up my skirt and took my knickers down. I could see he was getting worked up. So he sits down and takes his belt off his trousers, and makes me lie across his knee. Well, I didn't like being walloped, I'm not kinky. So before he can start hitting me, I reach across and give him a squeeze down there. Then he stops pretending, and puts his hand down between my legs. He says: 'Ooh, you're a lovely girl.' Then he tells me to sit up, and says: 'Listen, if you'll promise not to tell anybody, I'll give you five bob all for yourself.' I said: 'No, I won't tell anybody.' He says, 'Come on upstairs then.' Of course, I didn't realize what he wanted to do. I thought he just wanted me to play with him, same as

---

* Recreation ground.

49

Jim used to. I was scared stiff when he made me lie on the bed, but I didn't want to show it. He kept saying, 'I shan't hurt you, I promise.' When I saw the size of it, I nearly died. He tried hard to be gentle, I'll give him that."

"But he still raped you."

"Well, no, not that time. It hurt so much I asked him to stop, and he did. He gave me the five bob too."

I was amazed. I said, "You sound as if you still liked him, in spite of it all."

She looked surprised.

"Well of course. You couldn't really dislike him. He was quite a nice sort really."

"And when did you get a chance to be together in a house as small as that?"

"Saturday afternoons mainly. The young kids all used to go out and play. Jim and Ted worked as errand boys. Aunt Elsie used to go off to see her pal in the next road. Uncle Dick used to go to the pub until three o'clock, then he'd come back and I'd make him a sandwich. If he was too drunk, he used to cry."

"Cry? What about?"

"Oh, how ashamed he was to be doing such things to a young girl and all that." As I laughed, she said seriously: "I think he really was. You see, he was a very highly sexed man. And . . . well, you've seen Aunt Elsie. He just couldn't let me alone. I was like a wife. You'd be surprised how nice he could be. We'd go off to bed every Saturday, just like any old married couple, and sometimes he'd have me seven or eight times before it was time to get dressed. He used to say he saved it up all week."

"How did you feel about all this? Didn't it hurt?"

"Oh, only at first." She smiled, a sensual, reminiscent smile. "I'm pretty highly sexed too. It was better with Uncle Dick than with some fumbling teen-age kid."

"Then . . . you didn't have affairs with teen-age boys?"

"Well, not many, not what you'd call affairs. Naturally, there were plenty of lads at school who wanted it. And once you start having it regular, you get to want it all the time. And I only got it once a week, often not even that, because in winter the kids wouldn't want to go out and play. So I'd go with a boy occasionally. Uncle Dick once caught me in the entry, and half killed me. I didn't blame him . . ."

"Did your Aunt Elsie suspect?"

"Oh, I think she knew all the time. So did the eldest lads, because they stopped trying to get me."

"Now I want to ask you a rather . . . embarrassing question . . ."

She interrupted me, laughing. "You *are* funny. You sound just like a vicar."

I saw that she was a woman with no inhibitions. The gin may have helped; she was drinking her third glass. I said, "How about Arthur? What was his attitude to all this?"

She shook her head slowly. "That was really the worst part of it. He knew. He came in one afternoon when Uncle Dick was doing it in the kitchen."

"Having sex?"

"Well, not exactly . . ." There obviously were limits to her frankness. "He couldn't let me alone—he'd have to put his hand inside my clothes and get me to touch him." I said quickly, "I see. So Arthur knew about it. And how did he take it?"

"Well, very bad, I s'pose. He was jealous. But you see, Arthur wasn't like the rest of the kids. They was as sexy as rabbits. Arthur was . . . well, I s'pose he had sexy feelings, same as the rest of us, but he felt ashamed of them. He was—whatdy'e call it?—pure . . ."

"A puritan?"

"Yes, that's the word. And very affectionate."

"How do you know Arthur had sexual feelings?"

"Well, that's another story. You're certainly getting me to talk, aren't you?" She got up to light her cigarette, and when she sat down, swung her legs onto the settee. It was done without the intention of being provocative, but since her skirt was short, it was hard not to realize that her legs were very shapely. I found myself looking at her without actual desire, but with a deep interest that mingled the physical and the intellectual. This girl was a living equivalent of Joyce's Marion Bloom: intelligent in her way, very alive, naturally sensual. If I had wanted to sleep with her, she would not have treated it as a furtive piece of adultery; she would have removed her clothes for me as she had for her uncle, naturally and without shame. In her way, she was as naturally above her neighbors as if she had been born a princess.

She said: "You see, I was always a kind of mother to Arthur. Mam was at work when he was a baby—she went into

51

war work right at the beginning of the war. So I was the one who looked after Arthur and gave him his bottle. I 'spect he thought I *was* his mother."

I was suddenly beginning to understand. Pauline was his mother; Arthur's Oedipus fixation was directed toward her, not toward his foster-mother. And so when Uncle Dick became her lover, he became the natural object of Arthur's hatred and frustration.

I said, "Why did you turn against your uncle?"

"Turn against him? I didn't."

"But you gave the evidence that landed him in jail."

"No, I didn't. Arthur did it."

"What happened?"

"When I got pregnant, he told the welfare officer about it."

"Which welfare officer?"

"The one who came to see him. Arthur was always in trouble. He was on probation for burglary. He told the welfare officer that Uncle Dick was the father of the child."

"And was he?"

"I suppose so. Anyway, they came to the house—the police—and took him in for questioning. Then they told him that I'd given him away—that I'd accused him of it. They'd got me in the other room, two policewomen. So he admitted everything."

"What became of the baby?"

"I had it in a home for unmarried mothers, and it was adopted."

"Did your uncle know that Arthur had given him away?"

"Not until much later. He thought the welfare people had found out I was pregnant and heard rumors."

"Your affair was known outside the family then?"

"I suppose so."

I found her amazing. She had become her guardian's mistresss at twelve, she had lived in a tiny house with her aunt and cousins—I can imagine the atmosphere when the family began to realize what was going on—and it had left her unscathed. For her, it was all somehow natural.

I said: "But tell me about Arthur. You say he was a puritan—do you mean he never joined in the sexual games?"

"Well, he did . . . he couldn't really avoid it."

"But only with the younger children?"

Her lips parted in a serene smile.

"Oh, no. It was me he was fixed on."

"How do you know?"

"Well, to begin with, he'd simply cuddle up to me in bed. If he had to go bed before me, I'd give him one of my jumpers to hold against his face. He used to like to wear my clothes too. When he was very small, he used to ask for cuddles all the time—he'd put his arms round me and say, 'She's my sister, not yours,' and stick his tongue out at the others. Then he suddenly stopped all that."

"At what age?"

"Oh, about seven or eight. I can't remember."

"At about the time he discovered about you and your uncle?"

"I s'pose it could have been about then, yes, but I didn't think that had much to do with it."

"Why *did* you think he changed?"

"Well, children *do* change, don't they? I mean, they don't like to be laughed at and all that. He just didn't want to make an exhibition of himself anymore. But he'd come closer in bed. In fact, he had a funny habit. He'd try to get on top of me."

"You call that funny?"

"Oh, I don't think it was anything to do with sex—just that he wasn't satisfied to lie at the side of me. He'd feel more secure if he was using me for a mattress—like sitting on my knee. I'd wait till he dozed off, then slide from under him."

"Did he show any sexual interest in you?"

She laughed. "Well, he did later. That was when he started to grow up. He used to wait until he thought I was asleep, then try to feel me. Or he'd press himself against me."

"What did you do?"

"Well, I didn't want to upset him. I knew he felt jealous of Uncle Dick. So I'd pretend to be asleep. He'd try not to wake me. Mind, I'm not saying it was all his fault. Don't forget, I was . . . I mean, well, I used to have dreams. You see what I mean? I'd dream I was in bed with Uncle Dick, and I'd begin to move about. . . ."

For the first time that evening, she showed signs of embarrassment, although, even so, they were not acute. I changed the subject.

"What was Arthur's relationship with his cousin Aggie, if he was fixated on you?"

"Well, that was different. It was later, you see, when

53

Arthur began to change. About the time he was twelve, he got very queer. He'd read these morbid books all the time—used to lap 'em up. Anything about murder or torture and that sort of thing. There was a thing called *Marvo the Magician*—he used to read that all the time. Then I went off to have this baby. Then I went to Blackpool with this married bloke, and we lived together for about six months before his wife tracked him down. Then I went back to Warrington, but I slept in the other bed, with Aunt Elsie. And Arthur didn't seem glad to see me. He'd got all cold and distant. He started to use big words. Look, I've got a picture of him then." She rummaged in a drawer and drew out an album. She opened it, and found me a snapshot of Arthur, under which was written "Arthur, 1951." He had changed his hair style; the hair seemed to be plastered with brilliantine, and combed straight back. Since childhood, his face had become thinner. The bulging eyes stared at the camera. Altogether, it looked like a police photograph. "I didn't mind his odd ways —I just thought he was growing up. Then I found out what he was doing to Aggie."

"What was he?"

"Well, like Jane said, he treated her like a slave. He'd started this hypnotism lark with her."

"Are you certain of that? I mean, was he really serious, or was it just an attempt to imitate Marvo the Magician?"

"I think he was serious. He knew how to work it on Aggie."

"Did he ever try it on you?"

"No. But he did it on Albert—that was the youngest lad."

"Have you any idea how he went about it?"

"Yes. He made Albert sit down and put his hands on his knees. Then he'd tell him to think hard about his knees. Then he'd tell him to think hard about his fingertips. Albert said it made his knees feel all funny. He'd go on like that for a long time. Then he'd tell Albert he was getting tired, and Albert said he began to feel tired. Then he'd say his hands were getting lighter, they wanted to float up like balloons, and he said he couldn't stop them floating like balloons."

It was a technique I had occasionally used myself. But I was amazed that it should have been used by the thirteen-year-old boy.

"Tell me about Aggie. Why do you say she was his slave?"

"He'd got her into that state. He'd got her so he could make her do anything he asked. And it made him vicious."

"In what way?"

"He'd make her do things—well, things no decent person would force anybody to do."

"You mean sexual things?"

"Well, yes, mainly. But not just with himself. With other people."

"What others?" This was a new light on Lingard; I always thought of him as a lone wolf. I had to repeat the question; this was a subject she preferred not to talk about.

She said, "Well, I suppose I may as well tell you. One of them was this bloke—the one I went to Blackpool with."

Her method of telling the story was too roundabout and evasive for me to reproduce, but its substance was this. The man's name was Eugene Turner; he owned a garage in Stockport and raced his own cars. He was married with two children, but this did not prevent him from taking a series of mistresses. In the case of Pauline Lingard, he promised marriage before he took her to a flat in Blackpool, where she lived for six months, visited by her lover almost daily. He had deserted his wife by then. The size of her maintainence claim made him decide that it might be simpler to go back to her, so Pauline was persuaded to return to Warrington, where she continued to see him. One evening, Turner and Arthur Lingard got into conversation and became very friendly. And the following evening, to Pauline's astonishment, Turner offered to take them out for a Chinese meal—Arthur, Pauline, and Agnes. However, Pauline was still infatuated; she assumed it was simply a typical piece of generosity.

The restaurant was dark, and Agnes sat in the corner. Pauline noticed that she seemed pale and upset, but assumed this was shyness. Eugene Turner and Arthur were sitting on either side of Agnes. After a while, Pauline noticed that Agnes seemed uncomfortable, and asked her if she wanted to visit the ladies' toilet; Agnes blushed and said no. Later in the meal, Pauline kicked off her shoes—a habit she had in restaurants—and her foot encountered something soft under the table. She bent down to see what it was, raising the long tablecloth, and then saw with amazement that Agnes appeared to be naked from the waist down, and that Eugene Turner had one hand between her thighs. The object on the floor was a pair of knickers. Pauline, in her forthright way, asked what the hell was going on, and Agnes blushed and began to pull her skirt down. Turner only grinned broadly and said they were only having a bit of fun. Pauline stood up and marched out of the restaurant. Her lover followed her and explained that it was a bet; Arthur had told him that he could make Agnes do anything, and he had bet that Arthur couldn't make her remove her knickers in a restaurant and hitch up her skirt.

Pauline was shocked—less by the "bit of fun" than by the revelation of her lover's character—and marched off home. She broke permanently with Eugene Turner when Agnes later admitted—under pressure—that after the meal, they had gone to a park, where Turner had made love to her several times. She also quarreled with Arthur, and they stopped speaking to each other.

"Did Arthur force her to give herself to anyone else?"

"I only know about one, a bloke called Dagger."

"Another playboy type?"

"Well, no, the opposite really. He was a sort of old lag who'd been in and out of jail all his life. He was an ugly old sod who lived in the next street, nasty old man, the sort who'd offer you sweets to sit on his knee and let him feel you."

"What do you suppose made Arthur like him?"

"I dunno. See, I wasn't around much at the time. All I know is, he did it to Aggie as well."

"Did she tell you?"

"I s'pose she did. I can't remember." She yawned. I looked at my watch and realized it was nearly three in the morning.

"Just one or two more questions, then I'll leave you to get to sleep. Did you and Arthur make up the quarrel?"

"Sort of. He gave me a lovely gold watch once. I didn't like to ask where it came from."

"So it was Arthur who extended the olive branch?"

"Oh, yes. It always was. You see . . ." She hesitated. "He always had this thing about me."

"Even later?"

"Oh, yes. He wouldn't speak to me after I got married. He was really mad. Even threatened to kill me." She yawned. "I just laughed at him."

"You think he wasn't capable of murder?"

"Oh, it's not that. I wouldn't be surprised if he was. I

56

never really believed it was an accident with that farmer. But he wouldn't kill me."

"No, I suppose not." I looked again at the wedding photograph; it had a date underneath: January 19, 1960. She had married when she was twenty-eight, her brother twenty-three.

"What happened to this old man, Dagger?"

"I dunno. He died. I think he committed suicide, I'm not sure."

"I could find out. What was his other name?"

"Er . . . let's think. Odd name . . . Tebbut, that's it."

I felt as if someone had emptied cold water down my back. "Are you sure?"

"Oh, yes. You can't forget a name like that."

I stood up. "I'd better leave you. It's kind of you to give me so much time."

She stretched, and her skirt rose another two inches.

"You could stay the night if you like. There's a spare bed."

"I don't think I'd better. The neighbors might talk."

"They'll talk anyway. I don't care. I sometimes think I ought to charge entertainments tax. I dunno what they'd do if I moved out of the district. Oh, well, time for bed." She smiled dreamily, and arched her shoulders, and I noted the strength of her sexual aura. The interesting thing about her was that in spite of her sensual mouth and well-developed figure, she was not "obvious"; there was something restrained and distant about her.

I said quickly, "Please don't get up. Thank you again." She smiled mischievously as I hurried to the door, but she made no move to stand up. I let myself out of the front door, and closed it quietly. As I got into the car, I saw the bedroom curtains of the house next door stir in the lamplight.

FOUR

In spite of my fatigue, I found it hard to sleep. Too much had happened too quickly. The Arthur Lingard I had been discovering over the past twelve hours seemed to have no connection with the patient I knew at Rose Hill. It is true that I had already faced the possibility—which Pauline had confirmed—that the killing of the farmer had not been manslaughter, but deliberate murder. And I already knew that beneath the quiet surface, which had led two psychiatrists to describe him as "below average intelligence," there was a scheming mind and an obsessive will to power. But the stories about Aggie indicated something altogether more sinister—a sullen, violent aggressiveness. Again I found my mind running on the murder of Evelyn Marquis.

I kept reminding myself that all this might be pure imagination on my part. Arthur Lingard had been born into an affectionate, secure lower-middle-class home; and then, while still a baby, separated from his parents and thrust into an environment he hated. Under these pressures, the most easygoing character might have developed antisocial tendencies. Obviously, he was fixated on his sister, both sexually and emotionally. Now that I had seen Pauline, it was easy to see resemblances to the nymphomaniac girl of *The Kid from Louisville*. It must have come as a shock for Arthur—after five sex-starved years in prison—to come across this lurid description of a rape of a girl who sounded like his sister. His response—smearing the book with excrement—was at once a gesture of revenge, and of furtive possession. I would be prepared to stake my reputation that he achieved a sexual climax as he did it. All this remained something I could understand, and even feel sympathy for. Ever since I read the three-page psychiatric report on him, sympathy and pity had dominated my feelings about him. I saw him as fundamentally a victim of circumstances. But everything I had learned in the past twelve hours seemed to contradict this simple view.

I slept until eleven, and woke up feeling fresher. I paid my bill, and went to the coffee bar next door for a late breakfast. Afterwards, I sat by the window, watching the traffic in the street, and jotting down notes for my case report on Arthur Lingard. In the daylight, it all seemed clearer. The unhappy child, in a hostile environment, takes refuge in a world of imagination in which he is a magician. There is nothing unusual in this. Ian Brady, the moors killer, had been influenced by Superman comics and gangster novelettes; that did not make him a supercriminal. Arthur Lingard had also learned the trick of hypnotism—a very simple one—and used it to gain power over his cousin. But Agnes had been a victim type, and Arthur was naturally dominant. Their relationship was understandable enough, particularly if one took into account the overcharged sexual atmosphere in the house. The parallel that came into my mind here was Peter Kurten, the mass murderer of Düsseldorf, whose home background had also been a rabbit warren of incest and promiscuity. But Kurten's will to power had turned him into a sadist. There was no evidence that Arthur Lingard had sadistic inclinations.

What was it, then, that nagged at my mind when I tried to picture Arthur Lingard as another victim of Hitler's war? It was partly a formless intuition about a man I was beginning to understand, partly a definite sense of unease about the case of Evelyn Marquis. I consulted my map. If I took the A.628, just south of Saddleworth moor, my route would pass close to Stocksbridge, the home town of Evelyn Marquis. I phoned my wife and told her not to expect me back until late. Then I drove due east across the Pennines.

Stocksbridge is a pleasant, small town, typical of West Riding. I parked near the police station, and introduced myself to the sergeant on duty. He was not the man who had spoken to Frank Slessor a few days before. I asked him if he had actually worked on the case.

"Well, we all did, more or less."

"Do you keep the file on it here?"

"No, that's at the headquarters at Sheffield."

I asked him to give me his personal account of the case;

but what he was able to tell me added little to what I knew already. It had been a Saturday night; the Grove Hotel had been crowded, and no one had paid much attention to the man who asked where he might get a taxi. The reception desk recommended him to try the Marquis Garage on the Langsett road. Evelyn Marquis picked him up at ten forty-five, and drove off toward Dodworth. An hour later, a passing motorist near Ewden saw flames, and a man running away from a car that stood several feet off the road. He went to the car, and saw the body of a young woman lying beside it, her clothes on fire. The motorist beat out the flames, then saw that she was bleeding from a wound at the back of the head. The police arrived ten minutes later; but although police cars closed all roads leading off the moor, the man was not caught. The girl was later found to have been raped. The police eventually discovered that a known sex offender from Leeds had been in Stocksbridge earlier in the day, and his photograph was identified by the receptionist of the Grove Hotel. The man was eventually able to prove that he had spent the night in Sheffield, and he was released.

I asked the sergeant if he had heard of another suspect called Lingard. He shook his head. He knew there had been other suspects, but he knew nothing about them.

But he obligingly telephoned the Sheffield central police station for me, and I was invited to call there. The seven-mile journey took half an hour, and I was shown into the office of Superintendent Nutley, who had been in charge of the Marquis case. He had the file waiting for me. Before I opened it, I asked him, "Do you remember a suspect called Arthur Lingard?"

He frowned. "Lingard? I don't think so. . . . Oh, wait, was he the chap with eyes like a frog?"

"That sounds like him."

"Yes, but he wasn't really a suspect. What happened was that the hotel receptionist described the man as having piercing eyes and a round face. *The Yorkshire Post* reported that as "bulging eyes and a round face," and a police sergeant at Knaresborough rang us and said the description fitted this chap Lingard. So we got hold of a photograph of him and showed it to the receptionist. She agreed it was like the man she'd talked to, and we got the Manchester police to pull him in. He had some alibi—I can't remember what it was —

so we let him go. We were pretty certain we'd got the right man already. Why does he interest you?"

I told him briefly about Lingard's breakdown, and of my attempt to find what he was trying to hide.

"Well, I'm afraid I can't help you there. And I doubt whether you'll find anything in that file either."

I opened it casually—and again had the feeling of ice down my spine. I was looking at a photograph of Pauline Lingard. Then, when I looked closer, I saw it was not Pauline. This was a girl who was remarkably like her, although not so pretty and without her vitality.

The superintendent left me alone to glance through the file. I read the medical evidence. "The body was fully clothed, and all the clothes were found to be in place. In spite of this, a vaginal swab revealed the presence of semen, and further stains were discovered on the back of the underskirt, indicating that the knickers had been pulled down during intercourse, while a splash of mud near the elastic suggested that they may have been completely removed. The pubic hairs were also contaminated with semen. When the body was stripped for the postmortem examination, marks of teeth were discovered on the breasts, but the brassiere was untorn. The back of the skull was lacerated, and fragments of glass in the hair indicated that the weapon had been a bottle. A broken Vat 69 bottle was found in the back seat of the car. Examination for fingerprints was negative. Cause of death was suffocation, probably by the brocade-covered cushion that was found in the car, and that was identified by the victim's father as one she always used to give the driving seat additional height."

Evelyn Marquis was killed on February 28, 1960—nearly six weeks after the marriage of Pauline Lingard, whom she resembled. She was twenty-seven years old—a year younger than Pauline Lingard. She was the victim of a sex attack, but the attacker had taken the trouble to dress her carefully after the attack, and then to take her money (about two pounds) and a few rings, to make it appear that the motive was robbery. The police recognized this; it was one of their reasons for suspecting the known sex offender, who would naturally try to cover up his tracks, and probably a reason for dismissing the suspicions against Arthur Lingard, who had no record as a sex offender.

The superintendent returned, and I asked him if it would

be possible to borrow the photograph of Evelyn Marquis; I promised to return it when I had had it copied.

"Yes. You might tell me how this Lingard reacts when he sees it. Don't forget, this file is still open."

"I'll do anything I can. And incidentally, do you know the name of the policeman from Knaresborough who told you about Lingard?"

"No, but I think I know someone who does." He was back a few minutes later. "Sergeant Benham—he was Constable Benham then."

I thanked him and left. It was getting late, but I had one more call to make on my way home.

Sergeant Benham was not at the Knaresborough police station; but when I explained my business, the constable on duty gave me his home address, and told me how to get there. The man who met me at the door of the semidetached house on the outskirts of the town was younger than I expected, and the snub nose and heavy jaw made me think of a bulldog. The station had telephoned him to say I was on my way. He led me into a pleasant room, with windows open on the back garden, and offered me a can of beer. I was interested to note that the books on his shelf were not the usual *Reader's Digest* condensed novels or the lucky dip of the Book Society; there was Aldous Huxley, Hemingway, and John Gunther's "Inside" books.

The french windows were open on a lawn; two pretty children were playing lawn croquet.

I repeated my story about Lingard's breakdown—I had told it so often in the past twenty-four hours that it had been condensed to a few sentences. Benham, chewing at his pipe, said, "I'm not surprised."

"How well did you know him?"

"Well enough. We were in the same class at school."

"You lived in Warrington?"

"Ay. I was born there. I lived just around the corner from Arthur, in the Padgate Road."

This was a piece of luck I had not expected. I came immediately to the question that had occupied my mind for two days.

"Do you think he's a dangerous criminal?"

Benham shook his head, and I was surprised at the relief I felt, even though I was now certain he was wrong.

He said: "He *could* be, if the stakes were right. I think he's the criminal type. He's a loner, and a bit of a nut."

"In what way is he a nut?"

"He's not really with it. He lets his imagination run away with him. But he's not stupid."

I pressed him to explain further. He groped for words. Then his eye fell on the bookshelf.

"Do you know this?" He reached out, and took down a copy of Aldous Huxley's *Point Counterpoint*. "There's a character in here like Arthur." He opened the book. "Spandrell. Have you read it?"

"A long time ago."

"It's the same mentality, except Arthur's working-class and this bloke's rich. He wants to be a sort of criminal genius. The big bad wolf. But it's all a kind of show."

"And yet you thought he'd be capable of killing Evelyn Marquis?"

"That was the description in the paper. As soon as I read it—round face and bulging eyes—I thought of Arthur."

"Do you think he *could* have done it?"

He thought carefully before shaking his head.

"Not since I found out it was a sex crime. He could have killed her in a panic if she struggled when he was trying to rob her. But somehow . . . I don't think he's the sex criminal type."

"What makes you say that?"

"Well, I don't know, really. He'd think it beneath him. Besides, she wasn't his type either. He'd liked quiet pale girls, like his cousin Aggie."

"You knew about that, did you? Did many other people know?"

"Quite a few at school. He was always talking about hypnotizing people. He once got me to try it, but it didn't work. I don't believe he hypnotized anybody—not like he said, anyway."

"Why not?"

"Well, everybody knows you can't be hypnotized against your will. I don't know what he did to some of these girls, but I don't believe it was that."

"Were there others, then?"

"So he said. I only knew about one."

"Who was that?"

"Well, according to Arthur—I'm not saying I believe him

63

—it was the wife of one of our schoolteachers, a bloke called Mr. Grose. He taught gym, and his wife used to take a few of the older boys in music. She was a sort of pale little woman, not very attractive, the sort who wouldn't say boo to a goose. Arthur reckoned she was the type who could be . . . what do you call 'em . . . hypnotic subjects. They lived out at Widnes, and she used to come in by train. Anyway, Arthur said he was going to travel on the same train with her and see if he couldn't hypnotize her. I told him he was talking through his hat, and then one day he came and said he'd done it—hypnotized her on the train. I told him I didn't believe him, and he said: 'All right, don't.' I saw him walking to the station with her once or twice, so I suppose he got friendly with her on the train."

"Did he tell you anything more about her?"

"No. He knew I didn't believe him."

"But what did he claim to begin with? Why did he want to hypnotize her?"

"Well, the usual. I mean, that's what he said—that he'd been to her house and had her in bed. He was the biggest liar I ever came across."

"He actually claimed to have slept with her?"

"That's what he said. Mind, it's not completely impossible. A certain type of girl seemed to go for Arthur. But frankly, I don't think there was anything with Mrs. Grose."

"What happened to her?"

"Well, funnily enough, they got divorced. The rumor at the school was . . . well, she'd been trolling for trade." When he saw I didn't understand, he explained: "Soliciting. I suppose anything's possible."

"You don't think Arthur had any connection with the divorce?"

"No, I'm fairly sure he didn't. It was just one of his little fantasies. He liked to impress me because I was the captain of the cricket team. He liked to think that brawny people are brainless." He gave a grunt of annoyance, and his eyes roved over his bookshelves. "I couldn't stick him. He knew I thought he was a fool."

"What was your reaction when he was arrested for burglary?"

"Oh, typical. He was always in some kind of trouble. He had big ideas, but he didn't know how to carry them out."

I did not point out that this conflicted with his earlier

remark that Arthur Lingard could be dangerous "if the stakes were right." I thanked him, shook hands, and left.

Driving back to Hartlepool through the summer dusk, I had a sense of peace, of satisfaction. Sergeant Benham had handed me an important piece of the jigsaw puzzle—although he was unaware of this. I had begun by finding him a likable, levelheaded member of the British police force, solid, decent, and brighter than he looked. And no doubt all this was true enough. But his professed contempt for Arthur Lingard was a show. There was something about Lingard that disturbed him deeply. And evidently there was some sort of odd friendship between him and Lingard. The attraction of opposites? Lingard rankled. Five years after they had been schoolboys together, Benham thought that a description of a murderer sounded vaguely like Lingard. It was a long shot, but worth trying. It was not exactly malice; but if he had been right, it would have been a triumph for Benham, a vindication. And about twelve years later, that imputation "that brawny people are brainless" still rankled. In fact, Benham's "little learning" was worse than none at all. It was not true that people cannot be hypnotized against their will. In fact, the whole point of hypnosis is that it turns the will against itself. This is why intelligent people are often better subjects than stupid ones. If you tell a stupid man that his left foot itches, he simply doesn't believe you. The intelligent man doesn't believe you either, but he knows that your suggestion might induce an itch, and a part of his mind begins to fight against it, while the other half proceeds to induce the itch.

Arthur Lingard had boasted that he could hypnotize his schoolteacher's wife, and later told Benham that he had succeeded. Then he stopped talking about it. Benham preferred to believe this was because he could not be bothered to continue lying. I wondered whether there might not be another explanation: that Arthur Lingard had suddenly recognized the value of silence. Boasting is for the unsuccessful. Although Lingard had taken Benham into his confidence about hypnotism, Benham dismissed him as a fool and a liar. And that, in the long run, was probably what Lingard wanted.

The next day was busy; I had to fit in various appointments that I had canceled from the previous two days. There was a particularly demanding female patient who regarded my absence as a desertion, and had to be soothed out of a state of hysteria. I rang the prison at the first opportunity, and asked about Lingard. They told me he was no worse and no better, except that he had broken out in a painful skin rash. He had been asking after me. I told them to give him a message, saying that I would see him later in the day.

It was strange to see him again; for the past two days, I had become accustomed to another Arthur Lingard: a brooding youth, obsessed by crime and sex. He now looked slightly thinner than when I had last seen him, and his hands had been bandaged so that only his fingers showed. His face was covered with what looked like nettle rash.

He looked glad to see me, but did not ask me where I had been. He waited until we were alone, then said: "They're getting closer. That's why I've come out in spots."

"How far do they extend?"

"All over."

"You'd better undress and let me see."

Just as I suspected, his belly, genitals and inner thighs were covered with an unpleasant red crust. His penis and testicles had been painted with a purple silver nitrate solution and looked surrealistic. His inner thighs were suppurating.

"What do you suppose has caused this?"

"Actinic rays."

"Now come, Arthur, you know enough about physics to know that is impossible. Actinic rays are the rays in an ordinary light beam that affect a photographic plate. This room is full of them all the time." He frowned, and stared at his. hands.

A sudden absurd idea come into my head. I said, "Who painted your penis with silver nitrate?"

"The medical orderly. Berryman."

"Did you ask him to?"

"Yes."

"Why only your penis? Why not your belly as well?"

"Because it itched."

My suspicion seemed farfetched, but not impossible. Silver nitrate is the element on a photographic plate that responds to light—to actinic rays. Had he evolved some absurd notion that silver nitrate would counteract the effect of actinic rays? Or was the reasoning purely subconscious? The rash expressed some deep disturbance asssociated with his

66

genitals. Silver nitrate would disguise his genitals, and then the action of actinic rays on the silver nitrate would complete the disguise. Was this his reasoning?

I asked him about his dreams. He told me of several lurid ones about walking trees and dinosaurs. I wrote them all down, and kept asking: "Any more? How about women? Have you dreamed anything about them?" He frowned, and I had a feeling he was keeping something back. "You must dream of women sometimes?" He grunted something that sounded like assent. "Tell me one of them."

"She whipped me."

"Where?"

"Down here." His hands fluttered to the base of his stomach.

"On your genitals?"

"Yes."

"What did she look like? Describe her for me."

He looked at his hands and said nothing. I got a feeling he was digging in his heels.

"Was she big and strong?"

"No."

"Little, then? Small and pale?"

"Yes."

"Was it your cousin Aggie?"

He looked quickly at me. I expected him to ask how I knew, but he said nothing, only looked away quickly.

I said, "It was like her, wasn't it?"

"A bit."

I heaved a sigh of relief. This was progress. He had let me into the world of his childhood. And now my insights fitted together. His cousin Aggie—or another of the women he had bullied and dominated—had whipped his genitals. The past was rising up now that he was in retreat. For he had dared a great deal over the years; he had pressed forward ruthlessly, a man of purpose. Now his subconscious mind was in revolt; the fears he had suppressed, the guilt-feelings he had rejected were catching up with him.

I had a feeling that this was the time to press forward, to aim for a breakthrough.

I pulled my chair closer to his bed, and said: "Listen, Arthur, it's time you understood what's happening to you. You've been a lone wolf for years. You've been standing alone and keeping your own counsel. And now you feel you're losing your strength, and all your repressed fears are rising up from your subconscious. That's what's causing this rash, not the black guards. There aren't any black guards."

He said quietly, "How do you know?"

"Listen, you've got to understand. The way you're taking will lead to complete breakdown. You've been standing alone for too long, haven't you? Because you *daren't* take anyone into your confidence. Isn't that so?" He looked quickly at me. "But now you have become a victim of your own subconscious. You've got to learn to trust somebody." He was staring down at his hands on the coverlet, like a schoolboy being reprimanded. "Do you believe you can trust me?"

He hesitated. "Yes."

"Good. Then treat me as a doctor trying to help you. Don't think of me as someone working for the law. You can tell me anything you like, just as if I was a priest. Whatever you tell me is a secret between us." I saw the corner of his mouth twitch with a faint smile. I knew it was time for the major gamble, a gamble that could establish deeper communication or destroy all communication between us. Suddenly, I had to face the fact that he had become my obsession, and that I *had* to understand him. I laid my hand on his shoulder, ignoring his involuntary twitch.

"I'll tell you something that will prove I'm telling you the truth. I know that you murdered Enoch Benson [the farmer for whose manslaughter he was serving his prison sentence]. And I know you murdered this girl." I took the photograph of Evelyn Marquis out of my pocket and dropped it on the bed in front of him.

I could sense the impact it made, although I could not see his face. The hands began to tremble. When he looked up, his eyes did not meet mine, but focussed on the buttons of my jacket. The face looked gray and sick. I went on quickly: "I also know about Mrs. Grose, the wife of your gym master at school. I *have* to know all these things about you, because I'm a doctor, and it's my job to find out why you're sick." I sat down on the bed, and put the photograph back into my pocket. "She's like your sister Pauline, isn't she?" His face twitched; he looked as if he was going to burst into tears. "But there's nothing to worry about. If I'm going to help you, I've got to know everything. Why not tell me everything, frankly?"

His eyes were dull as he looked at me; his next sentence sounded completely dry and logical.

"And spend the rest of my life in jail?"

"I'm a psychologist, not a policeman. I'm interested in why you do things. I want to understand the way your mind works." This last was intended to flatter; but his face remained expressionless. I placed my hand on his forearm and leaned forward. "Whatever you tell me can't be used against you. At the moment, you're not legally sane."

An orderly knocked on the door; he had brought tea. I had always found that eating or drinking with patients has the effect of soothing their hostilities. I poured tea for the two of us, watching Lingard out of the corner of my eye. When I handed him his cup, his hand trembled so much that I had to put it on the bedside table. I could guess the conflict that was going on inside him. Five years of prison had broken down his resistance until he had to retreat into psychosis to avoid confiding in someone. I had made him aware of this; and now I was offering him an alternative. All my knowledge of human breaking strain told me I should be successful; either that, or he would retreat to a deeper level of psychosis where he could not be reached.

Another insight came to me.

I said: "You were thinking of confiding in Tebbut, weren't you? You wanted to take him into your confidence. Was that because he had the same name as old Dagger Tebbut?" This time, he flinched, but did not look at me. I had a sudden intuition that he was worried; I knew far too much.

I sat back in my chair, and sipped my tea, then said: "There's one thing that intrigues me. After you'd raped Evelyn Marquis, why did you dress her again? Didn't you know the pathologist would check whether she'd been raped?"

He said, "How do you know she'd been raped?"

It came out quietly, reasonably. Anyone listening to us would never guess that this man had been talking about actinic rays and black guards.

I said, "The pathologist's report proved it."

"How do you know she didn't have a boyfriend?"

"She didn't have a boyfriend. She hadn't been out with a man since her boyfriend jilted her and married the barmaid from the Grove. And even if she had a secret lover, he couldn't have had intercourse with her that evening. She'd been in bed all day with a bad headache."

He said nothing.

I said: "All right, let me guess. You raped her because you were raping your sister. But you didn't want your sister to guess. You were afraid that she might see the girl's photograph in the newspaper and guess it was you. So you tried to make it look like robbery. Is that the reason?"

He reached out for his teacup, and I saw that his hand was not shaking anymore. Before he put the cup to his lips, he said, "Does Pauline know?"

I experienced a huge rush of relief that made me feel dizzy for a moment. I had won.

He asked, "Have you talked with Pauline?"

"Yes."

I knew that now, for all practical purposes, he was sane. He had reached out and recaptured the parts of his personality that had escaped during the years in prison. Man's sanity is largely a function of his will, his sense of purpose. He is most himself when he pulls himself together, concentrates his will for some kind of effort. If a man who has possessed a strong will suddenly ceases to use it, he becomes mentally sick, just as an athlete who suddenly stops taking exercise becomes physically flabby. He develops a kind of mental dyspepsia, a feeling of internal heartburn, a sense of no longer being in control. But so long as he refuses to relinquish control, he remains fundamentally sane. The dancer Nijinsky developed a mental tension that made him difficult to live with; but he did not become actually insane until his wife's parents sent men with a straitjacket to his hotel room. Once in the straitjacket, he accepted that he was no longer sane; then he sank into catatonia. For years, Arthur Lingard had kept his own counsel, refused to accept defeat, kept his will rigid until his mind was sick with fatigue. Then some safety mechanism had taken over, allowing him to objectify his fears by identifying them with supernatural enemies, black guards. The will could go to sleep; the vigilant personality could relax. But he now faced another kind of danger—the strange dreams that come when reality dissolves. His waking sleep was a form of mental stagnation, and his mind became a swamp, a pool of stinking water.

I had restored him to Arthur Lingard, and I had offered him a chance to escape the mental torment. It may seem incomprehensible—why he decided to confide in me, when he knew that doing so meant the permanent loss of his freedom. For he must have known that my promise to respect his confidence had certain limits. As a public servant, I could not allow a man I knew to be a mentally unbalanced killer to go back into society. But it must be remembered that he was a sick man, a man whose whole mental life had become poisoned. With a single act of will—the decision to take me into his confidence—he could drain the mental swamp, escape the nausea that had paralyzed him for years.

He took the decision, but he did not put it into effect at once. The habit of reticence was too strong. I understood this, and made no effort to force him. I let him talk, encouraged him to talk, made no real effort to direct the flow of his conversation, knowing that he was trying to find his own way to release the tension.

As he drank his tea, I asked him, "Why do you hate your sister?"

"She broke her promise." I waited, making no further attempt to prompt him. "Before Dad went back to Alamein, he made her promise to take care of me. He said: 'Promise me you'll look after Arthur, whatever happens?' Paula said: 'I promise. I swear it.' But she didn't. She kept it for a while, then she forgot."

"But you were very close when you were small."

"Yes. When we first went to Warrington, we were very close." A long pause. "She was a pretty girl." Another pause, this time for five minutes or more. "Dad was a fool. He shouldn't have let us go there." He groped for words. "It . . . squashed me. I could have done anything. I'd got Paula, she'd got me. If we'd been left alone, everything would have been all right. I didn't have any bad thoughts about her. Everything went wrong from the start. Life didn't want to give me anything. First my mother died, then my dad. I'd got nobody except Paula. . . ."

I saw that he was drifting into a mood of self-pity, and from my point of view, this was excellent. Self-pity is a basically sane emotion, a way of adjusting an emotional balance, a method of catharsis.

I said: "Yes, you had a pretty rotten time of it. I suppose the war was to blame."

"We'd have been better off in London, or in Surrey or Dorset. So long as we were together, everything was all right. The two of us would have been all right even in an

71

orphanage." I could see that he was repeating something he had thought about many times: what life would have been like if they hadn't been sent to Warrington. I saw his point. All he needed was Pauline. They would have been happy together. He was an affectionate child who only asked to be loved and allowed to love.

I said: "Tell me about those early days in Warrington. Tell me with all the detail you can remember. How old were you when you went there?"

"Four. Pauline was nine."

"Tell me everything you can remember. What were your first impressions of your new home?"

Little by little, very slowly, it came out. He talked hesitantly and awkwardly, sometimes groping for the right word for minutes at a time. I resisted the temptation to prompt him because I could see he was suffering. He talked with his eyes closed, trying to visualize it all, to get it right, the sweat standing out on his forehead and running down his face.

What I was doing was dangerous; I was continually aware of this. All his later life had been a reaction against that childhood, against the emotions of helplessness and jealousy and disgust; he had created a personality to deal with these emotions: the enemy of society, the loner who took what he wanted. Now this personality had collapsed. He was like a man who has vomited himself into a state of exhaustion, and I was asking him to recall the meal that had made him vomit. This is why sweat stood out all over his face as he talked about his childhood, and each sentence came out as if painfully dragged up from his insides and tilted over his lips, like a barrowload of cement blocks. He didn't really trust me—although he would learn to when he understood how far I was committed to understanding him. But he had reached the breaking point, and he had to go on.

FIVE

When Arthur Lingard first moved into Penketh Street, the house smelled of fish. Meat was scarce in the second year of the war, but the sea was only a few miles away. The faint, nauseating smell of boiled fish hung over his childhood. It was unfortunate for Arthur that he had a natural dislike of fish; as a child in London, he would never eat it.

Five minutes after he and Pauline arrived in the house, escorted by their father (who had been given compassionate leave), the air-raid sirens wailed, and searchlight beams cut the sky into geometrical shapes. Ten of them—three adults, seven children—hurried out to the Anderson shelter in the backyard, and crouched in the cold, listening to the sound of bombers. Arthur and Pauline huddled together; Arthur was drowsy after the long journey; he could recall hearing Pauline and his cousin Maggie—the same age as Pauline (she died in 1949)—discussing dolls, as he fell asleep with his head in his sister's lap. Hours later, the all clear sounded; he woke up, shivering, and was carried into the house, and upstairs to his new bedroom, permeated by the smell of boiled cod. The bed was cold; he was no longer sleepy. The two eldest boys, Jim (age twelve) and Ted (age eleven) stood looking out of the bedroom window, staring at the reddening horizon. There was no light in the children's room ——it saved blackout curtains as well as electricity—but he could see the room clearly by the light of the fires. Liverpool docks had had one of their worst nights; in the morning, the sky to the west was a haze of smoke.

Arthur did not like his cousins, and they did not like him. I interviewed Ted Lingard some weeks later; he told me that Arthur was a spoiled mother's boy who screamed and howled when he was not given his own way. The Lingard cousins could hardly gauge the emotional upset due to the loss of his mother, and the disappearance of his father. Arthur found his cousins repellent. He set great store by physical attractiveness and vivacity. His two female cousins were pale and sickly, and Maggie had an unpleasant smell, the result of an ear infection. Albert, a year his junior, had a cast in one eye, and was subject to epileptic fits. Ted and Jim were lubberly boys with big front teeth and loose lips, and there was something about them that frightened him. Albert jeered at him for being a "crybaby"—with reason. For weeks after his father left, he was always in tears, until even Aunt Elsie's stock of goodwill ran out. After a week or so, Uncle Dick tried the experiment of dealing with his tantrums by removing the wide leather belt from around his waist and thrashing him. It was the first time he had ever been beaten, and he was so stunned by it that he forgot to cry.

That Christmas, his father visited them. In the course of three months, Arthur had become accustomed to his new environment; but the sight of his father aroused an intense longing to be back in London with his grandmother. He begged and sobbed, and told his father that Uncle Dick beat him with a belt. His father was disturbed and upset, and had a long talk with his brother. When he left, he said, "Now be a good boy, and perhaps you might be able to go and stay with your grannie for a while." For weeks, Arthur was comforted by this thought. One day when he was raging helplessly against Albert and Ted—who were calling him a crybaby—he told them that he would soon be leaving them forever to live with his grandmother. "Oh, no you won't," said Albert, "She's dead. She died in an air raid." He rushed to his aunt when she came home from work to ask if it was true. "I'm afraid so." His escape hatch was closed. He began wetting the bed, and Uncle Dick went back to beating him with the belt.

It was difficult to get him to talk consecutively about this early period. He would stammer, start all over again, contradict himself; finally, he developed a hoarseness that I guessed to be psychosomatic. He complained of a tickling in his throat, and would cough until the tears came into his eyes. This symptom tended to lessen if I sat on the far side of the room, as if it was my presence that caused the trouble.

I tried bringing him a battery tape recorder, and asked him to put down his memories on tape, but he seemed to achieve only hesitant mumbles.

The breakthrough was accidental. I had written to Pauline, asking her to write down memories of her childhood and all she could remember about Arthur. A week later, she sent me a twenty-page letter, full of reminiscences and anecdotes. I had these typed out on separate sheets of paper, with double line spacing, and half the page left blank. I handed these to Arthur, asking him to make corrections and comments. When I returned the next day, he had covered sheet after sheet with his spiky, irregular handwriting. (As the therapy progressed, it became less irregular, but maintained its spiky quality.) He had started by correcting Pauline's anecdotes, then decided that it would be simpler to give his own version. The result was amazingly detailed, full of names, actual lines of dialogue, recollections of exactly what he had seen and felt. The main outlines of his childhood emerged very quickly. If I dwell at some length on some of these events, it is because of the enormous, morbid impact they made on him. They are a clue to all that follows.

Before the arrival of Pauline and Arthur, the five cousins had slept in the same large bed in the children's bedroom; now Maggie and Albert moved into a camp bed in their parents' room, and Arthur and Pauline took their place in the huge brass bed. He slept at one end between Pauline and Aggie; Jim and Ted slept at the other end. Occasionally, he heard Pauline or Aggie say "Stop it," and a foot would be withdrawn; he always assumed that the boys were "tormenting" them by kicking and prodding.

Albert greatly admired his elder brothers, particularly Jim. He told Arthur: "Jim's got the biggest dick in the school." "How do you know?" "All the boys got together one day and took out their dicks. A boy called Goofy measured them all with his ruler. Jim's was the biggest." The thought of a boy with a ruler, taking hold of strange cocks and measuring them, filled Arthur with a sickly, fluttery excitement. But he did not share Albert's interest in male genitals; it disgusted him. When Albert talked gloatingly about playing on the recky with other boys, and allowing them to see his penis, Arthur was baffled. He could not see where the pleasure came in.

75

Not long after he and Pauline had moved to Warrington, their aunt and uncle went off for the day on a bus outing, leaving Jim and Ted in charge of the younger children. Arthur was playing peacefully with the building blocks when he realized that he and Albert were alone. He asked where the others were. Albert gave his squint-eyed grin. "Playing doctors and nurses." "Where?" "You can't go in. They don't want kids." Arthur went upstairs and banged on the closed door of his uncle's bedroom. Jim's voice shouted, "Go away. You kids can't cum in." "I *want* to come in," said Arthur, and proceeded to kick the door and scream. "All right," Jim said, "Let him in. But he's got to sit in a corner and be quiet." He was allowed in, Aggie was lying on the bed, her cardigan unbuttoned. Arthur watched, fascinated; so did Pauline, to whom this game was new. Ted came in carrying a shopping bag—it was supposed to be a doctor's black bag. "Now, what seems to be the trouble?" "She keeps fainting, Doctor," said Maggie, who was the ward sister. "I expec' she's got a clyster," said the doctor, "We'll soon find out." He unbuttoned the rest of her cardigan, and said, "Off wi' this." Then he pulled up her vest, and tapped her chest with a piece of hosepipe, listening to the other end. "Nothing wrong there." Aggie lay passively, staring at the ceiling. "We'll give her an examination." Pauline was instructed to examine one leg; Ted took the other. Aggie's calves and thighs were poked and slapped. Then Ted said, "I expect this'll have to come off," indicating her scotch plaid skirt. This was unzipped and removed; Aggie lay there in tattered cotton knickers, her vest still under her armpits. Ted listened to her stomach, announced that the source of infection must be elsewhere, and told his assistant (his elder brother) to remove her pants. Then Aggie was made to part her thighs, while Arthur craned his head, fascinated. He had often seen Pauline without her clothes, but he had never actually seen between her thighs. "Ah, yes," said Ted, "I think we've found it." He bent over close, and parted the lips of the vulva, peering inside. Jim also bent down. Arthur moved quietly to the end of the bed; he had not realized that girls were so different from boys. He watched Jim insert a finger into his sister, and Aggie wailed, "No, please, you're hurting." Ted pronounced that she needed ointment to ease the pain. He dipped his finger into a jar of ointment taken from the medicine cupboard, and rubbed it between his sister's thighs. "All right,

76

you can get dressed now." "Now it's my turn," said Maggie. "No," said Jim, "It's Ted's turn. He's been doctor twice." And Ted lay down on the "operating table," and allowed Maggie to unbutton his shirt. Arthur stole a glance at Pauline, and realized that she had forgotten his existence. She had a look of slightly horrified fascination, and was obviously determined not to miss a moment of this. Aggie and Maggie unbuttoned Ted's shirt, and the examination proceeded as before, with Jim, as the doctor, instructing his nurses. "Listen to his heart, sister. See if it's beating prop'ly," "No, nothing wrong there. Better have his trousers off." Maggie said, "Cum on, Ted, lift your bum." "I can't," said Ted, his eyes closed. "I've been knocked out in a street accident." The women had to tug off his trousers, and Arthur was not surprised to see that he was in a state of erection. "Ah, yes," said Jim, "That's the trouble. I think it ought to be cut off." He handed a wooden spoon to Maggie. "Would you mind doing it, sister?" Maggie grasped the penis firmly in one hand, and pretended to saw at it with the knife. "No good. This is blunt." She turned to Pauline. "Would you like a go?" "Oh, no," Pauline said, retreating. "Go on," Jim said, "Don't be a spoilsport." "No, I'd rather not." But Arthur noticed that she could not take her eyes from her cousin's erect member. And half an hour later, after Maggie had undergone an operation for appendicitis which necessitated inserting a finger inside her, Pauline was finally persuaded to help removing Jim's clothes. Suddenly, she experienced revulsion. "I don't want to go on playing this game." The others all appealed to her sporting instinct, and she finally allowed herself to be persuaded. She even helped remove Jim's shirt and vest, and listened to his heart. When he was wearing nothing but trousers, Ted said, "Nurse Pauline, I think we'd better have those off." "Oh, no." "Let me," said Maggie. The patient woke up from his trance. "No! Let Polly." Pauline's fingers were hesitant, and Maggie kept saying, "Go on, get on with it." The fly was undone, and the trousers tugged down. Arthur was repelled at the sight of the large brown-colored penis, and its predictable state of erection. Jim lay still, a faint smile on his face, while his womenfolk examined the wonder. "Does it hurt if I squeeze it?" asked Maggie. "It'd hurt if it went in there," said Jim, thrusting his hand up Maggie's skirt. Maggie stood still; Arthur looked on breathlessly, watching Jim's hand work its way into the leg of Maggie's cotton knickers. Ted observed Pauline's fascinated glance. "Go on, touch it. That's what the game's about. You're a nurse. He's lying there unconscious." "He wouldn't be like *that* if he was unconscious," said Pauline, but she allowed Ted to guide her hand. Arthur felt a sudden fury of jealousy as he watched his sister touching the brown object, pulling the skin back from the glans, prodding the tight scrotum with her finger. He went over to her, and tapped her leg with his fist. "Let it alone, Polly." She turned on him irritably. "You go away. You promised to be quiet." It was so fierce that he crept away to a corner, feeling his eyes prickling with tears. He sat there for five minutes, snuffling softly, with no one paying any attention; then he noticed that Albert had taken his place at the end of the "operating table," and went back to stand beside him. Now Jim's hand had closed around Pauline's, and was moving it up and down. And as he watched, Jim gasped and stiffened. So did Pauline. Then she snatched her hand away and looked at it in disgust. "What's this?" "That's cum," said Ted. "Cum? It's more like snot." She started to wipe it on the bedsheet, but Maggie stopped her. "Don't do that. Mam 'n' Dad'll find out what we've been doing."

Arthur confidently expected his sister to refuse to take her place on the bed. If she decided not to do something, no power on earth could persuade her, and he rather looked forward to the argument, with his cousins all calling her a spoilsport, and Pauline tossing her head and telling them she didn't care what they called her. "Sticks and stones may break my bones. . . ." When Jim was dressed again, he said, "Come on, now. It's your turn, Polly," and Arthur waited for the refusal. To his amazement, Pauline shrugged, and climbed onto the bed. By now, they were all slightly tired of the ritual of tapping the chest and examining the legs. Jim helped her remove her jumper vest, listened perfunctorily at her heart for a moment, then said, "Now, off with this," placing his hand on her skirt. For a moment, Pauline's hands went defensively to her waist, then dropped. Ted fumbled the buttons, and pulled one of them off. When Pauline protested, Aggie said, "Never mind, luv. I'll sew it on." The skirt came off. Pauline was wearing black school stockings— a relic of her London schooldays—and white rayon knickers that had belonged to her mother. They were slightly too large, but she had tightened the elastic at the waist and legs.

Ted rolled down the stockings and peeled them off; Jim, without even a pretense of examining her stomach, pulled down the knickers, and, as Pauline raised her buttocks to allow them to pass underneath, thrust his hand between her thighs. Arthur shouted, "Don't let him do it, Polly." Jim and Ted glared at him together, and Jim shouted, "You shurrup." Arthur realized that he would be evicted from the room if he gave way to his impulse to cry, and stood still, wondering why his heart was causing a pain in his chest, while Ted and Jim bent over his sister, avidly examining her. With her legs apart, he could see that the oval-shaped orifice was pink inside, and that there was something else beyond it, with petals like an anemone. Jim, peering inside, said, "Hello, what's this. Something's been in there already." Pauline shouted furiously, "No it hasn't, you dirty sod." All right, all right," Jim said soothingly, "I dint mean no 'arm." In spite of his rising feeling of misery and nausea, Arthur could not help feeling proud that his sister's body was prettier than those of her cousins, that the thighs were shapelier and whiter, and that there were two or three dark hairs at the base of her stomach. Ted was saying, "Yes, what we need here is a bit of ointment." He dipped his finger into the jar, and prodded its end into the orifice. And suddenly, with no feeling of preparation, Arthur vomited. He vomited the tomatoes he had eaten at breakfast, and the toast and dripping he had eaten since, some of it went on the back of Albert's head; the rest, as Albert dodged frantically, onto the bed. The others were so aghast that no one had the presence of mind to turn his head away. Pauline sat up, pushing away the hand that remained between her thighs, and said, "Go to the lavvy, Art, fer god's sake!"

The game ended for the day. Aggie and Albert were sick from the smell of Arthur's vomit; Pauline mopped up the bed and the floor, and later spent most of the afternoon with a bucket of soapy water, trying to get the smell of vomit out of the mattress. Finally, half an hour before the parents were due home, Arthur—who had recovered his emotional balance in the uproar he had caused—asked them why they did not simply turn the mattress over. No one had thought of this. Jim said gloomily that it would make no difference, because the sheet was wet, but Pauline, now she saw a way out, suggested that they should change it for the sheet on their own bed. It would mean an uncomfortable night, but it was better than being found out. Their annoyance with Arthur was forgotten. They set to in a hurry, unmade the bed, turned over the mattress—which proved to be only slightly damp on the lower side—and changed the sheet. The despondency lifted. Everyone—with the exception of Arthur —had felt that the disaster was some kind of judgment on their guilt; now the judgment was averted, they were all happy again. For Arthur, the day ended better than it had begun. But as he lay in bed, snuggled against Pauline, he was suddenly struck with the thought of what lay within a few inches of his hand, and felt sick again. Something disgusting and frightening seemed to have come into his life, and it aroused a feeling that he normally associated with worms and slugs. He wanted to protect Pauline from it, make sure that she was never again dragged into this swamp of slime and wickedness. His cousins had no business with her thighs and belly; they should remain decently covered with the thin sheath of rayon that at present enclosed them.

I have devoted a great deal of space to what was, after all, a fairly innocent childish game. There is no "corruption" in children being curious about one another's genitals, as the islanders of the South Pacific used to know. It is a curiosity that is better satisfied. But Arthur Lingard was five and a half, and an exceptionally innocent five and a half. He already had the feeling that there was something menacing about his male cousins, something leering and dangerous. And now he had a mental image to embody his fears. Arthur Lingard was a highly emotional child, but the emotions were unattached to definite objects; they were what Jaspers, in *General Pschopathology*, called "free-floating feelings." He explained to me that as a small child, he was always experiencing violent emotional states for no apparent reason; sudden deep anxiety, that made him wonder if some awful misfortune was about to happen; tremendous happiness that made him feel as though he was floating on air; strange, tingling excitements that made him feel sick (and that were obviously erotic in origin). He was a child whose "emotion factory" often overproduced. If, like the young Mendelssohn, he had been a part of a warm, close family life, and had been sympathetically schooled and trained from an early period, these free-floating emotions would have found various objects, and become easy to handle. This new, strange environment certainly provided an object for his fears. And this game of doctors and nurses provided a definite object for a much larger emotion. I mean the emotion—which is common to many sensitive children—of morbid excitement. It is an emotion that has something in common with poetry, for it tends to ignore the actual world, which is too commonplace and real to provide objects for it. Poe came to associate it with the death of beautiful women; Le Fanu with ghosts and vampires, Baudelaire with sin. Arthur Lingard was still young enough to feel that this family he had been forced into was inhuman and dangerous. Albert, with his swivel eye, seemed a kind of troll or troglodyte. He and his sister were a couple of royal children who had accidentally strayed into a peasant's hut. What Arthur would have liked was for his sister to enter an alliance against their cousins, to cling to him, to say, "We stand together among these horrible people. . . ." And instead, she entered their disgusting games. She actually touched the horrible genitals of her loose-mouthed cousin. And—most incredible and unbelievable of all—she lay still while this same slobber-lipped lout tugged down her knickers and reached greedily between her thighs. In retrospect, Arthur *had* to believe that it had all been against her will, that she had been frightened or forced into it. Otherwise how could she so degrade herself, allow these apes to feel her body? It was an emotional shock of a major order, whose basic component was a raging jealousy of the sister who was also his mother.

As he lay in bed that night, his arm round his sister's waist, he felt a foot disturbing the bedclothes, sliding up her leg. He reached down and felt it trying to insert itself at the back of her thighs. Arthur kicked frantically and shouted "Stop it! Stop it!" Pauline woke up and said, "What's a matter?" while the enraged Jim snorted, "You little bugger. I'll beat your brains out." "If you do," said Arthur, "I'll tell Aunt Elsie about your doctors and nurses." "You wouldn't dare!" From the next room came an angry male rumble, "What the bloody 'ell's goin' on in there?" "I'll tell him if he comes," said Arthur frantically. Pauline, aware of the gravity of the situation, soothed him and told him to go to sleep. Jim, frightened at the prospect of betrayal, said no more. Arthur lay awake half the night, wondering how Jim would try to kill him, and what his brains would look like when they were no longer inside his head. For weeks afterwards, he was terrified of Jim, who, in fact, had inherited his father's basic good nature, and in any case, hardly noticed the existence of his young cousin. But even when the fear had subsided, it left behind a residue of hatred and anxiety. Children soon adapt; within a few months, he was basically accustomed to his new environment. (His swift progress at school in reading is a proof of this; emotionally disturbed children tend to be backward.) But something had closed inside him. He stopped being the vulnerable little boy who wore his heart on his sleeve. They had robbed him of his sister's love, and it was a permanent grievance.

Pauline soon settled down in Warrington, although her father's death was a greater emotional shock to her than to Arthur. She had the kind of resilient temperament that can survive anything. She was also the kind who was not afraid of playing with fire. She later told me that before she lost her virginity to Uncle Dick, she allowed herself to be picked up by a soldier, and walked out with him along the canal bank, although a girl had been found strangled there the week before. She let him kiss her, fondle her breasts, and made no serious objection when his hand went inside her underclothes. Fortunately, he was not the rapist type, and when she told him she was a virgin, he contented himself by rubbing against her thigh until he reached a climax. Pauline told me all this with her unashamed frankness the second time I visited her at Stockport. It struck me then that she was one of the most remarkable women I had ever met. She had always thought sex was fun, and yet had a basic strength of character that prevented her from drifting into mere promiscuity. Her cousins soon persuaded her to touch their sexual members; she was good-natured, and saw no reason why not. She discovered that these games produced an excitement that could be soothed by Jim's fingers. She could produce the same effect herself, but somehow, her open, friendly character was averse to masturbation. She preferred a man's rough fingers. By the time she was eleven years old, her hips had widened and her breasts developed, and if she took a liking to a boy, she automatically thought how pleasant it would be to lie beside him and feel his hand making its way under her dress and into the elastic around her leg. Absurdly enough, the idea of actual sexual intercourse never entered her head; she assumed it would be an operation from which only the man would derive pleasure.

She obviously enjoyed talking frankly to me, treating me as a kind of Kinsey reporter to whom she could pour out the most intimate details without embarrassment. Sex was the center of her life, a subject of infinite interest, and she would have enjoyed writing a ten-volume encyclopedia about all its aspects. When I remarked that it was amazing she had not lost her virginity earlier, she explained that she had developed a manual dexterity that could bring a man to a climax in half a minute "whether he liked it or not," and showed me the wrist movement involved. I felt that she would have demonstrated it on me, purely to corrobrate her claim, if I had cared to suggest it; her attitude to sex was truly scientific.

All this makes it possible to understand why Arthur Lingard developed as he did. He was brooding, sullen, cleverer than his cousins (and his sister). By temperament, he was naturally inhibited. And since he despised his cousins, and, by association, despised their frank sexuality, his prudish tendencies were emphasized. He adored his sister; she remained a mother figure, and as her breasts and hips developed, this became increasingly the case. And even if she had been the soul of discretion about her amours, he would have guessed what was going on. As it was, it was all fairly open. Boys at school would develop a passion for her. She had a liking for athletic types, and was always ready to go to the cinema with anyone who could afford two ninepenny seats. One night, when she came in late, Arthur went down to the kitchen for a drink, and found her assiduously sponging her skirt; there was no need for him to ask what she was doing. He believed he was shocked by her immorality, but the emotion was probably less abstract.

It was a frustrating existence, and his dissatisfaction found expression in stealing and breaking things. From the age of six he stole so constantly—and so aimlessly—that a social worker suggested he should see a psychiatrist. Unfortunately, this idea was allowed to drop; it might have saved a great deal of trouble. The social worker told Dick Lingard, "All children go through a rebellious phase at the age of six or seven; they soon outgrow it." And in fact, Arthur seemed to outgrow it in his eighth year, when he learned to read.

I asked him, as a matter of routine, what were the first books he had read? He replied, *"Tarzan* and the *Punch An-*

nual." "Tell me about the *Punch Annual*." He shrugged. "There's nothing much to tell. I went to a jumble sale one day with Aunt Elsie, and a lady gave it to me." But for some reason, I was curious. A *Punch Annual* seems an odd thing for an eight-year-old to read. When I next went to Stockport to see Pauline, I asked her if she remembered the *Punch Annual*. "Oh, yes, I've still got it." She went to a cupboard, and took out a large, olive green volume; *Punch Annual for 1932.* "Why do you suppose Arthur enjoyed reading this?" "Oh, he didn't read it. He looked at the pictures." I looked at the pictures, and was intrigued; drawings of young men in golfing clothes tinkering about inside the bonnets of sports cars or ordering dinner at the club. ("You know, Benson, these lonely meals at the club are enough to drive a man to marriage." WAITER: "Yes, sir, but then, marriage drives most gentlemen back to the club again.") Was this what had interested him so much: the life of the English upper and middle classes presented in pictures? I asked Pauline if I could borrow the volume, and took it back with me that night.

I had told Arthur that I intended to visit his sister. When I went in the next afternoon, he struck me as more relaxed than usual. "Well, how was she?" "Fine. She sends her love." He looked startled, then suspicious. "Did *she* say that?" I assured him that she had. He brooded for a moment, then asked, "Did she say 'Give him my love,' like that?" "Yes." I handed him the *Punch Annual.* He opened it very slowly, as if afraid it would vanish. I went and stood by the window, and pretended to be looking at a sheaf of papers from my briefcase. Ten minutes went by, then he said, "It's funny—what it brings back." "What does it bring back?" "Oh, all sorts of things. Learning to read. . . ." I said, "Tell me about it."

When he began talking, I expected no special revelation; it was only after ten minutes or so that I realized he was offering me the central clue to his childhood.

There had been no books in the Penketh Street house, so although he had learned the rudiments of reading when he was six or seven, he had no incentive to improve. He liked looking at the comic strips in the newspapers his uncle occasionally brought back from work. On the first page of the *Punch Annual*, there was a picture of a waiter making out the bill. "Did you have the pea soup or the tomato, sir?"

CUSTOMER: "I don't know. It tasted like soap." WAITER: "In that case, it was the tomato. The pea soup tastes like paraffin." It struck him as one of the funniest things he had ever seen; he collapsed into a chair shrieking with laughter. A few pages farther on, there was a picture of a waiter saying to a studious old gentleman, "No, sir, I haven't charged you for the celery. You ate the daffodils." Again, it seemed incredibly funny. The more he stared at the picture, the more he got out of the joke. There, in front of the old gentleman, was an empty vase of flowers, and a vaselike dish containing the celery. An open book on the table explained why he had failed to notice that he was eating daffodils.

He had spent the following day in his bedroom, looking carefully at every picture, asking Aunt Elsie to explain the jokes he couldn't understand. The old *Punch* tradition of elaborately detailed pictures and keen observation of social types meant that he could learn a great deal simply by staring at the pictures. And—as I had suspected—it was a revelation of a world he had never known. The *Annual* became his most valued possession; when his cousin Albert hid it one day, Arthur became so savagely violent that Uncle Dick gave orders it was never to happen again.

What fascinated him at first were the jokes with children in them, children whose parents were obviously rich. He showed me one of a small girl pointing to a cow. ELSIE: "What's that, Daddy?" FATHER: "A cow." ELSIE: "Why?" But Elsie was a pretty, well-dressed little girl who wore a bonnet and ankle socks, and her father was a tweedy man with a cane under his arm and a little moustache.

I asked him, "Did you envy these children?"

"Not exactly . . ."

"What, then?"

"Well, they sort of intrigued me. Look. . . ."

He began to point out details in the drawings. The small boy's Eton collar. The two upper-class children playing tea parties, with a large doll's house and a toy car in the background. The fact that all of the mothers were slim and pretty. There was a picture of a small girl lying on a lawn, reading a book, with her mother sitting close by in a cane chair. "Is that a nice book, darling?" "Oh, it's lovely, but the ending's sad." "What happens?" "She dies, and he has to go back to his wife." She is lying under a willow tree, her back on a cushion. A Scottish terrier—obviously her dog—lies at

85

her feet. Beside the mother's garden chair there is a table that has been set for tea with flat, wide cups—obviously china —and a plate with cake. In the distance, across the lawn, one can see the house with flowers round the door. But I observed another detail. The small girl is lying with her skirt round her waist, showing her knickers; her knees are together, but her feet are apart, one plimsoll lying beside her foot.

When he had finished pointing out the social implications of the picture, I asked, "What about the girl?"

"What about her?" But his sideways glance at me showed he knew what I meant. He said nothing, only stared at the picture. Then he turned several pages. "That was my favorite." It showed a small girl lying on a settee, her head in the lap of her elder sister; she is asking, "I say, Mabel, do hedgehogs lay eggs, or do they have kittens, like rabbits?" I could see why it would fascinate him. Once again, the implication of luxury: the scroll-shaped arms of the settee and its elegant, curved legs. Both girls are beautiful, and Mabel's leg, folded back under her, is long and shapely; even the posture of the hand, dangling from the back of the settee, hints at a golden world of wealth and elegance. The older girl's face is beautiful and spoiled; the younger one's, open and angelic.

"Tell me about it."

"I used to daydream about those two. Her name's Angelina." He placed his finger on the younger girl. "I got the name from another joke."

"What did you daydream?"

"Oh, the usual things. About how I was really their long-lost brother and all that. Or rescuing this one from a mad bull."

"Did they attract you sexually?"

He gave a grunting laugh, deliberately coarse.

"Of course. I used to think: If I was standing there [he placed his finger at the end of the settee] I could see right up her dress as far as her pants. . . ." He laughed, but there was something in the way he said it that made me feel this was more important than he wanted to admit. I pressed him to go into details about his daydreams. And slowly, I began to understand. At nine years of age, he was romantically in love with these beautiful small girls; he had never seen anything so delightful and charming. Everything about them touched his imagination. They also touched a lower source of intensity. The pose of the girl lying on the lawn made him think of Pauline with her legs open as they played doctors and nurses. The first time he imagined tugging down her knickers and examining the pink orifice, it made him feel sick and ashamed. But the thought returned every time he looked at the pictures; his daydreams of rescuing the sisters from a mad bull, or discovering he was their long-lost brother, alternated with fantasies about finding them both asleep on the settee, and cautiously peering up their skirts. The younger one would probably wear pink or blue knickers, but the elder would wear brief things like Jane in the *Daily Mirror*. . . .

Obscurely, Arthur Lingard was aware that he was making a choice. He could either daydream innocently and idealistically about sharing their luxurious, pampered life; or he could allow the morbid excitement to take over, and imagine taking off their clothes. These fantasies made him feel guilty and soiled, but induced a sweet and poisonous excitement. They also gave him the feeling that he was not worthy to be a part of the world of the rich and beautiful. And increasingly, his fantasies were concerned with furtive entries into rich houses and the violation of Mabel and Angelina.

The choice was crucial. In this happy *Punch* world of well-dressed children and young men with canes, people did not think of sex all the time. He longed to be part of this world. It was only in the grubby, fish-smelling world of Penketh Street that the local roughnecks thought of sex all the time. But looking at these pictures, he could only think of sex; ergo, he belonged to Penketh Street. The very sight of their cleanness and prettiness gave him an erection. In his own eyes, he was incurably filthy-minded.

I asked him suddenly, "When did you first become so obsessed with panties?"

"What?" He started, and stared at me.

I pretended not to understand, "Were you always an underwear fetichist, or did it start at the time you were given the *Punch Annual?*"

He shrugged, avoiding my eye.

"I don't know. I think perhaps it was always there. But I didn't become aware of it until later."

It was the key; the clue I had been waiting for. His panty fetichism was the thread that ran throughout his later criminal activities. And as soon as he took it for granted that I knew about it, he began to speak with a new frankness.

It would be a mistake to think that the keynote of his childhood was his sexual preoccupation. On a bookstall in the marketplace, he discovered *Tarzan of the Apes,* and started to read it because he had seen a Tarzan film with Johnny Weismuller. Soon, he was gripped by a new emotion. He had never realized that a story could be so real and absorbing. Here was something with which he could completely identify; he was the young Lord Greystoke, stranded among apes in the jungle. . . . He bought more Tarzan books from the plump, talkative Jew who ran the stall, paying for them with money taken from his aunt's handbag, or Uncle Dick's pockets when drunk. He passed from Tarzan to *A Princess of Mars,* which again left him breathless. Then, allured by their sensational covers, he began reading the novels of A. Merritt, which the stall-holder sold him in a batch—*The Moon Pool, The Metal Monster, The Ship of Ishtar, The Face in the Abyss,* and the classic *Seven Footprints to Satan.* This could have been a turning point in his life, for this world of fantasy provided total escape from the enforced intimacies of Penketh Street. He might have become a dreamer, avoiding the real world, expressing his frustrations and aggressions through wish-fulfillment fantasy. But again, fate intervened. His uncle decided that he ought to interfere on principle; Arthur had become altogether too quiet. So whenever Dick Lingard caught him reading in the children's bedroom, he took away the book and ordered him out to play, on the grounds that he would ruin his eyes. Arthur soon learned to keep a book hidden in the coal shed, so that he could pick it up on his way out of the backyard. He found a quiet place on the canal bank, and spent the summer afternoons devouring Merritt and Doc Smith. He had chosen a spot between a fence and a bush, close to a bridge. On his first afternoon there, an American soldier arrived with a local girl. They lay down in a hollow where they were invisible from the canal towpath and began to kiss. Arthur hardly dared to move, convinced he would be seen; but they were too absorbed in each other. He saw the girl's hand move to the soldier's trousers, and start to undo the buttons. A moment later, her hand was inside. The soldier's hand went under her dress, but she said quite audibly, "You can't, it's my period." The soldier groaned. There was more kissing and fumbling, and then the girl disengaged herself, moved into a crouching position above his trousers, and bent forward. Arthur heard the soldier gasp, "Oh, that's terrific"; he could not see what was happening, but the movements of her head and the soldier's hips left no doubt. A few moments later, he gasped and groaned; the girl withdrew her head. Money changed hands; they got up and went off in opposite directions. Arthur sat there, shattered and electrified. In all his lurid sexual daydreams, he had never imagined such a situation. In his fantasies, it was always he who undressed the passive girl, never the girl who groped at his buttons. It seemed somehow infinitely more indecent that the girl should do such things to a man.

He needed someone to talk to, to tell about what he had witnessed. But he had no close friends. When he got home, there was only Aggie in the house; she was washing the dishes. Arthur had to tell someone; he broke the habit of years, and confided in Aggie. " 'Ere, you'll never guess what I just seen down by the cut." "No? Go on." He told her, and was gratified at her wide eyes. "Ooh, the dirty devils! I've 'eard about that Liz Morgan. But I didn't know she'd do that!" Aggie was three years his senior; he had always found her unattractive, but her amazement gratified his ego. "You mustn't tell the others." "Why not?" "Because you can bet Ted and Jim'd tell the ole man, and then there'd be 'ell to pay." She saw his point, and kept the secret. It was the beginning of the strange intimacy that developed between them.

Uncle Dick's reason for getting Arthur out of the house was not the one he gave: fear that Arthur would ruin his eyes; by this time, Pauline had been his mistress for six months or so, and they wanted the house to themselves on Saturday afternoons. Arthur sensed that something was happening; but he suspected that the recipient of Pauline's favors was his cousin Jim, or perhaps one of her numerous boyfriends from school.

What he had seen on the canal bank aroused a morbid degree of sexual awareness. He knew the girl slightly; she was known in the area as "Scabby Liz." And writing this nickname makes me aware of a point that must be kept in mind about the background of Arthur Lingard's childhood, and that tends to escape when the story is told in detached psychological jargon. There was an attitude—prevalent among his school friends—that was the reverse of Arthur's fastidiousness; a kind of delight in indecency, in subjects that would normally make one feel slightly sick. I asked him one day to make a list of the things he hated in childhood, and when I returned an hour later, he had written out a dozen or so dirty jokes; the point of every one of them was that sex was treated as actually degrading, and associated with vomit, with excretion, with scabs and boils; the most typical of them concerned an inexperienced husband on honeymoon who, when prompted by his wife to "do something dirty," had diarrhea in the bed. An eminent Russian psychologist has advanced the opinion that such stories express a "revolutionary" attitude to society; they are the poor man's revolt against his oppressors. I am inclined to agree that they express a fundamental cynicism, not only about society, but about life itself. Kings and queens go to bed, and commit the same furtive and "dirty" acts as a drunken sailor in a brothel; therefore, in a basic sense, they are no better than the sailor. Scabby Liz "gobbling" an American soldier is simply human nature without its disguises. Human dignity is a fraud.

But Arthur Lingard had an instinctive feeling of superiority to his environment, and the attitude behind such stories struck at the roots of his self-respect, and aroused a passion of rejection. It failed to take into account the feelings aroused in him by Tarzan and Captain John Carter and the heroes of A. Merritt. But then, of course, these things were fiction; Scabby Liz was real life. . . . And perhaps his sister was doing the same kind of thing with her soccer-playing boyfriends. She was as bad as any of them. Aggie's horrified incredulity showed that she had the right attitude to all this. But then, Aggie was so much less attractive than Pauline. . . .

That night, Arthur woke up from lurid, frightening dreams. He now slept on the edge of the bed, next to Pauline. Maggie and Albert were in the other end; Uncle Dick had moved Ted to a camp bed downstairs, and Jim to another one in their own room. Arthur lay awake in the dark, experiencing a conflict of emotions: of oppression and excitement, disgust and desire. Pauline was lying with her back to him; he put his arm around her and snuggled against her. After a moment, she muttered something, and turned on her back. She was wearing a nightdress. Since Ted and Jim had moved,

Micronite filter.
Mild, smooth taste.
For all the right reasons.
Kent.

America's quality cigarette.
King Size or Deluxe 100's.

Micronite filter.
Mild, smooth taste.
For all the right reasons.
Kent.

Regular or Menthol.

Kings: 17 mg. "tar,"
1.1 mg. nicotine;
100's: 19 mg. "tar,"
1.3 mg. nicotine;
Menthol: 19 mg. "tar,"
1.3 mg. nicotine
av. per cigarette,
FTC Report Aug. '72.

Warning: The Surgeon General Has Determined That Cigarette Smoking Is Dangerous to Your Health.

she had given up wearing her knickers in bed. And since her waist was bare, Arthur was aware that the nightdress had worked its way up her body. The thought frightened and excited him; his stomach felt so sick that he was not even capable of an erection. He allowed one of his hands to move, as if involuntarily, and rest on her thigh. She muttered something in her sleep, and her legs parted; at the same time, her hand moved on to his own thigh, and touched him. The result, he told me, was the most overwhelming emotion he had experienced up to that time. The action was not so much a sexual advance as a gesture of affection, of acceptance, from the mother-figure who had formerly rejected him. It made no difference that she was obviously asleep; it was a token of what *could* happen. She had turned away from other males, turned back to him. The emotion was so violent that he wanted to burst into tears. Her hand on his genitals induced sexual excitement and an erection, and she was making slight movements that were unmistakably caresses. He lay there for a long time in a condition of ecstasy, hardly daring to breath unless she woke up. There was no thought in his mind of trying to return the caress; that would have seemed indecent. He lay there for a long time, breathing regularly. Presently, she half woke up, realized what she was doing, and turned her back on him again. But this didn't matter. The only thing that now worried him was how to face her in the morning. But she had apparently forgotten; she hardly gave him a glance as she dressed, grumbling at the cold floor.

These two events, happening within a few hours of each other—the scene on the canal bank, the caress in bed—represent the dividing line between Arthur Lingard's childhood and adulthood. It is true that he was not yet ten years old; but for practical purposes, he had ceased to be a child. The fixation on Pauline had become specifically sexual. This, in turn, meant that his attitude toward what he had seen on the canal bank ceased to be one of rejection; he could openly acknowledge its fascination. If Uncle Dick Lingard had not sent him out on that Saturday afternoon in July 1948, his development might have been completely different. He would have retreated farther into his world of Martian fantasy, and continued to reject all thoughts of incest. He would have remained in a dream world where he was Captain John

Carter fighting the warriors of Mars, and where thoughts of Pauline's sexual activities had no place.

His fantasy world, of course, lost none of its fascination. *A Princess of Mars* remained the basic pattern of his fantasy: his daydreams always began with awakening on the bed of "yellow, moss-like vegetation" which stretched around for miles, with the warm Martian sun on his naked body. The idea intoxicated him: to awaken in a strange landscape *completely unlike the earth*, strange seas, strange cities, strange forests, and all of it infinitely distant from Warrington.

What happened was, I think, inevitable. The fantasy world provided him with an escape that increased his confidence. He was really Captain Arthur Lingard from Mars. These people did not even suspect the world with which he was familiar. But since he had now achieved a kind of detachment from Penketh Street, he had also gained a kind of recklessness. He returned to his hideout on the canal bank, and dragged more branches along to disguise it. He committed himself to spying on courting couples, instead of trying to do it "accidentally." And during that summer, his "sex-spotting" activities were remarkably successful. He watched couples engaged in everything from furtive caresses to actual intercourse. One evening while watching them, he pushed down his trousers, and found that the feeling of cool air on his nakedness increased the excitement. He had not actually reached the stage of playing with his genitals; he still felt some inhibition about this; it was the kind of thing the "dirty" lads at school did. He would press his loins into the ground and move his hips. In his daydreams, it was Pauline who lay beneath him.

About Pauline herself, he remained cautious; he was afraid that his activities might be discovered—he had the feeling that everybody must guess what he was doing—and so he made no attempt at further advances to her in bed. But his sexual excitement was renewed when Dick Lingard bought Pauline and Aggie their first sets of bra and panties. No doubt Aggie was included to allay suspicion; she was completely flat-chested. (The unfortunate Maggie died of bronchial pneumonia in the winter of 1949; she had been ill with various complaints since childhood.) In his voyeuristic activities, Arthur had noticed that his excitement was most intense when a girl was removing her knickers, or allowing a man to remove them; this act struck him as far more excitingly indecent than anything that followed. The thick woolen knickers worn by Pauline in her schooldays held no interest for him; it was something in the actual texture of silk or rayon that excited him. And when Pauline started to wear rayon knickers—which Uncle Dick apparently preferred too—his obsession with her became more specifically sexual. He would get up in the middle of the night, apparently to go downstairs to the lavatory, and take her knickers from the chair where she had left them. Downstairs, he would pull them on, and then rub his hands over his stomach and buttocks, delighting in the smooth feeling of his flesh under the silk, his erection making them stand out in front like a tent. Sometimes the excitement was so intense that he risked getting back into bed with them still on, to press himself cautiously against Pauline's buttocks. At these times he experienced the sense of being a supercriminal who has just pulled off some tremendous *coup*. She was unconscious that he had somehow stolen her intimacy. Fundamentally, it was a symbolic version of his imagined rapes of the girls in *Punch*.

But Pauline was not as unaware as he supposed. She became suspicious one morning when she found her knickers underneath the chair instead of on it. Arthur had apparently fallen asleep with them on, and woke when it was already daylight. He managed to slip them off in bed, and kicked them across the floor, hoping she would not notice. One night she was awake when he stole out of bed; when he was downstairs, she went to check on her clothes. I asked her how she felt when she found they were missing. "Well, sort of complimented. It didn't do me no harm, did it?"

It was at about this time that he suddenly realized that she was sleeping with Uncle Dick. Pauline had already described the episode to me: how Arthur had walked into the kitchen and found them in a compromising position. For a moment, he was hardly able to believe his eyes; Pauline's hand was in her guardian's fly, and his was under her dress. They separated instantly, and with a guilty air that left no doubt in his mind that his first impression had been correct.

Arthur was shattered. He had grown used to the idea of Pauline allowing her boyfriends various intimacies; but he was genuinely shocked to find her doing it with Uncle Dick. He was so upset that he could not bring himself to mention it to her. But two nights later, he woke up to find her hand on him again, as she stirred and muttered in her sleep. The idea that she thought he was Uncle Dick produced violent excitement; he was stealing something intended for someone else. Her thighs were open and her hips moved slightly. He placed his hand on her loins and pressed gently with his middle finger, and it came away wet. She stirred, and he took his hand away. When she seemed to be asleep again, he replaced it; but she was only pretending. Her hand reached down, and very firmly pushed him away. He whispered: "You started it," and then, seeing she did not understand, took her hand and placed it on his erection. She turned her back on him; but he had a feeling he had gained his point. The next morning, as they dressed, they avoided looking at each other. And yet, it seemed to Arthur, the ice was broken between them. . . .

His interpretation was not entirely correct, as I learned from Pauline. There was another reason, that Arthur had failed to take into account. Pauline was only fourteen; Dick Lingard knew that if she was subjected to a physical examination by a police surgeon, he could spend the next five years in prison. The thought that Arthur might mention what he had seen cost him a couple of sleepless nights. On the day after the episode just described, he asked Pauline: "Has he talked to you about it?" "No." "Have a word with him. You know how much he thinks of you. Tell him they'd put you in a girl's reformatory if he told anybody."

Accordingly, when Arthur was drying up the dishes that evening, Pauline joined him in the kitchen and took another tea towel. Neither spoke for a while; then she said, "You'll not tell anybody about it, will you?"

There was no need for him to ask what she meant. He shrugged and said, "I s'pose not." She passed her hand over his hair—a gesture of affection that dated from their childhood. "You're a good lad."

He asked the question that had been on his mind for days.

"But why him? He's an old man."

She smiled. "*Oh*, no he's not."

"But it's not right. He's your uncle."

"Why does that make it wrong?" She looked him in the eyes. "You're my brother."

He went pale. "What do you mean?"

She smiled and winked. "You know."

But the old feeling of closeness had been reestablished. Later that evening, Uncle Dick followed her outside when she went to get washing off the line.

"What did he say?"

"I think it'll be all right."

"Did he promise?"

"Well, no, not 'xactly."

"Well try and get him to promise. *Be nice to him.*"

Pauline put her own interpretation on those last words. I got the rest of the story from Arthur.

He woke up to find Pauline stirring with the familiar symptoms of unrest: the movement of the hips, and the wandering hand. He lay very still for a while, afraid to awaken her. Then his own excitement became too much. He cautiously reached down, raised the nightdress, and found the parted thighs. His finger pressed into the slippery warmth. She woke up with a start. He expected instantaneous rejection. She snatched away her hand, and lay there, obviously awake, her thighs closing on his hand. And then—he found it hard to believe his senses—her hand returned and touched him again. He bent his finger and felt it go inside her; there was a sharp intake of breath, and a movement of her hips. Her own hand was hardly moving, yet it was unmistakably caressing. He felt a rising tide of warmth, and turned toward her to press himself against her thigh. For the first time, he experienced an orgasm. Pauline's other hand pressed his own tightly, to prevent it from moving; and then she sighed, and relaxed. They fell asleep pressed close together.

For Arthur, this was not merely a pleasant sexual experience. It seemed to be a reward, a reward for years of unhappiness and refusal to be absorbed by Penketh Street. The earth mother had turned to him and treated him as a lover. His ecstasy was so intense, even after his orgasm, that he felt as though he was floating on a sea of peace. What did it matter if Uncle Dick was fucking his sister? What did it matter if every man in the street was? She was good and life was good, and everything came out right in the end if you hung on long enough. . . . He slept peacefully, and when he woke up, his hand was still on her thigh.

Pauline was also pleased with herself. She was now certain that he would be discreet about Uncle Dick.

95

SIX

When I talked to Pauline about the episode just described, it was clear to me that she had no idea of its importance in Arthur's development. For her, it was simply one more permutation in the sexual games that naturally occupied so much of her thoughts. She was unaware that she had created a kind of psychological landslide in Arthur. All human minds walk a tightrope between optimism and despair, trust and mistrust. A healthy mind, trapped in disagreeable circumstances, deliberately seeks out counterweights to its revulsion and rejection. Arthur had found the novels of Edgar Rice Burroughs and A. Merritt. His triumphant alter ego campaigned on Mars with John Carter, Ulysses Paxton, Jason Gridley, while the Arthur Lingard known to his family and schoolteachers remained stuck in the mud of Penketh Street and spied on lovers from behind bushes. It is possible he might have gone on to develop a split personality, like Thurber's Walter Mitty, contented to accept his "real" self as ineffectual and unlucky. I believe that the new relationship with Pauline changed all that.

But at this point there enters a third element, that has so far played no important part: his tendency to epilepsy. This was a subject on which I found him curiously reticent. I assumed that this was because he felt the residue of shame carried over from his schooldays: it cannot be pleasant to cry out and collapse in the middle of a crowded playground or a history lesson, and wake up surrounded by faces that wear an expression of curiosity mingled with disgust.

A few days after we had been discussing his Martian fantasies, my daily newspaper published a photograph of Mars taken by the Russian probe. I took it along with me to show Arthur. He glanced at the blurred photograph, then at the headline: "No Life on Mars, Say Russians," then tossed the newspaper on to the floor with a grunt of disgust. He said, "Idiots." I asked, "Why? Do you think there's life on Mars?" "I *know* there is."

I had been wondering for some time how far his fantasies about the black guards still retained a hold over him. It was a subject we had tacitly agreed not to discuss. This seemed an opportunity to probe. "*How* do you know?"

What he described—in a clear, rational manner—sounded like some strange dream or vision.

He had been sitting on the bank of the canal on a quiet Saturday afternoon, when most of the town's youth had gone to a local football match. He was making a map of an area of Martian territory in the kingdom of Jeddak—a series of interconnected lakes in a mountainous region, joined by fast-flowing torrents that disappeared underground. Periodically, he referred to one of the paperbacks of the Martian novels which he carried in his school satchel. On this particular afternoon, he was aware of a peculiar absorption in his game, a feeling of silence and concentration. Suddenly he began to feel something. (I asked him to be more specific. "A sort of shivery, prickly feeling.") An immense sense of contentment rose in him. Then, as he looked at the map of Jeddak, there was a strange sensation of *remembering* it. With a shock, he realized that this was not imagination; it was real. He had a sensation of dark hills rising above him, of cliffs that sloped inward, and had green, glassy markings on their surface, of trees whose foliage was black and glossy, of great red and purple fruits; at the same time, he clearly smelled the air, which was distinctive, and heard the sound of the flowing water. A sense of revelation came over him, of grasping something that was *true*. When the sensation—or vision—faded away, his sense of its reality remained. As he walked back to Penketh Street, among crowds wearing the colors of Manchester United, he kept thinking, "So *this* isn't true after all," meaning by "this" the reality around him.

I asked, "Are you *sure* it was Mars you saw?"

"Oh, yes, it was Mars all right."

"Could it—for example—have been some vision you experienced on the point of an epileptic fit?"

"No!" He scowled at me. "Why do you people want to drag everything down, just because you can't understand it?"

I said humbly: "I'm sorry. I didn't mean to drag it down. You must admit it's hard for me to understand."

"I suppose it is. . . . Still, it's true all the same."

"Did you ever experience it again?"

"Once or twice." But he was now unwilling to talk about it.

I pressed him about it later, when he had forgotten his resentment, and it became clear that the "vision" had been an event of great importance in his eleventh year. His own interpretation was that some latent power in him had been awakened, and had given him a telepathic glimpse of a real planet. His subsequent behavior confirms this; he borrowed books on the solar system from the library, and studied accounts of Mars and Venus. He was disappointed at first to realize that the real Mars must be a great deal colder than the fictional one, being some forty million miles farther from the sun than the earth. But then it struck him that even if this is true, there is no reason why the flora and fauna of Mars should not have adapted themselves to these lower temperatures, just as they have adjusted themselves to breathe a different atmosphere. As an alternative hypothesis, he was willing to admit that his vision might not have been of Mars, but of Venus. In any case, he never wavered for a moment in his certainty that he had seen, or remembered, a real place.

In my own view, the epilepsy theory provides the likeliest explanation. Some weeks later, I showed him one of Dostoevski's letters describing his sensations before an attack: the heavy feeling of oppression, followed by a sudden sense of total happiness and release, a feeling of some tremendous insight. He read it, agreed briefly that his own experience had "sometimes" been like this, then changed the subject. I realized that it was still important to him to believe that his "vision" had really been of another planet. It gave him a sense of uniqueness, of being "chosen."

I am also inclined to believe that the new relationship with Pauline played some part in the experience. Her acceptance of him caused a rush of pleasure, of optimism, a release of confidence, that reinforced his imagination, strengthened his identification with the Martian heroes. He also admitted frankly that his sexual obsession with Pauline led him to develop unusual powers of concentration. He described how, in the days when she first began to wear rayon panties, he often got an erection an hour before they went to bed. He would go to bed first, then lie awake, waiting for her. She always undressed with the light out, but there was often a light from the bedroom of the next door neighbor that made it possible to see. She always left her panties until last, and their actual removal always produced the same delicious thrill of "indecency" that he felt when watching couples by the canal. When she climbed into bed, he would lie awake, sometimes floating in a kind of suspended state of lust, waiting for her regular breathing to tell him she was asleep, so he could slide out of bed and grope until his hand touched the smooth rayon on top of her other clothes. He had no difficulty in remaining awake because his intense sexual excitement kept him concentrated on his objective. What surprised him most was that instead of feeling tired and guilty the next morning, he usually felt alert and brimming with energy, noticing the sights and sounds of the street with a sense of delight that was strange to him. He developed the conviction that most people sleep too much, and that anyone who really tries to develop his powers can throw off these limitations.

Pauline observed that her brother developed a new confidence. He no longer hid in corners, trying to conceal the book he was reading, or flinched nervously every time someone brushed against him. Uncle Dick thought that the amount of time he was spending outdoors was improving his health. He could hardly be expected to guess that his strange nephew was developing a superman complex, a sense of confident superiority to the people around him. Arthur was convinced that he was somehow living simultaneously on different planes of existence, one on earth and one on Mars—or Venus. The "visionary glimpses" of that other planet occurred whenever he was alone and in a state of peace that favored intense concentration, or occasionally on the edge of sleep. He read and reread Burroughs, and made elaborate maps and tables of Martian history.

It was this new sense of confidence that pushed him over the borderline into real crime; it provided the additional drive needed to turn fantasy into action.

The hot summer of 1949 became a rainy autumn, and Arthur no longer had the privacy for his Martian daydreams. Uncle Dick objected to him reading in the bedroom because he said it was a waste of electric light. He occasionally went to the reading room in the local library; but there was not enough privacy there either, and the sight of young girls going in and out stimulated sexual fantasies that broke the delicate eggshell of illusion. November was freezing and dull. It was in the late November of 1949 that he committed his first burglary.

He had returned home from school to an empty house. Sitting in front of the fire, he felt fatigued, resentful, and bored. The fire was low, but he could not summon up the energy to fetch more coal—Uncle Dick insisted that it would be "backed up" with damp slack coal dust—so that it would burn all day. He found himself wishing it was summer so he could go down to spy on the canal bank. The boredom frightened him more than anything, for it seemed to be an ironical comment on his pretentions to unusual powers.

One of his few friends at school was a boy named Duncan McIver; he was nearsighted, and had a withered arm; but he was also an addict of science fiction, and had a volume of Merritt that Arthur coveted called *Creep, Shadow, Creep*. He and Arthur loaned each other paperbacks, and sometimes made swaps. Duncan's parents were better off than those of the majority of his school friends—in fact, Duncan had attended a private school for a year; but his father, a self-made man, insisted that he was better off among the "ordinary lads" at the council school. Now Arthur recalled that Duncan had mentioned he was going to the cinema in Manchester after school, because his mother was driving in to do her shopping. He knew that Duncan had a sister in her late teens who was studying at a secretarial school, and that his father was often away all night. That meant there was a good chance their house would be empty. Arthur had returned there with Duncan one day after school and had seen him take a back door key out of the toolshed. There was an orchard at the back of the house, and the hedges were high, so that it was not overlooked by the houses next door. Duncan had told him he had a cupboard of books in his bedroom; that should not be too difficult to find.

As soon as he began to entertain this idea, Arthur felt a watery excitement in his stomach. It should be foolproof. He would go to the house with a book—pretending that he had forgotten that Duncan would be out. It would soon be dusk; his chances of being caught were slight.

The boredom vanished; he experienced again the excitement and tension he used to feel lying in bed, waiting for Pauline to go to sleep.

100

Duncan's house was two miles away; Arthur borrowed a bicycle belonging to Jim, and was there in ten minutes. He left the bicycle at the end of the street and walked up to the house. No lights were on. He mounted the steps to the front door and rang the bell. There was no reply. He went around the side of the house—now shielded by the hedge—and knocked on the back door. He tried the handle; it was locked. He went to the shed; the key was hanging behind the door. His heart was now beating painfully, but he felt immense exhilaration as he turned the key in the door and pushed it open.

The kitchen had green and white tiles on the floor and smelled of fruit. On the previous occasion, Arthur had waited at the door, but he had been struck by the cleanness and the pleasant smell. Now, inside the kitchen, everything fascinated him; a large refrigerator, a huge cooking stove, gleaming white; a double sink unit. He carefully locked the door behind him and put the key into his pocket. If anyone came into the house, he might be able to hide, and there would be no evidence that he was there.

He went out into the hall. A grandfather clock ticked peacefully in a corner. The place was warm; there were radiators against the wall. He peeped through an open door into a carpeted room with a grand piano, then went in, and looked out of the window. It was still daylight, but getting dark. There were photographs on the piano: of Duncan, his parents, and a pale, pretty girl, evidently his sister. She reminded him of Aggie.

The feeling of being in a strange house was the most exciting thing he had ever known, and he was tingling with sexual excitement. The pleasant smells intrigued him; furniture polish with a smell of lavender; an air freshener on the hall table. Even the lack of smell in certain rooms struck him as intriguing after the stale odors of Penketh Street.

He went upstairs two at a time. At the top of the stairs, a bedroom door stood open—Duncan's room, obviously, for he could see an open cupboard and the colored spines of paperback books. But at the moment, he was not interested in books. He opened the door of the next room, and looked into a large double bedroom, obviously belonging to Duncan's parents. The bed had been slept in—no doubt Mrs. McIver had taken a nap before setting out to collect her son from school. Arthur was scarcely able to believe his eyes. The

101

sheets were apparently made of green silk. Silk had a fetichistic significance for him; now he was so excited that he had to resist the temptation to remove his clothes and climb into bed.

He went out, and tried the door of the next room; it was a bathroom with sea-green tiles and a scented smell. The bars of soap were pink and oval, and this interested him so much that he washed his hands in the sink in warm water. At Penketh Street, they used large green bars of soap, cut into slices.

He explained that by this time all fear and tension had vanished. There were so many potential hiding places in this house that he was convinced he could conceal himself if anyone came home, and perhaps even wait until everyone was asleep before sneaking out. The thick carpets meant he could move silently. He peeped into a laundry basket to see if there was any female underwear; but there were only some sheets.

He carefully dried his hands on a folded towel, then replaced it in exactly the same position on a warm rail. He went along to try the next door. This seemed to be a guest bedroom; for although it contained a double bed, there were no signs of an occupant, and the drawers were empty. But the next bedroom, overlooking the front garden, was obviously that of Duncan's sister. Again, there was a double bed (Arthur was amazed at the extravagance of having a double bed for one person), and the sheets were again of green silk. This was too much for him; he undressed and climbed into bed. As he did so, he had what he described as "a marvelous feeling of indecency." It was her bed; a few hours ago, she had climbed out of it. Perhaps, in sheets like this, she slept naked; otherwise, what would be the point of silk sheets? They were cool against him, and he rolled around, gasping as though he had plunged into cold water. The thought of her naked body excited him, and he pressed his hips and thighs into the mattress. Almost immediately, he experienced a violent orgasm, *and,* with great distinctness, the sense of his Martian personality, of the vast plains and mountains that were his true home. This was combined with a hallucinatory sense of making love to Duncan's sister (whose name he did not know). He lay there for five minutes after it had subsided, feeling strangely confident and secure. The hall clock struck five fifteen. He got out of bed in a kind of daze, put on his clothes, and very carefully straightened the bed and smoothed out the pillows.

It was while he was doing this that he heard the key turn in the front door, and suddenly went cold with fear. He stepped softly out of the bedroom, thanking God for the carpets, and tiptoed along the landing. The door closed; he could not see who had come in. It could not be Duncan and his mother; he had heard no car; besides, it was too early. Whoever it was was alone. It could therefore be either Duncan's father or his sister. The refrigerator door slammed and there was a gurgling sound of milk being poured into a glass. Then, a few minutes later, a female voice hummed a few bars of a popular song called "Galway Bay." He experienced relief; if the worst came to the worst, he could deal with a girl, even if it meant attacking her.

Nothing happened for the next five minutes, and the pounding of his heart subsided. He began to wonder if it might not be possible to tiptoe downstairs and out of the front door. He opened the door of the spare bedroom, to provide a retreat in emergency, then tiptoed to the top of the stairs to survey the situation. He could hear her moving about in the sitting room. Then she came out, and he retreated. Her footsteps crossed the hall and began climbing the stairs. He expected her to look up and see him, and perhaps scream. He hurried into the spare bedroom and closed the door as far as he dared. She went past it and into her own room. The light clicked on—it was now almost dark—and he heard her draw the curtains. After this, he ceased to listen intently; his bowels turned to water, and his main concern was how to prevent himself from evacuating them into his trousers.

She came out of her bedroom and into the bathroom. A tap was turned on. She obviously suspected nothing, for she was still singing snatches of "Galway Bay." Then, to his immeasurable relief, the lock of the bathroom door clicked. It struck him that she was probably now taking off her clothes, so he hurried out, and applied his eye to the bathroom keyhole. But he could see nothing; she was out of range. At this point, it would have been sensible to leave the house; any other burglar would have done so. But this is where Arthur Lingard differed from the average burglar. He was sexually excited, and he had a sense of immunity and power. If the bathroom door had been unlocked, he might have attempted to assault the girl in the bath. The sound of water splashing around conjured up images of her soaping her breasts, and made him feel like a hungry wild animal.

He turned round and saw that her bedroom door was still ajar and that her clothes lay on the bed. Hardly able to believe his luck, he tiptoed to the room. A pink dressing gown that had been lying across the bed was gone; lying in its place there was a blue dress, an underskirt with a stocking dangling from it. He lifted the underskirt and saw that the other stocking was crumpled in the leg of a pair of white panties. He unbuttoned his fly, and pressed these against his tensed loins; their coolness brought an instantaneous climax that was so violent that he felt tempted to lie on the bed.

As soon as it was over, he felt panic; not fear of being caught, but of what he had been tempted to do: attack her in the bath. Now, in his relaxation, it was obviously absurd. He wanted to get out of the house, leave her to her bath. But first he opened a bedroom drawer, and took another pair of panties resembling those he had just dropped. He replaced the latter carefully inside the underslip, even crumpling the stocking and replacing it in the leg. Then he went downstairs. The sitting room door was open and the light was on. There was a bureau in the corner, and its top was open. He wanted another souvenir of his visit; he peered inside, saw a small, blue cardboard box in a pigeonhole, and thrust it into his pocket. Then he went out through the kitchen, unlocked the door and locked it behind him, and replaced the key in the shed. Now he was safe; even if Duncan and his mother returned, he could claim that he had called to exchange books. So he walked boldly round the house and out of the front gate. When he was halfway down the street, a car passed him, and stopped outside the house he had just left; a man got out to open the double gates that led to the garage. He had missed Duncan's father by a few minutes.

He felt so triumphant that he had no desire to go home. But physically, he was experiencing reaction. He cycled to the canal bank, and sat in his hiding place, although it was dark and cold, sat there with his eyes closed, reliving the whole experience, and, as he caressed the panties that he had spread across his bare thighs, suddenly feeling again that certainty of belonging to another world, another planet.

Before he went home, he dug a hole in the soft earth with a penknife, and carefully placed the folded garment and the blue box inside. He glanced inside the latter; it seemed to contain a pendant on a chain. He found a flat piece of stone, and covered the hole over. Then he went home. It was a cold, clear night, and he experienced an odd ringing sound in his ears (he described it at other times as "singing") associated with a feeling of expansion and happiness. He felt that he and his other "self" were communicating across millions of miles of space.

I must interrupt myself at this point to say a word about my whole approach to Arthur Lingard's obsessions. There was a time when I would have tried to interpret them entirely in sexual terms—sublimation of an Oedipus complex, and so on. But, as I mentioned at the beginning of this account, I have come to accept increasingly the views of certain "third force" psychologists—Frankl, Caruso, Maslow, Carl Rogers, Glasser—who recognize in man what might be called "higher instinctual needs." Of course, the basic mechanism of life is contraction and expansion, absorption and discharge of energy, like breathing in and breathing out. And there are undoubtedly many human beings of whom you can say that it doesn't much matter what they're doing so long as they're doing something. But most reasonably sensitive people prefer activities that they consider "worthwhile"—that is to say, in some way *creative*. It is a *need,* just as strong as the sexual urge.

Put it this way. Freud and most of his disciples see mental illness as the outcome of the frustration by the environment of certain basic needs, the chief one being the sexual need. A perfectly running human being ought to be like a perfectly running machine, somehow obeying the natural laws of his being. Neurosis comes from sand or rust getting into the works; it comes from outside, so to speak. But it has become increasingly clear to me that there is another kind of neurosis, that comes from *inside.* Human beings experience a need to develop, to mature, to *realize their potentials,* to become, if you like, more godlike (or more human—it's the same thing). And if it's true that inside every fat man, there's a thin man struggling to get out, so inside every dull, bored man, there's a brilliant creative man struggling to get out, like a chicken in its egg or a butterfly in its chrysalis. If circumstances frustrate his development, it may take strange turns.

Obviously, Arthur Lingard's sexual drives played an important part in his illness; but I believe they are only part of it. I do not believe that even his knickers fetichism can be explained simply in Freudian terms. His description of his absorption with *Punch* demonstrates this. What he wanted was a freer, richer existence, in association with women like the two sisters in *Punch,* who would bring out the best in him. Referring to the younger girl—whom he called, significantly, Angelina—he said that if he could have looked up her dress, she would have been wearing knickers of blue or pink silk. Why? Why not, for example, white silk, since Pauline had once worn knickers of that color that had belonged to her mother? Could it have been, perhaps, *because* he associated white silk with Pauline, and with the game of doctors and nurses that had so upset him? Blue and pink are the colors worn by babies, the colors of innocence. Silk, as compared to cotton or wool, is smooth, glossy, cool. Even his mention of the panties worn by Jane of the *Daily Mirror* illustrates the same point. The sex was being rendered pure and harmless by its association with pretty underwear and pretty girls. This is why his decision to indulge his violation fantasies was so important; he was deliberately placing his "higher instinctual drives" in abeyance, using his imagination to release aggressive tensions, destructive emotions.

All this explains why his Martian fantasies *intensified* after he had established a sexual relationship with Pauline, instead of vanishing, or becoming weaker. Sex with Pauline— and it must be borne in mind that it never reached the point of actual coitus—was an important release on one plane; but on another, it was asssociated with guilt. They played with each other like naughty children. Pauline, with her usual lack of embarrassment, told me in detail about their relations after that first time. It was accepted that he was allowed to place his hand between her thighs in bed, and he often fell asleep with it there (an involuntary gesture of protection?). She herself never made sexual advances, except involuntarily, in sleep, and this happened perhaps a dozen times during the year 1950. Arthur never, at any time, attempted sexual intercourse. I asked him why this was so; he said that he was afraid of awakening the other two who slept in the same bed. I believe it was the force of an incest taboo. Pauline was a mother figure; she caressed him as she might caress a baby's hair, and he touched her because she represented the mysterious source of life. But his role in relation to her was not that of the aggressive male, but of the child. And this also meant that his attitude toward her was bound to become increasingly ambiguous as he grew older. The child Arthur Lingard was turning into an adolescent with dreams of his own. She was not a mother who represented an unquestioned source of love, but a sister who had often hurt him and made him miserable. His Martian fantasies represented his "higher instinctual needs," and his ordinary sexual needs became increasingly obsessed by his fetichism. He was bound to turn away from her.

Pauline told me that Arthur became increasingly moody during the next year, and his attitude toward her often seemed irritable and detached. This was inevitable. Arthur was beginning to feel critical of her; she had allowed herself to be absorbed by her environment, to become a part of it. He wanted to dominate it—but not in the obvious way—making money, becoming successful. He had been bitten by the most dangerous kind of virus. If his teachers at school had known about it, they might have laughed. They would have been mistaken.

A few days after his burglary, Arthur opened *The Memoirs of Sherlock Holmes* at the story called "The Final Problem." He had read a great deal of Conan Doyle, and found him exciting, but not as fascinating as Burroughs or Merritt—until he read Holmes's description of Moriarty:
" 'Aye, there's the genius and wonder of the thing!' he cried. 'The man pervades London, and no one has heard of him. That's what puts him on a pinnacle in the records of crime. I tell you, Watson, in all seriousness, that if I could beat that man, if I could free society of him, I should feel that my own career had reached its summit. . . . His career has been an extraordinary one. He is a man of good birth and excellent education, endowed by nature with a phenomenal mathematical faculty. At the age of twenty-one he wrote a treatise upon the Binomial Theorem, which has had a European vogue. On the strength of it, he won the Mathematical Chair at one of our smaller Universities, and had, to all appearance, a most brilliant career before him. But the man had hereditary tendencies of the most diabolical kind. A criminal strain ran in his blood, which, instead of being modified, was increased and rendered infinitely more dangerous by his extraordinary mental powers. . . .

" 'As you are aware, Watson, there is no one who knows the higher criminal world of London so well as I do. For years past I have continually been conscious of some power behind the malefactor, some deep organising power which for ever stands in the way of the law, and throws its shield over the wrong-doer. . . . For years I have attempted to break through the veil which shrouded it, and at last the time came when I seized my thread and followed it, until it led me, after a thousand cunning windings, to ex-Professor Moriarty of mathematical celebrity.

" 'He is the Napoleon of crime, Watson. He is organiser of half that is evil and of nearly all that is undetected in this great city. He is a genius, a philosopher, an abstract thinker. He has a brain of the first order. He sits motionless, like a spider in the centre of its web, but that web has a thousand radiations, and he knows well every quiver of each of them. . . .' "

Arthur Lingard was reading the story in the cold front room on a rainy day in mid-December. When he reached this point, he began to tremble, and his hair felt as if it was trying to rise up. The sound of Aggie clearing away the breakfast dishes in the next room reminded him that he might be called upon to help with the washing up; he sneaked out of the front door, and closed it behind him. Then he hurried down to the canal bank, and into an old concrete bunker that smelled of stale urine. Sitting among broken bottles and used contraceptives, his collar turned up to cover his ears, he read the rest of the story, savoring each word. When he had finished, he chuckled. Holmes was dead. It had cost him his life to meddle with the great spider at the center of London's web of crime. He went back to the beginning of the story and read the description of Moriarty until he knew it by heart. By this time, he was so cold that he went out and walked along the canal, knotting his scarf around his head to keep off the drizzle. He looked at the sluggish canal, at the rusty tin cans on the towpath, the bedraggled washing flapping in tiny backyards; they no longer oppressed him. A Napoleon of crime was slowly uncoiling inside him, rising up, revealing its identity for the first time, and all this became unimportant.

It seemed incredible to him that a writer like Conan Doyle, so obviously on the side of law and order and respectability, should have been able to grasp the psychology of such a criminal genius as Moriarty. ". . . Hereditary tendencies of the most diabolical kind. A criminal strain ran in his blood. . . ." He thought of his autoerotic exercises with Pauline's underwear, of his burglary at Duncan's, and it was suddenly obvious. He was a born criminal, a man with some strange poison in his bloodstream. But was it a poison? Moriarty had a greater intellect than his fellowmen—greater than Holmes, certainly. Holmes had never written anything more difficult than a monograph on tobacco ash. Moriarty could see the truth about society: that it had been created for the protection of the rich and the exploitation of the poor. Its so-called law was really the law of the jungle, and it was on the side of the rich.

Arthur had no objection to the rich as such. He greatly preferred people who took baths at five o'clock in the afternoon to Dick Lingard and his aunt Elsie. But he had talked to Duncan's mother, and she had not struck him as a higher type of human being than Aunt Elsie. The human beings around him were little better than cattle; they were all stuck in the same mud.

What fascinated him about Moriarty was his capacity for remaining anonymous. " 'The man pervades London, and no one has heard of him.' " His cousins Albert and Ted had both been in trouble with the police, Ted for breaking into a radio shop and taking a portable gramophone, Albert for vandalism—smashing the basins in a public lavatory and cutting holes in bus seats. That type of "crime" was pathetic and downright stupid.

He was now soaking and cold, but so excited that he had no desire to go home. He stood on an iron bridge, and watched the raindrops making circles of water as they hit the canal. He had to face the fact that he was still too young to become a Moriarty at once. It was something that lay far ahead in the future. But it was not too soon to begin planning his campaign. He would train himself slowly and carefully. It was his destiny to be a supercriminal.

And what distinguished the supercriminal from the ordinary incompetent? Willpower and foresight. He had one enormous advantage where society was concerned: the advantage of secrecy. Like a guerrilla, he could strike unexpectedly, and withdraw before anyone was aware of it.

No doubt many other twelve-year-olds have had similar daydreams. But in Arthur Lingard's case, circumstances favored their realization. He was emotionally deprived; he hated his environment; he lived in a dream world. He was already aware that he was different from anyone he had ever met, that he had two selves, one of which lived on another planet. He did not *belong* to this planet. And now he saw why. He was born with hereditary criminal tendencies of the most diabolical kind.

Arthur Lingard's early sexual experiences had hurled him out of childhood into adolescence with a brutality that intensified the usual emotional problems. Such problems can usually be overcome, provided a human being has one strong personal tie—at least one. The more he is an integrated part of a warm family background, the easier he is likely to find it. Unfortunately, Arthur's only strong personal tie was already beginning to dissolve. He was beginning to reject Pauline. She was Dick Lingard's mistress. She had accepted the background of Warrington, allowed herself to become integrated into it. She had started to work at the age of fifteen, as a shop assistant at the local Woolworth's, and hung around with a group of girls who had loud, shrill laughs, and talked endlessly about "lads" and pop singers— Frankie Laine, Vic Damone, Fats Domino. One day in the summer of 1950, Dick Lingard had caught Pauline in the entry, having sexual intercourse against the wall with one of her ex-boyfriends. The recriminations were noisy and bitter, and every detail could be heard in every room of the house— how the youth—the captain of the school football team—had her panties in his pocket. Dick Lingard was frenzied with jealousy, but he could not allow this to become obvious. He kept saying: "I wouldn't mind if she'd tried to be decent, but a fuckin' knee trembler up against the wall . . . ! It's just dirty, like two dogs." Arthur smiled ironically. But he experienced a surge of jealousy that was quickly transformed into anger and disgust. Against the wall like two dogs. . . . And the boy had gone off with her pants. Pauline was becoming the district whore. . . .

Their first quarrel took place shortly after this. It was about the "acid bath murderer," John George Haigh, who had been executed in 1949. A Sunday newspaper ran a series of articles about murderers. After reading the piece on Haigh, Pauline had remarked that she couldn't understand why murderers seemed to be getting so inhuman. Arthur said that if what she meant by human was second-rateness and stupidity, then he supposed it was true. He said that as far as he could see, Haigh had only behaved with common sense and enterprise. He liked good clothes and fast cars, and he couldn't get these by working in a factory. So he had decided to take up murder as a business—murder of a few middle-class people who didn't matter anyway. He went on to say that the laws are intended to protect the rich and suppress the poor. Why shouldn't Haigh pay them back in their own coin?

Pauline made the mistake of jeering at this and telling him that he was too young to understand. This made Arthur furious, and his arguments became more dogmatic. If life was sacred, why did she eat meat and fish? Did she really think it was all right to kill a pig or a cow, but wicked to kill a human being who was just as stupid as a pig or a cow? Pauline said warmly that even the stupidest people could be kind and considerate, and Arthur said she was a typical woman, arguing with her feelings instead of her brain. Pauline brought up the Heath case, and asked him how he could justify the sadistic killing of two women. Did *they* deserve it? Arthur shrugged. He wasn't saying they did. But he could understand why Heath had done it. If a girl was pretty, and a man wanted her, why should he play the silly social game of taking her out for meals and buying her boxes of chocolates and telling her he loved her? Men were basically like wolves. They might convince a girl they loved her, but all they really wanted was to get her pants off.

This was too much for Pauline; she saw what he was driving at. She told him he was a disgusting pig and would probably end up like Heath and Haigh. And she flounced out of the house.

Arthur was upset; even his own sister was against him. Women were all the same: sentimental cattle. He would never allow himself to be enslaved by one.

I was curious to find out what happened at this juncture. Arthur, the ruthless loner, was suddenly seeing himself through Pauline's eyes—as someone who had become proud, intolerant, and vicious. It was a kind of crisis, a serious one for a twelve-year-old. I asked him what he did. At first he said he couldn't remember.

"Did you go out and do something?"

"No."

"Did you turn to Aggie for sympathy?"

"No," very sharply and contemptuously.

"Did you read?"

"I suppose I did."

I approached the subject again at a later session, and this time he admitted that he had taken a couple of his favorite books—*Seven Footprints to Satan* and *A Princess of Mars*—off to a hiding place on the canal bank—not the usual bush, but a more distant place, and read solidly for eight hours. And on this occasion, the sense of escape was more powerful than ever before. He roamed the deserts and forests of Mars; he plotted against the all-powerful Satan. And at some point during those eight hours, he cut the cord that bound him to Pauline. There was a world of adventure and terror that went beyond her female understanding. He had never met anyone who could enter it. The boys at school who also read adventure novels remained uninvolved; besides, most of them were weaklings. The only other boy who had read all Burroughs—Duncan—had weak eyes and a withered arm. Arthur set great store by not being a weakling. This is why he admired Pauline's athletic boyfriends, while disliking their stupidity. Strength or imagination—neither was effective on its own. It was necessary to possess both.

Reading about Haigh made him decide that he ought to study the methods of criminals. He spent evenings in the local library, reading volumes of the "Notable British Trials" series. He could have borrowed them and taken them home; but they would be seen by the family, who would wonder why he was suddenly reading true murder cases. That was not the way a master criminal went about preparing for his career. So he read them at a table in the library—Heath, Pritchard, Burke and Hare, Monson, Rouse, and so on. And he was confirmed in his view that most criminals are bungling amateurs. Even Haigh, on closer study, turned out to be a fool. His method was interesting and brilliant—to murder for possession of the victim's property, and dispose of the body by dissolving it in acid: a thought worthy of Moriarty. But the man himself seemed to be a fool, a show-off. Besides, anyone who disposes of his victim's property by forging deeds of conveyance is establishing a link between himself and the victim, and is bound to be caught sooner or later. Arthur had no objection at all to murder for gain. But the crimes of Haigh or Landru were really unworthy of a Moriarty. They were amateurish.

He was not thinking about crime for gain, but for its

own sake. The very word "crime" fascinated him; it sounded like "grime" and "slime." It was a way of reacting against this stupid society that he hated so much.

Later on, he rationalized this feeling about society into a kind of philosophy, and this is perhaps the place to describe it. He had read a book called *After London* by Richard Jefferies, describing some future date when industrial London has been destroyed, and been replaced by fields and woods. "When I read this great book," he wrote in his prison notebook, "I became convinced that all civilization is a mistake." Civilization has covered the earth with dirty cities; can it be surprised if the cities breed rats? The earth has been turned into a filthy rubbish dump. And since the invention of machines, everything has gone wrong. People have moved to cities, the population has increased, life has become a rat race.

Arthur Lingard liked to dream of a return to the Middle Ages—a rural England of woods and streams and pretty villages. If the people were as stupid as his cousin Jim, or Pauline's friends, it wouldn't matter, because they'd be living a healthy, simple existence, plodding home from the fields at night. The effect of civilization was to make worthless people more worthless by feeding them on cheap entertainment. Crime was simply a way of protesting about this messy civilization. Ideally, there would be great gangs of criminals, guided by a master mind, all devoted to throwing sand in the machinery of society. There was a block of luxury flats rising on the edge of the town, a new super-cinema being built, a pub with colored floodlights on its façade. Every time a venture like this was successful, it meant another step in the direction of urbanization. Even a fool like Albert felt an instinctive need to smash the floodlights, scrawl dirty words on the new flats, slash the cinema seats. One day, this instinctive protest would be organized and guided by a Napoleon of crime. The block of luxury flats would be dynamited the day after its completion. A poison gas would kill everybody in the cinema and turn it into a museum of horrors. A vial of cyanide slipped into a beer barrel would guarantee that the pub would become bankrupt. It could all be so easy. . . .

At the age of twelve, Arthur Lingard was a thin youth, with bulging eyes that indicated a thyroid condition, and a slight stammer. Excessive masturbation had made him pale, and his skin was always erupting into pimples or boils. No one liked him much. His sullenness was interpreted by school-masters as stupidity. Living mostly in a world of imag-ination, he paid little attention to keeping himself clean. He had a perpetual stale smell of urine. When alone, he had a habit of picking his nose, or scratching his crotch and then sniffing his fingers. He daydreamed of being the head of a criminal organization that would kidnap the most beautiful girls in town, take them to his room, and leave him to undress them and gloat over them.

His fascination with crime was basically sexual. Like sex, crime involved the forbidden; it involved furtiveness; it involved entering places you were not supposed to be in. In this sense, his dreams of being a Napoleon of crime con-flicted with his actual desires—to enter houses. His real incli-nation was toward burglary and rape.

How did a future Moriarty begin training himself for crime? The essence of crime, Arthur felt, was to be unde-tected, to look around carefully for opportunities. He needed an excuse to go to houses and ring the doorbell. At first, he considered taking a newspaper round, then recognized that this would not serve his purpose; paper boys went to the front door and pushed it through the letter box. But when he saw an advertisement in a local grocery store for an errand boy, he felt this was more promising. To the surprise of the Lingard household, he took the job.

It involved riding a carrier bike and taking boxes of groceries to houses in the area. He knocked at the back door, and took payment, and a small tip. On his first day on the job, he found a note pinned to a back door: "Please leave gro-ceries in outside lavatory. I will pay later." This was promis-ing. It meant that the house was probably empty—unless the woman had pretended to be out to avoid paying. He tried the door cautiously; it was locked. He went to the lavatory with the cardboard box. In the Lingard house, the door key was often left on a shelf in the outside lavatory if the house was empty. There was no such shelf in this one. But a careful search revealed a key tucked into a space between the door-jamb and the wall.

He was now experiencing the familiar sensation—the heart pounding, the bowels loosening, a sexual tension that made his loins tingle. He went to the back door, still carrying the groceries, in case some neighbor should be watching. He

114

inserted the key, and went in. Almost immediately, a child's voice yelled from upstairs: "Is that you, Ma?" He backed out precipitately, locked the door, and took the key—and the groceries—to the lavatory.

His second attempt at burglary had been a failure. But he continued to look around for opportunities. He soon noticed the houses that were not overlooked by neighbors, and made a mental note of them as possibilities. But luck was against him. On the few occasions when he received no reply to his knock, he could not find a key, although he would take the opportunity to search in the outside lavatory, coal house or garden shed. During six months as an errand boy, he made only one successful entry. He described it to me at a late stage in the analysis, when he had ceased to try to disguise the sexual nature of his drives.

In a house within two streets of Penketh Street, there was a young married woman who reminded him of Pauline —full-breasted, with a wide, heavy mouth and black hair. She had two children, aged about six and seven, and had a husband in the merchant navy. She was always pleasant and friendly, and always gave him a shilling tip—sixpence above the average.

One Saturday morning, he went to the hospital to have a boil lanced before starting work. On his way out, he met the married woman coming in with her two children. It struck him that she would be there at least an hour—the waiting room was full. The thought of being able to steal some of her underwear filled him with feverish excitement. He hurried back to the shop, getting there earlier than usual, and looked through the order book. He experienced disappointment; her name was not there. Then the shopman said: "There's one more to go in," and handed him a written order. It was the one he wanted. He was supposed to prepare the orders as they occurred in the book; instead, he immediately prepared the latest one. The shopman noticed and asked what he was doing. He said casually: "I thought I'd work backwards today, just for a change." The explanation was accepted. He placed two or three orders on the front of the bicycle, and rode off. It had been nearly an hour since he saw her at the hospital.

As he expected, the back door was locked, and there was no reply to his knock. He took the groceries to the outside lavatory, but a long search failed to reveal the key. Next he looked in the coal shed—and eventually found it in a jam-jar. He described to me how he burst out laughing with relief; he had been afraid that she had taken it with her.

He now went back to the door, and inserted the key. It turned in the lock. And, at that moment, he heard the sound of children's voices outside, and footsteps in the entry. He quickly removed the key, and as the gate opened and she came in, said, "I've just put your groceries in the lavatory." "Oh, that's nice of you. You're very early today." He mumbled something about having a lot to do, and, while she fumbled in her handbag, went to the coal house and opened the door. He quickly dropped the key in the jar, saying "Oh, wrong door," then went next door to the lavatory, and collected the box of groceries. His heart was beating so violently that he found it hard to return her smile as she gave him his tip, and it was hard to control the shaking of his hand.

He spent the rest of the morning in a daze cursing himself and cursing her. His belief in sympathetic magic inclined him to suspect that she somehow knew he meant to burgle her house, and had come rushing home. The failure seemed to him a sign that his luck was running out. And he felt angry and defiant.

But at midafternoon, he saw the woman waiting at the bus stop outside the shop. Both the children were dressed in their Sunday clothes. And while he worked on, preparing an order and speculating about this second chance, she hurried into the shop and asked for a packet of Earl Grey tea. "It's a good thing I remembered. I'm taking the kids to stay with their grandma for the night, and she can't get it where she lives." Suddenly, it was clear that the fates were with him after all. There was plenty of time. She would probably not be back for hours.

An hour later, he finished his deliveries, and hurried back to her house. There were a few children playing in the street, but no one paid any attention to him. When he reached the back gate, he discovered it was locked—evidently she had left the house by the front door. For a moment he felt fury; the fates were teasing him again. Then the doggedness reasserted itself. There was no one about; it was the work of a moment to climb the back gate. An old couple lived in the next house—he delivered there too—and they were not likely to notice.

He was afraid that the key would not be in the jar. If she had left by the front door, presumably she had locked the back door from inside. But the key was there. He went to the back door and tried to push it in. There was an obstruction. And suddenly he realized: this was a spare key, kept there in case of emergency. She had left the other key in the back door. And no matter how he pushed, it remained fixed.

The kitchen window was also locked; but he could see that the catch was inadequate. There was another outhouse beyond the lavatory; he went and looked in there. It proved to be a bicycle shed. On the floor, there were several muddy pairs of children's shoes. And beside them, on a sheet of newspaper, there was a kitchen knife that had been used to scrape the mud off.

He knew how to force window catches—he had occasionally had to do it at Penketh Street when Aunt Elsie forgot to leave the key in the lavatory. The blade slipped upward between the two window frames, then pushed the catch across. It opened easily. A moment later, he was standing in the kitchen, closing the window behind him.

This was not as exciting as the kitchen at Duncan's house. Basically, it was very like the kitchen at Penketh Street. But it was tidier, and did not smell of stale grease and squashed beetles. The furniture in the sitting room was new, and there was a cloth of some velvet material on the table.

He slipped off his shoes and mounted the stairs—he was afraid the neighbors might hear his movements through the thin walls. It was a two-bedroom house. The one overlooking the backyard was obviously the children's bedroom. A teddy bear and a doll were tucked up in bed. The other was her room, and over the back of a chair there was a peach-colored underslip.

By this time he was in a state resembling fever. Once again, he was swimming in his element like a fish—alone in someone else's house, in the bedroom of an attractive woman. His first objective was the drawer of her dressing table. It was just as he hoped. Like most young married women, she had an interest in what she looked like as she removed her skirt; there were panties and underslips in every possible color. He removed them from the drawer one by one and spread them on the bed. Then he investigated the laundry basket. (Seventeen years later, he was able to describe to me

117

the exact layout of the bedroom, and the colors of the panties; he closed his eyes as he talked, obviously seeing them all in imagination.) In this, he discovered a pair of black silk panties, inside out. And as he lifted them, he realized that they were slightly damp, and had the female-genital smell that he had noticed on Pauline's. This brought the excitement to a fever; he laid them out on the bed, removed all his clothes, and lay on them. The orgasm was violent and immediate. He lay there for ten minutes afterward, his cheek against a silky underslip, dozing, then turned dreamily on his back. The sky outside the window was very blue, with creamy clouds. Children's shouts echoed down the street. He felt completely at peace, supremely happy. She would not be back for hours. Meanwhile, this bedroom was his. He climbed between the sheets, and fell into a light doze.

When he woke up, he was hungry. He went downstairs, still naked—this was an additional touch of violation, of indecency—and went to the kitchen cupboard. He found milk and a tin of biscuits. This latter struck him as luxurious; at home, they only had biscuits at Christmas and on birthdays. He ate and drank, then carefully swept up the crumbs, and went back upstairs.

Now an idea came to him that brought back the fever. These garments were only a substitute for her. But supposing he could actually possess her . . . ? She would probably not be back until late. When she came back, she would go to bed. He could wait until she was asleep, and then attack her. One sharp, heavy blow with a hammer should knock her unconscious; then he could do what he liked with her. . . . The only problem was where to hide until she fell asleep. But that should not be difficult. There was the children's bedroom. It was unlikely that she would look in there when she came home.

The time dragged by. He had carefully replaced all her clothes in the drawer, folded neatly. In the drawer underneath, he found a bundle of pound notes hidden at the bottom of a box of hair curlers. He took two of them and replaced the rest. Then he climbed into her bed, and lay there, watching the sky turn dusky blue, then purple. After dark, he went downstairs, and out into the yard, to replace the key in the jar in the shed. Then back in the house, he went round with a towel, carefully wiping everything he had touched since he came in. He used a lamp from the bicycle to see his way. Finally, at about ten o'clock, he in-stalled himself in the children's bedroom, lying on an eider-down spread out on the floor. Lying beside him was a ham-mer he had taken from the coal shed.

It was toward one in the morning that he realized that she was not coming home. I asked him how he felt when this became apparent. "Cheated." "But didn't you also feel re-lieved?" He looked surprised. "Why should I? There wasn't much risk involved." "But you might have killed her with the hammer." He smiled mirthlessly. "I daresay I would've. I didn't have much experience in those days."

So the second burglary ended harmlessly. He left every-thing in order, returning the hammer to the coal house, where no doubt the housewife used it the next day, unaware that it had almost been the instrument of her death. His only spoils were two pairs of panties and two pounds. He wanted to take the black ones from the laundry basket, since they were pervaded by her physical smell, but realized they would be missed. He let himself quietly out the front door, and walked home to Penketh Street, where the back door had been left open for him. In some respects, it was a convenient house to live in. No one even asked him where he had been all evening.

Things were becoming chaotic in the Lingard house. Dick Lingard was subject to sudden storms of rage; in one of these, he gashed Aggie's forehead with his knuckles; on an-other, a flatiron aimed at Aunt Elsie went through the window. Pauline was the basic cause. As a pretty eighteen-year-old, she was attractive to men. She saw no point in being strictly faithful to Dick Lingard, particularly since she knew he still had relations with Aunt Elsie. Men were at-tracted to the soap counter in Woolworth's, where she worked, and they asked her out for meals, and to the cinema. One of these was a sunburned, bald-headed man called George Goldhawk, who had worked in the theater. Another was Eugene Turner, the garage proprietor who finally persuaded Pauline to go away with him. Pauline slept with both of them, flattered to be attractive to an older man. Dick Lingard tricked Pauline into admitting that she had had sexual relations with George Goldhawk by calling him "an old pouf." Pauline's *"Oh,* no he's not!" revealed that she knew better. George Goldhawk enlisted Arthur as a helper. He lived in a flat over a garage, and Pauline spent the evening there with him at least once a week. When this happened, Pauline was supposed to be at the cinema with Arthur, who would leave the house with her, and return with her late at night, discussing the film. Arthur would spend the evening alone at the cinema, and tell her the plot of the film on the way home. Dick Lingard was capable of going to see it himself, and then cross-questioning her. On one occasion, he followed them, but Arthur noticed him, and warned Pauline. They went into the cinema together, and half an hour later, she slipped out by a side entrance and went to her lover. Goldhawk soon began to treat Arthur as a friend and confidant; he was shrewd enough to recognize a good brain behind the pimples and eczema. They made no attempt to conceal the affair from Arthur. Arthur went in one evening when they were still in bed together, and he sat there talking with Goldhawk while Pauline dressed. On another occasion, Dick Lingard's jealousy became so obsessive that he refused to let Pauline leave the house. Arthur went to see Goldhawk, and the two of them spent the evening drinking beer and talking.

Goldhawk was an important influence—as I shall explain in a moment. He was killed in an accident, when a beam from a building under construction slipped from its chain and went through the roof of the car he was driving. Arthur saw him there before the car was removed, his face half obliterated, and the left shoulder torn loose by the force of the impact. He experienced a curious satisfaction, although he had liked Goldhawk. One more of Pauline's lovers had come to a violent end. . . . The captain of the school football team had been killed in a glider crash. Arthur felt immune.

Dick Lingard's jealousy was becoming a nuisance. Aunt Elsie had caught him fondling Pauline's breasts or buttocks so often that she could not remain in any doubt about the relationship between them. Strangely enough, she took the knowledge calmly. One day, when he was quarreling with her, Arthur referred to it, "I don't know how you can ignore what he's up to with our Pauline. . . ." But before he could go on, she had interrupted sharply: "You shurrup. Your uncle's a good man, and don't you forget it." "So was Hitler," said Arthur, with heavy humor. This remark was repeated to Dick Lingard, who decided not to tackle Arthur directly, but to wait for his opportunity.

One day, George Goldhawk told Pauline that he was expecting his divorce to come through shortly, and suggested that they get married. Pauline told me the full story of what followed, with her accustomed frankness. She decided that the best time to break the news to Uncle Dick was after sexual intercourse. On the following Saturday afternoon, Aunt Elsie went out. Pauline was drying the dishes in the kitchen when her uncle came in. He approached her in his usual way —unclipped her bra through the thick sweater she was wearing, then plunged his hands up the sweater, and felt her naked breasts. " 'Ow about it, lass. Goin' to let the old man 'ave a bit of cock?" She nodded without speaking. "Ee, you're a good lass." He raised her dress, tugged her panties to her knees, and felt her vagina. The pinching of her nipples had made her damp. "Niver mind the pots. Cum on upstairs." She stepped out of her panties and obediently followed him upstairs; he unbuckled his belt and slipped off his braces as he went up. In the bedroom, he made love to her immediately, in a state of wild excitement, and she increased his pleasure by inserting the end of her finger into his anus—a caress that always made his climax violent. Afterwards, he lay with his head on her breast, while she stroked his unshaven chin. He said: "Ee, lass, you cause me a lot of 'eartache, you know, I dunno what I'll do when you go away." "I'll have to get married someday, you know." "Ay, I know," he said gloomily. "Will you try to stop me?" He shook his head sadly. "No. I'm gettin' on. I know I can't keep you forever." "Suppose . . . I wanted to get married soon." "Soon?" He sat up, realizing that the conversation had been engineered in this direction, " 'Ow soon?" "George Goldhawk wants me to marry him in August." "What! That bald-'eaded pouf!" It was the unkindest cut. George Goldhawk was the same age as Dick Lingard. Dick had placed himself in a poor position, and he knew it. Ordinarily, he would have lost his temper and spanked her— it continued to give him pleasure to see her bare bottom reddening under his slaps—but having agreed that he would not stand in her way, it was hard to go back. He took the position that George Goldhawk would make a disastrous husband. Pauline pointed out that he had a private income and owned a boardinghouse at Bootle. That was unkinder still—Dick Lingard was sensitive about his poverty. "Well you'll not marry 'im while I'm your guardian, and that's

121

flat." "A fine guardian you are! It's a good thing they're not all like you." The wrangle went on; Dick Lingard burst into tears and went on his knees. He was a very powerful man, and Pauline knew better than to provoke him too far. She pretended to agree to leave it for the time being. Kneeling at her feet, clasping her knees, Dick Lingard became aware of her shapeliness, and a portion of his anatomy refused to abase itself. They ended back on the bed. But it was only a temporary reconciliation. For she had as good as admitted that she had been seeing George Goldhawk. And it struck Dick Lingard that Goldhawk probably exercised his privilege of undressing her more often than he did himself. He was in an agony of jealousy. When *could* she be seeing him? He kept a fairly careful check on her movements. It came to him that there was only one opportunity—her evenings at the cinema with Arthur. He taxed her about it, and she ended by admitting it. It was another black mark against Arthur's name.

The antagonism in the household became more open. Everyone was aware that sexual tension existed between Pauline and her uncle. It was a relief when one of the two was absent from meals. One day, Uncle Dick told Arthur darkly that he knew about the deception with George Gold- hawk. Arthur shrugged. "She's my sister. You don't expect me to take your side against her, do you?" Dick Lingard glared at him coldly; he was not used to defiance from the males of the household. "You'll get what's comin' to you. You mark my words." "I will?" said Arthur.

Pauline sent him with a message to George Goldhawk, explaining what had happened. Goldhawk offered him a beer, and went into a monologue of self-commiseration that made Arthur feel kindly contempt.

Finally, Arthur said, "If you want to marry her, you know the way. Get her pregnant."

Goldhawk looked up hopefully. "D'you think that'd work?"

Arthur was about to explain his reasoning—that the baby could be attributed to Dick Lingard, and that he would do anything to avoid this happening—but decided that Gold- hawk had better remain in the dark about Pauline's relations with her uncle. He might decide to throw her over. Even immoral men can get oddly moral about incest. Instead, Ar- thur assured him that Dick Lingard would probably allow her to marry rather than support an unmarried mother.

Later that day, Arthur broached the idea to Pauline. She seemed to like it.

Albert was in trouble. He had graduated from slashing bus seats and stealing from Woolworth's to stealing larger and more expensive items. He was caught trying to walk out of a stationery shop with a portable typewriter. The probation officer became a frequent figure in the Lingard household in the later winter of 1950–1951. And then Arthur made his first mistake. He had changed his weekend job from the grocer's to a television shop—more will be said of this presently—and he soon discovered that it was easy to "fiddle the till." The shop sold gramophone records and household appliances as well as radios and televisions. It was easy for Arthur to enter the wrong sum on the paper roll in the till, and pocket the extra. One day, glancing through Arthur's entries, the shopman discovered that he had undercharged for a television tube. By coincidence, the customer walked into the shop at that moment, and the shopman told him about it. The customer naturally mentioned the exact sum he had paid. Arthur was not in the shop at the time. His employer began to watch him closely, and soon realized that he was taking about two pounds from the till every Saturday. So one Saturday afternoon, as Arthur was about to leave the shop, the shopman asked him to turn out his pockets. Arthur refused indignantly. The shopman called a policeman who was passing, and Arthur, now intimidated, emptied his pockets, revealing that he had about two pounds more than his wages. He now understood why the shopman, pretending to be short of change, had asked him earlier, "Got any money on you, Arthur?" And Arthur had replied, "Only about half a crown."

Even in this emergency, Arthur kept his head. He realized that his possession of two pounds was no evidence against him. He could say he picked it up in the street, or that he had no idea how it got into his pocket, and no one could disprove it. But the shopman produced the roll from the till. He had been carefully watching Arthur when apparently repairing radio sets in the back room, and had made a note of every transaction that had taken place. Arthur decided he was beaten, and admitted the theft. "Do you want to take the case further?" asked the policeman. The shopman, who was not vindictive, said no. But he went to Dick Lingard and told him that he would prosecute if Dick refused to give Arthur a beating. Arthur submitted sullenly, raging at the indignity—but far more, at his own folly in being caught. The shopman watched with satisfaction as the heavy strap fell a dozen times on Arthur's bent behind, then said: "That'll be enough. That'll learn 'im," and walked off. Arthur left the house and stayed out half the night, walking up and down the canal bank, grinding his teeth and swearing. He continued to work in the television shop.

The Pauline situation did not improve. Dick Lingard lost his temper with her one day, and almost broke her wrist in his grip; the wrist remained swollen and bruised for a week afterwards. Pauline was so indignant that she went out the following Saturday afternoon. She spent it in bed with Eugene Turner (with whom she also carried on casual relations, usually in the back of his car). As he drove her home, she said, "You can drop me off at our front door." He gaped. " 'Ave you gone mad?" "No." She was adamant. Dick Lingard saw her from the upstairs window, and met her at the back door as she came in. "You filthy little slut. You're no better than a bitch in heat!" "You can talk!" She stared scornfully in the direction of his fly. This was too much. He grabbed her, dragged her into the living room, and held her across his knee, while he tugged down her panties. She expected him to spank her; all he actually did was to feel the cleft between her thighs, then thrust his finger into her. It came out wet. The stains on the crotch of her panties were unmistakable. He was now sobbing with rage and desire. "You filthy bitch, you think you can do what you like. I s'pose he didn't even wear a French letter?" "No," said Pauline, now enraged at this invasion of her privacy. "If you want to know, he pulled it out and came on me belly." She expected to be beaten, but the subtleties of male psychology were beyond her understanding. "If you behave like a bitch, you can have it like a bitch." At which, he forced her to bend over the arm of the chair, and, pulling open his fly with one hand, drove into her from behind. It was at this moment that Arthur came into the backyard. He looked in through the window, and paused, frozen. Uncle Dick saw him and shouted, "An' you can bugger off too!" As he shouted, he came, and the sentence had an odd, gurgling noise. Arthur turned and ran off. Dick Lingard then dropped on to his knees, made Pauline—naked from the waist down—sit in the armchair, and sobbed on her knees. She was too glad to escape a beating to reject him. But when his eye fell on her panties, with their stained crotch, lying on the rug, he groaned with genuine misery, "How could you do it to me?" and obviously felt that something terrible and irrevocable had happened. In his way, Dick Lingard was genuinely in love with her.

Two days later, Arthur was shocked when the probation officer appeared at school, and asked to see him. It was a gray-haired, middle-aged woman who had also dealt with Albert. What she told him was that the shopman had decided to proceed with charges against him. Arthur was indignant. "He can't do that. He promised." He described his flogging. The probation officer said: "All I can say is that he's changed his mind. Or perhaps someone changed it for him." Arthur understood. Uncle Dick!

It was true. Dick Lingard had gone to the shopman and explained that he would be doing everyone a favor if he proceeded with the case. Arthur was completely unmanageable. There is also reason to believe—although I have no proof of this—that he told the shopman that Arthur was having sexual intercourse with his cousin Aggie. This, as I shall explain in a moment, was true. The shopman was a moral man who was revolted by the idea of incest. He agreed to proceed with the charge.

I am inclined to doubt whether Dick Lingard would have taken this step—admittedly unfair—unless he had been half insane with jealousy about Pauline, and believed that Arthur was plotting to marry her off. It was an absurd thing to do, for, as a first offender, Arthur would certainly be put on probation. On the other hand, he might well tell what he knew about Pauline. Perhaps Dick Lingard felt safe on this score, since Pauline was no longer a minor, and it would be difficult to prove that he had seduced her six years ago. He had come to hate Arthur, who seemed so detached and contemptuous; he wanted to make him feel vulnerable.

The stratagem worked. Arthur appeared in the juvenile court on March 11, 1951, and was placed on probation for a year. The chairman of the bench told Dick Lingard sternly: "Your son [Albert] is already on probation. His bad example may have influenced this young man. It is your business to behave with enough severity to discourage further violations of the law." Dick Lingard had told the bench that Arthur

125

was completely unmanageable—sullen, disobedient, and violent.

Arthur was enraged; he could not believe that these silly indignities were really happening to him—the future Napoleon of crime. Dick Lingard achieved an important part of his purpose—he made Arthur feel the force of "contingency"; he made him feel vulnerable.

The result was total war in the Penketh Street household. Arthur loathed Dick Lingard and dreamed of killing him. Only murder could wipe out the feeling of indignity. His hatred made him careless, and he made a mistake that must have made Dick Lingard rub his hands with delight. He stole a revolver from a flat where he had repaired a television set. I think there can be no doubt that he stole it to kill his uncle. He was evasive about it, and I did not press him. From my knowledge of Arthur, I would guess that his intention was to keep the revolver hidden for a fairly long period, until it was forgotten; then to plan the murder carefully. He had no ammunition for it.

Unfortunately, the revolver was missed within a few hours of his stealing it. The police came to his home and questioned him about it. Arthur must have realized then that his murder plan had misfired. He should have thrown the weapon in the canal at once. But he was confident that it would not be found in its hiding place on the canal bank. He was reckoning without the Lingard family. Aggie had actually visited his hiding place behind the bush; she had told Jim about it. (She and Jim had been very close; he had been responsible for the loss of her maidenhead.) Jim was now married with two children—at age twenty-one—but when his father came to see him, he told him about the hiding place. Dick Lingard took a policeman with him, and they looked behind every bush within a mile of Penketh Street. The search soon revealed one that was obviously used regularly; the earth was trampled flat. And further search revealed a flat stone, carefully covered with earth, underneath which was a tin box that had been buried with a great deal of care. In the box there were six pairs of panties, several pieces of jewelry and trinkets, and the missing revolver. Among the trinkets was the locket on a gold chain that Arthur had taken in his first burglary; he had never tried to sell it.

Housewives in the area had been complaining about the

126

theft of underwear from clotheslines. The irony was that none of the garments in the box had been stolen from a clothesline. Some of the trinkets were identified by the owners of television sets that Arthur had serviced on Saturday afternoons. None was of any great value. (The locket and chain was never traced back to Duncan McIver's parents; neither, as far as Arthur knows, was it ever missed by them.)

Arthur's sullen and uncooperative attitude in court was probably an important factor in determining the length of his sentence. If he had been more cooperative, he might well have escaped with further probation. As it was, he received a sentence of two years at Earlestow, the approved school near Manchester.

This is a period that he refused to discuss with me. I am not surprised. Earlestow has the reputation of being the toughest school of its kind in the north of England. The sort of youths he met there probably filled him with contempt and loathing. He did tell me that, although fighting was theoretically forbidden, he was beaten up twice in his first fortnight there. The authorities apparently believed that this kind of thing did no harm: it took the fight out of a boy, made him anxious for peace at any price. If there was any chance of Arthur Lingard ceasing to be a criminal—and I am doubtful of this—it vanished during the six months he spent at Earlestow. I am inclined to believe that, in a certain respect, Arthur Lingard was a fairly well-balanced person before he went to Earlestow. When he left he was unbalanced; consumed with hatred, fear, and a savage determination to make someone pay. He succeeded. But the hatred and violence remained.

After six months, he escaped by climbing onto the roof of a garden shed and over the wall. He stole a bicycle and went back to Warrington—to the flat of George Goldhawk. The police went to Dick Lingard, who advised them to try Goldhawk's flat. Arthur was back in custody within sixteen hours of escaping. But the probation worker intervened; Arthur appeared in juvenile court again, prepared to have his sentence increased for the theft of a bicycle; instead, to his amazement, the magistrate ordered Dick Lingard to take the rebel back into his home, and make an effort to "keep him straight." Arthur had to promise solemnly to keep out of trouble. And, to complete his astonishment, the magistrate, a pink-faced, white-haired old man like something out of Dickens, caught his eye and winked. He learned later that this was his last case; he was retiring that day. He wanted to end his tenure with an act of clemency.

Three months later, Dick Lingard was in prison, for reasons that have already been explained. Arthur found revenge absurdly easy when it came to the point. The social worker asked him about Pauline's pregnancy, which was becoming obvious. (It was, of course, none of her business; she was simply curious.) Arthur told what he knew. The social worker was scandalized—particularly about the description of Pauline bending over a chair, with her guardian's brawny hands gripping the back of her neck and his frantic loins smacking against her exposed buttocks. She assumed—wrongly—that Pauline had been violated continuously—and unwillingly—since the age of twelve. Dick Lingard was arrested as he came out of a football match, where he had spent a gloomy and unsatisfactory Saturday afternoon. He made no attempt to deny that he had been Pauline's first lover when she was twelve; he believed she had already admitted it. Neither did he attempt to deny that he had spent most of the few hundred pounds that Arthur's mother had left to her children. He was lucky that a blood test proved that he could not be the father of Pauline's baby; he might have received ten years instead of three. But it hardly made any difference; his freedom meant nothing to him.

Aunt Elsie ordered Pauline out of the house; she had never doubted for a moment that her husband was entirely blameless.

SEVEN

On the day that Arthur described his second burglary—
recorded in the last chapter—I asked him casually, "Who
taught you about hypnotism?"

This was the first time I had mentioned the subject
openly; I had noticed that if I tried to get him talking about
his relations with his cousin Agnes, he looked at his fingers
and changed the subject. But I judged now that he was prepared to be frank. His answer startled me.

"Aggie."

"Your cousin Aggie? How?"

"She used to cure Maggie's headaches by stroking her
forehead. Maggie got terrible headaches before she died."

"Had you read *Marvo the Magician* by then?"

"Oh, yes, I read that when I was ten."

Marvo the Magician was a better book than one would
guess from its title. One of my favorite stories during my
teens was *The Haunters and the Haunted* by Bulwer-Lytton,
and it was fairly obvious that "Giles Percy," the author of
Marvo, had been heavily influenced by it. In *Marvo*, the
narrator is a member of the Society for Psychical Research,
who is asked to investigate the haunting of a Yorkshire vicarage. In a priest's hole he finds manuscripts more than a
hundred years old that describe a strange, sinister man who
has come to live in the area, and who has displayed various
evil powers. The "magician" had apparently forced the author of the manuscript to help him in certain magical re-
searches, and when the author finally escaped, decreed that
his spirit should haunt the vicarage every night through life
and death. The narrator then succeeds in talking to the
rectory ghost by means of table-rapping, and discovers that
the magician is still alive. (He is probably based on Maturin's

Melmoth.) He finds the man in Budapest—and is himself enslaved by him. The magician is hundreds of years old; his powers are immense; one of his favorite tricks is to cause rocks to shatter and trees to split apart by concentrating on them. The narrator and Marvo travel around like Faust and Mephistopheles, having all kinds of adventures, and Marvo is finally destroyed by a beautiful young girl he abducts, who turns out to be a rival magician in disguise. The most interesting feature of the book is a series of Marvo's discourses on hypnotism, obviously a subject about which the author had thought deeply. "All men have two souls, and the purpose of mesmerism is to turn one against the other. The easiest people to mesmerize are those who have nothing to do, because their boredom makes them suggestible."

This made sense to Arthur. At the age of eleven—when he began to masturbate excessively—he found that he could not urinate if someone stood beside him in the school lavatory. He could see that this was because the other person made him *self-conscious,* and this peering, conscious self had no power to order his bladder to release the urine. He quickly saw the implications of this. If you could make someone extremely self-conscious, they would not only find it hard to urinate, but to do almost anything that is natural and habitual. If a schoolteacher looks over your shoulder as you are writing, your handwriting begins to deteriorate, your hand feels stiff and awkward. One day a school friend said to him: "I love listening to your voice. You've got such a funny accent" (London, of course), and Arthur found himself stumbling in his speech. He got his own back by saying to the friend: "What really interests me about you is the way you walk. You remind me of my sister." "How?" "Well, you sort of swing your hips like a girl. Look, walk away from me now and you'll see what I mean." The friend did so, then blushed. "You're right. I never realized." After this, his walk became awkward, self-conscious, and distinctly feminine, and the more people remarked on it, the worse it became.

For weeks, Arthur amused himself with the power of suggestion. To a schoolfellow about to go to a new classroom: "I can't stand it. The chairs are made of sandalwood, and you'll find they make your bum itch and give you a funny feeling at the back of your knees." And to his delight, the friend came out in a rash at the back of his knees, and his parents sent a note to school asking that he should be allowed to have a different kind of chair. Or he would hand his pen to the person sitting next to him. "There's something funny about this pen. It makes your fingers feel all watery and weak." The friend would try it for a moment. "Yes, it's funny, isn't it?" The odd thing was that his own fingers began to feel watery and weak when he took the pen back and tried to write with it. "Do your eyebrows ever itch?" "No, I don't think so." But a moment later, the friend would surreptitiously scratch his eyebrow.

He found it worked best in the morning assembly, when the headmaster insisted upon everyone sitting silent for several minutes to "examine themselves" after prayers. Anyone caught whispering or fidgeting was harshly dealt with. Arthur fixed on a girlish, self-conscious boy, and as they were waiting to enter assembly, told him the old *Punch* joke about the soup that tasted like paraffin. The boy laughed. Then Arthur said seriously: "I shouldn't have told you that." "Why not?" "I always find I start remembering jokes when we're supposed to be examining our consciences, and it nearly kills me trying not to laugh. Then if I don't laugh, I start to itch all over and fidget." In the silent period that morning, he caught his friend's eye and shook his head seriously. Immediately, the friend exploded into a neigh of laughter. The headmaster looked up scandalized. The boy went purple in the face, trying not to laugh, then noticed Arthur scratching himself. He began to scratch, at first cautiously, then frantically. The headmaster startled everyone by roaring: "Ross, take five hundred lines: I must not fidget in assembly!"

He was deeply interested to observe the way that Aggie could cure Maggie's headaches by standing behind her and stroking her forehead. She always used the same movement, placing both hands in the center, then stroking outwards, in an upward curve, so that her hands followed the line of the hair. He asked Aggie why she used this movement. "I don't know. I used to stroke straight across, but she said it felt better when I did it that way." He said: "Try doing it the other way next time—move your fingers down a bit." He was present when Agnes tried it. Maggie gasped immediately: "Oh, don't. That makes it worse." "Why?" asked Arthur. "I don't know why. . . . Because it's the opposite way, I s'pose."

One afternoon, he was alone in the house with Maggie. He noticed that she was playing with the edge of the page as she read a woman's magazine. He said sympathetically:

"Have you got one of your headaches coming on?" "No, why?" "I can always tell when you have. You play with the edge of the page." "Do I? Was I doing it then?" "Yes." Within five minutes, Maggie's eyes were dark with pain. She buried her face in her hands. "Oh, it's awful. I wish Aggie was here." "I can do it if you like. Aggie taught me how." "Are you sure?" "Absolutely. You'll see." He was not overconfident as he took his place behind her, but he did not show it. He placed his hands firmly in the middle of her forehead, moved them outwards in a curve, and said soothingly: "There, you see? That's better, isn't it?" After a moment, doubtfully: "Yes." Five minutes later, the headache had gone.

Arthur was so fascinated by his new power that he took the opportunity of inducing a headache every time he was alone with Maggie, then curing it. The more often he did it, the easier it became. What pleased him far more was that Maggie, five years his senior, should begin to treat him with the respect due a doctor, and to give him slightly larger helpings of pudding when she had to prepare and serve the dinner.

One day, as he sat opposite her, reading *Tarzan*, Maggie yawned and stretched, and her grubby woolen jumper parted company with her skirt, revealing a few inches of flesh. He asked sympathetically: "Headache?" "No." But five minutes later, she was sighing and pressing her forehead. He said, "You know, somebody at school told me a much better method of curing headaches." "What?" "Pinching your nipples." "You're pulling my leg." "No, you try it." Maggie raised her hand doubtfully, and pinched her bare nipple through her jumper. "Doesn't it work?" "No." He stood up and went behind her. "Now relax." (This was always the signal for the stroking of her forehead.) "That's right." His hands pressed her forehead and stroked outwards for a moment, then reached down, found her breasts—small and flat—and began to pinch them. "Is that better?" "I don't know. . . ." She sounded doubtful. "You're not there. . . ." Her nipples were very tiny, and the wool was very thick. "Lift up your jumper." He knew the importance of giving orders, of making her do it. She tugged it up over the tiny breasts. Arthur leaned forward and pressed against the back of the chair, to satisfy the tingling in his loins, then began to pinch the nipples gently. "There, that's better, isn't it?" She said: "Ooooh!" and her breath was expelled in a long sigh.

"Better?" *"Lovely."* "You see, it's much quicker than stroking your forehead, isn't it?" "Yes, much quicker."

It was a pity that Maggie did not attract him physically. He was fixated on his sister. He would have given a great deal to be allowed to pinch Pauline's nipples, but the opportunity never arose; she seemed impervious to suggestion. "Got a headache?" "Headache? No, of course not!" And that was all. Maggie had a yellowish complexion—the doctor said something about her system's inability to deal with its poisons—and her body smelled unhealthy. It amused him to soothe her by pinching her nipples, and gave him a delicious feeling of power to order her, "Pull up your jumper." On one occasion when they were alone he said, "You'd better take it off." She did as he ordered without question. He unbuttoned his fly as he stood behind the chair, and pressed his loins against the wood. It was not that Maggie excited him sexually, but the indecency of the situation seemed piquant— his genitals exposed to the air, while a girl gasped gently as he pinched her nipples. The thought of raising her dress and putting his hand between her thighs produced a sense of revulsion. Maggie did not interest him; it was his power over her that gave him pleasure. He thought that it might be pleasant to beat her, but never fantasized about this. Two months later, Maggie took to her bed; she died in the autumn of 1949. Looking at her face as she lay in the coffin— so very obviously dead—Arthur was surprised when he felt a sudden rising sorrow that made tears roll down his cheeks. He discovered, with surprise, that to have power over someone also gives them power over you. He had never liked Maggie, always felt a certain revulsion against her; yet the contact with her body had forged a link between them. But the day after she was buried, he had forgotten her. That came as a relief. His sorrow had frightened him; it was not pleasant to feel weak.

Marvo had made Arthur interested in the subject of hypnotism. His cousin Albert read it too, and one day, when Aggie was in the room, Arthur suggested that he should try hypnotizing Albert.

He had made an interesting discovery. When he had been reading too much, he began to yawn, and his eyes became watery. When this happened, he sometimes locked together the fingers of his right and left hands, and then pressed the knuckles of his hands against the top of his head. One day, he tried pulling his hands apart in this position, tightening the grip of his fingers. As he did this, he experienced an odd feeling of lightness in his skull. The sun was shining through the window and was reflected on a cut glass bowl that stood on the sideboard in the front room. He suddenly came to himself as this light was temporarily eclipsed by a shadow passing the window. He had been "entranced" by the light for several minutes.

He told Albert to lock his fingers and place his hands on top of his head. Then he told him to pull as hard as he could. After a moment, Albert, now red in the face said, "I'm getting tired." "Never mind. Don't stop." As Albert's eyes became fixed from the strain, Arthur began moving his hand in a slow circle in front of his eyes. He said softly, "All right, that's fine, you can relax now." Albert relaxed, but his eyes stayed on Arthur's hand. "Now stand up." Albert stood up. "Can you hear me?" "Yes," said Albert. "Move your right hand." He touched the hand, since Albert was never sure which was his right and left, and Albert moved it. "Your right hand wants to rise up in the air, but you don't want it to. Try to stop it rising." The hand left Albert's side, and proceeded to rise. Albert looked startled and tried to press it down again. He succeeded for a moment; then the hand rose again at right angles to his body. "Try harder." Albert went red in the face. Aggie said: "Oh, please stop, Arthur, I don't like it." Arthur was as startled by his success as Aggie was. He could not know that he had stumbled upon one of the basic principles of hypnotism—to fatigue the attention—or the muscles—and then to take advantage of the momentary trance. The conscious self, the self that usually gives orders, falls asleep for a moment; the eyes become glassy; in this state, the hypnotist can issue the orders to the "instinctive self," bypassing the conscious self.

Arthur had no idea of how to get his cousin out of his trance. Snapping his fingers seemed to make no difference. But after a few minutes, Albert shook his head violently, and "came round."

As he thought about what had happened, he began to understand the principles behind it. His own brief trance state had been due to fatigue—fatigue of his eye muscles, followed by the fatigue induced by straining his arms. Fatigue had the effect of cutting you off from the outside world, so you ceased to notice things. In a sense, you were simultaneously awake and asleep. It was like being fast asleep in bed, yet capable of action, of obeying orders.

Albert was so puzzled by the experiment that he allowed Arthur to try it several times. Arthur devised other methods. Intense self-consciousness could have the same effect of fatiguing the attention. The trick was simply to make the subject intensely aware of his own body. Albert was told to sit in a chair and place his hands on his bare knees. "Now think about your fingertips. You can feel your knees under your fingertips. Which is warmest, your fingertips or the skin of your knees? Can you feel the little lines in your skin? Can you feel the hairs against your fingertips? Can you feel your fingertips with the skin of your knees." This kind of thing took longer than the other method. It was necessary to keep on suggesting feelings and sensations until Albert was frantically concentrating on the skin of his fingertips, and was prickling with self-awareness, the kind of unhealthy, intense self-awareness that Arthur had experienced when trying to urinate with someone beside him. When he reached this stage, it was enough to suggest that his knee itched for him to wince with pain; the itch became a stab of frustrated energy. After a little practice, Arthur could induce the trance state after about ten minutes of suggestion. When this happened, he could order Albert to do anything. On one occasion, he told him to strike a match and hold it under a finger of his left hand. Albert obeyed, staring at the flame with dazed unbelief until Arthur blew it out. Pauline—who was present at several of these sessions—asked him why he did it. Albert said he didn't know. "I know I'm doing it, and I try to stop myself. But my hand goes on doing it."

All this took place between the summer of 1949 and the summer of 1950. Arthur's first burglary was committed in November of 1949, soon after Maggie's death. It was not long after this that he discovered that Pauline was Dick Lingard's mistress. In the spring of 1950, he took the job as an errand boy, and the second burglary—when he contemplated rape—was committed in July. It was at about this time that Pauline began sleeping with George Goldhawk, and Arthur became the go-between.

George Goldhawk was an important influence on Arthur, in two ways. It was he who told Arthur that television would be the great money-maker of the future, and that Arthur could do worse than become a television engineer. The suggestion might have been ignored if he had not been brooding on the problem of how to commit burglary with a minimum of risk. A television repairman would have access to people's homes—particularly the homes of people like Duncan McIver's parents. Arthur persuaded the local library to order him a book on the subject. It is a proof of his natural brilliance that he mastered the essentials in a few weeks—inspired by the thought of riskless burglaries—and persuaded the local radio and television shop to take him on in a part-time capacity. The result has been described. By the time Arthur received his probation in March 1951, he was one of the most expert repairmen in Warrington. (It must be borne in mind that these were the early days of television, before it became as common as radio.) Immediately after being put on probation, he took a job with a television shop in central Manchester—having been given permission by the probation officer. And this, as he had hoped, gave him access to middle-class homes and hotel rooms. People were amused when the thirteen-year-old boy told them that he had been sent to repair the TV; housewives offered him tea and cake, and sometimes said: "I'm going out to the shops. Close the door behind you when you leave." Often, he was still there when they returned; they could not be aware that he was probably now wearing a pair of panties taken from the bottom of a laundry hamper. He would sometimes take pleasure in standing talking to the housewife, reveling in the thought that something that had been in contact with her genitals was now in contact with his. On these occasions, he moved his repair bag to conceal the rising erection. It was symbolic rape again, bringing a secret sense of power, of superiority.

George Goldhawk was important for another reason. He had worked in the theater as one of a group of five singers called The Melodairs, but his secret ambition had been to become a member of the Society of Magicians. His performing standards never became professional—or at least, he could never convince any management that they were—but he had a good amateur knowledge of the art of escape, as practiced by Houdini. Arthur pretended to be fascinated by the intricate problems of escaping from water-filled cabinets or air-tight safes; but what really interested him was Goldhawk's knowledge of locks. Goldhawk was happy to demonstrate his skill in opening locks. He showed Arthur how any ordinary Yale lock could be opened with the help of a simple instrument made of bent wire, and a strip of celluloid. A lock never fitted tight into the doorjamb; a piece of wire of the right shape could be inserted either above or below the tongue, and turned. If the door was a tight fit, the blade of stiff celluloid could be worked in to afford access. Arthur even worked out his own innovation: a narrow passage down the center of the cellophane strip, down which the wire could slide. For ordinary locks, Goldhawk showed him how to use a skeleton key, and how to judge what key would fit. He took it as a compliment when Arthur spent hours sitting at the table, examining locks and trying keys.

On the day George Goldhawk was killed, Arthur hurried to his flat, let himself in with a duplicate key (copied from one that had been given to Pauline), and took Goldhawk's collection of keys and other implements. This was exactly one week after he had pledged the magistrate to keep out of trouble for at least a year. He did not feel he was breaking his pledge; he had every intention of keeping out of trouble.

His seduction of Aggie was his first completely calculated act of its kind. This took place in the summer of 1951 at the time he was working as an errand boy. Duncan's sister played an important part in his sexual fantasies; after a while, so did Agnes. At fifteen, she was not unattractive, in a pale way. She and Arthur had been fairly close since the July of 1948, when he had confided about the scene he witnessed by the canal. She slept in the same bed as Pauline, Arthur, and Albert, but on the other side of Pauline. Albert slept at the other end.

One afternoon, Arthur returned from his grocery round to find the house full of steam. Aggie was doing the washing. This involved putting the soiled laundry into the copper, bringing the water to a boil, then poking it with a "copper stick." Aggie was not physically strong; after half an hour of this, she was sitting in the armchair, her hair plastered against her forehead in damp strands. She was reading *True Confessions*, and as she read, was pinching her right breast with her left hand. Probably this had no erotic significance; the perspiration had made her itch. Arthur said curiously: "What are you doing?" "Reading." "Pinching yourself." "Oh,

137

that." "Have you got a headache?" "No, why?" "I used to do that for Maggie when she had a headache. It made it better." "Did you?" This was the first Agnes had heard of it. Arthur went across behind her chair, and Aggie moved forward in alarm. "Oh, no. I don't want any of that ipmertism stuff." "I'm not. It's soothing when you're tired. Sit back." He reached down and touched her breast. "Where's your bra?" "In the wash." He had, in fact, noticed that she was not wearing it; this had given him the idea. He felt her tension and alarm, and pressed her back against the chair. "No ipmertism, mind!" "No. I'm only doing what you used to do for Maggie. That wasn't hypnotism, was it?" "No, I s'pose not." It was a thin, red cotton sweater (Arthur's memory for such details was always accurate). As he stroked her through the sweater, he slipped back into his mood when stroking Maggie, and the movements became slow and automatic. She relaxed. "Yes, that's nice." He placed his hands between her breasts, then stroked outwards firmly; the movement was completely unlike a sexual caress. She began to breath tranquilly and deeply; then, when she was completely relaxed, he began to pinch her nipples. "Is that nice." "Mmmm." It was a murmur of contentment. "Lift you sweater." He tugged it out of her skirt. She lifted it without protest. But her body was slippery with sweat, and it was less satisfying than stroking her through the sweater. But he continued for a few minutes more until there were sounds of footsteps in the entry.

The relationship proceeded slowly, since their opportunities of being alone were rare in the overcrowded household. But before the autumn, she had become accustomed to allowing him to stand behind her, stroking her, then pinching the nipples. Soon she ceased to object to the idea of hypnosis. As he stroked her, he would say: "Put your hands on your knees. Relax. Stroke your knees with your fingertips. Can you feel your stockings under your fingers?" He discovered that his own stroking distracted her. She achieved concentration much more quickly without it. The eyes became fixed. "There, now you can relax completely. It's like sinking into a deep feather bed. You're sinking deeper and deeper and deeper. Your eyes are closing. There, is that nice?" "Yes." Her voice was scarcely audible. He raised her jumper, and pulled up her bra—this was not difficult over her small breasts. He began to pinch the nipples. "Is that relaxing?"

"Yes." "Take off your bra." She reached behind her and took it off. "Now your sweater." He helped her pull it over her head. Her flesh felt cold. He said, "You're feeling warm, aren't you, very warm?" "Yes." "You'd better take off your skirt too. Undo the zip." Her hand went to her waist without hesitation, and the skirt fell at her feet. She was not wearing an underskirt. Her stockings were held up by bands of elastic, tied in a crude knot. He was familiar with the silk knickers. But the sight of them on her aroused violent lust. He put his hands on her waist and said, "Take your knickers off." It may have been his voice that alarmed her; suddenly, she was fully awake, and looking down dazedly at her naked breasts. Arthur, too excited to care, grasped the elastic, and tugged the knickers over her hips; her hands went up defensively. "No, Arthur." Her voice was weak and pleading, and he felt a tremendous gratification. He took his hands away from her. "Take them off." "No. . . . Why?" He knew he had won. She didn't want to take them off, but she had no definite reason for refusing; Jim had taken them off her many times. "Take them off." She looked down at herself, decided it was too late to object, and pushed them down to her feet. He was feeling a sense of power that he had never experienced before, watching her. She looked at him, waiting for his next move. He pointed to the homemade carpet of tufted rags. "Lie down there." "No. Someone might come." "Lie down." She sat down, looking miserable. He quickly unbelted his trousers, and stepped out of them. She knew what came next, and accepted it philosophically. She lay back, her knees parted, and allowed him to lower himself between them. He felt her; she was warm but dry. This was his first experience, and he was clumsy, although his self-confidence was unabated. "Help me." She reached down, grasped his member, and guided it. He thrust forward, and she gasped. He pushed hard, and felt himself slowly entering her. She gasped with pain. It brought his excitement to a climax, and he thrust hard and held her tight as it surged over him. When it was over, he said, "You're not very good, are you?" "I'm sorry. This is the wrong place." They lay together for a few more moments, then she got up and pulled on her panties. His excitement returned. He tugged her hand. "Lie down again." "Oh, no, not again." But she obeyed. He tugged the panties down so the elastic was below her crotch, then entered her again. This time she was easy to enter, and

139

he achieved a second climax. As he did so, he heard some-one enter the other room, and hoped that whoever it was would come in and see him in this position of power, lying between Aggie's meekly parted thighs. But no one came in, and they dressed undisturbed. He felt strangely clean and happy. The adventure was appropriate for the Napoleon of crime. Aggie seemed to take her new position for granted, like a horse with a new owner.

There can be no possible doubt that Arthur Lingard was basically sadistic; but the sadism never developed to the point of the enjoyment of pain. He needed to feel himself the master. Under different circumstances, this could have been harmless enough. If he had had some normal, social outlet for his need to dominate—as an organizer, for example, or in some legitimate business—it could have been a consid-erable advantage. Aggie was the sort of person who would have made a good wife for a businessman—patient, adoring, long-suffering. But his sexual desires were now so continuous and violent that his only thought was how to gratify them. This meant that they cut across what had previously been his real creative outlet: imagination. It is difficult to lead a heroic life on Mars if you are in a state of perpetual erec-tion and mentally undress every girl who passes in the street. He told me that in the days that followed his seduc-tion of Aggie, he was in a continual state of desire. Half an hour later, having tea, he thought of her removing her panties from her feet, and suddenly lost interest in food; nothing mattered but sex. When Aggie went upstairs for some rea-son, he followed her and made her lie on the bed, although the house was now full of people and they could have been interrupted at any moment.

"I decided I had to do something about it. I was want-ing her all the time. At first, I'd try to make signals to her to go outside or upstairs, but she would pretend not to under-stand. Then I saw the answer. It was in *Marvo*, where he makes Plunkett suddenly turn and stab the rajah on the mountain road, you remember? He tells Plunkett that when he raises his hand, as if to signal them to go slower, he's to stab the rajah—he tells him under hypnosis. It's called post-hypnotic suggestion. They can do it with people doing quite ordinary things like lighting a cigarette, or going across a room and doing something you told them to do when they were still hypnotized, at a given signal. So I thought I'd try this on Aggie. So it was a couple of days later and I got her to sit on the bed after I'd just screwed her. She didn't suspect anything, because I'd got rid of my load. She liked me to touch her, stroke her, she'd almost purr. Well, anyway, I did it then, I got her to go off, kept telling her she was tired and she wanted to sleep. Then, when she was so far gone she didn't move when I stuck a pin in her arm, I told her that if she saw me rub the end of my nose with two fingers, she would wait until I left the room, then follow me."

"Follow you where?"

"Anywhere. If it was warm, to the canal bank. We'd do it in the same place where I'd watched others so often. That was nice. But if it was cold, just to the outside lavatory, or the place behind the coal shed."

"But she couldn't lie down in a lavatory."

"No, we'd do it like I saw Uncle Dick with Polly. She'd bend over the seat and I'd get it in from behind. It never took long. Sometimes I'd shoot my load as soon as I went in. I'd make her pull her pants down, just halfway down her thighs, so I could keep my hands on them as I went in. I liked the thought that she was leaking my sperm onto them afterwards. Sometimes the thought excited me so much I'd make her go right out and do it again."

"Wasn't there a danger of her becoming pregnant?"

"She had a couple of scares, and after that she'd keep this sponge up inside her, soaked in something. . . . I think it was quinine, or vinegar would do."

"Were you in love with her?"

"Oh, no. I suppose I got fond of her."

"Did you kiss her?"

"Sometimes. She was nice to kiss. If it was her period, I'd kiss her while she tossed me off. She was good at that. I think Jim taught her and Polly how to do it."

"Did she satisfy you completely?"

"Sometimes. I'd think it was a pity there weren't more things I could do to her. It was this power thing. I'd make her kneel in front of me and suck me, and we tried it the other way a couple of times, but I didn't like it much. I'd enjoy giving her scares. Once we were on the top of a bus and I told her to take off her pants. She said she couldn't do it without being seen, but she managed it somehow."

"But you couldn't do anything on top of a bus."

"Oh, no, I didn't do anything. I just wanted her to take her pants off, for a joke."

From this above discussion, which I tape-recorded, it will be seen why I have not quoted him more often. His mind would go off on a different track from sentence to sentence. There were days when he was better than others, but for the most part, his ability to concentrate was minimal. Now that he was being natural, and not trying to argue intellectually, the level of self-expression was not high.

It will also be observed that his relationship to Aggie was not a good one, in spite of his assertion that he "got fond of her." She was used purely as an instrument of self-assertion. Such a relationship is not necessarily bad—there are many sadistic personalities married happily to masochistic ones—provided it is accompanied by emotional warmth. He had none to offer. When I asked about the danger of pregnancy, he replied, "*She* had a couple of scares," not "we," as most lovers would say. "It was a pity there weren't more things I could do *to* her." His orgasms upon entering her could not have given her any satisfaction. She was being used as an instrument, and she knew it. He admitted that she herself had normal orgasms if they were able to go to bed together or have sex without fear of interruption. Finally, there is his insistence that he would make her remove her panties "as a joke." He felt guilty about using her in this way. "I'd enjoy giving her scares." What he means is that it was a violent stimulation of his sexual appetite to see her wriggling out of her panties in a restaurant or on top of a bus, the satisfaction of a sexual urge that was almost all will-to-power.

It was from this point that my relationship with Arthur Lingard began to change.

This was, I now see, inevitable. When I first knew him, he was as helpless as a child, trapped by his own terrors. My relationship with him was the completely paternal one of doctor and patient. Even when I knew that he had murdered Evelyn Marquis, there was no question of moral disapproval. Why should there be? His murder was only another proof of his sickness, his need for help. In editing this account, I have deliberately cut out all references to my own psychological theories—which are humanistic rather than Freudian—because they made so little practical difference in the actual process of therapy. But there is one respect in which this is untrue. I have always believed firmly that the task of the psychiatrist is to identify himself as far as possible with the patient; there should be no attitude of superiority; only an attempt at total sympathy. In Lingard's case, this was not difficult. My wife came close to tears when I told her how Pauline and Arthur had watched their mother's body being removed from a burning building, and how, later, one of his cousins had told Arthur, in the course of a quarrel, "Your dad'll never come back. He's dead."

He was aware of this intensity of interest and sympathy— as unquestioning and uncritical as mother love—and in the early days of the therapy, he responded to it instinctively. After years as a loner, he was hungry for understanding.

The majority of mentally sick patients are not deeply interesting; their problems spring out of triviality and inadequacy. This can apply to intelligent as well as to stupid ones. Arthur's description of his absorption in the fantasies of Edgar Rice Burroughs marked a change in our relationship, a sharp deepening of my *interest* as well as sympathy. I was fascinated by his description of his strange aerial "vision" of Mars, and I even sketched out a paper on the subject: the intensifying of the imagination through mild epilepsy; it was the only case of its kind I had ever heard of. Inevitably, I began identifying with him. My own early years had been difficult enough; but compared to Arthur, I had been fortunate. I had good schoolmasters who helped me get to the university; Arthur was alone against the world. When I thought of his feats of imaginative identification with John Carter, I felt admiration as well as sympathy.

This was the "honeymoon" period of our relations. I spent hours every day with him, and wrote up my notes half the night. I read them aloud to my wife, and she agreed with me; here was the material for a case study that could become a classic of psychotherapy. At that stage, I intended to call it *The Dreamer*.

Arthur responded to this intensity of interest. He began to talk freely and eagerly. On the afternoon when he described his first burglary to me, it was almost as if our roles had been reversed. I listened like a fascinated child, drinking in every word, pressing for more details. I observed that he felt no shame in admitting that he thought of attacking Duncan's sister in the bath; there was even, perhaps, a kind

143

of pride. There came a crucial moment when he described using the girl's panties to induce an orgasm; there was a break in the flow, and he watched me doubtfully. I reassured him by nodding and smiling. Afterward, we discussed the episode intelligently, and he analyzed his "case" as detachedly as if it had been an unusual case of appendicitis. He was delighted that I saw its complexities, that I was so excited by the logic of his development; he was like an artist pointing out unnoticed subtleties in his masterpiece. He went on to tell me about his second burglary with the same excitement, and now we were like fellow conspirators. His description of the impact made upon him by Moriarty, and later by Haigh, moved and excited me more than anything so far, and confirmed my belief that here was my case of a lifetime, that he was the most interesting human being I would ever encounter. I reached a point where I would try to stop him from leaping ahead and referring to later events, because I wanted to savor every moment of this analysis. For weeks, I talked and thought of nothing but Lingard: I walked around on a cloud, like a lover. When he described his daydreams of a rural England, "after London," I saw him as a symbol of something fundamental in civilized man.

Certain changes began to take place in my attitude toward him when he spoke of using his television jobs as opportunities for burglary. I am not speaking of moral disapproval. But it was suddenly plain that he had made a decision that would fix his future. Here, I felt, he had made his mistake. The period at Earlestow confirmed this. It was at this point that my feeling of pity again began to predominate. Like the hero of some tragedy, he had made the wrong choice, and the results would follow inevitably. I wanted to shake my head and say, "No, that was a mistake. . . ." Whatever happened now, he was caught in a net of his own making.

And he himself was aware of this. In describing his seduction of Aggie, an element of self-assertiveness crept into his manner. He had ceased to expect my total, noncritical approval. I saw the danger—that he would begin to classify me with "them"—and went out of my way to reaffirm my interest. Yet when I left him that afternoon, I felt worried. *He* knew that his life had gone wrong after Earlestow, but he was not willing to face it. He needed my help in convincing himself that he had continued to do his best. It was a difficult choice I had to make. I had sympathized so deeply because I saw his problem as a problem of frustrated creative drives. I understood his logic in trying to express them through crime. But it was also clear to me that crime (or sexual aggression) is, by its very nature, a self-defeating way of achieving creative expression. The artist or the religious mystic can pursue his creative expression with the full approval of society. Arthur Lingard had decided that he could do without such approval. The result had been mental breakdown. The fact that he was now confiding in me proved the fallacy in his thinking.

There were two alternatives. Either he recognized this and continued to confide in me in the character of the prodigal son returning to the fold; or he would expect me to continue to treat his confessions with a blanket approval. I knew enough about Arthur Lingard to suspect it would be the latter. He had stood alone for too long to fall on his knees and do a mea culpa before society—or even before me.

Over the next few days, I recognized that this was so. He was no longer trying to gain my sympathetic understanding. On the contrary, he seemed to present himself—and his activities—in the worst possible light, as if he wanted to shock me into some gesture of disapproval. It was not difficult for me to avoid this; I only had to remind myself that this was the most interesting case of my career. I also tried to lure him into discussions of his motivations, or simply into philosophical arguments about hypnotism or the relation of society to the talented individual.

This seemed to work. The "honeymoon" period was over, but there seemed a good chance that, from my point of view, this new relationship would be just as satisfactory. My new role was that of an admiring but horrified priest listening to the confessions of a Corsican bandit.

I was not overoptimistic. I knew, and so did he, that all his past attempts to establish close contact with other people had been unsuccessful. My only hope was that, for the time being, he would prefer not to face this.

EIGHT

When Arthur returned from the Earlestow reformatory, Dick Lingard made him sleep in a bed in the front room—the bed that Jim—and then later, Ted—had occupied. Ted had married recently, having made a local girl pregnant. Dick Lingard knew about Arthur's relations with Aggie—there was no big discovery scene, but he was not blind—and probably suspected him of having relations with Pauline. (In fact, Arthur and Pauline had become close allies again, through the George Goldhawk affair.)

When Dick Lingard went to prison, and Pauline went to have her baby in a home for unmarried mothers, Arthur moved upstairs, and persuaded Albert to move down to the bed in the front room.

He discovered immediately that this was a mistake. To be able to have sexual relations with Aggie every night, like a husband and wife, was an anticlimax. And Aunt Elsie, the ever-adaptable, made no objection; it struck her that Arthur and Aggie might end by marrying. So when Albert had a bout of gastroenteritis in January 1952, and moved into the upstairs bed for a few days, Arthur seized the excuse to move downstairs again. Aggie did not object; she had accepted their nightly intercourse as a bonus; it was not expected to last. There was a brief occasion when they resumed nightly relations. Absurdly enough, Aunt Elsie found herself a male friend while her husband was in prison, and this man took her and the two-year-old Jane to Blackpool for a week. For that week, Arthur and Aggie slept in Aunt Elsie's bed. When she returned, he moved downstairs again.

I have mentioned that Arthur had two hiding places on the canal bank; one for wet weather, in a concrete bunker dating

146

from 1940. When the police uncovered the biscuit tin containing his spoils from burglaries, Arthur was relieved that he had never told anyone about the other place. There was another biscuit tin in the bank behind the bunker, and it contained a quantity of jewelry and money, carefully wrapped in panties. When he came out of Earlestow, he took care not to return there for several weeks. He was afraid his movements were being observed; he also knew that someone would be sure to notice if he started spending money. A few weeks after returning to Penketh Street, he found another job at a television shop in Liverpool—a forty-minute bus ride from Warrington—and very cautiously resumed his former activities. It was not that he needed money. It was simply that the excitement of entering a strange house or flat, and entering a woman's bedroom, had become indispensable to him. It was the only time he felt really alive.

It is worth pointing out that panty-fetichism has seldom been mentioned by Freudian psychologists, almost as if they were embarrassed by it. Stekel's classic two-volume work on fetichism never once discusses it. And yet it is probably the commonest, and most harmless, form of sexual anomaly. So that when Arthur Lingard bought paperbacks on sexual perversion from bookshops that specialized in erotica, he could still find no mention of his own obsession, and was inclined to believe that it was peculiar to himself, that he was far more abnormal than he, in fact, was.

When he resumed his burglaries in the early months of 1952, he seldom stole anything. If it was possible when he was repairing a television set, he went to the bedroom, used any panties he could find for masturbation, then carefully replaced them. For the first few months, he decided to take nothing. The police might suddenly decide to check on him as he returned to the shop one day; if they found jewelry or money in his pockets, it would mean return to Earlestow. That was something he was determined would never happen; if he was ever arrested again, he had decided to make a "suicide attempt" that would convince the magistrate that he was better at home. And if that failed, he would hurt himself so badly that he would be confined in a hospital. He would commit murder rather than go back.

After a month or so, he ran out of money, and wondered where he could sell some of the jewelry. He was aware that fences gave a bad price for it, and that they would certainly try to cheat a fourteen-year-old boy. But the stuff was of no use to him while it lay buried in a biscuit tin.

The answer came by chance. One day in June 1952, Jane, now a plump child of five, came home with a bag of sweets. At first she claimed to have found them; then she admitted that they had been given to her by an old man who had asked her to sit on his knee and allow him to kiss her. Finally, she admitted that the old man had put his "thing" between her thighs as she sat on his knee, and made her touch it. There had been no attempt at intercourse; he had not even removed her panties, although he had felt inside them.

Aunt Elsie was out spending the evening with her male friend when this happened; it was Aggie who persuaded Jane to tell the story. And Arthur, who came in shortly afterward, was shocked and enraged by it. He was violently intolerant of other people's perversions.

When Jane described the old man, Aggie immediately identified him as a Mr. Tebbut, who lived in the next street. In sunny weather, he sat by the open front door as the children came out of school, and often talked to them.

Arthur's first thought was to go to the police. Then it struck him that he had no evidence, and that it was the child's word against the grown man's. This made him still angrier. He kept repeating: "The filthy old swine. People like that ought to be put down like dogs." He did not know enough about the law to know that the police would take action on Jane's evidence. He and Aggie decided not to tell Aunt Elsie about it. If anybody went to the police, it would be Arthur, who would gain the credit for denouncing a pervert. . . .

The next day, at school, he approached Joe Benham—the same Benham whom I had interviewed at Knaresborough. Benham was not exactly a friend: he was an athletic type, popular and arrogant. But he was also the son of a policeman, and Arthur had always cultivated his acquaintance. With a grave, worried air, Arthur told Benham that he needed his advice. Benham was flattered. Arthur told him about Jane and the old man.

"Oh, yes, I know that Tebbut. He's a right swine. If I were you, I wouldn't tackle him."

"Why not?"

Benham implied that Tebbut was a dangerous criminal. Arthur objected that dangerous criminals do not take unnecessary risks by interfering with small girls. Benham said he was a "bit of a nut." And after lunch, he told Arthur more details about Tebbut—how he had been in jail several times for robbery with violence, how the police suspected him of innumerable other crimes they were unable to prove. But what really interested Arthur was the comment that Tebbut was suspected of rape. He asked for details. Benham said: "My old man wouldn't say much, but I heard him telling my mother something about finding a girl without any clothes on by the canal."

The surprising thing is that Joe Benham had apparently not told his father what Tebbut had done to Jane; or perhaps he told him, but nothing further was done. Such things were not uncommon in the area, and the child had come to no harm.

Arthur found himself unable to concentrate on his schoolwork. A really dangerous criminal! He thought of Moriarty in the center of his web. Perhaps "Dagger" Tebbut might be his first all-important contact with the underworld. What did it matter if he had messed around a bit with Jane? If it gave him a thrill, why not? Criminals lived according to their own laws. And the thought of this man knocking a girl unconscious from behind, then stripping her and violating her, struck a deep chord of sympathy. Given the chance, Arthur would have done the same to every girl in Warrington.

That evening, he received another shock when he asked Aggie to point out the house where Tebbut lived. It was next door to the place where he had committed his second burglary—had waited in the children's bedroom to attack the wife. Perhaps Tebbut had been home at that very time. (He learned later that he had actually been in Wormwood Scrubs.)

The following day was a Saturday; it was bright and warm. Arthur hung around Tebbut's house for an hour, hoping to see him, before it was time to catch the bus to Liverpool; but he saw no one. The following day was hotter still. And at three in the afternoon, Arthur walked to Prescot Row, and saw Tebbut sitting outside the house in a folding chair, absorbing the sun.

At first sight he was disappointing: fat-faced, with a curved nose like a bird's beak, pale, grayish complexion (the result of years in prison), round shoulders, dirty grayish hair, old slippers on his feet. Arthur began to feel calmer. He approached him.

"Mr. Tebbut?"

The man looked up and smiled amiably, showing false teeth, the amiability of the professional crook who wishes to appear harmless.

"What can I do for you, young man?"

"Can I speak to you?"

"Well, I'm here."

Arthur was disconcerted; he decided to take the plunge, "I've got something I want to sell."

"Oh? And what would that be?"

Arthur put his hand into his pocket. Tebbut said quickly, "Not here. Come on inside." And Arthur went into a very dark front room, very like his own, but full of cages of stuffed birds. Arthur put his hand into the lining of his coat and drew out a platinum ring with a small diamond in it. Tebbut took it and examined it.

"Where did you get it from?"

"Stole it." He had decided to tell the truth, although it cost a painful effort. Tebbut went on looking at the ring without a change of expression.

"When?"

"A year ago."

"Are you telling the truth?"

"Yes."

"Then why have you kept it so long?"

"I've been in reform school." He now felt rather proud of it.

Tebbut obviously suspected that Arthur was lying. He asked several more questions, then suddenly said, "Who told you about me?"

"My cousin Jane."

"What does she know about me?"

"She's the little girl who sat on your knee and let you feel her."

Tebbut was startled and shaken. Suddenly he looked dangerous. His eyes became very stern, and Arthur quailed.

"What do you mean?"

Arthur made an effort to conceal his nervousness.

"*I* don't care. You asked me, and I told you."

Tebbut seemed impressed by this answer. He sat down, and stared out of the window. Probably he was thinking what it would be like to be arrested for sexual interference with a small girl. Finally, he said, "Who is this girl?"

Arthur described her. He told Tebbut exactly what Jane had said when she came home.

Tebbut said, "What made you think it was me?"

"My cousin Aggie said it sounded like you."

"She could be wrong, couldn't she?"

"Yes."

There was another long silence. (Arthur's description of this first interview was as detailed and precise as usual.)

Then Tebbut said, "And you decided I might help you get rid of your stolen goods?"

"Yes. I don't know anybody else who might."

Tebbut seemed satisfied by this. No doubt he was relieved.

"What other things have you got?"

"Oh, one or two."

"Bring them all along to me this evening. I'll see what I can do."

"But what about that ring? What's it worth?"

If Tebbut had tried to convince him it was of little value, their relationship would have ended there and then. Arthur did not like dishonest smooth talkers. As a child, he had often collected rags at front doors, then sold them at second-hand clothes shops; he detested the sort of people who always try to swindle children. But Tebbut was not evasive.

"If you bought it in a shop," he said, "it would cost sixty or seventy quid—that's my guess. A fence couldn't get rid of it for more than twenty, or say twenty-five. That means he wouldn't offer me more than ten or twelve—offer *me*, that is, not you. He'd offer you ten bob. If I took the risk of selling it, I'd want sixty percent."

"That's more than half."

"Of course it is. What risk are you taking? If they catch you, you'll get another year in Borstal. If they catch me, I'd get two years for handling stolen goods, even if I told them you'd pinched it yourself. Is that fair or isn't it?"

Tebbut was a clever psychologist. His frankness was the right approach. Arthur agreed quickly that it was fair.

"All right. Bring the stuff along this evening, half past six." (Arthur discovered that the family who rented the room to Tebbut went to Sunday evening service.)

Arthur delivered the goods as promised. Tebbut exam-

151

ined them critically. Of some pieces he said, "You may as well throw that in the canal. It's not worth tuppence." But of a silver crucifix on a chain: "That's nice. It'd fetch fifty nicker on the open market. Pity to sell it under the arm."

The following evening, after dark, Arthur knocked quietly on the front door. Tebbut let him in. He handed him fifteen pound notes, and said: "Don't flash it around. Hide it somewhere and spend it ten bob at a time." Then he opened the door again, and Arthur left.

He was exultant. Tebbut was honest, and he treated him as a fellow criminal, not as a teen-ager. He was the contact he needed. A week later, he carried out a burglary he had been contemplating for a long time, at a new block of flats in Liverpool. He waited until after dark, and noticed which windows were lighted. He made a careful note of two flats that were evidently empty. When the porter was showing someone to the lift, he slipped in. Unfortunately, the porter saw him as he walked along the corridor. "Hey, you, where'd you think you're off to?" "TV repairs, someone called Jenkinson." He was on safe ground; he had repaired the Jenkinson's television a month ago. If the porter insisted on accompanying him to the flat, he could explain that he was making the routine check that the repair shop liked its workmen to make as a matter of courtesy. But the porter only said, "Flat twelve," and ignored him. He rang at the door of flat twelve, and asked the young housewife who answered it if her television had given any more trouble. She said it hadn't, and thanked him. He went upstairs, and found the first of the flats whose light had been out. He rang the bell. There was no reply. He waited for a few minutes, then opened his repair bag, lifted its false bottom, and took out his skeleton keys. A few moments later, he was inside. He switched on the light and made straight for the bedroom. But this proved disappointing. The flat seemed to be occupied by two men. There were no objects of value, and he was not interested in such items as electric razors or a portable radio. Without wasting time, he left, and located the second flat. This was altogether more satisfactory; as if to make up for his previous disappointment, it was evidently occupied by two girls—models, from their photographs. There was everything here to give him his sense of rich fulfillment; an untidy flat with the breakfast cups still on the table and bacon rind in the sink; discarded clothes on the bathroom floor, expensive nylon nightdresses on the unmade beds. He cleaned his teeth with both toothbrushes in the bathroom, drank the remains of the tea from the cups, even ate a piece of chewed bacon that lay on the side of a plate. When he left, half an hour later, he had two pairs of the most expensive panties he had ever seen—a thick, silky material—and some jewelry. There had been a considerable amount of jewelry, and he had only taken a few items that would probably not be missed for a few days.

He gave the panties to Aggie. They looked new, and he told her he had bought them; it gave him pleasure to take them off her before intercourse. He took the jewelry to Dagger Tebbut, who said frankly that it was probably worth a hundred quid, but that he couldn't expect to get much more than twenty. The following evening, when Arthur returned to collect his eight pounds, Tebbut asked him to sit down and talk. To Arthur's surprise, he advised him against taking up crime as a living. "When I was young, there wasn't much else to do if you didn't want to go 'ungry. But there's plenty of opportunity for you young 'uns nowadays. You could own your own TV business by the time you was twenty."

Arthur was convinced—when he told me the story—that this was simply cunning psychology. In his way, Tebbut *was* a master criminal; at least, he was well above average intelligence. He recognized unusual material in Arthur. If this young man was coached properly, he might be a future source of income. He already had the right instinct of cunning and caution.

Tebbut was clever enough not to sound too honest and decent. He told Arthur that people would get suspicious if they saw Arthur visiting him very often, particularly late at night. Why did he not simply bring his cousins along too—Aggie and Jane? Then it would look innocent enough. Arthur agreed, although he guessed the motive to be sexual. Tebbut was as obsessed by young children as Arthur was by panties. Aggie was reluctant; but it was easy to bend her will. Jane came happily to see the nice man who had given her sweeties. And when, a few days later, she came home with more sweeties, Arthur guessed that she had called to see him again. When Arthur called one evening, the curtains were drawn, and he could hear voices inside. Suspecting that it was one of the old man's criminal contacts, he waited outside for half an hour. But it was only a rather fat twelve-

153

year-old girl who came out. Arthur discovered later that one of the reasons Dagger Tebbut needed money was to pay a harem of Lolitas. For most of the children of the area, five shillings was a huge sum, and they were happy not to tell their parents what they had done for kind Mr. Tebbut to earn it. He never made the mistake of attempting actual intercourse, and he always took care that no seminal stains should get onto the children's clothes. Mutual fondling was all he asked, and if the child was inexperienced, it was enough for him to fondle her; he could achieve his satisfaction without her knowledge.

After seeing the twelve-year-old leave, Arthur knocked on the door and was admitted. Tebbut seemed to be in a mellow, relaxed mood. He reminisced about his early life, his prison experiences, and methods of avoiding detection. Arthur left that evening feeling that he was a lonely, harmless old man who could teach him a great deal. Soon, he began to talk voluntarily about his own methods and aims. They were fellow criminals; why should they not trust each other? He felt that he was gaining a hold over Tebbut. He said later, smiling ironically, "Like a rabbit gaining a hold over a snake." To increase his hold, he even asked Tebbut if Aggie attracted him. "Yes, she's a nice young girl. Why? Does she want to earn five bob?" "No, but she'll let you do what you like to her. You can go further than with the others." "When?" Tebbut's interest in children may have been the outcome of frustration rather than genuine pedophilia. "Tonight, if you like." "Are you sure?" "Quite sure." Arthur went home and fetched Aggie. She came willingly, assuming she was wanted as a "cover"; she knew that Arthur was engaged in burglary. Arthur turned the conversation to hypnotism, and offered to demonstrate to Tebbut. Aggie allowed herself to be put into a trance—Arthur could do it with a few movements of his hands now, like a stage Svengali. Arthur ordered her to remove her clothes. She did so quickly and naturally, while Tebbut watched, licking his lips and looking grayer than usual. As Aggie stripped off her panties, he began to tremble. Arthur, sitting beside Tebbut, ordered her to come closer, and told Tebbut to feel her. His hand shook as he reached out. "You see, she's all ready." He told Aggie to lie on the bed. She lay down obediently, and opened her legs. Tebbut began to sweat. "I can't do it while you're in the room. Go away." "She'll wake up if I do." This was not entirely true, although it was possible. Tebbut was fascinated by the slim, naked body; he went over to the bed and felt her again. This decided him. Keeping his back to Arthur, he opened his trousers. "Look the other way." He moved on top of her, and Arthur watched out of the corner of his eye as Tebbut fumbled, trembling, to get in the right position. After several minutes of hoarse breathing, he groaned, "It's no good, I can't," and moved off, buttoning his trousers. He sat in his chair, still trembling. "It's awful when you want it so bad you can't."

Arthur solved the problem by ordering Aggie to visit Tebbut alone. She protested. "It's all right, he won't try to do anything. He only wants to feel you. Give the poor old sod a little bit of pleasure." Aggie did as she was told. But when she returned, she looked miserable. "Well, it was all right, wasn't it?" "He didn't just want to feel me." That was all she said. But Tebbut increased Arthur's share of the takings to fifty percent next time. At least, he said he did.

Later that year, Arthur was almost caught. A husband and wife returned from the cinema while he was in the house. Fortunately, he had observed his usual precautions: locking the door behind him after entering, leaving no obvious traces of his entry. There was a moment of wild panic as he looked for somewhere to hide. The lavatory was closest, but he decided against it. This proved to be a good decision; a moment later, the husband came to the lavatory, while Arthur waited, tense, inside their bedroom door. He had had no time to return her underwear to the drawer; it lay on the bed. He decided that now was the time to leave. He pulled his cap low over his eyes, gripped a heavy spanner he carried in his bag, and hurried downstairs. Fortunately, the woman was in the kitchen; she called "Where are you going?" as he went out of the front door. It must have been a shock to her when her husband came out of the lavatory.

He was badly shaken. He had violated his first rule: never to leave obvious traces behind. The police might connect the panties spread over the bed with the half a dozen pairs in the biscuit tin that had led to his arrest.

Tebbut was disconcerted when Arthur told him he intended to lie low for a while. Arthur explained the circumstances—it was the first time he had told anyone voluntarily about the panties, but it was necessary, to explain his caution. Tebbut listened carefully. Then he said: "If you take my advice, you'll do another job right away." "Why?" "To get your nerve back." "There's nothing wrong with my nerve. I'm just being sensible." Tebbut fixed him with an eye like an Old Testament prophet. "Take my advice. If you don't, you needn't come back here." At first, Arthur could not believe he was serious. And when he became convinced, he went off feeling shaken and mutinous. He was so angry that he took a bus to a large block of flats he had been intending to burgle, walked in boldly, and went to the first flat without a light showing under the door. By now, his expertise enabled him to select the right key in minutes, and enter silently. This was as well; with the door open, he could hear the sound of a television set and someone moving around in another room. He closed the door quietly. He was feeling angry and reckless. If he was caught, he would give away Tebbut as his fence. He found another door without a light, and once again opened it. This proved to be on a chain; evidently, someone was in, and intended not to be disturbed. He climbed to the next floor and heard voices; a family party was coming along the corridor, and a man was carefully closing the door of a flat. It was too late to avoid them; he marched past them, carrying his bag, and no one paid the least attention. While the voices of the children were still audible in the distance, he opened the door and went in, switching on the lights. He marched straight to the bedroom, and walked in as if it were his own. He was feeling so tense that he did not even bother about underwear, although he looked in the drawer as a matter of habit. He emptied a jewel case into his bag, then went to the man's dressing table and systematically went through it, taking a gold watch, cuff links, collar studs, even a silver knobbed cane. Then he marched to the door of the flat, put out the lights, closed the door behind him, and marched out of the building, unchallenged by the porter, who was phoning for a taxi. As he walked down the steps of the building, the family passed in a Mark 10 Jaguar. It was his quickest burglary, and his most profitable to date. Even Tebbut stared with amazement as Arthur emptied out the haul in the bed. "My God, lad, did you rob a bank?" The only item he was dubious about was the gold watch; it was inscribed with the initials "P. L." Arthur said, "All right, I'll keep that," and took it, without a protest from Tebbut. He later presented it to Pauline.

Tebbut must have sensed that Arthur became reckless when angry; he lavished praise on him, and paid him fifty pounds as his share of the proceeds.

I asked Arthur, "But supposing you *had* been caught?"

"I wasn't." He said it so resentfully that I decided not to pursue the subject. But he had, in fact, told me what I wanted to know. He told me that he was so angry with Tebbut that he wanted to risk the whole enterprise. But if he had been caught, nothing would have happened to Tebbut, unless *his* fence was caught too. Arthur wanted to give up crime for a month or two; when Tebbut put pressure on him, he set out to get caught, or at least to play at Russian roulette.

Arthur's early crimes had been sexually motivated; they excited him because of their sexual undertones. Now he had become a professional, risking two years in reform school every time he did a "job" worth a few pounds. He continued to steal underwear; but he was losing the feeling of freedom, of enterprise. He was already up to his ankles in the same swamp that Haigh and Landru had drowned in. Burglary had become a "job" instead of a violation.

Something soured in his relations with Dagger Tebbut. And it was at about this time that he began to distrust him. He suspected that he was taking more than fifty percent of the proceeds. He also suspected that Tebbut would be capable of blackmailing him if he tried to sever their relations. In July 1952, Arthur still had another year at school; he made up his mind to save as much money as possible during that time and to leave for London at the end of it. He had no intention of being in Warrington when Uncle Dick came out of jail.

I asked him whether he was not attracted to other girls besides Aggie.

"Depends what you mean by attracted. There were plenty I liked. But most of the girls at school were a stupid, flashy lot."

"Did you ever try to hypnotize anyone besides Aggie?"

This was a subject he was not willing to talk about. (I was hoping he would tell me about the wife of the schoolmaster called Grose.) But he would only mention that there had been a boy at school. When he showed reluctance to talk, I never tried to press him; sooner or later, he would talk. But our sessions were closer to their termination than I expected. I never found out who the boy was. Pauline told me that she heard Arthur had tried to seduce a girl *through her brother*, but she knew no details. It might even have been Duncan McIver.

But a point *did* come when he was willing to talk about Mrs. Grose—Eileen, as he called her.

The gym master at the school he attended was a huge man with phenomenal acrobatic powers; he was also a fanatic about football; Arthur's feelings about him were, predictably, ambiguous. He told me he thought it was a pity that such a magnificent body should be wasted on such a fool. Mr. Grose was the most popular master in the school, and Pauline's boyfriend Walter (the one who was caught having intercourse with her in the entry) imitated his rolling, muscular walk.

"Drummer" Grose was unmarried when Arthur first went to the school in Slade Road. In 1950, he married a girl from Stockport, and the whole of the Slade Road football team—first and second elevens—attended the wedding and cheered him as he came out of church. Mrs. Grose was pretty in a birdlike way, and her head scarcely reached her husband's chin. All the boys who met her said how nice she was. She was a music teacher, and when it was announced that she would give afternoon classes in music at school, a number of sporting stalwarts decided to learn the piano. Most of them dropped out in a week or so.

Arthur saw her at close quarters for the first time soon after his return from Earlestow. The gym master asked him whether he knew anything about gramophones; the one she used in her musical appreciation class had gone wrong. Arthur was allowed to skip a late afternoon gym lesson to look at it. He soon discovered that someone had dropped the pickup head onto a record and broken off the point of the stylus. He told the gym master that it could easily be replaced for seven and sixpence; Mr. Grose handed over the money, and Arthur went out to the nearest radio shop for a new stylus. He returned when the school was closing. The music appreciation class was listening to Mrs. Grose as she talked about Beethoven. Most of them were the kind of boys

Arthur detested; he felt awkward and embarrassed as he put in the new stylus, feeling their eyes on him. Then Mrs. Grose turned on him with her birdlike smile. "Is it ready?" He looked at her and experienced shock. He was immediately aware that the brisk tone covered nervousness, and as her eyes met his, they wavered for a moment. He nodded without saying anything. "Could we try it then?" He started the turntable and put the needle on the record without speaking. The music came out very clearly. She said: "Marvelous! Why, that's far better than it sounded before."

Arthur told me: "It's nothing I could explain. It was one of those funny things. All the lads sitting there accepted her, but she knew I didn't. She knew it was no good putting on a show with me. I could see through her."

I suspect it may have been something to do with the admiration of the nonmechanical mind for the mechanical. Arthur's efficient taciturnity made her feel inferior. She asked him if he would like to stay and listen to the music; he said dryly that he had to go and work.

A week later, Arthur had to stay behind after school for being habitually late. On his way out of school, he saw her in the corridor. He was about to hurry past her when she stopped him. "Oh, you're the clever boy who repaired the gram. I'm so glad I met you." "Has it gone wrong again?" "I'm afraid so. Would you mind . . . ?" His heart was pounding in an odd way as he followed her. Something about her made him feel taciturn and masterful. She was not physically like Aggie, but he could sense something in common.

It took him less than five minutes to locate the trouble. In the back of the gramophone there was a socket that could be used for a spare loudspeaker or a tape recorder; she had plugged the spare loudspeaker into the recorder socket, cutting out both loudspeakers.

He pointed out what he had done. The gramophone stood on a table, and she stooped down to peer into the socket; as she did so, the cotton blouse she wore came out of the skirt, and he found he could see half an inch of pink nylon panties. He experienced a wild surge of lust that made him want to reach down and touch the smooth material. He also observed that he could see through the cotton blouse to the outline of the bra underneath. He went on pointing something out so that she would continue stooping. She asked some other question. His member was trying to rise, but was caught in the leg of his trousers. He was so absorbed in the thin line of pink nylon that he failed to notice when she straightened up. She brushed against him for a moment, and her hip rubbed against his rigid flesh.

He was not embarrassed. He again had the instinctive sense of being master of the situation. As she met his eyes, talking in her quick, nervous way, he stared into her eyes as he had often stared into Aggie's, pressing her with his dominance. He was taller than she was. Her legs were bare; he was thinking that if he ran his hand up over her knee, he would encounter the smooth silky material protecting her loins. He had a sudden conviction that if they were alone in a house, without fear of interruption, he could make her undress as he had made Aggie.

He was not listening to what she was saying; she had dropped her eyes. Then he said, "Well, I've got to get off." She smiled at him, a tense, quick smile, and then reached out and gave his hand a squeeze. "It's very kind of you. Thank you." The touch of her hand excited him; it was the first step in intimacy. He went home thinking, "That one's have-able." It was the power-feeling once again, Professor Moriarty imposing his will.

Nothing more happened for several weeks, although he saw her frequently, and she always smiled. Once she stopped to speak to him and said, "What a pity you don't like music." He said untruthfully: "I do. It's the other lads in your class I don't like." She said, "Perhaps I could give you a few private lessons?" and then suddenly caught his eyes and looked confused. As she hurried away, he said, "That'd be nice."

One sunny afternoon, he sat in an almost empty classroom, reading a book. The rest of the class was playing cricket. He hated sport, and had forged a note from Aunt Elsie stating that he was suffering from headaches and should be excused. The only other person in the room was Joe Benham, who had sprained his ankle. Benham said, "Mrs. Grose likes you, doesn't she?" "I dunno. What makes you say that?" "She seems very friendly." "I don't think so. I've repaired the gram a couple of times." Benham—who had stayed in the musical appreciation class—began to praise her. His view of her was so different from Arthur's that he experienced a sense of superiority. Benham seemed to think of her as the ideal Mother-Wife, clever, tender, understanding, sympathetic, the very person that a man like Drummer

160

Grose deserved for a mate. Arthur thought of the half inch of pink nylon drawn around her waist by elastic, and his loins stirred. He said cynically: "She's like all women. What she's made for is fucking. What she really likes is Drummer's big prick jammed right up her as far as it'll go." Benham was scandalized but, being a schoolboy, he was used to this kind of talk. "I don't think that's true. I don't think she's the type." He liked to think of her as pure and maternal.

It was unusual for Arthur to be able to feel so obviously superior to Benham. He thought of Aggie, who also struck strangers as a sweet, kind girl—which she was. She also melted with desire when Arthur pinched her nipple through her blouse. Arthur began to hold forth about the complexities of the female personality. When he saw that Benham was skeptical, he told him that Mrs. Grose was the sort of woman who could easily be dominated. She would make a good hypnotic subject.

Like most people who know nothing about hypnotism, Benham thought this was wild boasting, and said as much. And Arthur, not yet mature enough to control his annoyance at being disbelieved, declared that he would prove it by hypnotizing her.

He had not seriously considered it; he had enough on his hands with Aggie and Dagger Tebbut. But now the challenge was issued, he decided to treat it seriously. It was his view that most people achieve so little because they are cowards. Whatever his faults, Arthur Lingard was not a coward.

He knew she was due at the school on the following Monday. He took the afternoon off from school and traveled out to Widnes, ten miles away. It had been easy to work out the train she would travel on.

She looked surprised when she saw him on the almost empty platform. "What are you doing?" "Don't tell anyone. I'm supposed to be ill. I took the afternoon off to do an important TV repair job in Widnes." "Oh, I see!" She looked roguish. Before they got on to the train, she said: "You do television repairs, do you? I wish you'd look at ours sometime. The picture's always sliding." By the time they were sitting together in an empty compartment, they were on pleasant friendly terms.

She said, "I hear you suffer from headaches."

"No." Then he understood. He escaped sports by claiming to be a sufferer from chronic migraine. "I don't really. That's just to get off games. I'm good at curing headaches. . . ."

It was so easy that it was absurd. As soon as he led the conversation to hypnotism, she began to question him about it. He explained the basic principle—that it is due to perception-fatigue. She said, "I sometimes go into a sort of trance watching the telegraph poles go by the window and listening to the wheels of the train." "That's right. It's easy. I could put you into a light trance now." "Could you?" She was looking thrilled and a little frightened, the ideal state of mind for inducing a trance, since the upper levels of the mind are in conflict with the lower, and are therefore more susceptible to suggestion. "Would you like me to show you?" "If you like." The look was pleading and scared. She believed he could do it. She admitted later, his slightly bulging eyes always fascinated her. "Don't go tense. Just relax and listen to the sound of the wheels. Watch the telegraph poles go past. Just relax." He talked quietly and persuasively, and watched her tension ebb away. He began to stroke her forehead from side to side. Periodically she would start, and pull herself together. When this happened, he had to soothe her back into relaxation. She was already rather tired, having done a day's housework and shopping, and inclined to relax on the train journey to Warrington. Arthur talked on softly. "Your arms and legs feel heavy. You are completely relaxed. You are sinking backward, backward, backward, into a soft feather bed. You are more comfortable than you have ever been before. You can hear nothing but the sound of my voice. You are breathing deeply, deeply, deeply, deeply. . . ." He knew the value of sheer repetition. After five minutes of this, she seemed to be asleep. The sight of the Mersey told Arthur they were approaching Warrington. His voice was now very soft and very monotonous. He now began the dehypnotizing process. "Soon I am going to awaken you. Soon I am going to awaken you. When I count up to twenty, you will wake up feeling happy and refreshed. When I count to twenty you will wake up. . . ." As the train pulled into Warrington station, he noticed that her knees had parted as he had been whispering. He took the bottom of the skirt— a wide, orange one—cautiously in his fingers and lifted it. Her legs were bare. She was wearing white nylon panties, and through the thin material, he could see the shadow of

162

pubic hairs. The train was slowing. He dropped the dress, and counted up to twenty. Perhaps because his voice was tense, it had no effect. As they sat there, he went through the procedure again. "When I count to twenty you will wake up. One, two, three. . . ." This time, as he reached twenty, she sighed, stirred, and opened her eyes. She looked startled to see him. He asked, "How do you feel?" "Marvelous! Completely refreshed!"

As they got off the train, he asked her not to mention seeing him to her husband. She agreed immediately. The school was a short bus ride from the station. He asked her, "Can I come out and look at the TV next Saturday afternoon?" "That's not a very good time. James [her husband] has to take the cricket team to St. Helens and I usually go with them." "Make some excuse this time. Say you have a headache." She looked doubtful. The bus pulled up. He said, "What's your address?" "It's in the phone book." He took this to mean consent.

The week seemed to drag by. Every time he thought of looking up her dress, he experienced a feeling of intense will-power bordering on ecstasy. She had been sitting there, her eyes closed, while he could do what he liked. The master's wife, the woman on whom half the sixth form had a crush. What excited him most was that the circular legs of the panties had been bent upward slightly from being worn, no longer flat as they had been when she put them on. . . .

On Saturday morning the weather looked dull; he was afraid it would rain and the match would be called off. But toward afternoon it cleared. At three o'clock he was knocking on the door of a pleasant small house in Widnes, carrying his television repair bag—in case a curious neighbor noticed him—and wearing blue overalls. He thought she looked tired and nervous when she came to the door, and suspected that she had had second thoughts. He asked her how she felt.

"Miserable. I slept very badly."

For a quarter of an hour, he tinkered away with the television, which was showing a cricket match. There seemed to be nothing wrong with it. He called her in and asked her to watch it to see if it seemed improved. She sat down nervously, then said: "Yes, that seems better. You must let me pay you . . ." "No." He went behind her chair, and she sat up. "No, I don't really want . . ." He said soothingly:

"You're tired and nervy. Let me soothe it. You'll feel much better when you wake up." He had to talk persuasively for several minutes. Finally, she allowed him to stroke her forehead, but he could sense that she was resisting. In her own home, she was nervous; it was not like being on a train, where everything was somehow innocent. After ten minutes of failure, he grew impatient and decided to use the carotid procedure, which involves pressing a blood vessel near the ear; the brain is starved of blood, and the result is an almost instantaneous dizziness. He did this; she relaxed immediately. And now, although he was in a fever of desire, he determined there should be no mistakes. He went on for ten minutes more, suggesting that she was sinking into a deeper and deeper state of sleep, in which she could hear his voice. As he did so, he observed that her mouth drooped slightly open, and her thighs parted, as before. He began to feel certain of success.

A ring on the doorbell startled him, but she sat unmoved. After five minutes or so, footsteps went away down the garden path. He now proceeded to put his plan into operation. He suggested that it was evening, that she was tired and was going to sleep. "You're very tired. You want to go to bed. You stand up and go up to your bedroom." She followed his suggestions, and led him into a clean, light bedroom; to his surprise, there was only a single bed. "Now you undress. Your husband is in the room. He helps you off with your clothes." He was tense and excited as he helped her undo the buttons that ran all the way down the back of the sleeveless blouse. He watched her unclip the bra and throw it into a chair, then unzip her skirt. She slipped it off, together with a cotton waist slip. As he saw her lowering her panties, the pink ones he had seen before, he quickly took off his clothes, and moved against her as she stood, naked. She allowed him to kiss her, and one hand gripped his erection. They moved onto the bed. She lay there, passive, as he entered her, apparently sleeping. He had to order her to move her hips up and down before he could feel excited. As his climax approached, he found himself thinking how pleasant it would be now if her husband were to walk in and see him with her like this, her thighs spread apart, moving her body obediently to the rhythm of a stranger who was lying on her, engulfed by the warm mouth she had vowed to her husband. . . . It was one of his moments of supreme

164

certainty and insight, the nearest he ever came to total mental health.

After his orgasm, he moved around the room, looking through her drawers. She lay there with her legs still apart. Suddenly, he had an idea that seemed immensely exciting, the climax of the afternoon. He went back to the bed and said, "When I reach the count of twenty, you will wake up. . . ." He repeated it a dozen times. Then he moved on top of her again as he began to count. As he reached the count, she began to breath shallowly, then slowly opened her eyes. They dilated when she saw his face above her. She said, "Oh no!" This excited him so much that he began to move furiously on her. She tried to squirm from under him, then changed her mind; as he approached his climax, she began to move too; as he reached it, her eyes closed and she groaned, her vagina gripping him tightly. After a few minutes, he moved off her. She reached down and pulled the bedclothes over them both, then asked, "What's the time?" This was a disappointment; he had been hoping for tears, recriminations, pleading. He looked at the bedside clock and told her. "What time will your husband be back?" "Not for two hours or so." What baffled him was that she accepted the situation. And suddenly, he began to suspect that it was not entirely a surprise to her. The more he thought of it, the more obvious it became. She knew exactly what he wanted to do to her. That was why she looked so pale when he came; her conscience was bothering her. That was why she made the preliminary objections to hypnosis. When she woke and found him on top of her, it was too late to do anything; she could relax and enjoy it. It wasn't her fault after all. . . . In this respect, she was like Aggie; she took it for granted. Here she was, giving her body to yet another male. Men were like that. They wanted you, and you let them have you. Arthur began to feel that it was he who had been had. She had known how he felt ever since she brushed against his tumescence that day at school. . . .

He felt angry with her. He pulled back the bedclothes roughly, and sat up to look at her. She made no attempt to cover herself. He thrust his hand between her thighs, then reached out and pinched one of her nipples. She lay passively, and he began to rise again. He moved on top of her, and thrust into her. She lay passively for a while, then began to move under him. She went on moving, gasping and moan-

ing, for another ten minutes, until he reached his third
climax. Then, when he rolled off her, her hand reached down
and gently caressed his genitals as if she was saying, "Good
dog." She opened her eyes and looked at him. "You're rather
wicked, aren't you?" "So are you." "Yes, I suppose I am."
She sounded very complacent about it. He suddenly experienced a suspicion: it was a question he preferred not to ask.
Were there others . . . ?

When he traveled back to Warrington by the half past
six bus he felt tired and depressed. The great rape scene
had turned into a harmless intrigue. She had wanted to be
raped. And after she had given him food, she had persuaded
him to make love to her again, this time on the sitting room
rug. The woman was insatiable. The situation bore unpleasant resemblances to his relationship with Dagger Tebbut.
Perhaps it was that thought that depressed him most.

But his sexual urges were too strong to break with her.
He got her to give him the panties she had taken off in the
bedroom, and took them to school with him. He liked to
fondle them in his pocket during assembly, as he looked at
the gym master.

He spent another Saturday afternoon with her, and
placed her in a trance again, although she would obviously
have preferred to go straight to bed. He wanted to consoli-
date his power over her. She might be a nymphomaniac, but
she would do *his* bidding. It was disappointing that she
needed no persuasion or hypnosis to satisfy his various
whims. On their second Saturday together, she performed
an act of fellatio without being asked; she made no difficulty
at all about lowering her panties to her knees in the kitchen,
and bending over the chair while he entered from behind.
On one occasion, as she bent over a chair, he tried parting
the cheeks of her small, neat behind and pressing the swollen
head against an orifice that was obviously too small for it.
She shook her head. "That's no good." She straightened up
and went to the kitchen windowsill, took a tin of hand
cream, and handed it to him. "That will make it easier." As
he smeared it on her, he asked, "Has this happened before?"
"Of course. I'm afraid it's one of James's little eccentricit . . ."
Her voice choked into a wail of pleasure. Thinking over her
remark later, Arthur began to wonder what he had strayed

166

into. Was her husband's "devotion to the interests of the boys" more ardent than the Slade Street headmaster supposed?

The following Monday afternoon, he had an hour's detention again; as soon as it was over, he hurried to her classroom, and found Joe Benham asking questions. He waited until Benham left, then slipped his hand up her dress. "No, not here." "It's as good a place as any." A car hooted outside. "That's James waiting to take me home." "I want you first." *"Please,* Arthur. There's not time." He gripped her shoulders, and kissed her mouth very hard, then stared into her eyes. She looked helpless and weak. He said, "Come on." She followed him into the lavatory at the end of the corridor, and allowed him to pull down her panties as she bent over a lavatory basin. As always, she reached her climax with him. Unlike Aggie, she seemed able to enjoy sex anywhere and at any time.

This kind of thing satisfied him far more than the Saturdays in her house. Admittedly, her insistence on spending Saturday at home caused conflict with her husband, who wanted her to travel to matches with the team. But this in itself was a small triumph; it was simply that she preferred sex to sport. She told Arthur voluntarily that her husband was not good in bed; they had normal intercourse about once a month, and sodomy once or twice a week. He said he was afraid she might get pregnant; he admired her slim, boylike figure.

When the August holidays arrived, the matches stopped. But she had relatives at Bootle, New Brighton, and Southport, and often took weekends off to go and see them. Her husband would spend the weekend at home, coaching some of his favorite pupils in the nets. And Arthur and Eileen Grose would find a lonely beach or field, and make love.

It was her adaptability that worried Arthur. He could not feel that he was dominating her, because she did everything willingly. When he told her that his cousin Aggie was also his mistress she took the news calmly. He said with jocular malice, "Perhaps I ought to bring her round here one Saturday afternoon?" "Yes, why don't you?" "What, all three of us in bed?" "Why not? We could use James's bed—that's big enough." It seemed impossible to outrage her. But he discovered at least one trick that gave him deep satisfaction. She was so suggestible that he could induce sexual excitement in her by talking. He liked to do this in the snack bar at the station. He would sit beside her at the table in the corner, then slip a hand up her leg, and caress her through her panties. Then he would begin to talk softly. "I'm pulling them down slowly, pulling them down to your feet. . . ." It was amusing to see the misty, dreamy look come into her eyes, and her breathing come faster. "Now I'm kissing you there, pulling your thighs against my face. . . ." "Now I'm pinching your nipple as I slip into you. . . ." She would gasp as if he had entered her. "Faster and faster . . . you're moving faster and faster. . . ." Her buttocks began to wriggle on the hard chair. "And now I grip your bum, I pull it to me. . . ." Her eyes would close; she would shudder, and her face went pink. Then, very slowly, they opened, looking startled and happy. He would reach cautiously up her skirt, and feel the wet nylon between his fingers.

One day, he left her sitting at the table while he went out to the lavatory. When he came back, a young man was sitting at the table with her. He went to the counter and pretended to be studying the sandwiches. Then he caught her eye—the man was sitting with his back to him—and made a slight movement of his head towards the door. She joined him a few minutes later on the platform.

"What's happening?"

"Nothing. He asked if he could join me."

"Did you tell him I was with you?"

"No. I didn't think you'd mind."

"Why don't you take him home with you?"

She was startled. "How can I? I don't want to."

"Yes you can. Invite him back for a drink."

"I don't want to."

He stared in her eyes for a long time; finally, she turned away and went back into the café. He waited on the platform. Five minutes later, she came out. They left the station. He followed them outside and saw him open the door of a red sports car. She did not look back as the car drove away.

When he saw her a few days later, he was avid for news.

"What happened?"

"What you expected to happen."

"Where did you go?"

"He took me for a drink. Then we drove into the country."

"Not home?"

"No, it was too risky. Then he took me into a field."

"Was it nice?"

"Yes, of course."

"Did he give you anything?"

"No, of course not."

"That's pretty stupid, isn't it? What's the good of doing it if you don't do it for cash?"

"I . . . I wouldn't know how to go about it."

"No. Well I'll show you. Just stand on any busy corner in Manchester for ten minutes."

She colored.

"But I'm not a tart."

"Would you like to bet me?"

"No."

I asked him as he told me this, "You liked the thought of her being possessed by strangers?"

"Oh, no." He grinned, and I felt that he was acting a part. "I liked the thought of the money she could make."

"Are you serious?"

"Of course. She was a nympho. No man could satisfy her. She could have taken on all Manchester and still wanted more. Anyway, I knew she could make up to ten quid a time."

"But you didn't need money. You'd saved up the money Dagger had given you."

He shrugged, and again I had the feeling of evasion. I said, "So what did you do?"

"I made her take a room in Manchester, and showed her where to pick up men."

"You *made* her?"

"I suggested it to her."

"You mean when she was in a trance?"

"That's right."

He was resisting me, digging in his heels. So instead of pressing for details, I feigned lack of interest.

"And did she?"

He made a grunting, affirmative noise, and nodded. I remembered what Benham had told me, "She'd been trolling for trade—soliciting." Lingard seemed to be telling the truth.

"Did she actually give you money?"

"I made sure of that."

"And what happened to her after the divorce?"

He grinned. "He got her to go back to him, believe it or not. I told you he was kinky."

It was only later, when I had written up my notes on the episode, that I began to feel I understood it.

The sense of conquest had been vitally important for Arthur ever since he developed his elaborate fantasy of living on two planets at once. He had seduced his cousin, stolen his sister from his enemy Dick Lingard, and engineered his enemy's downfall. Eileen Grose should have been one of his most important conquests. And so she had been, according to his own account. He had seduced her by hypnotism; then, in due course, discarded her and turned her into a prostitute.

But how much of it was true? In order to know that, I would have had to find Eileen Grose and persuade her to speak as frankly as Pauline. And although I made a few inquiries, I never succeeded in tracing her.

But the facts were consistent with another version of the story. Eileen Grose was a highly sexed young woman, one of those bookish, mild-looking girls who seem to possess an unquenchable fire in the loins. No doubt she had had lovers before she met her husband. When she met him, she made the mistake of believing that he would be a magnificent lover, a sexual athlete. Within a short time, she had to recognize that he was emotionally fixated on his pupils, and preferred to make love to her in a manner suggestive of pederasty. She suggested teaching at his school because she wanted closer contact with these healthy boys who fascinated her husband. Two could play at that game. . . . Arthur Lingard may or may not have been the first to cuckold the gym master. Was she really hypnotized by him on that first Saturday afternoon, or was she only pretending? Was it Arthur who told her masterfully to stay at home on Saturday? Or did she ask him to come and look at the television set then, with every intention of seducing him?

He admitted the shock of discovering that she was sexually insatiable. To begin with, he probably didn't mind this. He was making love to the gym master's wife, and that was all that mattered. And no doubt she at first found it piquant to commit adultery with one of her husband's pupils. But a sexually insatiable woman is not likely to be satisfied with a schoolboy lover for very long. What she would like is a series of healthy stallions. Even if Arthur's power over her *was* as great as he said—and I was inclined to doubt it —the itch in her loins could not be satisfied by a schoolboy.

He must have realized this when he came back from the lavatory and found that she had picked up a young man. It is possible that he suggested that she should go off with the man. He was not sexually infatuated with her; she satisfied a sense of power; and if he ordered her to give herself to another male, he could still feel dominant and powerful. He may have followed this up by persuading her, or ordering her, to take it up professionally. But in doing so, he was only persuading her to follow her own inclinations, to revenge herself on the pansy husband with the athlete's body.

The affair had gone wrong, badly wrong. He salvaged what self-respect he could, and withdrew. It was a case of the biter bit. That was why he became evasive when he told me about it, or put on a boastful air. It was a matter on which he could not bear to be frank. Again, I had a sense of the slippery footholds and dangerous gulfs in our relationship.

During the winter of 1952, the relationship with Tebbut produced a growing sense of shame and frustration. He knew that, statistically speaking, he was bound to get caught if he continued. He prided himself on only one thing: he never allowed his hatred to appear. There was less than a year to go before he left school; when that happened, he could go where he liked. His probation would also be at an end; he could leave Tebbut behind forever.

And then, shortly after Christmas, he realized that this was an absurd dream. Tebbut had no intention of losing his source of income. He was an old man; in the winter, he suffered badly from asthma and congestion of the lungs. As soon as Arthur arrived at Tebbut's room, his first job was to empty the chamberpot that was half full of green bile. Then he had to sit and listen while the old man talked pathetically about his ailments, about not having much longer to live, punctuating his complaints with gasps and coughs, and occasionally spraying something into his mouth. But Tebbut had no intention of dying; his landlady, an immensely fat old woman who wore a straggly wig, told Arthur that he had been like this every winter for years. "I think he's better off inside. He gets bored sitting there with nothing to do." Tebbut was thinking about his old age; he wanted to spend it in comfort, and Arthur was his insurance. On December 28,

1952, there occured an event that put an end to Arthur's daydreams of escape.

It happened in the Grape Street area of central Manchester. He had spent most of a Saturday afternoon repairing a television set in a penthouse there. It was a warm, luxurious place, close to the opera house; the carpets on the floor were thicker than he had ever seen, and the bar in the corner seemed to contain as many bottles as a real pub. There were two television sets, one in the sitting room, one in the bedroom. The owner of the flat was a handsome, gray-haired man of about fifty, the kind who appears in advertisements for expensive cars: "You don't need a director's salary to drive a director's car. . . ." A manservant had let him in. The gray-haired man, whose name, according to the job card, was Simon Banks, offered him a glass of beer, which he refused, and showed him the defective set—the one in the bedroom. While he was working at it, he heard the door slam, and a girl's voice said: "I'm so sorry, I couldn't get away. I'm going to miss my train . . ." "Not if you hurry." "But I've got to change first." He peeped out of the bedroom and saw a pretty blond, about sixteen years old, flinging off her coat. As he watched, she unzipped the side of her skirt, then hurried into the bedroom next door. He heard snatches of conversation as he worked; she was apparently the daughter—or niece—of the gray-haired man; she lived here, but she was going to see her mother. Her voice charmed him; it was a spoiled, expensive voice, the voice of a girl who had been sent to the best schools and knew Switzerland and the Riviera better than Manchester. He heard her say: "Oh, damn, now I've broken my shoulder strap. That's what I get for rushing." The man said soothingly: "Don't rush. There's plenty of time. Give me your bag. I'll get the car started." He went out. No longer able to restrain his curiosity, Arthur went into the other room—he had left his bag of tools there— and glanced round. The girl was standing with her back to him, wearing a blue underslip; she was pulling up one of her stocking. Arthur's lust was instantaneous and violent; he wanted to hurl himself on her and push her onto the bed. Then she straightened up and passed beyond his range. He went back into the other bedroom. A few minutes later he heard the door slam. He waited for a moment, listening for noises. The butler seemed to be washing up glasses in the kitchen. He went quickly into the room next door. The clothes she had taken off were on the floor. There were stocking but, as far as he could see, no underwear. He crossed the room and looked into the washbasin. A pair of white panties lay there. His heart leaped with joy. He picked them up; they were of a heavy, expensive silk. He was about to thrust them into his pocket when he heard the slam of a door. He crossed the room, and was in the sitting room, bent over his bag of tools, when the butler came in with a tray of glasses and arranged them under the bar. He went back into the bedroom, and went on testing the television set, waiting all the time for the butler to leave the room, so he could return to the soft, smooth garment whose silkiness he could still feel against his fingertips. But the butler began to tidy the sitting room, then her bedroom. And a quarter of an hour later, the owner came back. He heard him say, "She just caught it!"

Before he left the bedroom, he heard the butler ask, "Will you be needing me this evening, sir?"

"No, thanks, Robert. I'm going out to dinner. You can leave when you've finished that."

"Thank you, sir."

When Arthur left the flat ten minutes later, the butler had already gone. The gray-haired man had made some friendly remarks to him, renewed his offer of a beer (again refused), and tipped him a pound.

At nine o'clock that evening, Arthur opened the door that cut off the penthouse from the rest of the building, and mounted the stairs. He rang the doorbell, as a matter of precaution, then, when there was no reply, tried his skeleton keys until he found the right one. He pushed open the door —and then stood blinking in the light. The gray-haired man was sitting on the settee, looking calm and amused. He said: "Well, well, so it's you." Arthur stood there, gaping foolishly. He had drunk two bottles of beer on the top of a bus before coming here—he found that a small amount of alcohol increased his confidence and relaxation without affecting his judgment. Now he felt oddly calm, in spite of the unexpectedness of the situation. The man was obviously not about to attack him.

"Do close the door and come in, won't you?" Arthur's mind worked quickly. If he fled, the man might give chase and catch him. If he stayed, and the man called the police, he could deny that he had broken in. He had simply rung the doorbell and been admitted. . . . But the man did not look as if he intended to call the police.

He was saying: "Yes, it's a strange thing, but I seem to have a sixth sense about such things. When I looked at you this afternoon, I knew I'd be seeing you again. Not quite so soon, of course." He was completely confident. He was bigger than Arthur, more strongly built. "I phoned the shop to find out your name. Arthur Lingard. I like that. It has literary associations . . ."

"You phoned the shop?" Arthur was alarmed.

"Only to tell them what an excellent job you'd done on the television." There was something about his manner that puzzled Arthur, something he could not place. "I thought I'd ask for you next time something went wrong." He stood up. "Now, can I offer you that drink you refused this afternoon?"

Arthur, deciding that he was going to get away with this after all, said thank you.

The man crossed to the bar.

"Would you like a beer? Or something else? Why don't you choose?" He gestured at the bottles. Arthur was still too unsure of himself to make up his mind. He said vaguely, "Oh, anything." The man mixed several things together—Arthur watched him with a sort of numb fascination—including orange juice and soda water, and ended by shaking it up in a long silver vessel with ice. He poured it into a pint mug. Arthur tasted it. It was sweet, sharp, and very pleasant. It tasted harmless.

The man asked him suddenly, "What did you intend to take?"

Arthur was caught unawares, and choked. The man repeated the question. Arthur decided that the truth would not be amiss: he was anxious not to be taken for a common sneak thief.

"Your daughter's pants."

"What!" He could see that he had succeeded in amazing the man. "You're not serious?"

Arthur nodded.

"But *why*, for God's sake?" Arthur felt himself going red. The man said: "Well, well, well, well, well. . . ."

Arthur took a long drink. The man kept murmuring: "I see. . . ." He came and sat beside Arthur, on a high bar stool.

"You find these garments attractive, do you?" Arthur nodded. "Which color do you prefer?"

Arthur said hoarsely, feeling a clod, "The ones she took off were white."

"Ah, so that's it." He helped himself to another whisky. "Of course, the ones she took off. She changed while you were here. Did you see her?"

Arthur nodded. "I went out to get a screwdriver out of the bag, and she was pulling her stockings up."

He was deliberately exaggerating his embarrassment. The man would obviously feel better if he believed that Arthur only intended to steal a pair of panties. Even rich people do not like to lose more expensive items.

Arthur thought he had the man weighed up. He was obviously kindly and rich. He was not vindictive. And he was fascinated by this embarrassed young man who had glimpsed his lovely daughter in her underwear, and had come to steal her panties for a token, like a lover stealing a lock of hair. . . . It was all rather sad and pathetic, and not at all a matter for the police. . . . And Arthur, with the correct pauses to indicate embarrassment, told of how he had gone into her bedroom after she had left and looked in the washbasin.

The man said: "Oh, the washbasin. Well, why don't we go and look?" Arthur followed him into the bedroom. The washbasin was empty. "I expect Robert tidied up before he left." He looked into a pink and gold-sprayed wickerwork basket. "Ah, here they are." He took out the white panties, and held them at arm's length by the elastic. "Yes, they are made of a rather nice material, aren't they? Well, I daresay Diana won't miss them." He held them out to Arthur, who took them awkwardly. "Thank you." "There are others if you're curious. Let's see." He pulled open the drawer of the dressing table. "How about these." He held up a black pair. For a moment, Arthur suspected that he was being mocked. But the man seemed perfectly serious. Then he said: "Look through them yourself. Take any you want to. I can get them replaced before she comes back." This struck Arthur as the height of absurdity. Open-mindedness was all very well, but. . . . He began to feel a kindly contempt for the man. He said, "It's very kind of you, but these will do." "Because she's worn them?" Arthur nodded. "And what will you do with them? Masturbate with them, I suppose?" Arthur blushed

175

and nodded. "You don't have to be embarrassed. Everyone masturbates. I do myself at least once a day. Do you wear them when you masturbate?" He led the way back into the other room. The man sat at the bar again. "How very sad. And there's Diana, probably climbing into bed with some half-witted rich idiot, or having her cunt felt in the back of a car. I wonder what she'd say if she knew how much you wanted her?" Arthur was startled at the crudeness of the man's language, but it made him feel more at ease. He laughed, and finished his drink. He was feeling strangely happy and excited.

He asked, "Don't you mind her sleeping with rich idiots?"

"What can I do? Her mother's exactly the same. They encourage each other. Both of them ignore me."

There was something in the manner in which he said this, with a limp wave of his hand, that brought a seed of suspicion to Arthur's mind. But he was feeling too happy about his situation, and how well everything was turning out, to let it worry him. He accepted the offer of another drink, and watched with interest as the man made it. The man called the ingredients. "There, a little vodka . . ." It struck Arthur as rather a lot of vodka. "White Cinzano, a touch of brandy, a touch of Campari, a slice of lemon, orange juice, ice. Shake it all up in the cocktail shaker. Then add soda water to fill up the glass." Arthur found himself thinking how pleasant it must be to be rich. But, with his imagination inflamed, it was easy to conjure up the day when he would be rich. "Ah, Duchess, have you met Professor Moriarty? Such a brilliant man."

Half an hour later, he was calling the man Simon, and hearing himself called "my dear Arthur." He felt the urge to boast about his burglaries, his hypnotic powers; obviously, Simon would listen to anything he said with sympathetic interest. But that might lose him the ground he had gained. Instead, he talked about his childhood in Penketh Street, about how Jim had seduced Aggie when she was eleven, about how Dick Lingard had seduced Pauline when she was twelve. He could see that the talk of sex obsessed Simon. He seemed to enjoy using crude four-letter words when speaking of it. He talked remarkably freely of his wife, describing her infidelities with a frankness that made Arthur feel as though they were old friends. And he was obviously fascinated by the glimpse into another world that Arthur

176

afforded. At one point, the phone rang. Simon said: "No, not this evening, my dear. As a matter of fact, I canceled one appointment. I had a dreadful headache. But it was worth it. I've got a most charming young friend here with me. . . ." He smiled at Arthur. "Well, tomorrow night, perhaps? Yes, I'll tell you all about it, every bit. Good-bye, dear."

He came and sat beside Arthur again. "Are you hungry? Have you eaten since this afternoon?" Arthur said he hadn't. "Well, let's see what we can find in the fridge." He went into the kitchen, leaving Arthur alone. Obviously, he trusted him. It seemed odd to be in a strange apartment, with no temptation to look into ladies' dressing tables. He had already seen the range of Diana's underwear, although, given a chance, he would like to examine it more closely. He took the white panties out of his pocket, and his loins stirred. He strolled into the kitchen and found Simon making a salad, taking cardboard cartons of prawns and shredded crab out of the refrigerator, and putting them on to a plate with lettuce and radishes. He ate the meal at the bar; it seemed he had never tasted anything so delicious as the creamy mayonnaise on his hard-boiled egg. He was beginning to wonder whether he might not strike up a permanent friendship with Simon. It would be delightful to be allowed to return here at any time. . . .

Simon was saying: "Tell me more about these cousins of yours. Did this Jim ever try to play with you?"

For a moment, Arthur failed to understand.

"Oh, no. He was a lot older than me. I used to play with lads of my own age."

Simon laughed. "I don't mean *that* sort of play. I mean this." He reached over playfully, and squeezed Arthur's penis through his trousers.

"Oh, no. We didn't go in for that sort of thing."

"Never? Not even the boys at school?"

Arthur noticed that Simon's hand remained where it was. He said: "Oh, yes, some of the lads at school. We called 'em fairies."

Simon took his hand away.

"And hated them, I suppose?"

"Oh, no. We didn't hate them. But, I mean . . ."

"Yes?"

"Well, it's a bit daft, isn't it, one lad with another? I mean, you can't do much to another lad, can you?"

"Why not?"

"Well, I s'pose you could. . . ."

Simon smiled in his kindly, superior way.

"But you never have?"

"Oh, yes. I've done it a few times." He was thinking of Eileen Grose in the kitchen.

"Really? But you just said . . ."

"Oh, not with a lad. With a gel. 'Smatter of fact, with the wife of one of the teachers at school."

Simon sighed. "Ah, lucky wife. You sodomized her, did you?" When Arthur looked dubious, "You stuck it up her arse?"

"Oh . . . er . . . yes."

"And did it hurt her?"

"No. Her husband used to do it. Anyway, she used hand cream."

"Yes, of course. You would. You must be very large. Do you mind if I see?"

He reached over and began unbuttoning Arthur's fly. Arthur, full of food and drink, felt no objection; he was naturally polite. Simon undid his fly from the waist downward, so it fell open. He never wore underpants. His sexual parts were well developed for his age. This was evident though his penis was now limp. Simon grasped it roughly, then caressed it with both hands. "Ah, beautiful. How beautiful young boys are. Never be ashamed of your body, my dear Arthur. It's the most beautiful thing in the world. And it can give you exquisite pleasure." He suddenly climbed off his stool, bent over, and took Arthur's still limp member into his mouth. He began to suck hungrily and greedily, occasionally removing his mouth to gasp, "The most delicious thing in the world." It was a funny sensation, the warm mouth, and the tongue tickling him, not unpleasant, but not pleasant either. He felt embarrassed that he had not washed it recently. He knew his testicles smelled, because he had been scratching them on the bus and sniffing his fingers. Simon did not seem to mind. Arthur looked away from the smooth, gray hair, thinning on top, and across the room. He thought how delicious it would be if this were Diana, in her white panties and expensive blue underskirt, trimmed with lace, kneeling between his legs and murmuring hungrily. He began to get an erection. Simon's head began to rise up and down. Arthur wished he would stop; he wanted to go and pee. Simon had unbuttoned his own trousers now, and was masturbating with one hand and he fondled Arthur's testicles with the other. He gasped, and Arthur watched the sperm rush over his fingers. He sat back on his heels; his face was red. Then he stood up and pulled up his trousers. He bent over Arthur, and, before Arthur could turn away his face, kissed him, thrusting his tongue into his mouth. "Thank you, dear boy. That was marvelous." He went over to the settee and lay down, his eyes closed. Arthur looked down at his limp penis, and saw that Diana's panties were hanging out of his pocket. He said, "Can I find your bathroom?"

"Yes, the door to the right."

After relieving his bladder, he took off his trousers, and masturbated with the panties, kissing the damp crotch. Then, feeling better, he went back into the other room. Simon smiled at him dreamily.

"Would you like to sleep here, Arthur?"

"Er . . . well, I orter be off."

"Would you like some money? More money than you could earn in a week at repairing televisions? Fifty pounds?"

"I . . . er . . . I s'pose so."

"Good. Let's go to bed. I don't want anything more to drink. I'm almost incapable as it is."

They undressed in the room where Arthur had repaired the television, and he reflected on the strangeness of fate. Simon had an erection, he saw, and when Arthur was naked, he came over and held him, kissing him. Then he felt the end of Arthur's penis, and knelt down. "Ah, a little sperm. So my efforts were not entirely fruitless." He covered it with his mouth. Arthur saw the panties sticking out of his trouser pocket, and felt embarrassed; he hoped that his host's "sixth sense" was not working.

They climbed into bed; Simon switched off the light. He had a well-made body, although his stomach was too fat; the hairs on his chest were dark, not gray. Arthur heard the noise of a tin clicking on the glass-topped table. He asked, "What are you doing?"

"I don't want to hurt you." A finger, covered with scented cream, touched his anus. He squirmed, then lay still. Simon took a long time. He kissed Arthur for ten minutes or so, and fondled his behind and genitals. By thinking about Diana, Arthur managed another erection. Simon sucked him again, then finally said, "Turn over." Arthur did so, unwill-

179

ingly. He wanted badly to say: "Look, that's enough. You've had your fun. I don't want any more." He lay there, tense with rejection. But Simon seemed not to notice. He inserted a finger into Arthur's anus, and said, "Relax." That struck Arthur as so funny that he did, in fact, relax. When the end of Simon's penis entered him, he felt distended, and thought he was going to bleed. But it seemed less painful after that. He felt it all inside him, a strange sensation, while Simon's other hand groped around at his testicles. He seemed to take a very long time; finally, after convulsive jerks, he came. Arthur found himself thinking: "So that's what it feels like to be a girl. Oh, well. . . ."

Simon did not seem to be at all sleepy. After a few minutes when he seemed to doze, he woke up again, and began whispering endearments. Then he said, "How would you like to be in this bed with Diana?" "What, all three of us?" "Why not? You on top of her and me on top of you?" Arthur giggled. "That'd be hard on her." "Oh, no. I'm sure she'd love it." Arthur could remember the spoiled, Roedean voice, and his desires rose. Simon whispered. "You can never tell, perhaps I'd convert you." "Convert me?" He hadn't realized Simon was a Christian. "You can have as many pairs of her knickers as you like. I'll save you the ones she takes off." Arthur felt suddenly disgusted. This filthy bastard thought about nothing but sex. Simon was holding his penis again. "Listen, dear boy, could you bring yourself to push that in me?" He felt revolted. "No, I'm sorry, but . . ." "But what?" "Well, you're not a girl. I'd stick it in Diana quick enough." "Please try. Just try." "No." Simon kept on for ten minutes. Finally, Arthur agreed. He lost his erection as Simon applied cream to himself, but recovered it by thinking of Diana. But when he came to climbing on to Simon, he lost it again. He felt like crying with rage. "I'm sorry, but I just can't. I've never done it before. I can't do it—not this time, anyway." He wanted to hold out some hope. "Would you like to come back here?" "Yes." "You're a sweet boy." He ran the tip of his tongue into Arthur's ear. Arthur began to feel sick.

He drifted into a doze. When he woke up, he was sleeping with his back to Simon, who had one arm around his waist. He realized he had an erection. But Simon's breathing seemed to indicate he was asleep. It all seemed very strange now, and the evening seemed to have taken place a long tim

180

ago. His stomach felt heavy, and he wanted to pee again. He thought of how Aggie had stood on the rug and removed her panties for the first time, then lay down obediently, her knees bent, opening her legs. His teeth clenched. He was Arthur Lingard, the spider at the center of the web, not a fucking fairy.

Simon's hand moved on him, up his stomach, an automatic caress. He felt an iron wave of fierce contempt. This vile, sickening, corrupt rich bastard, with his "dear boy," "dear Arthur." How *dare* he call him "Arthur" in that possessive tone? He was Arthur Lingard, whose real soul dwelt in the cold canyons of Mars, and this filthy fool would never understand the terrible force of the willpower behind those eyes. . . . He felt suddenly cold and pure. He had allowed this man to make love to him, to use him, but only because he willed it. Only because he wanted to lull him into sleep, into a sense of security. He had made a stupid mistake, breaking in before making sure the flat was empty. And he had paid for it. The master criminal had acquired another valuable piece of experience. And now it was time to go. On the other hand, this man knew his identity, knew where he lived.

Without thinking, in a cold daze of action, Arthur got out of bed and went into the other room. He bent over his tool bag, and found the heavy hammer he had brought for such emergencies. The feeling of it in his hand calmed him. Suddenly, he became detached. Now was the time to prove his mettle. He went back into the bedroom. His eyes had accustomed themselves to the dark now, and the light of a neon sign leaked in from behind the curtains. He could make out Simon's head against the pillow, and hear the level breathing. He smiled, and felt a sudden warm gush of power, of happiness. He raised the hammer carefully, and brought it down with all his force. He felt it strike, felt bone crunch under the impact. Simon seemed to jerk, then lay still. Arthur took the blanket, and pulled it up over Simon's head, felt the shape under the blanket, then struck again, then again. The third blow sank in, like hitting a soft orange.

Suddenly, he experienced something strange, a childlike feeling. He wanted to say: "I'm sorry. I didn't mean it. It's all right, isn't it?" He repressed it and felt sick. He rushed to the bathroom and vomited. He went on vomiting until his stomach was empty, and knelt there, with his cheek against

181

the cold porcelain. When he felt better, he flushed the toilet, then switched on the light, and saw that his hands were bloody: not covered with blood, as he had always imagined a murderer's hands would be, but very lightly smeared, as if he had picked up a piece of raw butcher's meat. He washed carefully at the sink, then went and dressed. He found the hammer, and washed it in the bathroom, drying it on a towel before he replaced it in the bag. He did not look at the shape in the bed. He checked carefully to see that he had left nothing behind; he dropped his glass, and the knife and fork he had used, into his bag, then spent five minutes with a towel, wiping the top of the bar and any other smooth surface that he might have touched. The television did not matter; his fingerprints were supposed to be on that.

A clock was striking five as he left the flat. He had not searched for money; he only wanted to get away as soon as possible. Outside, it was drizzling slightly. He started to walk back toward Warrington. He was halfway there when he remembered that he had told Dagger Tebbut that he meant to burgle the flat of a rich businessman in Grape Street. Moriarty had blundered again.

NINE

It was strange to wake up the next morning and remember that he was a murderer. The first thing he did was to go over his movements before he left the flat, trying to recall whether he had left anything behind, left any clue. When he felt certain that he hadn't, all anxiety disappeared. In the clear air of daylight, there was no more remorse; on the contrary, there was a certain exaltation. He was justified in killing Banks; the earth would be a better place if all such men were dead. What really frightened him, and caused a constriction of the stomach, was the sense of putting out to open sea, of

182

ceasing to be a child who could always retreat into a cocoon of imagination. Nothing he had done so far struck him as irrevocable; if the worst came to the worst, a couple of years in reform school would pay for the burglaries. But the cost of murder would be many years' detention, far more than he was willing to pay under any circumstances. Adulthood lay ahead and there could be no going back.

He was prepared to be questioned by the police. He could see that he was a natural suspect. The butler would mention that he had been at the flat that afternoon, and had left him alone with Banks. And no doubt Banks was known as a homosexual. The first thing to do was to get rid of the hammer, which could be tested for bloodstains. That was no problem. Within an hour of waking up, he had dropped the hammer into the canal, together with the knife and fork; he smashed the glass and threw it over a wall. His alibi, he decided, would be that he spent the evening at the cinema. The local one was reshowing *This Gun for Hire* with Alan Ladd, and he had seen it twice.

The alibi was never called upon. The following week, the proprietor of the television shop said, "Did you see in the paper that that bloke Banks got killed?" Arthur felt that he acted surprise brilliantly. "What? When?" When the proprietor had given the details, he said: "Funnily enough, he rang me up to say what a good job you'd done of his set. Even wanted to know your name."

And it was due to this absurd chance, I learned from Detective Inspector Cornock of the Manchester C.I.D., that Arthur was never even suspected of the murder. If Banks had rung the shop to ask Arthur's name, then obviously, he had not become friendly with Arthur in the time they had been alone together; the first thing he would have asked would have been Arthur's name. And Arthur was back at the shop some twenty minutes after the butler had left at four fifteen, and had gone out to do other jobs. Banks was queer—"one of them 'omosexualists," said the proprietor. "A murder of this sort is almost impossible to solve," Inspector Cornock told me, "because a man like Banks has so many contacts. And living so close to the center of Manchester, he might simply have picked up someone from off the streets and taken him back home."

The police did not suspect Arthur. But Tebbut did. Arthur decided not to go to see him on the Sunday after the murder. There had been other occasions when he had returned empty-handed because the flats he had marked down were occupied; Tebbut would assume it had happened again. He seldom read newspapers; perhaps he would not even hear about the murder.

On Monday evening, Arthur went out to do a private repair job near Walton Lea, and on his way back, noticed a house without lights. In twenty minutes he had collected a quantity of jewelry. He called at Dagger Tebbut's on his way home, anxious to get rid of the stuff.

Tebbut looked at it approvingly. "Nice little lot. Where did you get it?"

"Place down in Manchester . . ."

"Oh, yes, that place in Grape Street."

Arthur said quickly: "No. There was somebody at home. So I found another place."

Tebbut smiled at him in a kindly, sad manner, shaking his head.

"Now come off it, lad, you wouldn't lie to your old pal?"

"What do you mean?"

"You know what I mean, my boy. If you'd pinched this stuff on Saturday you'd 'a brought it to me yesterday." He placed his hand on Arthur's shoulder. "You don't have to lie to me, lad. I'm on your side. I know what 'appened on Saturday."

Arthur had been prepared to rebut accusations; but this friendly paternalism slipped past his guard. His face gave him away. The old man exuded concern and sympathy.

"I'm not just the bloke that gets rid of the stuff for you. I'm 'ere to steer you right, make sure you keep out of trouble. That's my job." [This was news to Arthur.] "I suppose he caught you at it and made you drop your trousers, eh?"

Arthur did not tell him the whole truth. In his version, Simon Banks had blackmailed him, forced him into bed with the threat of the police, and then, after crudely violating him, ordered him to reappear the following week. Tebbut nodded gravely.

"Well, I don't suppose you can blame 'em, that's the way they're made. But if you'll excuse me sayin' so, lad, you might've done worse than to keep in with that chap. He was rich. Might've been a good contact. . . ." He was obviously thinking in terms of burglaries. "What did you do with the 'ammer?"

"Threw it in the canal."

Tebbut shook his head and clicked his tongue.

"That was a mistake. If they suspect you, they'll drag the canal for miles. Well, let's 'ope they don't." He gave Arthur a great deal of useless advice, such as warning him never to confess if the police questioned him, and wished him better luck next time. When Arthur left, he knew he had made a mistake. Tebbut was interested in only one thing: retaining his hold over him. During the nine months of their association, Arthur had never met any friend of Tebbut's. He still had no idea of how or when he disposed of the stolen goods. The old man knew he was on to a good thing.

One piece of useful advice emerged from the episode. Tebbut told him: "If you're going to cosh somebody, don't use a hammer. It makes the blood spray nearly as bad as a chopper. The best thing's a piece of lead pipe wrapped in cloth, or a spanner with a big end. Don't carry anything that *looks* like a cosh."

In March of 1953, Tebbut's landlady died, and Arthur was surprised how much it upset him. At first, he hoped that this was a reprieve; when Tebbut talked pathetically about being forced into an old folks' home, he found it hard not to show his delight. But the district welfare officer somehow arranged for him to stay on in the house, and an old lady next door agreed to cook him two meals a day. "And I suppose Aggie could come in and do a bit of cleaning for me now 'n' again?" Aggie hated him; she said that the smell of him made her physically sick. Arthur sympathized, but persuaded her to help him; he wanted to stay on good terms with the old man until he saw his chance to escape. A week later, Aggie came home sobbing and declaring she would never go back there. Tebbut had grasped her by the neck and forced her to perform an indecent act on him. She said she didn't really mind him fumbling up her dress every time she came near him, but this was too much. "He's so strong. He's got a grip like iron. I was afraid he'd break the bones in my neck." Tebbut was becoming sex-starved; his endless snuffling and spitting was too much for the children who used to sit on his knee. Even Jane declined to be taken there on visits.

Arthur went to see him to explain. He expected Tebbut

185

to understand. But to his surprise the old man became bitter and very fierce.

"They're all the same. All they think about is themselves. Nobody ever thinks about anything but themselves." He glared at Arthur. "Well, she *got* to come back. You can make her."

"How can I?"

"Don't give me that!" The old man sounded like Napoleon reprimanding a general. "You can make her do what you like."

"You don't want me to hypnotize her into sucking you off, do you?"

"Of course I do, you bloody fool! What's wrong in that? It doesn't do no 'er 'arm. Where would you be if it wasn't for me? . . ." The tirade went on for a long time; Tebbut seemed to have surrendered to an agony of self-pity. The threats were veiled, but Arthur knew him well enough to know they were meant.

He said finally, "Well, if I get her to come back, will you let her alone for a while?"

Tebbut grumbled but agreed. Arthur kept his promise: he put Aggie into a trance, and suggested that she should feel pity for the lonely old man, who was so much like an older version of her father. This worked. For a few days, Tebbut also kept his promise; then he insisted that Arthur should persuade the girl to "do something for him." Arthur tried. But as soon as he suggested it, Aggie came out of her trance in a state of distress and refused to return to Tebbut's on any terms.

Arthur was in a state of fury. It all seemed a waste of time. He even considered running away to London with Aggie, taking the money he had saved—now nearly five hundred pounds. But while Tebbut was still alive, that was out of the question. Arthur had no doubt of what would happen. The police would receive an anonymous letter about the murder of Simon Banks, and a tip to drag the canal for the weapon. They had only to find the knife or fork—bone-handled, with a peculiar flower pattern—to know they had found their man. He was not sufficiently familiar with the law to know that such purely circumstantial evidence could never convict him.

He toyed with plans of murder, but they were not serious. The odd truth is that he detested violence and had a natural revulsion from the whole idea of murder. The conviction he had reached from reading the Notable British Trials was that murder is always a mistake. His killing of Banks was a case in point. Tebbut could not have many more years to live; although only sixty-five, he looked ten years older. He daydreamed of putting ether into the atomizer Tebbut used for his asthma, or slipping a poison into his food. But in practice, he knew he would prefer to wait for the old man to die naturally.

The end, when it did come, was absurd and unexpected. Early in the evening of April 3, 1953, Tebbut spent an hour persuading him to bring Aggie along to see him. "Let *me* talk to her. . . ." He was in a good mood. He had persuaded one of the local children to pay him a visit. He had tidied his own room up, hidden the slop basin out of sight, sprayed the room with a scented air freshener (risking an attack of asthma), and finally lured a ten-year-old girl into his room. The outcome had been satisfactory to both of them; the girl had gone off with ten shillings, a box of chocolates, and a promise to come again. Things were looking up. He tried to convince Arthur that he only wanted Aggie to keep the room tidy so that future visits would be equally successful. Now the summer was on its way, he saw his health improving, and a more active sex life. Arthur asked him frankly: "Why not pay a prostitute? They wouldn't object." Tebbut glared indignantly. "And pay five or ten quid! Not likely. Anyway, I don't like 'em." He inserted a hot poker into his jug of beer. "I'm not one of these persons that interferes with kids. I'm just an ordinary man with natural desires. I never do 'em no 'arm. All I want 's a little affection. We all need love." He was obviously sincere. Arthur decided that he would never understand the mysteries of human self-deception. He knew there was no chance of Aggie returning, unless he bullied her into it (which he did not intend to do); but for the sake of keeping the old man in a good mood, he agreed to go home and try. As it happened, Aggie had gone to bed with a headache. That would do as an excuse. He returned to Tebbut's, knocked on the door for several minutes, then, getting no reply, went round to the back of the house. As he passed the outside lavatory, Tebbut's voice called, "Is that you, Arthur?" "Yes." "Is Aggie there?" "She's in bed with a headache." There was a grunt of disgust. Arthur went on into the house and sat down. He had often wondered where Tebbut kept his money hidden, and suspected the mattress. Now the room was empty, he raised the mattress and felt underneath it. There was a great deal of brown paper there, for some reason, but no money. At this moment, he heard the back door slam. He quickly rearranged it and sat down. Tebbut came in, looking sour. "Make the fire up, will you?" He sat down in the armchair, and his eye fell on the bed. Arthur's tidying would have deceived most eyes, but not Tebbut's. "'Ello, 'ello. What's this?" "What?" "You know what!" He pointed to the bed. "I don't know what you're talking about!" The old man grew angry. "Don't you come that with me. You know as well as I do. I'm not daft. Well, listen 'ere, the day you catch Dagger Tebbut napping 'll be the day he's in his coffin. . . ." His fierce, red-eyed glare always had the effect of cowing Arthur. "You an' I 'ave got along all right so far, but if you start trying to cheat on me, you'll rue the day." Arthur felt cautiously defiant. He said: "It seems to me I'm the one who has to do all the trusting. I've no way of checking up on you." "No, and no more you won't 'ave, the way you're goin' on." "Why *don't* you trust me? If you gave me the address, I could get rid of the stuff and you wouldn't have to bother."

Tebbut stood up and came and bent over Arthur, prodding him in the chest—a favorite trick when he wanted to intimidate. "I'll tell you why I don't trust you. Because I know you don't treat *me* fair. Don't tell me you never find cash when you're 'elping yourself to jewelry. A lot of women keep their spare cash among their underwear. But you make sure I never get any of it, don't you? We're supposed to be partners, remember?"

Arthur was furious. It was true that he pocketed the cash he found; but he felt that this was his own. His arrangement with Tebbut only concerned things that needed selling.

He said: "Why shouldn't I? The cash is nothing to do with you!"

"We're partners! And if that's the attitude you're goin' to take, then bang goes your fifty percent. Don't try and lie to me. You've just admitted it. From now on, you keep the cash and I take seventy-five percent!"

He nodded to emphasize the words, then moved backward and sat on the bed. He immediately leaped up with a yell, and a cat shot from under him and out of the door. Arthur had half noticed the thing coming in. He had left the back door open when he came into the house; it must have wandered in, and then, finding the door of Tebbut's room open, come in to share the warmth. Tebbut looked so funny, with his wild leap, that Arthur burst out laughing. Tebbut went red with rage and roared: "Can't stand cats! Who let it in?" He always claimed that cats brought on his attacks of asthma. "I didn't. It must have wandered in the back door. I'll let it out." He found the cat by the back door and allowed it to slip into the yard. When he came back, he found Tebbut coughing and gasping into the slop basin. The atmosphere was full of smoke—Arthur's slamming of the door had made the smoke from the fire billow into the room. Tebbut pointed to the shelf, where he kept his inhaler, and Arthur handed it to him. He stood watching the old man cough and splutter into the basin, sitting on the edge of the bed, his attempts at speech lost in the gasps and wheezes. And quite abruptly, it struck Arthur that the old man was at his mercy. He was far too powerful for Arthur to have attacked him under normal circumstances. But now, as he coughed and vomited phlegm into the basin, and tried to work the atomizer with the other hand, he was obviously helpless.

It was one of those decisions of a moment that came without calculation. He had hated Tebbut for a long time and had suppressed it until he loathed him with every atom of his being. And he had the weapon to hand. His bag stood behind the door—he had brought a few stolen items earlier—with a heavy spanner wrapped in a yellow duster. One good blow ought to do it. . . . Moving deliberately, so as not to attract attention, he bent over the bag and took out the spanner. Holding it behind him, he went over to Tebbut, an anxious and sympathetic expression on his face, the weight of the spanner giving him reassurance. At that moment he was determined to kill Tebbut, even if it meant a struggle and battering his skull to a bloody pulp.

Tebbut must have felt some intimation of danger as the spanner came down, for he looked up, so that the blow caught him on the right temple instead of on the back of his bent head. To Arthur's amazement, his eyes remained open, and he started to stand up, the basin of phlegm spilling over Arthur's legs and shoes. Arthur found himself striking automatically, with a kind of horror, wondering whether the old

189

man had a metal skull. After the second blow, Tebbut fell back on the bed, but he continued to try to force himself back up. Arthur aimed at the forehead, striking with all his strength, wondering if Tebbut would manage to force out the scream that seemed to be choking in his throat. He lost count of the blows. The end of the spanner came out of the yellow duster, drawing blood, and he stopped. Tebbut's eyelids were still fluttering. Arthur was feeling sick again. He had been afraid that his blows were having no effect. And even now, when he felt exhausted, the old man was still alive. He was apparently unkillable.

Ten minutes went by. The old man seemed to be unconscious, and his breathing was scarcely audible. Blood had run from the split in his forehead onto the coverlet of the bed, and bruises were beginning to appear. Yet he was alive. Arthur thought of trying to suffocate him with a pillow, but felt he had no strength in his arms. Outside, rain was beating against the windows, and the wind had sprung up. A gust of smoke came out of the fire and blew into the room.

Arthur shook himself out of his apathy. He saw suddenly that he had one chance. If the old man died, he would be the first suspect . . . unless it appeared accidental. The face was bruised, but not badly cut, thanks to the yellow duster. But if he fell with his face into the fire, that thick white smoke would probably suffocate him, and the death would have a good chance of appearing accidental.

The fire was burning through; it was a low grate, almost on floor level. Arthur shoveled on more coal. Then he crossed to the bed. He was afraid Tebbut would struggle again when he tried to move him, and was prepared this time to use the naked spanner on him. It proved to be unnecessary. He dragged him off the bed and on to the floor, noticing the odd rigidity of his right arm (from which I would infer that Tebbut had suffered a stroke or brain hemorrhage), then half lifted and half pulled him across to the hearth. The most difficult part was placing his face in the fireplace; although the body was inanimate, it seemed to have a will of its own, and rolled out into the hearth. He finally achieved what he wanted by pulling the grate forward with the poker, and although it slipped back as Tebbut's head rested on it, the head stayed in place.

He stood there, looking down at the body stretched out across the floor, the head surrounded by white smoke, expecting him to choke and move. He was also afraid that the old lady next door might have heard the noise and suspect something. When the body lay still, he went over, and tried to feel the heart, then the pulse. As far as he could tell, Tebbut was dead. He tried to bend the right arm upward, so that it would look as if he had tried to protect himself as he fell, but it refused to stay in place, and the head seemed about to slip off the unburned coal. He decided to leave things as they were. Before he left the room, he remembered the bedspread; it had a few spots of blood on it. He folded it carefully and put it in his bag. Then he made his way through the kitchen and out the back door. It was nearly midnight.

Back in Penketh Street, he burned the bedspread in the firegrate with paraffin. He dropped his trousers into the copper, and washed his shoes in the sink with cold water. In the night, he woke up several times, and was tempted to go to see what had happened to Tebbut. But whenever he thought of the room, he felt revulsion. The next morning, he woke up feeling feverish and sick, and vomited for half an hour, until his stomach seemed to be twisting in nervous convulsions. Then he lay on his bed in the front room, his eyes closed. At half past eleven, Aunt Elsie came into the room and said, " 'Eh up, your friend's dead." "What?" "Old Tebbut, he's been found dead." "What happened?" "He fell in the fire. They say there's nothing left of his face."

The inquest showed that Tebbut had collapsed into the fire after a mild stroke. Arthur was not even questioned. The whole thing seemed anticlimactic. He should have felt enormous relief to be free of Tebbut. Instead, he felt empty.

I have explained that his description of the seduction of Aggie seemed to constitute a turning point in our relationship. I tried not to allow this to become obvious; I redoubled my efforts to make him feel that I understood and sympathized with him. But I had a sensation of walking on a tightrope—a sensation I could not fully understand when I tried to rationalize it. When he had described to me his sexual obsession with Pauline, his first burglary, his excursions into Martian fantasy, I had a feeling that this was a catharsis that left him stronger and healthier. He once referred jokingly to me as his biographer; and to a large extent, this was true. It was as if the book I intended to write about him would be

191

his apologia, his ultimate justification. As our sessions continued into August, this ceased to be true. He talked less willingly, was inclined to repeat things he had already said, or to waste whole afternoons rambling about his likes and dislikes. He might begin: "You know the trouble with the English, don't you? They're stupid and lazy. They've got self-confidence and nothing to be confident about. This bloke who used to run Earlestow. . . ." And for the next hour he would tell anecdotes about the headmaster of the reform school, digressing every minute or so to refer to things he had already told me, or to read aloud some pseudophilosophical passage from his notebook. He spent days describing the books of Burroughs and Merritt, quoting whole pages from memory, and insisting that this was "real literature," not the "snob stuff they teach in schools." Whenever he became self-assertive and argumentative, I felt that he was playacting, and that he was trying to conceal something.

He was particularly elusive when I tried to persuade him to talk about the period between the murder of Tebbut and his attempted rape in late 1953. He admitted that he had been severely depressed for most of the year. What happened, I believe, is that he had pushed himself to a point of emotional exhaustion. The past year had been too much for a fifteen-year-old; he did not have the resources of will or emotion to meet it. So instead of experiencing a sense of happiness and release after Tebbut's death, he sank into a state of exhausted inactivity, and experienced a sense of meaninglessness. He needed someone to comfort him and provide an emotional outlet; in fact, he needed Pauline, and she was no longer at home. Aggie was no substitute; his dominance meant that he felt a kindly contempt toward her. When I tried to get him to talk about Aggie, he became evasive. He was interested in some other girl who reminded him of Pauline, but I never learned her name, or whether the interest was returned. I assume not. He felt permanently tired and depressed, and seemed to become accident-prone. In February, he collapsed on the pavement during an epileptic attack and cut his forehead so badly that he needed eight stitches in it. Later in the year he spilled a kettle of boiling water on his foot and could not walk for several weeks. He told me that he committed no more burglaries during 1953, but that he began stealing panties from clotheslines. He felt will-less and defeated. In this state, the sexual itch became more violent. One day when he was creeping through someone's backyard, he saw a twelve-year-old girl having a bath in a tin tub in the kitchen, and he again began to have fantasies about rape. He had read of an American youth who had committed some hundreds of rapes before he was caught, and began to wonder whether this was not an indispensable experience for a future Moriarty.

In July, he left school, and the probation officer congratulated him on keeping out of trouble for so long. He found a job with a radio shop in Warrington. The shop already had an engineer who traveled around in a van putting up aerials and bringing in sets for repair; so Arthur spent most of his time in the back of the shop. Occasionally, he went out in the van with the engineer; but he was always overlooked when in strange houses. He found he enjoyed putting up aerials on roofs; the sense of being up above the city, even on a windy day, produced a momentary exaltation. But he had the chance only when the other engineer was ill. He received a bonus, "danger money," and liked to do the job himself. For reading, he turned to Jeffrey Farnol, Richard Jefferies, and the animal books of Henry Williamson. This gave him momentary satisfaction and acted as a kind of drug. But he could not understand the perpetually tense and dissatisfied feeling, like wearing wet clothes. Even the news that Aggie was pregnant failed to arouse any interest. He felt it was irrelevant. He told her that if she could find an abortionist, he would pay. She did nothing about it, but after five months, she had a miscarriage, and burned the fetus in the copper fire.

His only crimes in the remainder of 1953, apart from the occasional underwear theft from a clothesline, were a rape, a near-rape, and an attempted rape.

The rape occurred one winter evening when he was returning from the cinema, walking along the canal bank. He liked to walk this way, in case he passed backyards with washing on the line. While he was peering over a fence, trying to distinguish the ouline of clothes on a line, he heard a boy and a girl say good-night. A few minutes later, the girl passed him, walking quickly. She was startled when she heard his footsteps behind her, and walked more quickly. He had no weapon with him, but she seemed small. He walked with quick strides, and she suddenly broke into a kind of trot, her hands in the pockets of her coat. A hundred yards farther along, she could turn into a lighted street. He overtook her, and grabbed her shoulder. She said, "Oh, no, please." He pulled her round, and pressed his lips to her face. She tried to push him away, halfheartedly. "Please, you can't. It's my period." There was almost no roughness involved; she was obviously terrified. He said, "I won't hurt you," and bent her backward by tightening his arms round her waist. She allowed herself to be lowered to the bank. He began to unbutton her coat—they were enormous buttons. She lay there numbly. Impatient, he pushed up her dress, and experienced a surge of ecstatic lust as he felt the bare flesh above the stockings. She tried to hold his wrists as he fumbled with her knickers; they seemed to be crepe nylon briefs. He said, "Stop that, or I'll hurt you." He was talking in a deliberately guttural voice, so as not to be recognized. She made no attempt to keep her legs together; he even got the impression she opened them voluntarily. When he felt her genitals, he found they were wet and slippery. He said, "I'm not the first tonight, am I?" "Yes, you are." But it was obviously untrue. She was too easy to enter, and after two thrusts, he came inside her. As he lay, relaxed, on top of her, she said, "Please, can I go now?" He rolled off her, lying down. "Please, could I have my knickers?" He groped around and found them. She snatched them, and rushed off, saying nothing. It was pleasanter in retrospect than in actuality. There had been no surge of triumph as he entered her, but thinking later, "I've raped a girl, right after her boyfriend had done it," he felt again a flickering of the old Moriarty feeling, the sense of power. It lent sweetness to his onanistic fantasies. He wished he had remembered to ask her name; it would have been pleasant to look at her by daylight.

The success of this first venture might have turned his energies in the direction of rape; but his second attempt made him aware of the risk. He began to hang around on the canal bank late at night, hiding behind his bush, trying to keep warm. He could seldom stand the cold for more than an hour. Courting couples came past, and occasionally girls who were alone; but there was usually someone within hailing distance. One night, cold and angry, he was walking back home when he heard someone approaching. He stood back against the supports of a bridge, and could hardly believe his luck when a girl came past. He walked behind her, as he had before, and she looked around nervously, and said, "Who's that?" He reached her in two strides and grabbed her. This one fought and kicked, so that he finally threw her down on the canal bank and hissed, "I'll kill you if you don't lie still." This made her quiet. She asked, "What do you want?" and he said, "You know what I want." He unbuttoned his fly, and lay on top of her. She said: "I know you. You're Arthur Lingard." "Who are you?" Then he recognized her face in the half-light: it was the plump thirteen-year-old girl who used to visit Dagger Tebbut. He was tempted to let her go, but felt that he would regret it afterwards. He said, "Well, you won't mind what I do to you after what you let him do." "Who?" "Mr. Tebbut." "Oh, you're a liar. He never did that to me." She knew what he meant; he now had his hand up her skirt, in spite of her resistance. She seemed to be wearing woolen school knickers with elastic in the legs. He said: "Come on. If you let me do it, I'll give you more money than he ever did." "I don't want to." "Come on, I'll give you two quid. I'll give it you now." He put his hand into his jacket pocket and took out the two pounds notes he had there. "Here, take 'em." "No." But she took them. While her hand was engaged with the money, he succeeded in getting past her guard and penetrating the elastic. "No, you can't do it that way. Just the same way he used to." He felt violent and angry, prepared to strangle her and throw her into the canal if necessary. His bare stomach was getting cold and he was losing his excitement in all the bargaining. He said, "You'll do it the way I like it, you bloody little whore." She evidently decided it was not worth the struggle. But she had been telling the truth. She was a virgin. When he thrust into the tight orifice, he met an obstruction. He pushed against it while she gasped, "You can't." The end of his member seemed to bend, as if pushing against a wall. He decided to admit defeat. "All right. Well do it for me like you did for Tebbut." "Let me get up then." "No, lie there." She held him as he pushed against her stomach, and seemed to experience a certain excitement as his seed covered her fingers. When she had pulled up her knickers again, and he had buttoned his trousers, he took her by the shoulders and kissed her, pushing his tongue into her mouth. She responded with her own tongue, and said: "Why didn't you do that to begin with? Givin' me a fright like that. . . ."

But as he walked home, he sank into deep depression. Rape was not what it was cracked up to be. It was not the ecstatic plunge into the receptive warmth of a woman's most private spot, but a messy fumbling with clothes and flesh and buttons. Moreover, she stank, a stale smell that reminded him of the white mice Albert used to keep. He thought of Aggie, and suddenly felt so sorry for himself that he wanted to cry.

One day, Aggie came in and said, "Vera Widdup reckons you raped her." "What!" The name of the thirteen-year-old schoolgirl was Peggy Childs; so obviously, Vera Widdup was the other. Presumably Peggy Childs had repeated the story of the attack until it had reached the ear of the other girl. He was now known in the district as a rapist. Nothing further happened; no one accused him. But he began to feel that people were looking at him oddly, that shopkeepers deliberately ignored him or gave precedence to other customers. Aggie's low vitality angered him; he felt she was a drag on him. For no reason at all, a feeling of watery fear would invade his stomach. Worse still, with normal parole, Uncle Dick would be out of prison in a month or so.

He found some relief in the reading of pornography. In Salford, he found a shop run by an old Cockney that allowed him to purchase a paperback edition of *Pauline, The Memoirs of an Opera Singer* for five pounds, and then exchange it when he had read it for other classics, all printed in Holland: *Memoirs of Dolly Morton, The Pearl, Teleny, Fanny Hill,* De Sade's *Justine,* and medical volumes on sexual perversion. Then he began to observe the child who lived next door to the church at the end of the street, a slim, blond little girl named Iris Franklin. He had seen her in shops; she struck him as exceptionally lovely, and she began to play a part in his sexual daydreams. It began to seem to him that it would be very pleasant to have intercourse with a child of that age. But he was aware of the danger. He was now sixteen, old enough to be treated very severely. There was a great deal of juvenile violence in the Manchester area in 1954, and judges were handing out long sentences.

The girl occupied his thoughts a great deal of the time. He watched her movements closely. Her father worked nights at an engineering firm in Salford, so she was often allowed to play until well after dusk. The church was seldom used in the evenings. If he could drag her into the yard behind it, he would be sheltered by a high wall. . . . But the risk struck him as too great. Then it occurred to him that perhaps he could ensure in advance. The probation officer still came to the house—Albert's latest exploits included selling lead from a church roof and breaking into a grocery store —and often remarked that Arthur was looking tired and rundown. The next time she made this observation, Arthur said darkly: "No wonder. I daren't eat anything in this house." "Why ever not?" "Somebody's putting poison in my food. I get sick after nearly every meal." For a while, the officer took him seriously, and asked Aggie whether she had ever seen Aunt Elsie sprinkling a white powder on Arthur's food. Aggie told Aunt Elsie, who confronted the probation officer, and said indignantly, "Either he's batty, or he's got his own reason for telling lies." The gray-haired lady said: "Oh, but I'm sure he's not lying deliberately. He's mentally sick."

When this was reported back to Arthur, he knew he had achieved his object. One evening, walking down Penketh Street at dusk, he saw the child picking Michaelmas daisies in the yard of the church building. She was alone and there seemed to be no one else around. He stood watching her, then said, "There's prettier ones around the back." She smiled at him. "Are there? Wouldn't anyone mind?" "I don't think so." "I'll go and look in a moment." He hurried back home. His bag of tools was in the living room, and Aunt Elsie and a neighbor were in there. It would look obvious if he rushed in and grabbed the bag. But there were flatirons on the kitchen shelf. He grabbed one of these, pushed it into his pocket, and went back up the street. The child was still there. He stood on the opposite side of the street, watching her. Suddenly, he had ceased to feel bored and miserable. He was the hunter, tensing all his faculties for stalking. It was beginning to get dark; if she stayed out ten minutes longer, he might risk attacking her in the front of the church. Then he saw her go around the side of the church. He waited for a moment, then went across the road. He walked quietly along the gravel path, and peeped around the corner. She was standing with her back to him, breaking twigs off a laurel brush. He took the iron out of his pocket and leaped forward. But he had not noticed the bent iron bar that ran from the corner of the church into the ground—some kind of support. He tripped, then recovered himself; but she had time to turn round. He had not realized that a child could scream so piercingly. He raised the iron and struck her on the forehead; she dropped to the ground. But he could already hear someone saying, "What was that?" and a moment later, a woman's voice screamed, "Iris!" He ran around the other side of the church, and jumped over the low wall that separated it from the main road. He deliberately slowed his pace as he walked along the lighted street, his heart thumping.

When he returned home half an hour later, he knew something was wrong. Two or three people outside looked at him. And the police were waiting. Aunt Elsie said, "What have you done with that iron?" "Iron? I don't know what you're talking about." But it was no use. An old busybody had been watching him out of an upstairs window as he stood waiting for the girl to go into the backyard; she saw the bulge in his pocket as he stood there, and saw that he was watching the child. The girl herself could not identify him as her assailant—she said it had happened too quickly—but she was able to say that he had advised her to go and look for flowers in the backyard of the church. She had been rather suspicious then, for she knew the backyard far better than he did, and knew there were only a few weeds and laurel bushes.

His "insurance" paid full dividends. The probation officer testified that he had been mentally deranged for weeks before the attack, refusing to eat and believing that his food was poisoned. His "unfortunate background" was brought up, and the story of Uncle Dick's misappropriation of their legacy and seduction of Pauline was told in court. The inference was that Arthur was under mental strain because of his fear of what would happen when Dick Lingard came out of Strangeways. The judge remarked that he could not see why such anxiety should take the form of an attack on a child, but in general, he was sympathetic. Fortunately, the child had been unharmed except for a bump on the forehead. Arthur was placed on further probation, on condition that he was given psychiatric treatment.

TEN

I had the story of the attempted rape, not from Arthur himself, but from the probation officer, Miss Ramsay, who had retired to live at Blackpool. Arthur's account of it had been evasive and confused, and I could perfectly understand why. It was not something he would care to remember, even though he had, in a sense, outwitted the police.

And this, it seemed to me, explained the relative failure of our sessions during the first two weeks of August. From now on, his career ran downhill; the master criminal lost his touch, and allowed himself to be caught in two minor burglaries and a crude attempt to swindle housewives. Then there was the *crime passionel,* the murder of a girl who reminded him of his sister, the subsequent murder of an old farmer in the course of a burglary, and the gradual breakdown. Yes, I could understand the breakdown now. His enormous ambitions had collapsed into this boring and humiliating reality. It certainly explained why he had played this elaborate game of pretending to be stupider than he was; it must have provided a certain satisfaction to feel that he was still an unknown quantity to his jailers, a potential Netchaev planning their downfall. . . .

As I now saw it, my task was to persuade him to face up to his failure as a crook. I had to make him see that he had been a victim of society, and that, even at this late stage, society could make amends. The war had deprived him of his parents and of the secure, middle-class childhood that was his right. What would have happened if he had remained in Barnet and there had been no war? He would have done well at school, obtained a scholarship to a university, perhaps turned his imagination to account in becoming a writer. I had to make him see that it was not too late. The Master

Criminal idea had been a childish daydream, understandable enough in its context; but where, in fact, had it led him? Into this cul de sac of criminality. He had committed murder—four times. But he had been under age when he killed Banks and Tebbut; they were crimes of immaturity. And he had paid for the murder of the farmer with eight years of his life. That left the *crime passionel*. What he did about that would be his own affair. My own feeling was that if he was to be cured completely, he would have to be persuaded to confess. In view of his subsequent history, a plea that it had been committed when his balance of mind was disturbed would be almost certain to be accepted. If he confessed now —when he still had time to serve—there was a good chance that he might escape a further sentence. And then there would be a chance of rebuilding his life, making him turn away from the paranoiac daydreams. There was no reason why he should not marry and have children.

I tried putting this idea to him—very cautiously—after his description of his second attempted rape. I pointed out the absurd gap between the daydream of rape and the reality. But he shrugged, as if I had made a remark that was too platitudinous to consider, and changed the subject. He was jumpy and nervous, and his forehead twitched as he talked. He was aware of this, and kept trying to hold it still with his hand. Before I left, I decided to give him a sedative. As I searched, I glanced up from my bag, and caught him regarding me with active dislike. He looked away quickly.

August 15 had been a thundery, oppressive day. The tall weeds that overshadowed the stream at the end of my garden were drooping limply. I sat on a deck chair opposite my wife, listening to the distant shouts of children at the swimming pool, and tried to concentrate on a novel about Maigret. I was trying to ignore an apparently irrational feeling of foreboding. The telephone rang, and I started nervously. My ten-year-old son called, "It's Mr. Slessor for you, Dad." I did not look at my wife as I stood up; she sometimes has an uncomfortable capacity to read my thoughts.

Frank Slessor said: "I'm afraid this is serious news. Lingard has attacked one of the guards. We've had to put him in a straitjacket. Could you come over here right away?"

"Of course. Is the guard all right?"

"Only just a slight stab wound in the neck."

"Thank God for that."

I tried to throw off the feeling of depression and guilt as I drove out to Rose Hill. I had not seen Arthur Lingard for two days. After the last interview, I had wondered if perhaps I was seeing him too often. So I decided to leave him for a week, let him think back over what he had told me, and make up his mind how much more he wanted to tell me. I had to talk myself into it; something told me it might be an evasion. Now I knew my instinct had been right.

The governor was waiting for me at the gate. As we passed the window of the recreation room, I saw that the other prisoners were standing in groups, talking; no one seemed to be watching television. Lingard's latest outburst obviously provided material for endless gossip.

I went to see the guard, who was in bed in the governor's house. The knife had penetrated the soft part of the shoulder near the neck, severing the muscle; it would be painful, but not dangerous. The guard's name was Hyams, a middle-aged man who got on well with the prisoners and was well liked. He called Lingard by his Christian name.

It seemed that Arthur had allowed him to read his notebooks—Hyams had vague literary ambitions. But two nights ago, Arthur had come out from the lavatory and found Hyams looking at something he had been writing. He had snatched the book from him and called him a spy. Hyams apologized, and Arthur calmed down. On the previous day he had been sullen and quiet, but said little. But he had apparently been using a small piece of a sharpening-stone to grind down a hacksaw blade into a knife. He had plunged this weapon into Hyams' back as he left the room, carrying a food tray.

Hyams looked very pale and tired, understandably. The prison doctor had just finished bandaging him. He confirmed that the wound was not dangerous, but that the guard was suffering from shock.

I asked Hyams, "Did you see anything in the notebook that explained why he was so angry?"

"No. It seemed to be a morbid sort of poem called 'Preparations for My Burial.' I couldn't see anything wrong with it."

I asked the governor, "Do you know whether he's destroyed it?"

"He tried to. He seems to have sliced the pages up with the knife. It's over there."

To say that Lingard had sliced the pages up was an understatement. He seemed to have turned them into a fretwork of tiny pieces, many of them shaped like a splinter of glass—a long, pointed triangle. I looked at the curious-looking heap in bewilderment. If he had wanted to destroy the pages, why not flush them down the lavatory?

I was shocked when I saw Arthur Lingard. His face was badly cut and bruised—it had taken three guards to subdue him, and they had done it very roughly, believing that he had killed Hyams—and he was lying on the bed, his arms tied across his chest, his feet strapped together. But his eyes were as dull as lead. All intelligence had gone out of them. He was breathing in a shallow, irregular manner. And as I looked down at him, I knew that he had retreated into some dark world of subjectivity. Perhaps he was wandering through the forests of Mars?

I tried talking to him; it was useless. I questioned the guards who had been with him over the past forty-eight hours. They could tell me very little; he had been sullen and taciturn, and had apparently been writing or drawing much of the time. Some of the drawings were lying around. Most of them were of women, some naked, some dressed. The only curious thing about them was that they seemed to be elongated, so their curves were scarcely noticeable.

There was nothing more I could do. I told the governor to ring me if there was any further development. Then I drove home very slowly. What had happened? What had gone wrong? Where had I made my mistake?

Back at home I brooded over the drawings, and tried to put myself in his place. He had been telling me a great deal about sex. It may seem that some of my descriptions have been overdetailed, but they are sexless compared to the accounts he actually gave me. He went in for minute physical detail, details of smells, of textures, of his actual procedure. (Of his rape, for example; he had mentally photographed every detail: the girl's panties, her underskirt, her breasts, the amount of pubic hair, the lack of development of the vulva, the slackness of her mouth, the goose pimples on her thighs; he even claimed that the angle of her vagina was slightly different from that of Aggie or Eileen Grose.) I had assumed that this excess of detail was due to

202

frustration; he had been deprived of sex for several years. But could it have been simply that this strange power of imagination, that enabled him to recite pages of Merritt and Burroughs, had captured every detail of his sexual experiences, so that he was merely trying to be precise? Then with such a detailed memory of the past, his sexual drives must have achieved a painful intensity. His sexual motor was overheating; I saw these drawings as an attempt to cool it down, to change women's bodies into Modigliani-like abstractions.

Then I began to understand my first mistake. Although he had stated several times that his sexual desires were so strong that he wanted to rape every woman in Manchester, I had never tried to grasp this literally. My own sexual desires are normal, I suppose, but not uncomfortably strong; I had been making an unconscious assumption that his were the same. They weren't; they were a perpetually raging furnace, like an intense pain. He could not conceive that they could ever be satisfied. Nature was to blame, God was to blame, the world was to blame. It wasn't his fault that he possessed this perpetually rigid tumor between his thighs, always throbbing and aching, longing to release its heat and tension in the moisture between a girl's thighs. And I—I was to blame too, as I sat by his bed taking notes. For all my pretended sympathy, I didn't understand either.

I set about the slow, painful business of piecing together the fragments of his notebook. It was an incredibly difficult job, for they were just so many slivers of paper covered with biro ink. Luckily, some of them were still stuck together. It was also lucky that my son and daughter are both jigsaw puzzle enthusiasts; they were able to help me. Otherwise, I think I might have decided the whole thing was a waste of time.

What finally emerged was baffling enough. It was called "Notes for My Funeral" (Hyams had remembered the title wrongly). It seemed to be a poem in free verse, printed in large, precise letters, so that a page contained only half a dozen lines. The first page read:

> I knew a man called Jack
> Jack, John, James, Jock
> Watched the beetles walking over the floor

While the knife got hot.
Jock bit Zoe's tight tits
And scissored Sarah's cunt
Haw haw haw hee hee hee.
That's two for me.

The other pages were not numbered, so it was difficult to guess their order. They made no more sense than the first page.

Through carnage to joy
And up Joy to Jannifer
Warren wouldn't like it
Warren wouldn't like it.
I dont expect the bugger would
Neither will you
11 December 1959.

Another page contained only the lines:

Give Polly my knife
She'll know what to do with it.

One page, fairly certainly the last, contained the line,

Signed Jolly John Jack James hee hee hee.

The first thing that caught my eyes was the date. Presumably it afforded some clue? Where was he in December 1959? I had a vague idea that he had been in jail, serving his second sentence for burglary. But a check with the records revealed that he had been out of jail since mid-November.

I decided that it might be worth checking. I telephoned Detective Inspector Cornock in Manchester, and asked him if he could find out for me whether the date had any significance for the Manchester police. Had there been a murder committed on that day? Or a burglary in which female underwear was taken?

The result was discouraging. Within an hour, he was back on the phone to me; the answer was no.

I sent Pauline a telegram, asking her to ring me. When she phoned, I told her that Arthur had lapsed back into a catatonic state, and asked if she could spare the time to come and see him.

"Are you sure that's wise?"

"I don't know. It's worth trying."

"All right. Will Thursday do?"

I said it would.

The following day I met Pauline at the bus stop in Darlington. I had spoken to her once—by telephone—since my first meeting with her. I felt a certain disappointment when I saw her now; she was more heavily built than I remembered, and her skin looked sallow by daylight. But within ten minutes, I had forgotten this; her vitality was like an electric current.

I told her about the poem, and handed it to her. There were still two pages that had not been reconstructed. I had managed to salvage another two lines:

> Lady Mary Monchelsea
> Dropped her drawers and did a pee.

When Pauline came to this page, she laughed:

"I know what that's about. Aggie went to live at a place called Boughton Monchelsea near Maidstone. She married a consultant to a big engineering firm. Arthur used to call her Lady Mary Duckmuck."

"Aggie married?" For some reason, I had always assumed that Aggie was dead. It was not a matter I had pursued, because I expected Arthur to tell me about it in due course. "When did she marry?"

"Oh, I dunno, about, let's see, it must have been 1955. But she was engaged to this chap for two years."

Two years. That made it 1953—when Arthur was sixteen.

"What happened?"

"Oh, I dunno. She met this bloke Brian, Brian Roll. I think it was at a dance in the park."

"That must have been in the summer, then?"

"That's right."

"How did Arthur react to that?"

"Well, I wasn't there so I can't tell you. He was dead jealous. Aggie got really upset because he used to threaten to cut this bloke's cock off."

"This Brian Roll—he couldn't have been an engineering consultant in those days, I presume."

"No, he was still a student at the Manchester Tech. A nice quiet sort of chap—I met him a couple of times."

"But why didn't Arthur try to use his power over Aggie to break it off?"

"He did. That's why she left."

"She left?"

"Yes. This bloke met her after work one day with a car and said, 'You're not going back home.' She was older then of course. She'd turned into a nice-looking girl, in a sort of pale way."

"Where did he take her to?"

"To live with his mother, I think. They lived out at Tyldesley, near Bolton."

"And can you remember if this was before or after his attack on the little girl, Iris Franklin?"

"Oh, before, I know. I always thought that was something to do with it."

I said, "You were probably right."

I drove on in silence. So Arthur had lost his pale, submissive cousin to a student of the Manchester Tech, a "nice" young man who intended to get on, who *had* got on. It must have been an unbelievable shock. If there was one thing he was sure about, it was that Aggie would always be there to sympathize and allow him to use her body. And then, at the end of one of the most depressing years of his life, she deserted him. No, that was not quite true. The "nice" young man stopped his car and said forcefully: "You're going away with me. From now on, you're mine." And Arthur was alone. No doubt the young man was so nice that he didn't even have sexual intercourse with her before they were married.

Pauline said, "I didn't tell my husband I was coming."

"No? Does he still dislike Arthur so much?"

"Well, it's not that. I s'pose Arthur'll get out of jail sometime, won't he? I'm not sure I want him dropping in on us every time he's in trouble."

"Did he do that before?"

"Well . . . to do him justice, only when he was really fed up. And he never asked for money."

I was driving along, thinking about this, when I was suddenly struck by the question I should have asked.

"When he came to see you . . . was he still interested in you sexually?"

She said casually, "Oh, I s'pose so."

"But you said that you stopped liking each other after you left Penketh Street?"

"Only for a while. Blood's thicker than water. He knew I was fond of him."

"But how did he express his sexual interest?"

"Oh, I don't know that I ought to talk about it, with him like he is."

"Please. It may be important."

She lit her third cigarette. "God, you must think I'm awful." She giggled, then became serious. "Well, I told you, he used to be a very affectionate little kid as a baby—always wanting kisses and cuddles, always saying 'She's my sister, not yours.' And he used to be the same when he came to see me—I was living in Southport at the time—I had a marvelous job as the manageress of a café. That's how I met Ernie and George. I'd give him a meal, then he'd come and sit in my flat upstairs. The first time he came, he looked so forlorn, like an overgrown schoolboy, you know the way he can look with his curly hair, and his hands hanging between his knees. So I just sat on the arm of the settee and sort of ran my fingers through his hair and said, "Well, how's the Lightning Kid?" —that was a comic character he used to read about. Then he put his head against me" (she indicated her right breast) "and said, 'She's my sister, not yours,' just like he used to." I could just imagine Arthur trying to sink into Pauline's motherly arms, to forget that he was no longer a child, that he had done things for which even Pauline could not give him absolution. "Well, then he put his head in my lap. I didn't mind that, and after a while, he puts his hand up my skirt. I said: 'Hey, that's enough of that,' and he says, ' I just wanted to see if you still like frilly pants'—he always had a thing about pants, you know. So I said something like, 'That's not what brothers do to sisters,' and he said, 'Well, it's what we always did, isn't it?' Well, to cut it short, we ended lying on the settee."

"You had intercourse?"

"Oh, no. He said, 'Do it like you used to, Polly.' So I did—we sort of pretended we was still in bed like in the old days. I know you won't believe this, but it wasn't so much sex as a sort of sentimental thing. Well, for me, anyway. It sort of reassured him, made him feel better. I could see he was low."

Yes, I could believe it. That was typical of Pauline. She knew her brother was low; it seemed common sense to offer what she had without shame. She would have given her body to any man who really needed it in the same way, without wantonness.

"Did this happen often?"

"Oh, no. Once or twice, that's all. The last time was when I told him I was going to marry George."

"I thought you married Ernie?"

"I did, but I thought about marrying George first. Anyway, that was the only time Arthur ever tried to . . . do it properly."

"To rape you?"

"Well, it wouldn't've been exactly rape, would it?"

"But he didn't?"

She giggled. "He tried to, but I was too clever. I told you I could make any man shoot his lot—nasty phrase, isn't it? What d'you really call it—organasm or something?"

"Orgasm."

"Yes. Well, that's what happened."

She lapsed into silence, her frankness temporarily exhausted by this revelation.

I said, "What was his reaction to that?"

"Well, funny really. He said, 'That was a dirty trick, wasn't it?' I just told him not to be so daft."

"And was this when he threatened to kill you?"

"No. He came back again. But I was a bit fed up. I wouldn't even let him up to the flat. 'Smatter of fact, George was in bed. So I told him to b——— to go away."

"So in fact, you and Arthur never actually engaged in incest? Not in the technical sense?"

"No, we never did. Not that Ernie believes it. That little bitch Jane dropped a few words in his ear."

So I had another clue to Arthur's later years: the attempt to return to old relationships, to the supreme security of Pauline's caresses. And he wanted to possess her—just once. He wanted to feel that Pauline had been his, that she had allowed him that final liberty that she had allowed Uncle Dick. But—for whatever reason—he never achieved it. Knowing Pauline, I cannot believe she would have refused it if she had known it was so important to him. I remembered Arthur telling me how he had felt, in those early days, that *he* was the true husband, Uncle Dick merely the lover.

And I knew again, with total certainty, that in some way Pauline was the key to Arthur Lingard's whole life. Not the sole key, perhaps. Yet a very important one. For Arthur, she symbolized something supremely important, the primeval mother who knows all and will forgive all.

It made me ask her, as we drove through the gates of Rose Hill, "Did Arthur ever admit to you that he'd committed a murder?"

She looked surprised.

"No. When?"

"At any time?"

"No. He was far too smart for that."

So Arthur had not risked telling her everything. But— and suddenly I wondered if I was being carried away, or whether this was a basic insight—he had told *me,* after he knew I had been to see Pauline. He had told someone who might tell Pauline. . . .

I saw the prison doctor as I got out of the car.

"How is he?"

"He seems to be repeating the same cycle as before. He's in a state of catatonic excitement. It isn't acute yet."

I noticed that Pauline tried to appear composed as we went into Arthur's room. But she was tense, and her hand trembled so much that she threw away a cigarette she had only just lit.

The doctor said: "He still hasn't eaten. If it goes on much longer, I think we ought to force-feed him."

He knew I disapproved of that, particularly in Arthur's case. A tube forced down the throat might remind him of Simon Banks's penis, or of Harry Tebbut's.

He was still in his straitjacket, lying with his back to the door. He did not move as we went in. Pauline walked around until she could see his face, then looked shocked. I understood why.

I said: "You mustn't assume he's worse than he is. He recovers very quickly. I think his body tends to reflect his mind far more than in most cases." I was thinking of how quickly he had recovered last time.

She stooped down beside the bed, and said, "Arthur, it's me, Pauline."

The doctor went quietly out. I understood why. I felt like an intruder too.

She said, "Arthur, do you know me?" Then she looked at me. "Could we take him out of this?"

"It could be dangerous."

"Not to me."

I knew it was no use arguing with her. A paranoiac like her brother could be passive one moment and violent the next. I went across to the bed, and helped her untie the tapes. As I did so, I thought that Arthur glanced at me. I stood back and let Pauline finish it. If he *had* glanced at me, it could mean that he preferred Pauline to untie him. I was uneasy; his face was covered with sweat, and he was trembling like a horse after a race. But if he recognized her, knew she was helping him, it was an important step.

She took a damp flannel from the washbasin, and wiped his face. I moved out of his range of vision, but stayed inside the door in case of emergency. She dried his face on a towel, then bent over him. I could not hear what she was whispering but I could guess—words of reassurance, perhaps of love. Her lips came very close to his face. I think she kissed him. I moved quietly to the door and outside, leaving it open a few inches. I knew Pauline was a strong woman, and that she knew something about judo. If Arthur attacked her, she could defend herself until I arrived.

I heard her moving around. I looked through the crack in the door, and saw she was filling a glass with water at the sink. Then she went back to him. He propped himself up on the pillow and drank the water, while she stood beside him. Then, as I watched, he reached out and touched her leg. She had good legs, as I have remarked, and she was wearing sheer stockings. I watched his hand move up the leg, under the black skirt. There could be no doubt where it had reached. She glanced across at the door. Arthur looked at it too. Then she crossed the room and closed it. I felt relieved. I didn't enjoy playing Peeping Tom.

Only about two minutes had passed by, with no sound from the room, when the governor, Frank Slessor, walked along the corridor.

"Hello? What's happening? Everything all right?"

He had a loud and cheerful voice.

I said, "His sister's visiting him."

"Oh, good." He came closer, and dropped his voice.

"Don't mind me interfering, but I think you ought to keep the door open, even though he is under restraint."

He turned the knob and pushed it open. Pauline was still standing by the bed. I must confess that I had half expected to see her in it. As the governor looked in, she nodded at us, and I saw Arthur made an abrupt movement, as if to hide something.

Pauline said: "I think he's hungry. Have you got any milk?"

I hurried off to get an orderly. Within five minutes, he was sitting up, eating the semolina pudding she spooned into his mouth. I went out with the governor.

He said: "Well, you took a bit of a risk removing the straitjacket, but he certainly seems better. What's happening? Do you think he'll keep on having these breakdowns?"

"I couldn't say. You see . . . he's got an almost insoluble problem. Do you remember a story of Henry James, where he talks about a child waking up in the middle of the night and seeing a ghost, and waking her mother? But the mother's just as terrified as the child? He's rather like that. As he comes back to everyday sanity, he sees something that makes him want to retreat into catatonia. That's the problem."

"Do you think he'll ever recover?"

It was the kind of question I could not answer; I had not even thought about it. I thought about it now, and could still see no answer.

I said: "I hope so, but I don't know."

"Then don't you think it might be better to have him moved to Broadmoor? I understand your problems—you'd rather keep him here. But he worries the other prisoners. And you know what that means."

I knew what he meant; it was a pity to endanger the success of Rose Hill, which was still in its probationary period, for the sake of one psychopath. If Slessor had known what I knew, he would have called the Medical Superintendent of Broadmoor in five minutes.

I said, "If he doesn't improve within the next day or so, I promise I'll go into it."

"After all, he could be transferred to Rampton. That's only half a day's drive from here, or a couple of hours by train. You could still see him regularly."

Pauline came out.

"I think I'd like to go now."

I looked back into the room. Lingard was fast asleep, lying on his side, his body bent into the fetal position. I thought I detected a tension in his breathing, but apart from that, his sleep seemed normal.

I told the governor to put him back in the straitjacket if there was any sign of overexcitement. Then we left.

As we drove out of the gates, she said, "Poor devil." Her voice was full of compassion.

"What do you think?"

"He's bad, isn't he? I wish I knew what was eating him?"

"Don't you?"

"No. Do you?"

"I've got an idea. I'll try to explain later."

Pauline had agreed to stay overnight. My wife was not too happy about the idea. The things I had told her about Pauline made her feel she was the scarlet woman from Revelation. But it was too much to expect Pauline to travel back to Stockport the same day; and I wanted her close, in case Arthur asked for her again.

As we drove back into Hartlepool, she said: "Would you mind stopping by Marks and Spencers?"

"No. But it's around the block. We'll have to turn back."

"Oh, never mind. This place'll do. Could you park?"

I watched with curiosity as she went into a lady's lingerie shop. Five minutes later, she was out again with a small paper bag.

I said, "Excuse my asking, but what . . . ?"

She opened the bag, and took out a pair of black nylon panties.

"Do you mind?" She slipped them over her feet, and pulled them on, arching her body in the seat. I kept my eyes firmly on the road. "I feel uncomfortable without pants."

"So that's what Arthur was hiding?"

"Yes."

"Do you mind telling me what happened?"

"Well, he put his hand up my leg. So I closed the door. When I came back he sat up on the bed and pulled my pants down. He wanted me to lie down beside him; I shook my head and pointed to the door. Then we heard voices outside, so he snatched them up off the floor and lay down."

"Did he . . . do anything after removing your pants?"

"Only the usual—put his hand up for a feel, and took it out of his pajamas."

I said nothing as we drove back home. I found myself wondering seriously whether it would be of therapeutic value to persuade Pauline to spend a night with her brother, or at least half an hour or so. Impossible, of course, and completely unethical.

My wife eyed Pauline as if she might explode at any moment. But Pauline put on her best ladylike manner: "How do you do, Mrs. Kahn. What a pretty house. You *are* lucky." And, as I had expected, they were behaving like old school chums within ten minutes; I kept expecting them to put their arms around each other.

My son called, "Dad, it's Inspector Cornock for you."

I took the phone. Cornock's voice said: "Hello, Doctor. Sorry to disturb you on a Saturday afternoon. I've just had the copy of that stuff by Lingard." I had sent Cornock a carbon copy of the "poem."

"Yes?"

"Do you happen to have the original thing near you, by any chance?"

"Yes, it's here in the room."

"Could you get it? This typescript has: 'Through carnage to joy, and up Joy to Jannifer.' Is it supposed to be Jannifer of Jennifer?"

I looked at the paper, held together with cellotape.

"It could be either, but I'd say it's an 'a'."

"That's interesting. It's an odd name, and my sergeant here tells me he remembers the murder of a girl called Jannifer Tass back in 1959."

"Where?"

"She disappeared at Annsdale—that's near Southport. Apparently they found her body a few days later at Ormskirk, ten miles away."

I sat down on the nearest chair, suddenly feeling as if my legs had lost all their strength.

"Do you know any more details?"

"Not much. I'll check up, of course. The sergeant says she disappeared on her way back from seeing her grandmother."

"Has he any idea of what month?"

"No, but it was midsummer."

"Because Lingard was in prison from June until November that year."

213

"I'll find out and ring you back. How is he now? Would he be able to answer questions?"

"Not right at the moment. He hasn't spoken since he had an attack two days ago."

When I hung up, I poured myself a whisky and drank it straight down. I stood and stared out of the window. My wife and Pauline were having tea on the lawn; my son was turning somersaults on a trampoline, and my daughter was practicing her guitar in the hammock between the apple trees. I felt as if someone had hit me on the head with a sandbag. I looked at the paper again. Jannifer. It was definitely an "a." How could I have been such an idiot? For some reason, it had never entered my head that Lingard might have committed more murders than the ones I knew about. And now I found myself staring at the names in the "poem." Zoe, Sarah, Joy, Jannifer. "Through carnage to joy." And one of them was a schoolgirl who had been murdered near Southport—where, as Pauline had just been telling me, she had worked in 1959. Arthur Lingard was a sex killer. It all followed: the panty fetichism, the rapes, the rape-murder of Evelyn Marquis. Crime and sex were indissolubly associated in his mind. And now there was no way out. An absurd thought came into my head. A few weeks before, I had found Lingard doing one of those children's puzzles that showed two houses standing in back gardens. The problem was to work out six paths between the two houses so that none of them crossed. I spent five minutes at it, and convinced myself that it could not be done; the maximum number possible was five. But Arthur Lingard had been working at it for hours and when I returned the next day, he had made several copies of the puzzle, discarding each one as it became a tangled mess of lines. At the time it had struck me that this showed his inability to reason clearly. Now I saw it as a frantic determination to solve an insoluble problem. He needed to confess to keep his sanity. But if he confessed, the price would be a lifetime in Broadmoor. The only question that remained unanswered was: What had caused the original collapse?

I sat there, dazed. I could not bring myself to go outside and face Pauline. For—although this sounds an odd thing to say—the bond between us was that we were both fond of Arthur. The reader of this account may find it impossible to believe that he excited anything but revulsion. But this is to miss the point that a psychologist's job is not to condemn but to understand. I had quite deliberately developed toward him the basic approval and protectiveness that a parent feels for a child. I thought I had come to understand how he became what he was. And now I had to recognize that I had been missing the vital point about him. And the enterprise that had occupied all my thoughts for two months collapsed and vanished. There could no longer be any question of curing him. Cure him for what? For a lifetime behind bars? *He* understood the problem: that a complete confession would be the equivalent of suicide. And in a sense, he had chosen suicide. Now I understood why he had called the poem "Notes for My Funeral."

My son came into the room. I told him that one of my patients had asked me to call and that I would be back in an hour. I wanted a chance to think. I went to the park, and sat on a bench in the hot August sunlight. I reread the "poem" a dozen times. The last line stirred a memory: "Signed Jolly John Jack James hee hee hee." Jolly John Jack. . . . Then it came back. Surely one of the Jack the Ripper letters in Madame Tussaud's had a similar phrase; something like "Dear Old Boss, You'll be hearing more about jolly Jack's work tomorrow. . . ." And was it the same letter that had some such phrase as "I'll clip off the lady's ears, ha ha. . . ." "I knew a man called Jack" was the first line of the "poem," "Jack, John, James, Jock." Why this talk of knives? Had he actually killed some of the girls with knives? Or was it another reference to the Ripper? "Give Polly my knife/ She'll know what to do with it." I was reminded of his cry about Harry Tebbut, "Don't let him stick that up me. . . ." Knives and penises—they had somehow become identified in his mind. Hand it to Pauline—this insatiable urge to commit rape, to violate every attractive girl in the world, and let her hide it inside her. . . .

When I stood up again, my doubts had vanished, I saw clearly that I had no choice. If Arthur Lingard was a multiple sex killer, it was no longer my affair; it was the concern of the police. The first thing to find out was whether he could have been the killer of Jannifer Tass, and whether the other names in the "poem" could be identified.

The first question was solved within the hour. When I arrived home, there was a message from Cornock asking me to phone him. He had the details of the murder of Jannifer Tass.

The notes—which I wrote down from his dictation—read as follows:

"June 28th, 1959. Jannifer Tass, age fourteen and a half, left home at five thirty to have tea with her grandmother, who lived in a cottage a mile away. She left her grandmother's at seven forty-five and cycled back in the direction of home. Her route took her along the edge of a golf course. Sometime toward eight, a man on the links thought he heard a scream, but assumed it was teen-agers 'larking about.' At ten thirty the girl's brother called at the grandmother's house and was told she had left. On his way back home, he found her bicycle lying in the ditch near the golf course, the front wheel slightly buckled. On the grass verge nearby there were the marks of tires. One of her shoes was found near the bicycle. Nothing more was heard of her until her body was discovered on the morning of July 1st, lying in a ditch near Ormskirk. The body was clothed, and was lying on its back, the arms by the sides, the legs together. On closer examination, it was discovered that she was wearing only socks, her school blazer, and her navy blue school uniform. Stockings, a nylon petticoat, and her panties were missing. The pathologist's report stated that she had been subjected to considerable sexual interference, traces of semen being found in the vagina, rectum, and mouth. Her forehead was badly bruised, and she had been strangled. She had been dead for about two days. No one reported seeing a stranger in the area of the golf course on the night of her disappearance, and no arrest was ever made." The medical evidence revealed, incidentally, that she had not been a virgin for a very long time.

Cornock told me he had also checked on Arthur's prison record. He was caught breaking into a radio shop in Southport on July 2, and sentenced to six months in jail. He came out in late November.

Cornock said, "I think I'd better come over and talk to you on Monday."

I was relieved that he was giving me a day's grace.

Pauline came into the room as I sat reading and rereading what I had just written down.

I asked, "Can you remember where Arthur was living before he went to prison in 1959?"

"Yes, in Preston."

"Was he working?"

"Yes. He had a job as a TV repairman."

"Have you any idea of his address in Preston?"

"It's probably in my address book." She found the small leather address book in her handbag. Arthur seemed to have had various addresses in Manchester, Leeds, Glasgow, London, and Preston; all had been crossed out. The Preston address was 14 Heather Grove, Walton le Dale.

She said: "I went there once. He was living there with two blokes. I can't remember their names. I think he'd met them in prison."

"What sort of a place was it? Quiet? Was there a landlady?"

"No. The two blokes had the house, and Arthur had a kind of holiday chalet in the garden. He said he liked it because it was so quiet. Why? What's it all about?"

I decided there was no point in keeping silent. I showed her the "poem," and told her what Cornock had told me. She was as amazed and shaken as I had been.

Her first reaction was, "Oh, no! He may be a bit of a lad, but he'd never do a thing like that."

"Are you quite sure of that? You told me you thought he'd deliberately murdered that farmer."

"Yes, but that's different. I mean, he wouldn't kill a girl for sex."

I said, "I'm afraid you're wrong. That's exactly what he did." I told her about the Evelyn Marquis case. There was only one thing I omitted to tell her: about her own resemblance to the murdered girl.

She kept repeating: "I can't believe it. He's such a gentle type of person. I just can't believe he'd be capable of a thing like that."

I thought of the sister of the Boston Strangler, who had said the same thing about her brother. And I understood Pauline's incredulity. But with the facts I now had, it was impossible to doubt that Arthur had killed Jannifer Tass. It had happened on a Saturday. Perhaps he had been to Southport to see Pauline. It was the frustrating period that she had described to me; he was angry and jealous. Driving along a quiet country road, he had seen the schoolgirl pedaling along on her bicycle. He had started to pass her, then deliberately swerved and knocked her into the ditch. She screamed—Arthur leaped out at her, and struck her on the forehead with something heavy. He picked up the unconscious girl and dragged her into the back of the van. Then he drove off to Preston. He may have strangled her there and then, or later that evening. He took her to his "chalet," and kept her there for twenty-four hours, or perhaps longer, acting out his sick fantasies with her body. Then, with the caution that was peculiar to him, he dressed her carefully and placed her back in the van. Why? Because a naked body is more likely to be noticed than one with clothes on, if someone peeped into the van. On Monday night he drove her back to a spot within ten miles of the place where he had found her—so that it would be assumed that she had been in the area ever since her disappearance—and carefully laid her out in the ditch, her heels together, her arms by her side.

It was as I thought about this that its full horror suddenly hit me. This was not a case of an impulsive murder committed in a rage. He wanted the schoolgirl on the bicycle. He made a deliberate act of choice. He could have driven past her; instead, he swerved. He could have raped her in the back of the van, and thrown her out, unconscious, in some other place. He could even have blindfolded her and kept her tied up while he possessed her. He discounted all these alternatives and killed her. For the first time since I had been dealing with Arthur Lingard, I had a sense of deliberately chosen evil.

Pauline's reaction was as healthy and straightforward as I might have expected. "If he did those things, then he's no good. He just shouldn't be alive."

As she said it, I suddenly understood Arthur's breakdown. His childhood had been unhappy. Yet unhappiness could never really touch a person like Arthur, for two reasons: he had his imagination, and he had womenfolk. And then there were those moments of absolute coziness and security when the whole world became sweet, when he felt lapped in the arms of some eternal mother. It was this basic sense of security that had given him the confidence to face the world alone as a "master criminal."

But the murder of Jannifer Tass was not the crime of a "master criminal"; it was the crime of a human fox thinking only of the satisfaction of his appetites. If the evidence had not seemed so clear, I would have said that it was precisely the type of crime that Arthur would never commit. It was not the kind of crime that could be magnified by the imagination until it became a romantic protest against society. It was the crime of a man who no longer has the self-confidence given by rich, romantic daydreams: who does something that he knows can never be justified in the eyes of his fellowmen.

What had happened, then, to turn the romantic dreamer, the lord of Mars, into a vicious child molester?

I had my answer. Pauline had given it to me earlier that day. The source of his pride and self-confidence had been crippled by the desertion of his women. The murder of Jannifer Tass had taken place when he was quarreling with Pauline about her projected marriage; the murder of Evelyn Marquis had taken place a few weeks after her marriage. And Aggie had deserted him to live with a respectable young engineer. And a few months later, he attempted his first rape murder—the twelve-year-old Iris. The pattern was perfectly clear. Arthur Lingard was taking his revenge on women. His hero was no longer Professor Moriarty, but the vindictive, semiliterate Jack the Ripper.

That evening, with Pauline's help, I settled down to make a list of all the significant dates in Arthur's life. It read as follows:

Born, November 12, 1937.

Mother killed April 1941, father, early 1942.

Evacuated to Warrington, September 1941.

Generally rebellious behavior begins in 1944, when he is seven. This was the year Pauline became Dick Lingard's mistress. Although Arthur did not discover this until December 1949, I believe he somehow sensed it.

Maggie died October 1949. Arthur's first burglary followed in November.

His first period of probation occurred in 1951, and was followed by the sentence to Earlestow, of which he served only six months, arriving back in Penketh Street in February 1952. Dick Lingard was arrested in March 1952, and was released in November 1954. The affair with Eileen Grose lasted from May 1952 until January 1953. (The seduction of Aggie had occurred about August 1950.)

The murder of Simon Banks occurred on December 28, 1952. The murder of Dagger Tebbut followed in March 1953.

Arthur's breakdown seems to date from this period. Aggie had met her future husband about May 1953, and had "eloped" with him in November. The two rapes Arthur had described to me occurred sometime during that autumn or winter, and the attempted rape-murder of Iris Franklin occurred a month after Aggie's "elopement," in December 1953.

It was after this that the dating became more difficult. Arthur had remained in the Penketh Street house until October 1954, shortly before Dick Lingard was released from jail. He had committed two more burglaries in 1954—at least, in confessing to the second one, he asked for another to be taken into account. He was warned that if he was caught again, he would be sent to prison. Pauline had the impression that he had moved to Scotland when he left Penketh Street, but the earliest of the addresses in her address book was near Clapham Common, London. She thought this was in early 1955. She was living in Blackpool at this time, working as a night club hostess, and carrying on affairs with several men. Arthur wrote to her there—she was unable to recall how he found her address. In September 1955, he wrote to her from Wormwood Scrubs; he had been caught burgling a house in Muswell Hill. On his release from prison in February 1956, he again wrote to Pauline, this time from an address in Putney. It was during his period in prison that he reestablished contact with Aggie, who wrote to him when Pauline told her he was in trouble. Aggie had been married since the previous August, and was now living at Boughton Monchelsea. He apparently visited Aggie there several times between coming out of prison, and being arrested again in September for the washing machine fraud.

After this, the dates again became vague. He served the sentence for fraud in Brixton. Early the following year, he moved back to the north, this time to Doncaster, where his address was The Dairy Farm Caravan site, near Armthorpe, and where, Pauline seemed to remember, he again worked as a radio and television repairman. He moved from Doncaster in December 1957, and Pauline heard no more of him until some time in 1958, when she found a letter from him waiting for her in the Penketh Street house. (By this time she had moved to Southport and was apparently seeing a great deal of the man she later married.) He told her in this letter that he had turned over a new leaf, and hoped to make a fortune by starting a business that would sell portable Turkish baths. He came to visit her at Southport for the first time at Christmas, 1958. She thinks that at this time he was living in Liverpool. But in early 1959, he moved to the Preston address, and worked for a firm called View-Hire with branches in Blackpool, Southport, and Lancaster. This meant that he covered the whole of northern Lancashire in his van.

The murder of Jannifer Tass occurred in June 1959, and soon after this, Arthur was serving another short term for petty theft. Pauline married in January 1960, and the Marquis murder occurred five weeks later. After this, Arthur apparently decided that he preferred Yorkshire to Lancashire. He was angry about Pauline's marriage, and made no attempt to contact her before March 1962, when they met accidentally in Salford, where she was then living.

It was in June 1962 that Pauline began to suspect that Arthur was becoming "queer." He had visited her several times at Salford—although her husband disliked him and wanted Pauline to break with him—and often talked vaguely and glowingly of future plans to make a fortune. On the afternoon of June 28, 1962, he arrived in a strange mood, and Pauline had the impression that he had been drinking or taking drugs. He talked of a plan for setting up a night club for sexual perverts in Glasgow, something that would cater for every possible taste, and asked Pauline to come with him as his manager. Pauline said vaguely that she might. Then, quite suddenly, Arthur picked up a photograph of her husband from the mantelpiece and hurled it into the fire. Pauline was indignant, and bent to pick it up. As she did so, he struck her on the head with something, and then began to wrestle with her. She was determined not to scream —her neighbors were too inclined to gossip even then—but she fought hard and determinedly. Arthur's strength amazed her. At one point, as they lay panting together on the floor, he tried to force her legs open. She told him angrily to stop it. The result terrified her. He suddenly made a very real attempt to strangle her, and when she fought back, hit her on the face several times. She scratched him badly. Then, quite suddenly, he burst into tears, begged her forgiveness, and left.

There was no doubt in her mind that he was attempting

rape. I asked her, "But you were quite determined that you didn't want him?" She shrugged. "It wasn't that. Perhaps if he'd gone about it in a different way. . . ." She stared into the empty fireplace for a long time, and sipped her third gin and tonic. "I knew then there was something wrong with him. He'd changed. I could see he'd got used to grabbing what he wanted."

Her husband flew into a rage when he found her with a black eye and other bruises and scratches, and went straight to the police. Arthur was arrested the next day at his lodgings in Stockport. But by then, Pauline had talked her husband into dropping the charge. She promised never to see or speak to Arthur again. And she heard nothing more from him until the following year, when she read that he had been arrested for the murder of the farmer.

Pauline decided to stay with us until Monday, so that Cornock could interview her at our house. On Monday morning I rang Rose Hill. Arthur was so wild and confused that they had decided to put him back into a straitjacket. Cornock asked me if I was still determined not to have Arthur transferred to the criminal lunatic asylum at Rampton. I said I would like more time to think about it. I was inclined to go out and see Arthur before Cornock arrived— so that I could give him a firsthand report. But when I asked Pauline if she would like to come, she shook her head firmly. "I couldn't face him . . . not knowing what he did to that girl." So I also decided to shirk it.

Cornock and his sergeant came in time for lunch, which we ate at a local restaurant. When I showed him the typed report—which I have quoted above—he said, "You ought to be a detective." Pauline laughed and said, "Didn't you know? —that's just what he is."

The problem that faced us should not have been abnormally difficult in a country like England. England's murder rate has remained remarkably constant throughout the twentieth century, in the area of one hundred and fifty murders a year. Of these, the greater number are solved, and even in cases where the file is still officially open, the police may be reasonably certain of the identity of the murderer, or that he has committed suicide.

It meant, then, that Cornock had to check on every unsolved sex murder in England between, say, 1955, when

Arthur left Warrington, to 1963, when he was arrested for the farmhouse murder. Cornock had come armed with a list of all such murders, and we sat side by side, looking through it. We had four names: Sarah, Zoe, Joy, and Jannifer, and we knew the identity of the last. It took us less than five minutes to arrive at a tentative identification for Sarah. On Friday, June 7, 1956, Sandy Lewis, a seventeen-year-old student at the London School of Ballet, set out to hitchhike to her home in Maidstone. With her were a twin brother and sister named Plassett, who lived in Sittingbourne. Her violated body was found in the early hours of the next morning near Wateringbury on the A.26.

There was only one other girl whose Christian name began with S, and she had been murdered in Glasgow in August 1959, when Arthur Lingard was in prison. It seemed a reasonable assumption that a girl called Sandy was probably really a Sarah. Cornock was able to telephone the Maidstone police from my home after lunch and verify this. Later in the day, he was able to speak to the detective who worked on the case, Detective Inspector Gifford of the C.I.D., and obtained full details of the murder.

Sarah Lewis often hitchhiked home for the weekend, in company with her two friends from Sittingbourne. On June 7, they took a train to Bromley, and set out to hitchhike. Within five minutes they were picked up by a man in a white minicar. He was young, well dressed, and described himself as an electronics engineer. They all talked pleasantly on the drive down. He dropped the brother and sister at a bus stop near Sittingbourne, then drove on toward Maidstone, with only Sarah Lewis in the car. It was about three o'clock on a bright afternoon; there was plenty of traffic on the road, and her friends felt no anxiety about her.

Sarah Lewis should have been home before four o'clock. When her friends, John and Margaret Plassett, rang up at six, her parents became anxious. The Plassetts reassured them. The young man had seemed polite and intelligent; perhaps he had persuaded her to drive down with him to the coast. But at nine o'clock, the Lewises notified the police, and the search for the white minicar began. It was found a few minutes before midnight by a police patrol car, on the A.26. It was empty, but there was a pair of torn panties on the floor. In the ditch, on the other side of the hedge, they found the body of Sarah Lewis. She had been strangled

223

manually and sexually assaulted, vaginally and anally. The murderer must have spent several hours with her since, as in the case of Jannifer Tass, she had obviously been assaulted more than once. Two minor facts were suppressed in the newspaper reports of the murder. Her left nipple had been bitten through, and the skin between the anus and vagina had been cut with scissors. "Bit Zoe's tight tits and scissored Sarah's cunt."

I told Cornock to ask Detective Inspector Gifford if he knew what the panties were made of. The answer came back immediately: "Yes, cotton." That explained one thing that had puzzled me; that they had been left behind in the car. If they had been of nylon or rayon, Arthur would have taken them as a trophy.

I could have no possible doubt that Arthur *was* the killer, even though the description given by the Plassets did not mention bulging eyes. (After all, the passengers in a car are in no position to stare at the driver's eyes.) Arthur Lingard had been living in Putney at the time, and often visited Aggie at Boughton Monchelsea, not far from Maidstone. And he had told his passengers that he was an electronics engineer—the profession of Aggie's husband. The white minicar had been stolen that morning from a street in Croydon. Arthur was, at this time, involved in his washing machine fraud, and his victims included three women from Bromley.

It was clear to us that, from Cornock's point of view, the case was solved. All he had to do was to send a photograph of Arthur to the Plassetts, and find out whether this was the driver of the white minicar. This, in fact, is what happened; their identification was quite definite. This meant that no matter what happened, Lingard would never be a free man again.

It may seem strange that the Lewis case had remained unsolved. Arthur had a criminal record, and the identikit drawing that was issued after the murder—and published in most newspapers—certainly resembled him (although the eyes were too far apart, and the chin too long.) The answer is that he had no criminal record, as far as sex crime was concerned. Apart from the attack on Iris Franklin in Warrington, he had no record of physical violence either. There were no fingerprints in the car—he had worn gloves all the time (which is no doubt one of the reasons why he committed the assault outside the car; he wanted to remove his gloves.)

A few days later, Cornock showed me a photograph of Sarah Lewis, and I was greatly struck by it. She was beautiful: slim, white-skinned, with red-gold hair. Her face was very delicate, and the mouth gentle and rather weak. Her parents were apparently fairly well-to-do middle-class people. I was beginning to see a pattern. Arthur Lingard seemed to be violently attracted by two types of women; or rather, his desires were directed toward two ideals: the physical and what might be called the "spiritual." His description of Iris Franklin made it clear to me that she also belonged to this latter type. So did Diana Banks, the girl he glimpsed in her petticoat in the bedroom, and Duncan McIver's sister. Perhaps "spiritual" is the wrong word here; such girls seemed to have a Scott Fitzgerald kind of glamour for Arthur. He longed for them as a symbol of some superb fulfillment, connected with his longing for a rural England without cities; girls with grace and loveliness and culture, girls who took baths at five in the afternoon. Pauline and Eileen Grose —and, I assumed, Aggie—were physical relationships that appealed to his need for dominance. What now struck me as significant was that he had tried to rape the child in Warrington. It was as if he decided that this kind of beauty would always elude him, unless it was seized by force. I had sensed, when he told me about his attack on the child, that it was far more important and complex than he wanted me to guess. It is also significant that he began to show definite signs of the latest breakdown after this admission. Up to this point, the pattern of his life had been a search—perhaps a search for the mother he had lost in an air raid. Now he had suddenly decided to give up the search, to take the short-cut of violence. It was impossible not to see the connection between this decision and Aggie's elopement with her electronics engineer.

What puzzled Cornock—and myself—was the problem of "Zoe" and "Joy." There were no murder victims of either name on the list. It was Frank Slessor who provided the key to the first part of the problem. On Tuesday, August 25, the day after I had talked to Cornock, I showed him my chronology of Lingard's life, and a copy of the list of unsolved murders. I left them with him while I went to see Arthur.

I detected a slight nervousness in myself as the guard unlocked the door of his room; but it was unnecessary. He lay on the bed in his straitjacket, staring dully at the ceiling. When I asked him how he felt, he ignored me. Although his eyes looked dull and withdrawn, I had a feeling that he was sane enough, and knew exactly why I was there. His tired, blank stare seemed to imply that anything we said would be meaningless. I had to shake off a feeling of depression when I left him, ten minutes later.

Slessor was on the telephone when I came back. He was saying: "I thought I was right. She was found buried in a field, wasn't she—an orchard, was it? Could you get me the details? Yes, I can hang on." He put his hand over the receiver. "This address at Armthorpe rang a bell. I remember reading an article about it in a Sunday newspaper a few years back. They found a girl's body buried in an orchard near there. I'm talking to the chief of police in Doncaster." Ten minutes later, he had the details.

The corpse had been found in May 1959, buried under an apple tree at the side of a stream. Saponification had set in: that is to say, the moisture of the ground had caused the fatty constituents of the body to change into the substance known as adipocere, a yellowy white fat that looks like washing soap. The consequence was that although the face, which had been partly exposed, had been eaten away by ants, the limbs, breasts, and buttocks had been virtually mummified. She was a well-made girl with dark hair, and she had never been positively identified. The body had been fully clothed, except for bra and panties (although inevitably, the clothing had rotted). It was too long after death to determine whether she had been raped; but the nipples of both breasts had been bitten through.

I was standing behind Slessor, watching him write down the details. As he wrote this, I quickly took the typescript of Lingard's "poem" out of my pocket, and pointed to the line "Jock bit Zoe's tight tits." Slessor nodded. He said into the telephone: "I think we may have the solution of your murder. Was there a Zoe among the suspected victims?" He looked at me and shook his head. "Could you give me a list of the women it might have been?"

The second name he wrote was "Bella Paisely, last seen December 10, 1957." Again, I pointed out a line of the "poem," "11 December 1959." Slessor said into the phone:

"Do you have any more details about this second girl? For example, was she nicknamed Zoe?" The police chief said he'd ring back.

I said: "I think it has to be this girl. She disappeared on December 10 from Doncaster. Arthur was living in the caravan at Armthorpe up to that time, and according to Pauline, he left Doncaster in December."

"Except that the date she disappeared was December 10, 1957, not December 11, 1959."

"She disappeared on December 10. Perhaps she spent the night with Arthur and he killed her the next day, or perhaps he kidnapped her as he did Jannifer Tass. The body was found in 1959. Perhaps he made a slip, or perhaps he deliberately put in the wrong date to confuse the issue."

When the Doncaster Superintendent rang us back, half an hour later, it was clear I had hit upon the right explanation. Bella Paisely had worked in an all-night coffee bar, and had preferred to be known as Zoe. She was twenty years old, and had a good figure. (I checked on the newspaper files in London; the *News of the World* published a photograph of her that made her look remarkably like Pauline; the same outthrust breasts, the same rounded, child-bearing hips, even the same way of tilting back her head when being photographed.)

A few days before her disappearance, Bella gave notice at the coffee bar, telling them that she had met a "smashing fellow" who had offered to get her into drama school in London. (She had dreams of being an actress.) She was not, apparently, a virgin, although she was certainly not, as one newspaper implied, a prostitute. Several men were interviewed after the discovery of the body in the orchard. One of them had actually had intercourse with her a few hours before she left the coffee bar for the last time. She told him she was going to drive to London that night with a man called Nigel, who had only just rung her to confirm that he had arranged an interview at RADA. She came to the coffee bar at eleven o'clock on the evening of December 10 to say good-bye, then went off to meet "Nigel."

What happened then will never be known. My own guess is that Lingard took her back to his caravan and killed her. He killed her because she was like Pauline, not because he wanted to sleep with her—he had probably already slept with her. He may have buried her that night, or kept her there for several days. A police check later revealed that Arthur had lived in the caravan—rented from Mr. L. Manners of Dairy Farm—from March 1957 until December 28. During most of that time he worked for a television hire firm in Balby, and drove their van. He undoubtedly used the van to transport the body from his caravan to the orchard, two miles away. The orchard was a part of a farm that had been untenanted since the previous July. Arthur probably borrowed the spade to dig the grave from the tool shed near the gate of the orchard.

This murder seems to me to pose some of the strangest psychological problems in the whole case. In 1957, he was on good terms with Pauline. After his prison sentence, he continued to exchange letters with her, and visited her twice at Southport. At this time, she was living with a married man who was more than twice her age; but this did not seem to trouble Arthur. On the contrary, he and her lover apparently took a liking to each other, and on one occasion, sat up until the early hours of the morning getting drunk together.

And yet in November, he met the pretty waitress who reminded him of Pauline, went to a great deal of trouble to seduce her (she told a friend that "Nigel" took her to expensive restaurants), lied to her about his job and his theatrical contacts, and planned to kill her. This was a great deal riskier than the murder of Jannifer Tass, or Sarah Lewis. Since he worked in Doncaster, he might bump into her at any hour of the day, and his TV repair van would hardly support his story of being a young business executive. If she said too much about him, or even described his appearance, the police might easily track him down after her murder. The thought of killing her excited some morbid erotic nerve, and he ignored the risks.

But *why* did he kill her? If his intention was to sleep with her, he could have achieved it without murder—even without telling her lies about himself. A television repairman would have been a perfectly eligible wooer. I have to assume that this was too aboveboard for Arthur. The seduction of a promiscuous waitress by a television repairman would not have fitted the Moriarty daydream. He wanted to be the mysterious criminal, the ruthless killer.

And this in itself reveals something important about his psychology. He was no longer dramatizing himself as the Napoleon of Crime—this was hardly possible in view of his lack of success even as a petty swindler—but as some deadly black spider, to whom girls were the flies he carried off to his lair. In other words, he had *consciously decided* to be a super sex-criminal. He had killed Aggie in Sarah Lewis. Now he killed and violated Pauline in Zoe Paisely. It was a murder of revenge—revenge upon his substitute "mother." Hence the mutilation of the nipples. In the case of Sarah Lewis, the mutilation had been of the genitals, symbolizing his determination that she would never give herself to another man.

The jigsaw puzzle was now missing only one piece: the identity of "Joy."

Looking over my chronology, it struck me that a likely date for a murder would be in 1962, after Arthur's attack on Pauline. I read carefully through the list of unsolved sex crimes for that year. There was no Joy. Then I saw it: Martha Apjoy, murdered July 17, 1962, in Leeds. "Through carnage to joy/ And up Joy to Jannifer." I had been puzzled by this phrase. How could one get at Jannifer by going "up Joy"? Now it was clear: it was an absurd pun. Her name was Apjoy and he had been "up" her.

I rang the Leeds police for details of the murder, and knew that I had found my missing link. Martha Apjoy, age eighteen, was found strangled with a silk stocking in the yard of St. Mary's Church, Leeds. She fitted my categories perfectly: the daughter of wealthy parents, slim and blond: about to start at St. Anne's College, Oxford. She had been seen for the last time visiting the Leeds hospital, where her boyfriend, Warren Machen ("Warren wouldn't like it . . ."), to whom she was engaged, was recovering from a tonsil operation. Martha Apjoy had been driving a red Standard Triumph, which had been parked in Thoresby Place, near the hospital. Her boyfriend had stood at a window and watched her climb into the car and drive away. The car was found abandoned the following day on the moors between Leeds and Bradford. In the back was a child's toy pistol.

My reconstruction of the crime is as follows. Arthur may have seen the girl leaving the car and been attracted by her, or he may have observed that it was a girl's car—most women leave feminine articles in their cars—a Kleenex stained with lipstick, a woman's magazine. Arthur climbed into the back and lay on the floor. She got in without noticing him, and drove off. At some point, he pushed the gun

229

into the back of her neck and ordered her to drive on. She was forced to take him to some lonely spot on the moors, where she was sexually assaulted. He strangled her, placed the body in the car, and drove her back into Leeds, where he left it in the churchyard.

Why should he do that? The risk was insane. Cornock believes that the answer is that Lingard was, in fact, insane, and had no clear idea of what he was doing. He cites Pauline's description of her brother's visit—a month earlier—as evidence.

My own view is more complex; it also, I think, explains a great deal more than the mystery of why he returned to Leeds.

The medical evidence revealed that Martha Apjoy had been a virgin before this assault. It is also clear that she did not arouse Lingard to the same degree of sexual frenzy as previous victims. The body was unmutilated, and semen was found only in the vagina.

While she drove out to the moors, with the gun—which she thought real—pressed against her, she must have pleaded with him, perhaps told him she was a virgin. After this personal contact, he could no longer treat her simply as an object of lust. It is true that he also had personal contact with Sarah Lewis, Zoe Paisely, and Evelyn Marquis before he killed them; but in each case, he was playing a part, waiting for the moment to knock them unconscious. He was the cat watching a bird hopping unsuspectingly on the lawn. In this case, the girl was frightened, and she knew what he wanted. She told him about the man she was engaged to ("Warren wouldn't like it . . ."). In spite of this, he forced her to strip (the evidence showed that her clothes had been removed, and later put on again). No doubt he enjoyed the sensation of power when he watched her remove her clothes. And yet she was a person, not an abstract object of lust. He made her lie down, flung himself onto her—and encountered again the problem he had encountered with the girl on the canal bank. In spite of this, he went through with it; and, during the course of the next few hours, repeated the act at least twice. Cornock is of the opinion that she was unconscious at the time—the back of her skull had been cut open with a heavy blow, apparently from the toy pistol, which was expensive and heavy. I cannot accept this view; for even if Lingard had stunned her before she got out of the car, she would not have remained unconscious for more than an hour. I believe that he talked with her, and that perhaps she even showed sympathy and interest in him. She was convinced that when it was all over, he would let her go. He allowed her to believe this, but he knew it was untrue. She would only have to mention his description to the Leeds police, and he would be in custody within hours. Sometime after dark —probably after midnight—he made her drive back into Leeds, while he sat in the back seat. They stopped in the silent street near St. Mary's churchyard, less than half a mile from her home. One violent blow on the back of her skull made her slump forward. He looked both ways to make sure the street was empty, then dragged her out into the churchyard, and strangled her. She had been dead about eight hours when she was found at nine the next morning. Then he began to wonder: Had he left anything out at the scene of the rape? This seems to me the only plausible explanation of why he drove back to the moors. The other possibility is that he was living at Bradford. To take the car all the way back to Bradford would divert the search there; so he left it halfway, and walked through the rest of the night.

If this reconstruction is true, then I believe it would have important psychological repercussions on him. Here was a case where the whole crime had gone sour. It was intended to be an explosion of lust; it had turned into the bullying of a rather sweet and pathetic girl, and even the rape itself had been spoiled by her virginity and her nervousness. The characteristic of Arthur's kind of crime was that it had to fit into his dream world; this one was too real. He did not want to kill her—otherwise he would have killed her on the moor, and saved himself a great deal of trouble. He killed her purely out of calculation, because he could not accept her assurances—which she must have given—that she would not betray him. As he walked back home that night, he must have wished heartily that he had never seen the red sports car, and that Martha Apjoy was at present comfortably tucked up in bed. The crime left him feeling soiled and vicious.

What evidence is there for this view? Well, there is the fact that this was the last of his sex crimes, although he had another year of liberty before him. This in itself is remarkable. Most sex criminals continue until they get caught, and their crimes become more frequent. Arthur Lingard com-

231

mitted five sex murders between June 1956 and July 1962, and then stopped. I have tried to show that in all these cases, the motivation was revenge—on Aggie and Pauline—as much as sex. With the murder of Martha Apjoy, reality entered the paranoid daydream, and the murders stopped.

On August 26—while Cornock was still trying to find out the identity of "Zoe"—Frank Slessor rang me to say that he wanted to transfer Lingard to the Broadmoor Extension at Rampton immediately. As one of the guards had been removing his straitjacket—before feeding him—Arthur had leaned forward and bit his finger. He bit hard, and his teeth sank to the bone. He went on biting, in spite of frantic punches in the face. When his teeth were finally forced open, the guard fainted, and Arthur spat out a mouthful of blood, then scattered the food tray on the floor.

I agreed to the transfer immediately. The truth is that Arthur was in a straitjacket not simply because he was inclined to violence, but because it would have been too easy for him to escape from Rose Hill if he had really made an effort.

On August 27, he was transferred to Broadmoor. I did not accompany him—the Broadmoor authorities sent a van to collect him. Two days later, when I rang the governor to ask if he would like me to visit Arthur, he told me that it would probably be better if I stayed away for now. Arthur had settled down quickly, showed no sign of violence, and was capable of carrying on sensible conversations.

The day after this report, I traveled to London with Cornock, at the invitation of Scotland Yard. I also wanted to look through the newspaper files at Colindale. (It was there that I realized the striking physical resemblance between Pauline and Zoe Paisely.) Cornock hoped to trace Arthur's movements during the periods for which Pauline had no addresses—during 1958, and between June 1962 and his arrest for the farmhouse murder the following year. It was during my second day in London that I made a discovery about Martha Apjoy in Leeds—while looking through Scotland Yard's unsolved murder file. From that time on, the matter was in the hands of Cornock and of Chief Inspector Hawkins of the Yard. I now decided to take a day off to pursue an interest of my own: I wanted to meet Mrs. Roll—the former Aggie Lingard. I must admit that I felt no great curiosity about her. Pauline was the interesting one of the two; Agnes drifted passively, allowing things to take their course. She was evidently one of those quiet, unquarrelsome women without remarkable vitality or intelligence. But it seemed a pity to go back to Yorkshire without seeing her.

I drove down on a Thursday afternoon, reflecting that I was following the route that Arthur had taken when he drove the white minicar.

The countryside looked green and peaceful; orchards were full of apples, gardens bright with flowers. There was no trace of autumn in the air. I found The Meadows half a mile beyond the village, a pleasant bungalow, obviously built within the last twenty years. There was no reply when I rang the front doorbell, and for a moment, I was afraid that my unheralded visit would be a waste of time. But I heard voices in the garden, and walked around the side of the house. A huge boxer saw me and started barking; I knew better than to retreat, and walked on; at which it sniffed me and walked quietly beside me.

The back lawn was large, and three ladies were sitting in the shade of trees, drinking tea. Several children in bathing costumes were splashing in and out of a stream that ran past the end of the garden. A willowy lady in white and blue stood up and came to meet me. Her face reminded me of portraits of Virginia Woolf—the same large eyes and eyelids. Her smile was exceptionally sweet; this was partly due to her eyes, partly to the very white front teeth, one of which slightly overlapped the next.

"Is Mrs. Roll in please?"

"Yes, I'm Mrs. Roll. What can I do for you?"

I looked at her in amazement. The hair was light blond, almost ash-blond. Somehow, I had always pictured Aggie as having dark hair, like her cousins, and sallow skin.

I felt myself stammering as I said: "My name is Kahn, Dr. Samuel Kahn. I wanted to speak to you about your cousin Arthur."

She went pale.

"What about him? Where is he?"

"In Broadmoor, I'm afraid. He's had a severe mental breakdown."

"Oh, my God!" The accent was perceptibly Lancashire; it was a pleasant, silvery voice. She looked around the lawn in a bewildered manner. "Will you come inside? 'Scuse me a minute while I tell my friends."

I was curious about her friends, so I walked with her down the lawn. A pretty blond girl of about seven shouted shrilly: "Mummy, Arthur's hitting me with his water pistol." Aggie ignored her. She said to one of the women: "Mary, this gentleman wants to talk to me about my cousin Arthur. Would you mind keeping an eye on the kids?" She looked at me in a confused, vague way, as if she had suddenly forgotten why I was there—I would have guessed that decisiveness and efficiency were not her chief virtues—then decided I ought to be introduced. "Mr. Kahn—I mean Doctor Kahn. Mrs. Mercer, Mrs. Adams?" One woman was young and very pretty—she might have been the wife of a junior executive; the other was about fifty, and looked—and apparently was—a vicar's wife.

Aggie said, "Would you come into the house, Doctor?" I followed her, noting that her small son, Arthur, was as unlike his namesake as it was possible to be: large, sturdy, and blond.

She led me through the french windows into a pleasant room with good furniture, and shelves of records above a stereo record player.

I apologized for calling at an inconvenient time. Then I sketched out the story of my relationship with her cousin, taking care to say nothing of the murders. She listened in a wide-eyed, troubled way, and I found myself wondering how much she was taking in. But when I had finished, she said, "Arthur's done something terrible, hasn't he?"

I nodded. "He killed a girl."

She stared at me blankly, so I wondered if she understood. Then she said, "I always knew he would."

"How did you know?"

She said, "He wanted to kill me."

"What!" I gaped.

"That's why Brian—my husband—told him never to come to the house again. He said he was convinced Arthur intended to come and kill me one day when I was alone."

"And what did *you* think?"

"I thought . . ." She looked troubled. "I thought he could. Do you . . . do you know about Arthur?"

I completed the sentence. "I know you were lovers, yes." She smiled palely. "Not lovers. He never loved me."

"But you loved him?"

She nodded gravely. "Of course. I still love him."

She had the art of staggering me by saying things as if butter wouldn't melt in her mouth. While I was still collecting my wits, she said, "How many did he kill?"

We were interrupted by her small boy, who rushed into the room, hooting. When she shook her head at him, he explained he was a train. He came and stood by her knee.

"What are you both talking about?"

"Your Uncle Arthur."

"Is he dead?"

I said, "No, he's still alive."

The boy said cheerfully: "Well, that's all right then. Mummy, why won't Mary let me hold her teddy bear?"

I experienced a sense of shock. Yes, it was all right. So long as you are alive, it's all right. So what had gone wrong with Arthur? How could he become so negative?

As I stared at her, caressing her child's hair, I had a sudden vision of her lying down naked on the rug of the front room at Penketh Street. It had the vividness of an hallucination. It struck me suddenly; Arthur could never have believed that this tender, docile girl would ever desert him. Of course she still loved Arthur. She was the kind who, once she has given her love, never withdraws it.

As the child ran off again, I asked, "Did Arthur come to this house?"

"Oh yes, seven or eight times. That was soon after we married. I was having Mandy at the time."

I could see it. Aggie, in a maternity dress, in this golden house, Aggie, soft and contented with the hormones of motherhood, smiling with gentle fondness at her husband who had carried her off like a knight. And Arthur, the outsider, with his dreams and visions of Mars, and the sordid reality of his everyday life of crime. And the result? He had decided to become a gentleman crook, a swindler, instead of a burglar.

The vicar's wife tapped gently on the french windows.

"Oh, excuse me . . . I think we ought to go. Robin's fallen in the water and got soaked."

Aggie got up, excused herself, and went out. I sat looking out of the window. It was amazing to realize that Aggie was, in her way, as delightful as Pauline. She was less vital, perhaps, but more feminine; one could not imagine her being

235

angry. And this life obviously suited her. I could see the greenhouse behind the apple trees in the garden; her small hands were brown and rough, the hands of a woman who enjoys digging and planting. If her skin had once been unhealthy and sallow, it was now a warm golden color, the skin of a woman who spends much of her life outdoors. She was the sort of girl that certain men—fatherly men like myself—want to pat and cuddle. Her figure was very good—slim and lithe—and her breasts were still firm. She had been giving herself to men ever since she was a child; she felt it was their right to take her. She would allow them to make love while her mind remained fixed on its own desires: children, a house with a garden, strawberries for tea on Sundays. She was Blake's "soul of sweet delight" who can never be defiled. What would she know of the black loathings and rages that Arthur was releasing as he drove into her? If I had seen her sitting in the garden with the two other women, pouring tea and keeping an eye on the children as they splashed in the stream, I would have assumed she was the daughter of a county family. She had a thoroughbred air.

Arthur needed her. In a sense, he needed her far more than Pauline.

I saw that a pretty schoolgirl of about fourteen was now playing with the two children on the lawn; they were apparently trying to pull both her arms off.

Aggie came in. She said: "It's the girl from next door. She helps me with the house sometimes." She sat down, and stared past me.

She said, "What will happen to Arthur?"

I said, "Nothing. He'll stay in prison."

"Will they put him on trial for the girl?"

"If he recovers his sanity, yes."

She began to cry. I had to restrain the desire to go and stroke her hair. To distract her, I took the "poem" out of my pocket and handed it to her. Like a child, she wiped away tears with the back of her hand, and looked at it. She seemed to read it without understanding.

She said, "But it's signed Jock . . ."

"Jack the Ripper?"

"Oh yes. I know now. I understand that line about the beetles."

"Tell me."

"It was a book about Jack the Ripper. It was by a man

called Manners . . . no, Matters. He sat in the kitchen reading it, and there was a nest of black beetles in a hole in the corner. He read that book until it fell to pieces. . . . I remember another thing. It was Christmas, and Arthur found the wishbone in the chicken, and we pulled it, and he got the big half. Then he said, 'You wish, it's no good me wishing.' So I asked why not. He said, 'I can never have the thing I want most.' I asked, 'What's that?' 'To know who Jack the Ripper was,' he said."

I had no idea whether I had found a vital clue, or merely stumbled on another false trail. Jack the Ripper, the only English mass murderer who was never caught. Was this the image that replaced Moriarty when Aggie left him?

She looked vaguely at the paper in her hands. "Why is it all cut up?"

I said, "Because he couldn't decide whether he wanted to tell me or not."

What was the fear at the back of his mind as he trembled in the corner of his cell? The dog? Aggie's dog? Suddenly, another image flashed into my head. It was of this house late at night, with one window still lighted. Standing by the gate, staring at it, is Arthur. His eyes are bulging, and sweat runs down his face. In his hand, he holds a knife.

I asked her, "Do *you* believe Arthur would ever harm you?"

She smiled at me, almost pityingly. "No, of course not."

I stayed with Aggie for the remainder of the afternoon. She had one thing in common with her cousin Pauline: a strange frankness. I had noticed the open way she told the vicar's wife that I had come to talk about her cousin Arthur, the jailbird. . . . It obviously seemed to her, quite simply, that nothing was worth concealing or lying about.

Her husband came home just before six o'clock, driving a Jaguar saloon. He was a good-looking young man, with fair hair and a clean-cut profile. His hobby, he told me, was music, and both his children had piano lessons. It suddenly struck me clearly: this was Aggie's real background, not Penketh Street. She had been as out of place there as Arthur. That was why he loved her.

Her husband walked me back to the car I had hired for the day. I asked him what he thought of Arthur.

"Funny type. I never really liked him. The way he looked

at me always made me think of a snake. He often came here."

"Yes, in 1956. Your wife mentioned it."

"Yes, that was it. Aggie was carrying Mandy at the time. Mandy's the eldest—she's at boarding school. I got the feeling Arthur hated us both really. That was why I finally told him to stay away." He shook his head. "To be honest, your news is a relief. I think he's better off in jail. Of course, Aggie always loved him. She insisted on calling our youngest after him."

He shook my hand through the car window. "Mind, I never wished him any harm. If he gets out, he's welcome to come here—for Aggie's sake."

"I'm afraid he won't."

Aggie waved to me from the front door; the small boy was pummeling her thigh, trying to attract attention.

Arthur Lingard was killed on September 12, 1967, two weeks after his transfer to Rampton. The man who killed him was also serving a sentence for sex crimes: Charles Dooley, "the Dublin Strangler." Dooley was literally a lunatic, a man who experienced the urge to strangle women at the time of the full moon. He made no attempt to hide the bodies or conceal himself.

What happened is still not clear. The two men seemed to like each other. They were under the supervision of a guard, talking in the garden. The guard wandered off to exchange words with another guard. When he looked around, he saw that Arthur was on the ground, with Dooley's huge hands at his throat. He died later, without recovering consciousness. Dooley would only say obstinately, "He started it." Another prisoner claimed that Arthur had leaped at Dooley and started hitting him with his fists. The cause of the quarrel, apparently, was a pair of black panties that Arthur claimed Dooley had stolen from his locker.

I was glad to be back home with my family. When I came into the house, my son rushed over to hug me, and the book he was reading fell on the floor. I picked it up for him. It was the copy of *A Princess of Mars* that I had picked up from under Arthur's bed at Rose Hill, on the last occasion I was in the room.

I glanced at the page it was opened at, and experienced

a shock of tension. The chapter was called "Through Carnage to Joy"—the line of the poem that had so far evaded me. I read through the chapter to see whether it had any special significance for Arthur, but could not detect any.

When I came to the end, I saw the title of the next chapter: "From Joy to Death."

Arthur knew the book too well not to have noticed it.

NOTE TO LINGARD

Back in 1963, I wrote a play called *71 Mettmannerstrasse* about Peter Kürten, the Düsseldorf mass murderer, for Theatre in the Round at Scarborough. The late Stephen Joseph found this attempt at a nonfiction play too jarring for the nerves of holiday audiences, and I do not even know whether a copy still exists. But the idea stuck in my mind: an attempt to transpose reality literally—in this case, Berg's classic book on Kürten, *The Sadist*—into a fictional form.

When Capote's novel *In Cold Blood* appeared, I felt that his talk of a "nonfiction novel" was a red herring. As practiced by Capote, it is fundamentally no different from novelized nonfiction—for example, Fülop-Miller's "biography" of Rasputin (if he attempted to apply it to any field other than crime, I suspect this would become obvious). But I still felt that a genuine nonfiction novel should be possible. Professor Berg has shown the way. He was the psychiatrist appointed to examine Kürten in prison. His book about Kürten is as compelling as a novel; but it also has a clinical realism that gives it a brutal impact far beyond the range of fiction. I tried to transfer this to the stage; and apparently the experiment was not successful. In this novel, I have made another attempt to capture the impact of Berg's book on Kürten.

Arthur Lingard is not based on any single murderer, although Peter Manuel was the model at the back of my mind when I started the book. The childhood background is closer to Kürten, the burglaries and underwear fetichism to William Heirens, the Chicago murderer, the imaginative instability to Hans Van Zon, the recent Dutch murderer, who seems to have lived a Walter Mittyish fantasy life. Psychiatric details have been lifted wholesale from Medard Boss's *Psychoanalysis and Daseinsanalysis,* Erwin Straus's *Phenom-*

enological Psychology, Robert Lindner's *The Fifty Minute Hour*, Frederic Wertham's *The Show of Violence* (the latest edition of which contains some interesting remarks on Speck, the murderer of the eight nurses in Chicago), and Ludwig Binswanger's *Case of Ellen West*.* It is true that I have "selected" from all this material; but I have not attempted to fictionalize it or tone it down. Only in dealing with Lingard's hypnotic powers have I diluted material from Paul J. Reiter's *Antisocial or Criminal Acts and Hypnosis* (Munksgaard, Copenhagen), since some of the details sound frankly incredible. (I am not suggesting that they are; in fact, I know they are not.)

Whether the result of all this is a genuine nonfiction novel I do not know; but it is the closest I can get to it. And if someone should point out that it reads more like a shilling shocker than a nonfiction novel, I would not dispute this; the two are not incompatible.

But I must here acknowledge a fundamental debt to A. E. Van Vogt. Most people think of him as a writer of science fiction; but his most important book, *The Violent Man*, is a straight novel. While writing it, he anticipated that it would be misunderstood, and went to the trouble of preparing a pamphlet, in fourteen short chapters, to explain his basic theory. The book was not misunderstood; it was treated as another work by a writer of science fiction, and ignored. The pamphlet remains one of the most important and revolutionary statements I have ever read.

"In 1956," writes Van Vogt, "when I already had the behaviour of the violent type of man accurately outlined, I asked a psychologist friend to tell me of any unusual husband-wife relationship that he had observed, with emphasis on selfish male behaviour. He told me of a man who had brought his former wife for treatment five years before.

"This man's story—as the psychologist related it to me—was, in brief: He was divorced, and had set up his ex-wife in a suburban home. Her role, as he planned it, was that for the rest of her life she would be the perfect mother for their son. She was not to re-marry. The man saw nothing wrong in her playing this role.

"This viewpoint was so one-sided that the psychologist was

* In the symposium *Existence* edited by Rollo May.

not surprised at the story of male subjectiveness that the wife told him.

"She had been a nurse, and had had two affairs with doctors prior to her marriage. When her future husband proposed to her, she told him of these relationships. The man almost went insane with jealousy and hurt. He arrived at her home the day after her confession with a legal document in triplicate for her to sign. He refused to let her read what was in the paper, demanding that she sign on the grounds that she owed it to him. He was in such an obviously disturbed condition, and she felt so guilty, that she finally signed, sight unseen. . . . Shortly after she signed, they were married.

"As a married man, he roamed the country, literally reporting home whenever he pleased. He was always driving his secretaries to and from work and taking an unconscionable long time to do it, or visiting one or the other of his women employees in their apartments. Any questioning by his wife . . . put him into a rage that often included violence. . . ."

After further illustration of this one-sided, near paranoiac behavior, he says:

"My years of observation of other males of this type tempts me to speculate that in [the document] she agreed that she was a prostitute, and that in marrying her he was raising her from the status of a fallen woman, but she must agree that she had no rights as a wife except those he bestowed on her."

This, says Van Vogt, is the "violent man." He also calls him "the right man" because he has an obsession about being "in the right," and will not, under any circumstances, admit that he is wrong. The personality, in this respect, is rigid. Van Vogt points out that this is an exaggerated version of the usual male attitude to woman, the result of millions of years of evolution in which the male was dominant. In Italy in 1961, two women were sentenced to a year in jail for adultery. They pointed out that their husbands were self-acknowledged adulterers, but the Supreme Court upheld the sentence on the grounds that there is a legally accepted double standard in Italy.

Van Vogt goes on to quote several cases of "right" males, men whose relationships with their wives involve flagrant double-standard behavior, and who fly into insane rages if the wife attempts to protest. But the most curious part is still to come. It is Van Vogt's contention that if the "right man" is deserted by his wife—his whipping boy—he may die, or become seriously ill, or become a drug addict or alcoholic. Because his life-world of dominance, will-to-power, is built upon the body of a woman, the whole structure becomes tottery if she gets out from under it. "If she leaves him or starts divorce proceedings, he presently goes into a frantic emotional state. The death-thought begins to show; tears, wild appeals, desperate anxiety: 'Don't leave me, I love you more than life.' Only after many bitter disillusionments do a percentage of wives refuse to accept this madness as love.

"If she leaves him with any kind of finality, thoughts of murder vie with thoughts of suicide in his unstable mind, for he must control his woman or die, except . . . he can leave *her* and live. If he does the leaving, he may still try to control her. . . ." He cites several more cases in which the "right man" has murdered or attempted to murder his wife. In China in 1950, the communist regime introduced a law designed to weaken the ancient tradition of total subjugation to the male; "in one district alone, in 1954, 10,000 wives were murdered by their husbands for attempting to take advantage of the 1950 law."

Van Vogt goes on to argue, brilliantly and convincingly, that Hitler, Stalin, Mao Tse-tung, and Khrushchev were all violent men. I was at first inclined to wonder if this was not a case of American anticommunism; but study of his arguments has convinced me that this does not enter into it. I have come to believe that he is right. His theory of the "right man" is particularly interesting when it relates to dictators, because the characteristic of the "right man" is to refuse to recognize that he has ever been in the wrong. His wild outbursts of rage are always justified later on the grounds that he was tried past all endurance, that the most sweetly reasonable of men would have done the same, etc. He will rationalize convincingly, distorting the facts as necessary. And such distortions become the ground for further action—in the case of Hitler or Stalin, bloodlettings. Given power, "sickly, suspicious men" tend to become paranoiac; they may go completely insane, like Caligula.

I suspect that most male readers of this account will feel that the cap fits, to some extent. Everyone has his amour propre and, when this is violated, is liable to get on his high horse and impose his own interpretation on the "facts." But the matter is of special interest to me, since I approached it from a different angle in *The Outsider*. One of the main points in that book is that it is often very difficult to draw the line between the highly gifted man who fails to fit in because he "sees deeper" than most people, and the ungifted crank with a capacity for rationalizing his crankery as genius. Any artist of high individuality is saying, essentially: "*I am right.* This is what life is really like." And since the artistic spectrum extends from the optimism of Blake, Shaw, Whitman, and Chesterton to the gloom of Andreyev, Greene, Beckett, and Céline, it is clear that they cannot all be right. And that is one of the odd things about art. When Céline says: "Man is only himself on the lavatory or on his death-bed; all the rest is histrionics," we may reject what he says, while still being impressed by the power of *Voyage au Bout de la Nuit*. Perhaps it is relevant to comment that Van Vogt himself is a gentle and modest man whose central interest is psychology; he can therefore examine the "right man" dispassionately through his microscope without much involvement. I am personally not as mild, modest, or detached as I would like to be; therefore I see ambiguities where he sees sharp outlines. The problem, as I see it, is this. I may, on occasion, be capable of acting with the self-righteous anger and rationalization of the violent man. It is also possible that my anger arises from the fact that I happen to be, in some particular matter, in the position of Wells's hero in the country of the blind, actually *seeing* something that others refuse to believe exists. A necessary characteristic of creativity is the kind of assertive drive that also characterizes the violent man. Martin Gardner wrote a delightful book, *Fads and Fallacies in the Name of Science*, in which he discusses all kinds of crank theories; but he seems to imply that there are perfectly simple and obvious rules by which any sane person can distinguish between a crank theory and sound science. Moreover, what is also implied is: "If everyone were like me—level-headed, skeptical, logical—the world would get on much faster." And this seems to me a doubtful proposition. In science as well as art—and politics—the great originators are often self-assertive, noisy, and wrongheaded, and these qualities sometimes lead to inspired flashes. Newton himself was a sour, suspicious man. Wagner was such a cad that it is hard to see how he rationalized his bad behaviour toward women and patrons.

This is worth saying, but it does not clarify the issue. For obviously, I am not saying that "right men" are really "right." I am saying that Van Vogt's observations ought to be the basis for further investigation and discussion. They are a bold foundation, but not a complete theory of "right-motivated" violence. Not only do we need to modify it to fit in Newton and Wagner; we even need to modify it to fit in Hitler and Stalin. Whatever one's feelings about these two, one cannot deny that they were more vital politicians than any in the world at the moment. In Hitler's case, his Wagnerian political visions involved the belief that Jews and Negroes are an inferior type of human being, actively plotting against the higher type. This is a typical "right man" rationalization. A thoroughgoing anti-Nazi would attribute *all* Hitler's drives and theories to the insane self-assertion of the "right man," and he would be talking nonsense. What we need is a comprehensive theory of the violent man that can make some distinction between creative self-assertion and paranoiac egoism. And the answer is not that creative self-assertion is always modest and reasonable.

Van Vogt's "violent man" theory is the key to *Lingard,* and *Lingard* is also a questioning of the theory in the form in which he has expressed it in the novel and the pamphlet. I accept the existence of the violent man type. I would even accept his assertion that the traditional male dominance of the female provides a psychological atmosphere in our culture that is "thousands of times more significant than any other environmental factor" (i.e., Oedipus complexes, economic motivations, the class war, the clash of male against male, religious beliefs, and so on). Most important, I accept that the withdrawal of the female causes such a psychological shock that the result is a death wish, directed either at oneself or other people. But the whole point about the "right man" is that one of his basic drives is to make his "life-world" a *logical* structure. One might say that while most people drift on cheerfully from day to day, accepting life as something "given" (as we did as children), the "right man" feels a compulsion to question. Personal problems are not dealt with one by one, as they arise, but are treated as a part of some larger pattern. The results of this attempt at pattern-making are unpredictable. I have known a charming and intelligent man who was unsuccessful in his chosen profession—as an actor.

(There is a full-length portrait of him in my *Adrift in Soho*.) His first response to this lack of success was to create a theory to the effect that modern society is an intolerable straitjacket for "free spirits," and that an amoral "bohemian" existence was the only answer. As the problem became more acute he became a racist who felt that England had no place for his talents because it was run by "nigs" and "wogs" and "yids" (who, he felt, were also responsible for the attacks on my own work). He hanged himself in Bonn jail last year, having been arrested for smuggling cannabis. I was sad to hear of his death; but I could honestly think of no way in which he could have adjusted himself to the reality of the world he lived in.

The need to erect a logical structure need not lead to this kind of subjective self-assertion. Edward Upward has described in his novel *In the Thirties* how various personal problems seemed insoluble in terms of art or poetry, and how he came to accept Marxist dogmas: that the economic structure of society was the reason for his personal miseries. This acceptance led, as he admits, to artistic sterility. The test of a "logical structure" is not whether it enables one to fit in with social reality, but whether it is ultimately conducive to the expressions of one's best abilities.

In Arthur Lingard, I have tried to show the development of a "right man" who is also an outsider in my sense: that is, who, in certain respects, *is* more imaginative and talented than those around him, who *does* possess more will and drive than they do. His life is not tragic in the Greek sense of inexorable doom, but only in the sense of wrong choices, made freely, that end by frustrating his creative potential. He does not fit the pattern of Van Vogt's violent man, or of my own outsiders—most of whom are genuinely creative; and it is because he falls between the two stools that I find him so interesting—that I find the problem of the criminal mentality so interesting. (This novel should be regarded, with *Ritual in the Dark* and *The Glass Cage,* as the third of the criminal trilogy.) Most criminals are not "right men"; they are drifters. But the worst criminals are: a Kürten, a Manuel, a Haigh. Van Vogt remarks: "most right men deserve some sympathy, for they are struggling with an almost unbelievable inner horror." And his final remarks, while they do not actually solve anything, open up an interesting field for discussion. He believes that a democratic political

247

system is one safeguard against "right men"; for they can impose their "logical" dominance in the home, or even in the office if they happen to be boss; but not in a political arena, where they have to clash with other determined persons. And this, in turn, leads Van Vogt to assert that the real objection to all totalitarian systems is that it is usually—no, always—the "right men" who end up in power. It is an interesting concept: that the most important difference between human beings is the difference between the sensible, stable persons who are ultimately good "adjusters" to problems and threats, and the "right men" who rationalize frantically and then swing into paranoiac violence. The fundamental problem of our society, if he is right, is to learn to distinguish the "right men" and induce them to develop inner checks. *Lingard* might be regarded as a willful complication of the problem: an attempt to point out that "right men" are not necessarily and completely wrong.